OXFORD WORLD'S

PETERSBURG
MARRIA
THE GOVERNMEN

NIKOLAI GOGOL was born in the village of Greater Sorochintsy, Mirgorod province, in 1809. He began to write in his teens, studied painting at the Academy of Fine Arts, and entered the Civil Service as a scribe in 1830. He soon moved to a post as a history teacher, followed by a brief and unsuccessful stint as Assistant Professor of History at St Petersburg University. All the stories in this volume, except for 'The Overcoat', were written during this period. In 1836 the first performance of *The Government Inspector* was an instant success. Working on *Dead Souls*, Part One, he travelled in Switzerland, France, Italy, and Germany in the late 1830s. He continued to travel and write in the 1840s; in his self-imposed exile he dedicated himself to recreating the land he had left behind. Gogol never married, although he proposed marriage to the sister of his dear friend Prince Vielgorsky, whom he had nursed through his last illness. In 1848 he moved back to Russia, living under a cloud of religious introspection. His last significant act as a writer was to burn the manuscript of *Dead Souls*, Part Two, on which he had worked during the 1840s and early 1850s. He died in 1852 and was buried in Moscow's Danilov Monastery; his remains were transferred to the Novodevichy Cemetery in 1931.

CHRISTOPHER ENGLISH is a translator based in Zimbabwe. He attended Oxford and Moscow universities and has worked as a translator and teacher in the USSR, USA, and Zimbabwe. His translation of Gogol's *Dead Souls* is also available in Oxford World's Classics.

RICHARD PEACE was Head of the department of Russian Studies at the University of Bristol. His books include *The Enigma of Gogol: An Examination of the Writings of N. V. Gogol and their Place in the Russian Literary Tradition* (Cambridge, 1981).

OXFORD WORLD'S CLASSICS

*For over 100 years Oxford World's Classics have brought
readers closer to the world's great literature. Now with over 700
titles—from the 4,000-year-old myths of Mesopotamia to the
twentieth century's greatest novels—the series makes available
lesser-known as well as celebrated writing.*

*The pocket-sized hardbacks of the early years contained
introductions by Virginia Woolf, T. S. Eliot, Graham Greene,
and other literary figures which enriched the experience of reading.
Today the series is recognized for its fine scholarship and
reliability in texts that span world literature, drama and poetry,
religion, philosophy and politics. Each edition includes perceptive
commentary and essential background information to meet the
changing needs of readers.*

OXFORD WORLD'S CLASSICS

NIKOLAI VASILYEVICH GOGOL

Petersburg Tales
Marriage
The Government Inspector

Translated and edited by
CHRISTOPHER ENGLISH

With an Introduction by
RICHARD PEACE

OXFORD
UNIVERSITY PRESS

OXFORD

UNIVERSITY PRESS

Great Clarendon Street, Oxford OX2 6DP

Oxford University Press is a department of the University of Oxford.
It furthers the University's objective of excellence in research, scholarship,
and education by publishing worldwide in

Oxford New York

Athens Auckland Bangkok Bogotá Buenos Aires Calcutta
Cape Town Chennai Dar es Salaam Delhi Florence Hong Kong Istanbul
Karachi Kuala Lumpur Madrid Melbourne Mexico City Mumbai
Nairobi Paris São Paulo Singapore Taipei Tokyo Toronto Warsaw

with associated companies in Berlin Ibadan

Oxford is a registered trade mark of Oxford University Press
in the UK and in certain other countries

Published in the United States
by Oxford University Press Inc., New York

Translation, Note on Texts and Transliteration, Table of Ranks, Chronology,
Explanatory Notes © Christopher English 1995
Bibliography, Introduction © Richard Peace 1995

The moral rights of the author have been asserted

Database right Oxford University Press (maker)

First published as a World's Classics paperback 1995
Reissued as an Oxford World's Classics paperback 1998
Reissued 2008

British Library Cataloguing in Publication Data

Data available

Library of Congress Cataloging in Publication Data
Gogol', Nikolaï Vasil'evich, 1809–1852.
[Selections. English. 1995]
Petersburg tales ; The government inspector ; Marriage / Nikolai
Vasilyevich Gogol ; translated and edited by Christopher English ;
with an introduction by Richard Peace.
1. Gogol', Nikolaï Vasil'evich, 1809–1852—Translations into
English I. English, Christopher. II. Peace , Richard Arthur.
III. Title. IV. Title: Government inspector. V. Title: Marriage.
VI. Series.
PG3333.A6 1995 891.73'3—dc20 95–21752

ISBN 978-0-19-955506-2

16

Printed and bound in Great Britain by Clays Ltd, Elcograf S.p.A.

CONTENTS

CONTENTS

INTRODUCTION

Gogol's stories 'Nevsky Prospect', 'The Diary of a Madman', 'The Nose', and 'The Overcoat' all have as their setting the city of St Petersburg, and it has become conventional to refer to them as the 'Petersburg Tales', even though the title is not Gogol's own, and they were published separately and at different times. The setting which links them is that of the 'fantastic city', a concept that would receive further development in the works of Dostoevsky and Andrei Bely among others. The theme had already been launched in Pushkin's poem 'The Bronze Horseman' (1833) in which we first see the figure of the humble civil service clerk as a lone individual undergoing torment, persecution, even succumbing to madness, on the streets of St Petersburg. At the same time it is true to say that the theme of the 'fantastic city' had already been adumbrated in Gogol's earlier writing. In 'Christmas Eve' (1832) the blacksmith, Vakula, flies to St Petersburg on the devil's back.[1] Once there, the devil changes into a horse and, as they gallop through the streets of the capital, Vakula is overawed by noise, bustle, and lights: a fantastic confusion that looks forward to the depiction of St Petersburg in 'Nevsky Prospect', where the unreal quality of the city, it is suggested, is actually the work of the devil himself. In *Mirgorod*, too, Gogol had given us another fantastic perception of the city-scape in Taras Bulba's visit to another capital, Warsaw, with its bizarre Jewish ghetto.[2] In turning his attention to St Petersburg, Gogol shows that its hard streets and tenement houses are just as much the home of demonic forces as the reflecting rivers and lush countryside of the Ukraine.

Against this background two stories first published in 1835, 'Nevsky Prospect' and 'The Portrait', project a common theme of 'art' and the 'artist' and in matter and manner they exhibit more than the others the influence of the German writer E. T. A. Hoffmann. Yet Gogol's earlier procedures are also in evidence; for

[1] *Village Evenings near Dikanka and Mirgorod* (trans. Christopher English, World's Classics, 1994).
[2] Ibid.

structurally both rely on the technique of the double story. Thus in
'Nevsky Prospect', as in the earlier story from the Dikanka collection 'A Night in May, or the Drowned Maiden', two plot lines
drawn in parallel provide a mutual commentary. However, in 'The
Portrait' Gogol adopts a structural technique he had used before in
'A Terrible Revenge'. The source of evil conditioning the action of
the main plot is to be found in another originating story, which
although chronologically (and causally) anterior to the main plot, is
presented in a structural appendage as its key and explanation.

   This idiosyncratic structure is a sort of 'riddle plot': the significance of the main story cannot be disentangled without its apparently unrelated key. The unilinear plot, by contrast, contains its
own inception of the action (i.e. in Russian *zavyazka*) which cul-
minates in the denouement (i.e. *razvyazka*), but the 'riddle plot'
exhibits the typical Gogolian device of inversion: the main story
substitutes *zagadka* (the 'setting of the riddle') for *zavyazka* and
the origin of the action is in effect not *zavyazka* but *razgadka*—its
'unriddling'. The concept of the 'riddle' is important for an understanding of Gogol's presentation of reality (in particular of causal-
ity) in these stories, and whereas for most the 'riddle' can be solved,
the story 'The Nose' appears to present the reader with a riddle
without resolution: *zagadka* without *razgadka*. The very title 'Nevsky
Prospect', the chief thoroughfare of St Petersburg, hints at a technique that would increasingly typify his art—the rhetorical device
of synecdoche, in which the part is substituted for the whole, and
a salient feature assumes the totality of the person or object. Such
a device has great comic possibilities, but because of its inherently
reductive nature it may also imply authorial comment. Here the
Nevsky Prospect suggests in microcosm the fantastic city itself, yet
at the same time those who pass along it are reduced to mere
external features: to hats, dresses, scarves, moustaches, swords. The
effect is comic, but in reducing human beings to the status of objects it is also dehumanizing: it suggests they are empty people, 'dead
souls', whose vanity (and in essence their personality) centres on
some fashionable feature of their external appearance. The double
plot on which this story depends provides the vehicle for a stock
romantic theme—the contrast between idealism and philistinism,
but it also reveals a Gogolian preoccupation—woman as the agent
of man's downfall. The two chief protagonists, the painter, Piskaryov,

and the lieutenant, Pirogov, walk together at night down the Nevsky Prospect. Both notice, and are attracted to, different women, and it is in their pursuit of them that the plots diverge. Piskaryov sees his woman with a painter's eye: she is 'The very image of Perugino's Bianca'. 'The entire bearing and the lines, and the cast of the face—unbelievable!' In a world of synecdoche where external values are accepted as inner worth, he dismisses the idea that she could be a prostitute on no better grounds than that 'her cloak alone must have cost eighty roubles'. It is this billowing cape which he follows down the Nevsky Prospect, and as he does so fantasizes more and more about the beauty it conceals, until he finds himself in a brothel.

Shocked at this unexpected revelation of the gulf between external and internal beauty, Piskaryov returns to his garret, where, despite his confrontation with reality, he manages, through dream and the use of opium, to sustain his idealized view of the woman on the street, even seeing her as his wife and painterly muse. Drunk on his own idealistic illusions, he returns to the brothel to offer his hand in marriage, but when he is mocked he returns home and commits suicide.

The plot line involving Lieutenant Pirogov is a clear contrast to the story of Piskaryov and a commentary on such idealism. His is the lascivious pursuit of a foolish, but stolidly respectable lady, the wife of a German tinsmith. The shock, which he too receives as a consequence of this pursuit, is not spiritual, but crudely physical: he is soundly beaten by her husband and his friends. Nevertheless, for all his initial sense of outrage, after eating pastries, reading the *Northern Bee*, and dancing a mazurka, Pirogov can easily shrug off this shock to his person and pride. Both have been deceived by the surface of reality, but the blows of disillusionment are far more deadly for the idealist than for the smug, self-satisfied philistine; indeed for an artist, failure to perceive discord between outward form and inner content betrays an aesthetic which is essentially flawed.

Yet who is to blame for such misreadings of surface signs? It would seem that, each in his own way, both protagonists themselves bear responsibility for confusing appearance with reality. This does not, however, seem to be the view of the narrator, who, as in the earlier Ukrainian stories, sees in all this the hand of the devil. Thus in Piskaryov's first dream it is as though some demon had chopped the world into little pieces and jumbled them up. At night on the Nevsky Prospect 'the devil himself is abroad, kindling the street-lamps with one purpose only: to show everything in a false light'. Moreover, distinct as the two plot lines are, even here there is an implied 'jumbling up'; for if Pirogov had pursued the prostitute he could quite happily have become identified with the 'gleaming boot and spur and the red piping of a uniform' glimpsed by Piskaryov in the brothel. Moreover, had Piskaryov followed the German blonde to the house of Schiller, nominally at least, he could have been in the house of a great artist and idealist, except, of course, that Schiller was 'not the Schiller who wrote *Wilhelm Tell* and the *History of the Thirty Years' War*, but another Schiller, one tinsmith residing at Meshchanskaya Street'. His friend Hoffmann was 'not Hoffmann the writer' (just as his other friend, Kunz, presumably was not C. F. Kunz, the publisher and friend of E. T. A. Hoffmann). Of course, even with such an outcome, Piskaryov would still have been deceived, and in musing on these two stories the narrator himself comments: 'What an amazing world we live in!... How strange, how inscrutable the games fate plays with us. Do we ever attain the object of our desires?' The world depicted by Gogol is indeed amazing, its workings strange and inscrutable, but in a story in which description is so dependent on synecdoche the tragic and comic consequences of mistaking the part for the whole, surface for content, have an artistic logic of their own.

'The Portrait', like 'Nevsky Prospect', was first published in the collection *Arabesques*, but Gogol was not happy with the original 1835 version, particularly as it had been dismissed by the influential critic, Belinsky, as an imitation of Hoffmann. Gogol rewrote the story between 1841 and 1842, toning down its more overtly super-natural features and presenting it less equivocally as a parable on the vulnerability of the artist to the evils of wealth. On finding money within the frame of the strange, diabolic portrait he has just purchased, Chartkov is faced with two choices: to spend it either on study to develop his undoubted artistic talent, or to set himself up as a society painter. It is the latter course which he chooses and in the process he impoverishes his art for the sake of accumulating riches. Nevertheless, as a socially acclaimed artist, he is suddenly confronted by the genuine art of a contemporary, who has chosen the way of study which Chartkov rejected. Chartkov undergoes a crisis; he tries to paint in his old manner, but to no avail, and the inimical relationship of money to art is further underscored by the fact that he then proceeds to use his wealth to buy genuine works of art, merely to destroy them. He dies a madman haunted by the eyes of the diabolic portrait.

The second, elucidatory, plot line also begins by emphasizing the mutual antagonism of money and art. It begins in an auction room where images of death, vultures, and funerals point to the baleful effect created by financial haggling over works of art. When the diabolic portrait comes up for auction, the whole process (somewhat improbably) is suspended, while the son of the artist who painted it tells his story. Unfortunately, the device, though reinforcing a point, is scarcely convincing as realistic narrative from the lips of the young man himself, let alone one capable of diverting its audience from the business in hand. Its detailed descriptions and moralizing bear the marks of Gogol's later, more oratorical, style. By the time the young man has finished, the portrait itself has mysteriously disappeared. Perhaps, it is suggested, it was stolen as the silenced bidders listened to the young man relating how his father had painted the portrait of a strange, mysterious money lender, whom he considered a fitting model for the depiction of the devil himself. The young man goes on to relate how the portrait had brought misfortune to those who later possessed it, and how his own father had expiated his guilt for painting it by becoming a monk and, after rigorous mortification of the flesh, had managed to paint a remarkable icon. Thus the diabolic portrait and the holy icon are the two symbolic poles of artistic potential. The earlier version of 'The Portrait' had been even more explicit in its examination of art as a vehicle for evil as well as for good. It had also stressed the related concept of the relationship between surface and content in the artistic process, and here one can see a parallel with the problem central to 'Nevsky Prospect': the very nature of beauty itself—the relationship between outer form and inner worth. Although in both stories the art in question is painting, one may sense Gogol's own neurosis concerning the nature of his own art, which was also one of deceptive surfaces. In the earlier Ukrainian stories the bright reflecting surfaces of rivers, lakes, and mirrors had often distracted the reader's vision from darker depths beneath. Yet the more Gogol became obsessed by religion and his own divinely sanctioned mission, the more he felt the need for art to have an illuminating, positive message, and if he were ever to become the seer and prophet he longed to be, his writing would have to move away from surface and express real inner content. The moralistic tone of the young man's narrative reflects this desire, and the artistic precepts on inner meaning, handed down by his reformed father, are really Gogol's own: 'Examine and study everything that you see, submit all to your brush, but learn to seek the inner meaning to everything, and above all endeavour to fathom the great mystery of creation. Blessed are the chosen few who hold the secret.'

The typical inhabitants of the 'fantastic city' are not, however, artists, as Gogol makes clear in 'Nevsky Prospect' when he introduces the artist Piskaryov with the words: 'A strange phenomenon, do you not agree?' A more characteristic denizen of the capital city was a figure who, like Gogol himself, though in a different sense, owed his living and his status to his ability to write. A vast army was required to copy out the forest of official documents that kept the empire running. Everybody in the civil service had a rank; even the lower grades (from rank 14 to rank 9) were 'ennobled' by their service—they were officially *blagorodnye* 'well-born', however poor and humble they might be in reality. Within this hierarchy, rank 9, the grade of titular councillor, marked a career threshold: promotion to rank 8, collegiate assessor, depended, in theory at least, on the successful passing of examinations. For holders of this rank and above the status of 'noble' became hereditary. It is significant that in his depiction of the minor civil servant Gogol focuses precisely on this borderline. Poprishchin, the hero of 'Diary of a Madman', is a titular councillor, the unfortunate Akaky Akakievich of 'The Overcoat' is described as an 'eternal titular councillor', whilst Kovalyov, in 'The Nose', who appears to have crossed the threshold, gained his promotion, not by examination, as is made clear, but in the Caucasus, a frontier area of the empire, notorious for its civil service corruption. In order to give himself more weight, therefore, Kovalyov assumes the title of major—the military rank corresponding to his civil service grade. Anxiety about status lies at the heart of Gogol's depiction of the St Petersburg civil servant (the *chinovnik*). Ground down in the bureaucratic mill, poorly paid, and housed, and although dehumanized by the mechanical chore of copying, he is somehow considered 'noble': for the Gogolian *chinovnik* the external identity of rank replaces the inner content of personality. The only rebellion against the structural order of his official existence appears to lie in madness.

Madness was a romantic theme in the literature of the time, and Gogol's original idea for 'Diary of a Madman' appears to have been a Hoffmannesque tale about a mad artist (in this case a musician). However, for a story set in the fantastic city of St Petersburg it was perhaps more appropriate for his madman to be a civil servant. Poprishchin, whose very name hints at 'career' (*poprishche* is 'career', 'area of activity') begins his 'diary' in a disarmingly sane manner. Yet, even from the outset, it is obvious that he is a prey to anxiety. Thus he admits that his section head criticizes his behaviour and his copying skills: 'Sometimes you dash around so wildly and get your work into such a tangle that Satan himself couldn't sort it out, with small letters where there should be capitals, and no date or number at the top of the page.' Poprishchin obviously cannot measure up to his job, yet it is one which brings him status, as he is only too keenly aware: 'Yes, I must say that if it weren't for the nobility of the job I would have left the department long ago.' Thus Poprishchin's dilemma is that his 'noble' status depends on his ability to 'write', yet his ability as a writer is seriously called into question. There is, nevertheless, a straw at which he can clutch; he has been transferred to the director's office to sharpen quills, and although this is obviously a demotion to carry out more menial tasks, in view of the incompetence he has shown in copying skills, Poprishchin himself can view it as a mark of special favour—he is now working in close proximity to the most important man of all. Such inversions of reality typify the progress of Poprishchin's madness, and his vulnerable pride can here effect a further inversion: the hostility of his head of section is not provoked by Poprishchin's incompetence, it is mere envy of his new-found favour.

As he sets out to work on 3 October, he again reveals his unreliability as a clerk. He is already late and confesses that he would not have gone to the office at all if he did not need to ask for an advance on his salary. His descent into madness occurs in increasingly marked stages, and for all its absurdity is logical, if one bears in mind the psychological mechanisms through which he seeks to overcome his own inadequacy: the inversion of his true position and its projection on to people and phenomena of the outside world.

His difficulties seem to begin after he has projected his own secret desires on to the only other 'noble' man on the street, a fellow civil servant observed at the crossroads. But Poprishchin's comforting assertion about the boldness of civil servants in sexual matters is immediately challenged by reality, when he himself is confronted by the sight of Sophie, the director's daughter, descending from her carriage to enter a shop. Shrinking back and unnoticed, he seems to be in a similar position to Madgie, her lapdog, left outside on the pavement. At this point there occurs another projection of his inner world, even more hallucinatory than his musings on the civil servant at the crossroads. Its object is now two dogs, Madgie and her friend Fidèle, who appear to initiate a conversation on a topic relevant to Poprishchin's own relations with Sophie: misunderstandings and a breakdown in canine communication. This is the first real sign of Poprishchin's madness, but the mechanism prompting his hallucination can be readily glimpsed: he is distancing the problems of his inner world by loading immediate phenomena of the external world with his own psychological freight.

The next phase of his madness comes over a month later after increasing tension in his relations with his section head, the director and his daughter. He is in the director's household, but not of it. Access to the domestic life of Sophie and her father can only be granted through further hallucination, and this focuses on the all-important issue of writing. On first learning that dogs could write, he had expressed his surprise in a revealing oath: 'I swear—I'd stake my salary on it!—never in my life have I heard of a dog that could write. Only a gentleman knows how to write properly.' Not only Poprishchin's salary but his 'noble' status depend on his own ability to write, and the letters of the dogs assume the added interest of an entrée into a forbidden world.

The letters maintain the social gulf between the two dogs, and their formal correctness in spelling and punctuation is seen by Poprishchin as a reproach to that critic of his own lapses in such matters—his section head. Yet in terms of content Poprishchin finds the letters increasingly less satisfactory, principally because, whenever the name of Sophie is mentioned, he himself internally vetoes the subject. In the real world Sophie is about to marry the young courtier, Teplov, but the letters project this as the courtship of Madgie herself by the dog Trésor, whereas in another admirer, the 'terribly coarse mongrel . . . who imagines that he's some kind of noble being', we have a canine parody of Poprishchin himself. Thus the 'letters' provide a psychological device allowing Poprishchin to come to terms with painful truths, yet he has still not learned what he wished to hear. In desperation he calls for human beings not dogs. The next letter gives him the plain unvarnished truth: Sophie is to marry Teplov, and she regards Poprishchin himself as a comic figure, little better than a servant. Wanting to know cannot be reconciled with not wanting to know, even through fantasy. Letters, which at first seemed a rebuff to the section head, now appear to have been inspired by him. This nonsense must now be rejected; for the device, by which Poprishchin sought to distance truth and yet come to terms with it, is satisfactory on neither count.

Shattered by his discoveries and even more aware of his abject worthlessness, he now finds salvation through the very inversion of this condition, and thus enters the third, and final, stage of his madness—megalomania. He reads in the papers of the constitutional crisis in Spain. Spain has no king, yet, he argues, there must be a king—he is in hiding. Once more consciousness of his 'noble' status comes to his rescue; for there are many examples in history of people of lowly birth, even peasants, turning out to be important people: 'if that could happen to a peasant, just imagine what a gentleman could turn out to be?'

Once he has discovered that he is the king of Spain, his diary entries show no inhibitions about the shortcomings criticized by the section head: dates become increasingly jumbled and nonsensical. His behaviour in the office shows that he feels himself superior to everyone, and he is able to interpret the events which then overtake him as regal, rather than penal. The men who take him to the asylum are the deputation from Spain; the asylum itself is the Spanish court, and the inmates with their shaven heads are Capuchin monks; the chief warder is the Chancellor, who soon becomes reidentified as the Grand Inquisitor—indeed, because of the tortures to which Poprishchin is subjected, he fears that the court has fallen into the hands of the Inquisition. Poprishchin's delusions are comic, yet steeped in pathos. His diary ends with a moment of lucidity, in which he fully appreciates the position he is in, only to fall back into madness with his concluding remark: 'But did you know that the king of France has a wart right under his nose?'

'Diary of a Madman' is a prime illustration of the Gogolian formula: 'laughter through tears', and is unique in his *œuvre* as a sustained piece of first-person narrative: Gogol's only attempt to get inside a character. Yet, significantly, the inner world of this character merely proves to be the random phenomena of the outside world, flooding into this inner world and becoming 'psychologized'. 'Nevsky Prospect' presented the reader with an absurd procession of ill-assorted objects; the inner world of Poprishchin is a similar procession, only internalized, and now clearly identifiable as madness. The causes of his insanity may seem to lie in his impossible love for Sophie, but they go deeper: Poprishchin is more impressed by her father, and in the daughter he prizes status above all else. This is clearly seen when he rushes to pick up her handkerchief; for what impresses him most is that it is positively redolent of 'generalship'. Once he has become 'the king of Spain', he can despise her—the roots of his insanity lie in his own sense of insecurity and his search for status.

In ending his diary, Poprishchin leaves the reader with a 'nose'—that of the king of France. The Russian expression 'to leave someone with a nose' (*s nosom ostavit'*) suggests that he has been made to look foolish, and the reader has even more cause for concern on reaching the end of the story which actually bears a 'nose' as its title. Here we enter a world of total absurdity, in which cause and effect are completely dissociated. Even the author declares himself at a loss to understand what it means and, even more provocatively, asserts that 'hardest of all to understand is how authors could take such incidents as their subject-matter'. With a final twist of irony he then challenges his reader: 'Whatever you might say, such things do happen—rarely perhaps, but they do happen all the same.' Pushkin described 'The Nose' as a joke, and if it is a joke, it is one at the expense of the reader: a Sternean story of 'a cock and a bull'.

To explain the bizarre world of 'Nevsky Prospect' Gogol had suggested diabolical intervention. The absurdities of 'Diary of a Madman' are explicable as mental illness, but the even more incredible events of 'The Nose' are a riddle: complete absurdity thrown back at the reader himself, who, unless he is content 'to remain with a nose', must search for his own explanation.

Originally Gogol had provided an 'unriddling' by explaining in his concluding sentence that all this had occurred in Kovalyov's dream. Although he later decided to eliminate this explanation, commentators have pointed to the fact that the Russian title *Nos* ('nose') is merely the inversion of *son* ('dream'). To see it in these terms makes sense; for the inverted logic of this world is in essence that of nightmare. In the earlier Dikanka stories the dream of Ivan Shponka is inherently no less absurd, and yet it can readily be interpreted as the manifestation of Shponka's anxiety at the thought of marriage. The shallow, self-important Kovalyov, on the other hand, does not seem capable of anxiety. Yet if we follow Gogol's sly suggestions his 'hero' emerges in a different light.

As a civil servant, Kovalyov has crossed the career threshold from rank 9 to rank 8, and yet he is a 'Caucasian' as opposed to a 'learned' collegiate assessor: he has gained promotion in a remote corner of the empire without passing any examination. Gogol slyly suggests the insecurity he feels about his status through a logical *non sequitur*: 'He had only been a collegiate assessor for two years and thus thought about it every minute of every day; to give himself greater weight and a sense of nobility he never called himself Collegiate Assessor but always Major.' Thus a civil servant who cannot for one moment forget that he is a collegiate assessor never calls himself such, but reinforces his sense of being 'noble' (the quality of *blagorodstvo* which had so obsessed Poprishchin) by assuming a military title. In the further course of the story such disconnected logic (which, nevertheless, makes 'psychological' sense) will take more free-floating forms.

To make matters worse, Kovalyov has come to the capital, where qualifications are taken seriously, in order to search for a better position (the word in Russian is the same as 'place', *mesto*, which allows for further suggestive punning concerning the nose and its 'place'). In terms of 'place' Kovalyov's ambition seems overweening: he has a vice-governorship in his sights, no less. Looked at objectively Kovalyov is a poorly qualified nonentity, with ideas above his station, who is seeking to better himself in the least advantageous of circumstances, and although he calls himself only 'Major' rather than the 'king of Spain', his predicament, in essence, is not dissimilar to that of Poprishchin. It is therefore most galling to him, on losing his nose, to discover this foolish, yet prominent, part of himself riding in a carriage on the Nevsky Prospect, mocking his own military pretensions by wearing a sword, and parodying his own ambition by being three ranks his senior. To make matters worse, the nose highlights Kovalyov's own lack of education, by claiming (in a phrase full of punning irony) that he himself serves in education. The echoes are those of jeering synecdoche; for, taken literally, the nose's 'place' in education is 'serving according to the learned part' (*ya zhe po uchenoi chasti'*).

Seen as a nightmare, 'The Nose' begins to assume some meaning, and as in a nightmare, the lines of plot and logic are constantly being fractured. There are essentially two plot lines: that of the barber, Ivan Yakovlevich, who appears to be responsible for the loss of the nose, and the plot line of Kovalyov himself. The relationship between the two is ostensibly the same as in the 'riddle plots' of 'A Terrible Revenge' and 'The Portrait': that of *razgadka* to *zagadka* (see p. viii) but here Gogol appears to be mocking his own device; for the story of Ivan Yakovlevich never properly fits the story of Kovalyov. Thus, for example, the nose apparently cut off by the barber is thrice dead: it has been severed from a living face; baked in a roll of bread; drowned in the river Neva. The nose pursued by Kovalyov is very much alive; it rides, walks, speaks, and even prays.

In the first plot line Ivan Yakovlevich is apprehended by a policeman after he has just thrown the nose into the river, but at this point the narrative dissolves into mist. Nevertheless it is this very same police officer who apparently provides the link (and explanation) between the two stories. Yet the link is entirely absurd; for although the policeman accuses Ivan Yakovlevich of the 'theft', it is nevertheless the living nose that he has apprehended, as it was about to get into a coach bound for Riga, with an old passport of an official in its pocket. Despite this information the nose that he actually returns to Kovalyov turns out to be the dead one: a small object 'as stiff as wood [which] fell to the table with a strange noise, as if it were made of cork'. Unfortunately this dead nose defies all Kovalyov's attempts to fix it back in its rightful place.

The two plot lines link up again when the nose unexpectedly attaches itself once more to Kovalyov's face thirteen days after its mysterious disappearance. It is at this precise moment that Ivan Yakovlevich returns to shave him, but, although the police officer had roundly condemned the barber as the culprit, and had actually put him in prison for cutting off Kovalyov's nose, Kovalyov himself makes not the slightest reference to this allegation, and is seemingly more concerned about the cleanliness of the barber's hands. If this is the logic of nightmare, it seems significant that both plot lines begin with sleep and that each protagonist is brought into the waking world (which is in fact a dream world) by his nose (*nos*—the inversion of *son* 'dream'). It is the smell of baking bread which rouses Ivan Yakovlevich, just as it is a pimple on his nose that obsesses Kovalyov as he wakes up in bed. In the first case Kovalyov's nose is an unwelcome presence in the bread which Ivan Yakovlevich had smelled baking; in the second case it is an unexplained absence, when Kovalyov seeks reassurance about the pimple in the mirror.

If the two stories, like the nose itself, are severed and cannot easily be put into place, the internal logic of each plot line itself is no less bizarre. Normal responses are inverted. Thus it is not Ivan Yakovlevich who is annoyed with his wife, when he finds a nose in the roll she has just baked, it is rather she who scolds him. Kovalyov, for his part, treats the loss of his nose, not as a medical matter, but one deserving the attention of the police.

The nose with its association of foolishness is, as we have seen, a comment on Kovalyov's overweening ambition. Gogol himself was characterized by the length of his nose, and in as much as Kovalyov's runaway nose serves in education it may also have psychological significance for the author himself, who at the time of writing the story was acutely aware of his own incompetence as a university lecturer—a post for which he had no formal qualifications and to which he had been appointed by 'Caucasian' methods. Gogol's letters at the time reveal his sense of anxiety in the 'learned' world, yet, like Kovalyov, his ambition had been even higher—the Chair of History at Kiev University, no less. Such autobiographical overtones are strengthened by the fact that on three occasions in his manuscript Gogol made the slip of writing 'collegiate professor' for 'collegiate assessor'.

On the other hand some critics have seen the story as an expression of a different kind of anxiety. They have pointed to the fact that the loss of Kovalyov's nose also harms his marriage prospects, and have interpreted the bizarre plot as a fantasy about a castration complex. Nevertheless, as we have seen in the case of 'Diary of a Madman', a story with which 'The Nose' has much in common, anxiety about status can also be linked to sexuality. Even the overt sexual motif of 'Nevsky Prospect' serves as a vehicle for other

themes. The same is true of the last, and most famous, of the
Petersburg Tales: 'The Overcoat'.

In this story, another civil servant is again faced with a sudden
loss, and again seeks its restitution through those in authority, but
here the lost object, an overcoat, has more explicit erotic associa-
tions. When the poor clerk, Akaky Akakievich, dreams of acquiring
a new overcoat even though he has to scrimp and save, his feelings
towards it seem clearly sexual: 'his whole existence became somehow more fulfilled, as if he had got married, as if there were some
other person with him, as if he were no longer alone but attended
by some fair companion who had agreed to step down life's path
with him.' The external wrapping of clothing, as so often in Gogol,
has more the feel of the material of psychology. The coat produces
a change in Akaky Akakievich: it displaces his other 'love', the
mechanical copying out of letters, and when he is invited out to a
party on the first night of its acquisition, his passage on foot through
the 'fantastic city' from the empty, unlit streets of his own quarter
to the greater light and 'life' of the main thoroughfares, the movement seems more like one of spiritual awakening than a real journey. In contrast to his earlier obliviousness to surroundings, he now
appears to be looking for the first time, and his 'awakening' has
clear sexual connotations. He pauses to examine a titillating picture
in a lighted window, and chuckles, though the self-consciously
inept narrator seems at a loss to know why. On his return from the
party he almost chases after a woman in the street, yet seems at
a loss himself to explain such promptings. The way back is the
reverse of the outward journey. It is now from light and life to
darkness and isolation, and, when daring no longer to look he closes
his eyes to cross a dark, lonely square, it is then that he is deprived
of the pledge of his awakening: he is robbed of his coat by thieves
whose masculinity is emphasized by their moustaches, and whose
words: 'Hey—that's my coat you're wearing!' seem to place his
assumed mantle in its true perspective. His return home to his aged
landlady underlines his defeat by evoking in ironic terms the details
of that titillating picture which had first stirred something unknown
within Akaky Akakievich himself. In this scene of the homecoming,
the bewhiskered man peeping in at the door of the earlier picture is
now replaced by a dishevelled Akaky Akakievich himself; the young
girl with a shoe on only one foot—by a similarly shod old woman,

who has just sprung from her bed and is 'modestly clasping her nightshirt to her bosom'.

From now on Akaky Akakievich is in sad decline. His efforts to have the coat returned are fruitless, and the important person to whom he finally turns so devastates him by his words that he goes home and dies. That it is words that finally destroy Akaky Akakievich should not surprise us; all his life he has been obsessed by words— but only their outer form: the letters in which they are clothed. Copying words has not only been Akaky Akakievich's work, it has been his one source of leisure. Yet the essence of words, their meaning, has always eluded him. At work he could not cope with the skills of rephrasing a document, but could only reproduce its form, and in everyday life he exhibited similar difficulties with the functional use of words, expressing himself 'for the most part with the use of prepositions, adverbs, and all sorts of particles which have absolutely no meaning at all'. The life of Akaky Akakievich is in all senses bereft of significance. He is at the mercy of those who use words to significant effect—in the first instance the tailor Petrovich who 'liked to say things which would shock and then slyly watch the expression which these words brought to the face of his stunned listener'. Akaky's second, and final, confrontation with those who use words to effect is even more devastating. The important personage, for his part, is 'delighted with the effect of his words, which had surpassed even his expectations, and quite entranced by the idea that his word alone was sufficient to scare the living daylights out of another person . . .'. Yet this voice of authority is also copied; before his promotion the important personage had to practise these phrases in a locked room before a mirror, and the very designation—important personage—(*znachitel'noe litso*) conceals a pun: it may also mean 'significant face'. Thus the insignificance of the little clerk is such that he can be crushed by the mere mask of verbal significance.

As is usual for Gogol's 'riddle' stories, there is a secondary plot. A ghost which steals coats appears on the streets of St Petersburg. It is recognized by the important personage as that of Akaky Akakievich, and is only laid to rest when it has stolen his coat. It does so in circumstances which echo the loss of Akaky's own coat. Thus the important personage is returning from a party, at which, like Akaky, he has drunk just two glasses of champagne, and, like the little clerk, has amorous thoughts in his mind (he intends to visit a certain Karolina Ivanovna). Thus poetic justice is done in terms of 'situation rhyme', and revenge is exacted, not on the original thieves, but on vacuously authoritarian 'significance'. As a result the important personage mends his ways.

The effect of this fantastic coda is to subvert the apparent realism of the main plot. Yet on closer examination the details of this plot, if not supernatural, are no less fantastic. Akaky's poverty is not credible in real terms: he has no dependants, no outside interests, and saves money through a diligent system of self-taxation. The further economies he effects (walking on tiptoe and removing underwear) are comic rather than realistic, yet this titular councillor seems poorer than more junior clerks. More striking is his spiritual poverty: Akaky's outward indigence is a metaphor for his inner world.

The coda makes punning play with the concept 'dead and alive', and its depiction of Akaky Akakievich suggests that he is more decisively alive when dead than he was when alive. The ambivalence of 'dead and alive' characterizes Gogol's presentation of the nose in the story of that name; it haunts the view of art expressed in 'The Portrait', and in a sense it is relevant for all the characters who walk the streets of Gogol's 'fantastic city'. It is a theme which will receive major prominence in his *magnum opus—Dead Souls*.

The setting of 'The Carriage' is not the fantastic city of St Petersburg, but the tawdry reality of a small southern provincial town. The reader may feel that Gogol has taken us back to Mirgorod and the ambience of a story such as that of the two Ivans. The difference, however, is in the narrative tone. The comic hyperbole of the earlier tale, which elevated a puddle in the square to the status of a lake, is here replaced by a more realistic evaluation of the dilapidated squalor of the provincial setting.

Nevertheless, there is a consonance of setting and action. As in 'The Overcoat' the streets of this town assume metaphorical significance for the psychology of the central figure. Thus we are told that before the advent of the cavalry regiment the low houses produced such a despondent effect, that a passer-by felt as though he had lost at cards, or had inadvertently committed some foolish act. To this extent the setting anticipates the action: for Chertokutsky, seduced by the card table, omits to make arrangements for the hospitality he has just offered the general and his officers, and consequently he too has inadvertently committed a foolish act.

In yet another respect psychological presentation in 'The Carriage' has affinities with 'The Overcoat'. In both stories an inanimate object is the focus for the 'hero's' self-esteem; here it is the carriage, but Chertokutsky unlike Akaky is not deprived of the object which gives him significance—at the end of the story he is discovered curled up inside it, after the carriage itself has been reduced to its true worth by the devastating criticism of the general and his officers. Before the advent of the regiment animals appear to have replaced people in this town. 'You would not meet a soul on the street', but you might see a cockerel, or pigs wallowing in the mud (which through the coarse, jingoistic humour of the mayor are elevated to 'Frenchmen'). The values of the officers are not much different; as a cavalry regiment, it is the horse which symbolizes their prestige. The general criticizes the town merely because of its stables, and his own horse is given human attributes: it is 'like a southern belle', and actually bears a name and patronymic, Agrafena Ivanovna, as though it were a real person. For their part, the local gentry are characterized by animal, or even plant, imagery. Thus Chertokutsky, wishing to kiss his wife, is likened to a calf searching for its mother's udder, and another local squire has arms like potato shoots. All this mockingly suggests the vegetative, animal-like, existence of provincial life, and it is just as depersonalized as the world of St Petersburg. Here, too, people are designated by occupation or rank. The only two actual names in the story are those of a horse and the central figure himself. Even here the reader may be aware of Gogol's sly allusive irony; for Chertokutsky's Christian name and patronymic are both those of a philosopher noted for his doctrine of the transmigration of souls—human to animal. Pifagor Pifagorovich is literally 'Pythagoras son of Pythagoras'.

Indeed, Chertokutsky's reactions are more akin to those of an animal. His behaviour owes little to reason, but like Pavlov's dogs his actions are motivated by psychological 'triggers'. Thus when he sees a glass of punch, he drinks it, just as he pours from a bottle, if one happens to be before him. His vain boasting to the general is similarly activated; having praised the general's horse, he seeks to assert his own prestige. When he asks the general whether he has a carriage to match his fine horse, his desire to assert comparability with himself might be uppermost in his mind, but he has committed a solecism. As an ex-cavalry man himself, he should know that Agrafena Ivanovna is not a carriage horse. To cover his confusion he boasts about his own carriage, and ends up by inviting all the officers to lunch the following day to view it.

There is no consistency in what Chertokutsky says about the carriage. First he claims that he paid 4,000 roubles for it, then almost immediately says that he won it at cards. His statements are without consequence. The invitation to lunch and to view a prized possession is a 'mirror' reaction to the hospitality offered by the general himself, but it is a gesture without implementation. Nevertheless, the discrepancy between cause and effect is not the fantastic dislocation to be found in a story like 'The Nose', it is a lack of consequentiality on the level of the mundane.

In the Petersburg Tales the fantastic city itself generates a sense of the grotesque in which supernatural forces seem a distinct presence. Humour in 'The Carriage' is more naturalistic, though none the less bizarre. At the same time objects characterize people, and there is a similar use of synecdoche. Moustaches not only typify members of the regiment, but take on all their masculine attributes. The general is characterized by his pipe, and his speech is punctuated by its 'puff, puff, puff' until he himself disappears in a cloud of smoke.

The short two-act play *Marriage* reads like the dramatization of a typical Gogolian story. Its setting is St Petersburg, and although some of its protagonists are civil servants, the milieu is essentially that of the merchants—a social group noted for two chief attributes: wealth and adherence to traditional values. Concern about the first meant that marriages were often more in the nature of business contracts, hence the prominence (often comic) given to the details of Agafya Tikhonovna's dowry. Wealth often attracted noblemen to make such matches, when all they could offer in return was status. The idea of a 'noble' suitor appeals to Agafya Tikhonovna and the merchant suitor, Starikov, is given short shrift. Her aunt, however, champions the merchants against the apparently superior claims of the nobles (Act I, scene xiii). The merchants' adherence to traditional folk values meant that marriages were arranged through matchmakers, and that formulaic pretences of purchasing goods were used to gain access to the house of a potential bride, in order to inspect the real goods on offer. Such devious substitutions and pretexts suit Gogol's comic style admirably and the play abounds in his own reductive imagery of objects: clothes, footwear, food, carriages, and parts of the body.

The play may seem little more than a farce, but all Gogol's bright surfaces have a darker undertow, and in essence *Marriage* is about sexual anxiety. Podkolyosin, like Ivan Shponka in the earlier Dikanka stories, is being bullied into marriage against his will by a domineering figure—Kochkaryov, who claims to be a friend. Kochkaryov takes on the role of amateur matchmaker himself, and although his bullying and machinations manage to get rid of the other suitors, at the last moment he loses his own candidate, who takes fright, jumps out of a window, and escapes in a cab.

The vividness of the language reveals Gogol's ear for idiosyncratic dialogue at its most acute, and in recognizing the comic potential of the merchant milieu, and putting it on stage, he laid the foundations for the later plays of Ostrovsky.

The staging of *The Government Inspector* was a remarkable event. During the reign of Tsar Nicholas I censorship, particularly for stage performance, was extremely strict, and a play which dealt with venal civil servants had little chance of gaining approval. However, the friends of Gogol at court carried out a campaign to influence members of the royal family and gain their support for the play, showing them extracts and suggesting that as the play was not only very funny, but dealt with corruption in the provinces, it would appeal to the tsar himself and his known concern to stamp out corruption. So successful were they that the play gained the tsar's approval and completely bypassed the censors. Even more remarkably Nicholas himself graced it with his presence on the opening night.

This, by any standards, was a personal triumph for the author, but Gogol was far from happy. The tsar laughed loudly during the performance, but on leaving is reported to have commented: 'Everyone has caught it, and I more than most.' Nevertheless, he urged his ministers to see it, though they were far less happy than he to see civil servants, albeit provincial ones, pilloried on stage. It was perhaps the sense that his play was too sensitive politically that caused Gogol's unhappiness. He left Russia shortly afterwards, but in his writings returned more than once to his play, attempting to elucidate his intentions in terms of both theatre and message.

In the traditional nineteenth-century view the play's theme was social criticism—an interpretation reinforced in the twentieth century by Soviet critics, and as a reaction to this commentators in the West, notably Vladimir Nabokov, have tended to dismiss the play's social dimension. Nevertheless, the way in which Gogol's highly placed friends conducted their campaign shows that they were aware of its social and political implications. The reported remark of the tsar himself is even more suggestive: Nicholas had 'caught it'. The theme of inspection itself was near home. Nicholas regarded it as his duty to inspect institutions and towns of his empire in person. His regime was based on his personal predilections which were principally military, and he expected to see 'order' (*poryadok*) in everything. On that first night, with the tsar in the audience, Bobchinsky's request that Khlestakov should tell the tsar that he existed must have been electrifying (Nicholas himself certainly remembered it later), but there is another oblique reference to him, which alludes to military values and the much prized quality of 'order'. At the beginning of Act IV the judge tries to assemble the civil servants in fitting 'order' to meet the supposed government inspector: 'Look, for heaven's sake, gentlemen, hurry up and get into formation. And let's have a bit more order! Don't forget this is a man who visits at the palace, God help us, and tears strips off the Cabinet. Get on a military footing, now—you must be on a military footing!'

This word 'order' is a magic word, it is a talisman which the civil servants of the town feel will protect them from official wrath. The word is constantly on their lips in their dealings with Khlestakov. The official in charge of the paupers' hospital (the 'charitable institution') actually suggests that his patients are cured by it rather than by medicine, and Khlestakov's manservant, Osip, knows what to say when he is cross-questioned about his master—he is a lover of order. Yet the practices of the town itself give the lie to the much vaunted order which the tsar wished to see in his empire. This is most glaringly the case in the behaviour of those enforcers of order—the town's policemen, who in the interests of 'order' end up drunk or gratuitously hand out black eyes.

Each of the town's functionaries exemplifies a negative aspect of official order: the judge—the muddled state of the laws themselves; the postmaster and the warden of charities—the opening of private mail and the denunciation of friends and colleagues: two of the least attractive practices of Nicholas's own police state. In the all-pervasive climate of official suspicion education was particularly vulnerable to outside meddling, a fact commented on by the most nervous of all the officials—the inspector of schools. The mayor's concern about the mannerisms of one particular teacher must be seen against the background of the tsar's own inspection of schools during which he could fly into a rage at the slightest hint of slovenly comportment by the pupils. Hospitals are in danger of being considered inefficient on purely statistical criteria (during the cholera epidemic of 1830–1 the tsar had interpreted high death-rate statistics as inefficiency in a hospital too conscientious to falsify them). In the interests of showing efficiency Zemlyanika is advised to discharge most of the patients in his care. Above all, it is the mayor himself, the chief representative of 'order' in the town, who is at the very centre of its corruption and maladministration.

Gogol himself stated his intentions in social terms: 'In *The Government Inspector* I made up my mind to gather together into one pile all that in Russia was bad, as I then knew it, all the injustices, such as are done in those places and on those occasions, where most of all justice is demanded, and in one go to laugh at everything.' Nevertheless, after its performance, he began more and more to move away from such a view, and his growing concern with religion prompted another interpretation. Ten years later he wrote a coda for the play which, he claimed, was its true denouement. This ending seeks to present *The Government Inspector* as a moralistic parable, in which the town is really the soul of man and its inhabitants are corrupting passions, easily capable of buying off the false conscience represented by Khlestakov. At the end of the play they have to face the real inspector, who is true conscience—the conscience that each must face on his death-bed as he prepares to meet his maker.

It would be easy to dismiss all this as a fanciful afterthought, but there is internal evidence in the play to support it. Structurally there is a clear parallel between the arrival at the end of the play of the real inspector (true conscience) which strikes all those on stage into dumb poses and the effect produced in Act II, sc. viii, when the mayor first meets Khlestakov (the false conscience). Here the stage directions read: 'Mayor and Khlestakov stare at each other in terror for several minutes, goggle-eyed.' This moment of dumb-show is particularly emphasized; for if the stage directions are taken literally it lasts for 'several minutes', whereas the final dumb scene is directed to last for 'almost a minute and a half'. In Act II the interpretation that the mayor sees in Khlestakov the advent of conscience is further strengthened by his subsequent behaviour. For all his much-vaunted astuteness, he immediately blurts out his guilt, for no apparent cause, and, in spite of much evidence to the contrary, persists in seeing Khlestakov as the government inspector up to the very end of the play. For the mayor Khlestakov does seem to represent conscience, even if it is only a spectre within his own mind (and in his own mould) with which deals can be done. Real conscience, however, is waiting in the wings.

On a formal level it is possible to see *The Government Inspector* in another light, as a parody of the classical comedy in the form canonized by Molière or the Russian eighteenth-century playwright, Fonvizin. Mistaken identity is a stock comic plot device, but Gogol's play mocks it by emphasizing its sheer implausibility. In the first place Gogol eliminates deception from this central device: his plot is based on double misconception. Khlestakov is an idiot abroad, who is not aware, until perhaps the very end, that he has been mistaken for someone more important. He is such an overweening nonentity that he accepts all marks of toadying and special favour as merely his due. Deception is part of the play, but as it is predicated on misconception, it is always misplaced and ludicrous. Wishing to impress, Khlestakov reveals details about himself (particularly in the drunken scene in Act III, sc. vi) which if Gogol's intentions had been realism, would completely explode the myth of his identity. Yet the more Khlestakov reveals, the more the civil servants are impressed. When Khlestakov says that they even wanted to make him a collegiate assessor (a high ambition for one at the bottom of the table of ranks) the functionaries, quite improbably, insist on standing in the presence of such a rank, yet they are obviously of comparable or higher rank themselves. The mayor continues to address Khlestakov as 'Your Excellency' even though Khlestakov's own servant addresses his master by the more humble title of 'Your Honour'. A glaring example of this occurs in the offstage departure scene at the end of Act IV. Thus through parody Gogol is mocking the very material from which comedy itself is constructed.

A somewhat tiresome feature of the classical comedy is the sub-plot devoted to a frustrated pair of younger lovers; Gogol's play has no sub-plot—the love interest, as such, is swept up into the action of the main plot, and is grossly parodied. The younger generation is represented by Khlestakov himself and the mayor's daughter, but Khlestakov is prepared to make advances indiscriminately to both daughter and mother, and the romantic nature of his declarations is put into comic perspective through bathos. When kneeling before the mother he is told that the floor is dirty, and his campaign against the daughter is conducted through the advancing and with-drawal of chairs. The typical 'discovery' scene is doubled and paro-died when each woman in turn finds Khlestakov on his knees before the other, and each utters a similar cry: 'Heavens! What's this?' Khlestakov has the primitive psychological responses of Chertokutsky in 'The Carriage', but in his case it is the mere presence of a woman which produces a conditioned reflex. The classical comedy ends with the triumph of its sub-plot and the prospect of marriage: the final act of Gogol's play is the unmaking of a marriage.

Another tiresome feature often found in the classical comedy is the figure of the *raisonneur*, who explains the moral aspects of the action to the audience and contributes to its positive ending. Such a figure in Russian eighteenth-century comedy is Starodum in Fonvizin's play *The Minor*. *The Government Inspector*, by contrast, not only lacks a *raisonneur*, but is devoid of all positive figures. If there is a positive outcome to the action, it can only be in the mathematical sense that a minus in opposition to a minus gives a plus: one set of negative characters (the functionaries of the town) are defeated by the negative Khlestakov and his servant.

None of Gogol's characters is quite the stock figure of classical comedy. The comic foreigner in Russian comedy was a German who spoke with a heavy accent permitting *doubles entendres*—a figure such as Vralman (*vrat'* means 'to lie') in Fonvizin's *The Minor*. In Russian the verb *gibnut'* means to perish, and Gogol gives his Ger-man doctor the name Huebner, which transliterates into Russian as the comically evocative Gibner. In the drafts he had toyed with the idea of having Huebner actually speak in German, but his final solution is a total parody of this stock figure: he reduces his comic speech to the absolute absurd by making his only utterance a sound 'somewhere in between "ee" and "eh"'.

The Government Inspector, like most of Gogol's writing, contains an element of concealed authorial confession. Later he would liken his own behaviour in publishing *Selected Passages from Correspondence with Friends* to that of Khlestakov. Nevertheless, the central issue surrounding Khlestakov in the play is the question of identity, and it is refracted in the other characters, notably in the dual identity of Bobchinsky/Dobchinsky. Although its presentation is comic it reflects an anxiety which Gogol undoubtedly felt during this period: he had failed in his role of university lecturer and believed that he had yet to find his true identity as an artist. His later interpretation of the play as the working of 'conscience' again reflects an issue which touched him personally during his later more religious phase. Yet it seems significant that his projection of conscience in the play is not unlike his portrayal of guilt and responsibility in the earlier stories—it, too, like the devil, or the world of the supernatural, is an external force, ostensibly divorced from the inner world of the characters themselves, and apparently producing only externalized reactions.

The Government Inspector is a remarkably well-constructed play. From the letter which initiates its action to the letter which closes it, its mechanisms operate with the balanced precision of clockwork. Yet the surface it presents to the world seems guilelessly naïve, and in this it exhibits characteristics we also recognize in the short stories. Gogol's art, both as storyteller and playwright, is disarmingly deceptive.

NOTE ON THE TEXTS AND
TRANSLITERATION

These translations are based on the fourteen-volume edition of Gogol's collected works published by the Academy of Sciences of the USSR, known as the 'Academy edition' (N. V. Gogol, *Polnoe sobranie sochinenii*, Moscow-Leningrad, 1937–52). Volume three of that edition, which incorporates all the stories included here, was edited by V. L. Komarovich, volume five—containing *Marriage*—by A. L. Slonimsky and volume four—devoted to *The Government Inspector*—by B. V. Tomashevsky.

Most of the stories in this volume are based on translations originally commissioned by Progress Publishers, Moscow. They appeared in two volumes: Nikolai Gogol, *A Selection*, and Nikolai Gogol, *A Selection II*, published in 1980 and 1981 by Progress, with whose kind permission they have been used for this edition. In this collection, however, I have extensively reworked the translations, where necessary bringing them in line with the text of the Academy edition, and adding endnotes.

The system used here for the transliteration of names is that generally followed in the World's Classics series, and is designed to be readable rather than academically precise. Where greater precision has been necessary, such as in the explanation of some names in the endnotes and introduction, a more academic system has been adopted. Place names are given in transliteration rather than translated form (Nevsky Prospect is in fact 'Neva Avenue'), and where possible are indicated on the maps of St Petersburg on pp. xxxviii–xl.

My intention has been always to reflect the original as closely as possible: this has persuaded me only to transliterate names, and not to translate them (with one unavoidable exception in *Marriage*). A different approach might be taken, however, in a stage production, where the information carried—or suggested—by a character's name needs to be conveyed more directly to the audience. Where I felt it useful and necessary, I have glossed the semantic force of the name in an endnote.

I have reproduced the stage directions and editorial presentation of the plays exactly as in the Academy edition, even where there are inconsistencies (such as failure to indicate the exit of a character from the stage). The only deviation from this principle has been to introduce some uniformity in the references to characters, as Gogol frequently switches between characters' names (e.g. Derzhimorda) and their function (Constable). I have considered it more appropriate to give the reader as close as possible a reflection, in English, of the standard Russian edition of the text than to attempt to improve on the work of earlier editors.

Lest the text might seem overburdened with endnotes, the English reader can perhaps take comfort in the knowledge that modern and popular Russian editions of Gogol also contain extensive endnotes: Russian readers do not necessarily know the Table of Ranks, or the titles of courtiers, or the former names of streets and bridges—to say nothing of nineteenth-century opera and Masonic texts.

SELECT BIBLIOGRAPHY

BIOGRAPHY

Lindstrom, Thais S., *Nikolay Gogol* (New York, 1974).

Magarshak, David, *Gogol: A Life* (New York, 1960).

Setchkarev, Vsevolod M., *Gogol: His Life and Works*, trans. Robert Kramer (New York, 1965).

Troyat, Henri, *Gogol: The Biography of a Divided Soul*, trans. Nancy Amphoux (London, 1974).

GENERAL STUDIES

Bely, Andrey, 'Gogol', trans. Elizabeth Trahan and John Fred Beebe in *Twentieth-Century Russian Criticism*, ed. Victor Erlich (New Haven, Conn., 1975).

Erlich, Victor, *Gogol* (New Haven, Conn., 1969).

Fanger, Donald, *The Creation of Nikolai Gogol* (Cambridge, Mass., 1965).

Gippius, V. V., *Gogol*, ed. and trans. Robert A. Maguire (Ann Arbor, Mich., 1981).

Karlinsky, Simon, *The Sexual Labyrinth of Nikolai Gogol* (Cambridge, Mass., 1976).

Maguire, Robert A. (ed. and trans.), *Gogol from the Twentieth Century: Eleven Essays* (Princeton, NJ, 1974).

——, *Exploring Gogol* (Stanford, Ca., 1994).

Mersereau, John Jr., *Russian Romantic Fiction* (Ann Arbor, Mich., 1983).

Nabokov, Vladimir, *Nikolay Gogol* (London, 1973).

Peace, Richard, *The Enigma of Gogol: An Examination of the Writings of N. V. Gogol and their Place in the Russian Literary Tradition* (Cambridge, 1981).

Rowe, William Woodin, *Through Gogol's Looking Glass: Reverse Vision, False Focus, and Precarious Logic* (New York, 1976).

Shapiro, Gavriel, *Nikolai Gogol and the Baroque Cultural Heritage* (University Park, Pa., 1993).

Tertz, Abram [Andrei Sinyavsky], *In the Shadow of Gogol* (London, 1975).

Woodward, James B., *The Symbolic Art of Gogol: Essays on his Short Fiction* (Columbus, Ohio, 1982).

Zeldin, Jesse, *Nikolai Gogol's Quest for Beauty* (Lawrence, Kan., 1978).

ON THE STORIES

Driessen, F. C., *Gogol as a Short-Story Writer: A Study of His Technique of Composition*, trans. Ian F. Finlay (London, 1965).

Grayson, Jane, Wigzell, Faith (eds.), *Nikolay Gogol: Text and Context* (London, 1989).

A CHRONOLOGY OF GOGOL

1777   Birth of Gogol's father, Vasily Afanasievich Gogol, minor land-owner, possessing some 400 souls.

1791   Birth of Gogol's mother, Maria Ivanovna Kosyarovskaya.

1805   Vasily Afanasievich Gogol and Maria Ivanovna Kosyarovskaya marry (she is 14).

1809   Gogol born on 20 March,[1] in village of Greater Sorochintsy, Mirgorod province. His parents ask the village priest of Dikanka to pray for a safe delivery. Contemporaries remember him as a sickly, introspective child, serious beyond his years.

1821   Enters the Nezhin Lyceum.

1825   Shortly after the birth of his second daughter, Anna, Gogol's father dies. Gogol's first literary ventures can be dated to this period.

1827   *Hans Küchelgarten* (an idyll, in verse).

1828   Completes studies at the Lyceum, gaining membership of the fourteenth (lowest) class in the Petrine Table of Ranks.

1829   First published work, a five-stanza poem 'Italy', appears anonymously in the review *Son of the Fatherland*. *Hans Küchelgarten* published anonymously at the author's own expense. When the work is ridiculed by the critics, Gogol gathers up all the unsold copies and burns them. Leaves for Germany in July, returning in September.

1829–30   Works on literary reviews, publishing *St John's Eve* and other stories which are later to be collected in *Village Evenings near Dikanka*. Studies painting at the Academy of Fine Arts. Enters the Civil Service on 10 April, working as a scribe in the cadastral department.

1831   Publishes his first piece under his own name: an article entitled 'Woman'. Leaves the Civil Service and takes a position as an assistant history teacher in a girls' school. Makes the acquaintance of Alexander Pushkin. *Village Evenings near Dikanka*, Part One, published, and praised by Pushkin.

1832   *Village Evenings near Dikanka*, Part Two, is published.

1832–3   Works on *Mirgorod* stories.

1833   Completes *The Story of How Ivan Ivanovich Quarrelled with Ivan Nikiforovich*.

---

[1] Dates are given in the old style, according to the Julian calendar (to convert to the new style, or Gregorian, calendar, add twelve days).

1834   Appointed Assistant Professor of History at St Petersburg University; his lectures are lacklustre and ill prepared, and attendance declines rapidly.

1835   *Arabesques*, a collection including *Nevsky Prospekt*, *Notes of a Madman*, and *The Portrait* published (January). *Mirgorod* published (March). Completes *Marriage*, and works on *The Government Inspector*, developing an idea suggested to him by Pushkin. On 31 December leaves his position at St Petersburg University.

1836   More stories published, including *The Carriage*. *The Government Inspector* has its first performance on 19 April and is a sensational success. Tsar Nicholas attends the première, laughing often and loudly, which is fortunate for the other spectators, as etiquette prohibits them from laughing unless His Majesty laughs first. Leaves for Germany, spending the rest of the year there and in Switzerland and France.

1837   Works on *Dead Souls*. Rome, associating with Russian painters, and Baden-Baden.

1838   Continues work on *Dead Souls*, travelling between Rome, Naples, and Paris.

1839   Rome, Vienna, Hanau, and Marienbad, returns to Moscow in September. In May his friend Prince Vielgorsky, whom Gogol nursed in his final illness and to whom he is thought to have had a romantic attachment, dies.

1840   Travels to Rome, where he prepares the first volume of *Dead Souls* for publication.

1841   Rome, Frankfurt, and Hanau, then returns to Russia (mid-September).

1842   *Rome* published. First printing of *Dead Souls* (2,400 copies). Travels to Badgastein, then Venice. Winters in Rome. *Marriage* has its première on 9 December.

1843   Spends the summer in Germany and travels south to Nice for the winter. Works on *Dead Souls*, Part Two.

1844   Nice, Frankfurt, Ostend; continues working on *Dead Souls*, Part Two.

1845   Paris, Frankfurt, Hamburg, and Carlsbad. Gogol takes the waters, to recuperate from a serious illness. Develops a fear of death. Travels between Prague, Berlin, Rome, also visiting Badgastein, Salzburg, Venice, Florence, and Bologna. By the end of the year his health improves.

1846   Rome, Genoa, Paris; works on *Dead Souls*, Part Two, and on *Selected Passages from Correspondence with my Friends*. Moves to Naples.

1847   *Selected Passages from Correspondence with my Friends* published
        (January). Bad Ems, Ostend; works on *Author's Confession.*

1848   Visits the Holy Land, then travels on to Odessa, where he is
        quarantined for a time because of the cholera epidemic, and to St
        Petersburg.

1849   In May Gogol writes of a 'serious nervous disorder' and 'spiritual
        distress', complaining of his inability to write anything and of
        general listlessness. *Dead Souls*, Part Two, according to the mem-
        oirist I. Arnoldi, is virtually complete in manuscript at this time.

1850   After a correspondence lasting a number of years, proposes mar-
        riage to Prince Vielgorsky's sister, but is refused. Visits the reli-
        gious community of Optina Pustyn, near Kaluga, and travels to
        Odessa for the winter.

1851   Makes the acquaintance of Ivan Turgenev, who had been one
        of his students during his disastrous year as a history lecturer.
        Conducts a correspondence with one of the coenobites in Optina
        Pustyn and visits other monastic communities.

1852   Informs Arnoldi that he has completed *Dead Souls*, Part Two. On
        the night of 10–11 February burns the manuscript of *Dead Souls*,
        Part Two. Dies on 21 February (4 March by the Gregorian cal-
        endar, or new style) and is buried in the Danilov Monastery in
        Moscow. In 1931 his remains are transferred to the Novodevichy
        Cemetery.

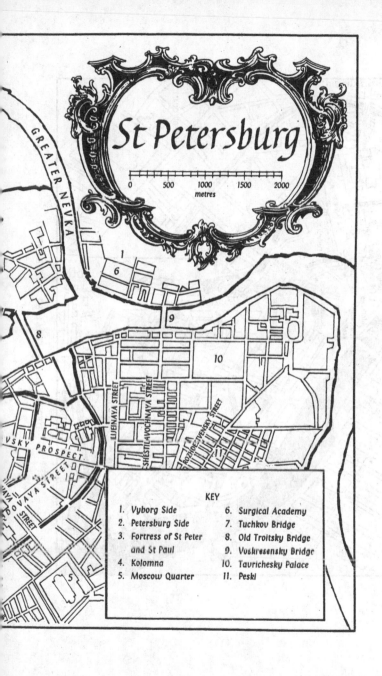

St Petersburg

0   500   1000   1500   2000
metres

GREATER NEVKA

1

6

9

8

10

LIJEINAYA STREET

SHESTILAVOCHNAYA STREET

ROJDESTVENSKY STREET

VSKY PROSPECT

DOVAYA STREET

NAYA STREET

5

KEY

1. Vyborg Side
2. Petersburg Side
3. Fortress of St Peter and St Paul
4. Kolomna
5. Moscow Quarter
6. Surgical Academy
7. Tuchkov Bridge
8. Old Troitsky Bridge
9. Voskressensky Bridge
10. Tavrichesky Palace
11. Peski

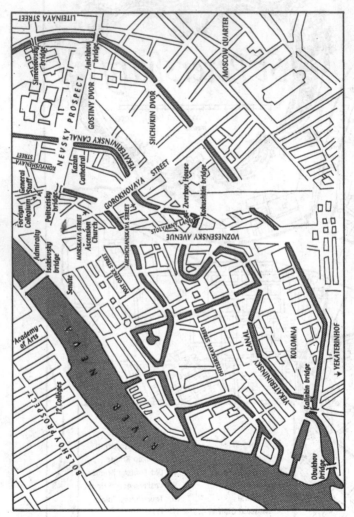

DETAIL OF CENTRAL ST PETERSBURG

TABLE OF RANKS

The Table of Ranks was instituted by Peter the Great in 1722, on the model of the system of civil service ranks employed in Germany. Originally, membership of the 14th class gave personal gentry status and of the 8th class hereditary gentry status. The correspondence between the civilian and military ranks changed as reforms were carried out in the respective services; this table reflects the situation prevailing at the time Gogol was writing—the 1830s. Civilian officials could use the corresponding military title, thus Collegiate Assessor Kovalyov in 'The Nose', while not a military man, styles himself Major Kovalyov.

Class	Civilian rank	Military rank (land; naval)
1	Chancellor	Field Marshal; Admiral of the Fleet
2	Actual Privy Councillor (Class I and II)	General; Admiral
3	Privy Councillor	Lieutenant-General; Vice-Admiral
4	Actual State Councillor	Major-General; Rear-Admiral
5	State Councillor	Brigadier; Commodore
6	Collegiate Councillor	Colonel; Captain
7	Aulic (Court) Councillor	Lieutenant-Colonel; Commander
8	Collegiate Assessor	Major; Lieutenant-Commander
9	Titular Councillor	Captain; Senior Lieutenant
10	Collegiate Secretary	Staff-Captain; Lieutenant
11	Naval Secretary	Lieutenant; —
12	Gubernia Secretary	Second-Lieutenant; Midshipman
13	Provincial Secretary Senate Registrar Synodal Registrar Cabinet Registrar	Ensign; —
14	Collegiate Registrar	— ; —

PETERSBURG TALES

NEVSKY PROSPECT

Nothing could be finer than Nevsky Prospect,* at least not in St Petersburg; it is the be-all and end-all. It positively gleams and sparkles—the jewel of our capital! I know that not one of the city's pallid functionaries would exchange Nevsky Prospect for all the riches of the world. By this I mean not only the young fellow of 25, sporting splendid moustaches and a remarkably well-cut frock-coat, but also the old gentleman with white hairs bristling on his chin, and a pate as smooth as a silver dish—he too is in raptures about Nevsky Prospect. And as for the ladies!—The ladies are even more enamoured of Nevsky Prospect. Mind you, who wouldn't be enamoured? No sooner do you step out on to Nevsky Prospect, than you are swept along in its unending carnival. You may have had some pressing business to attend to, but the moment you step on to Nevsky you will forget all your commitments. This is the only place where people will appear without any special reason, where they are driven neither by mundane need nor by the mercantile interest which pervades all St Petersburg. The person you meet on Nevsky Prospect is likely to be less of an egoist than his counterpart on Morskaya, Gorokhovaya, Liteinaya, Meshchanskaya, and other streets, where you can read avarice, cupidity, and opportunism on the faces of the passers-by and the occupants of the carriages and droshkies flying by. Nevsky Prospect is St Petersburg's main artery. Here the resident of the Peterburg or Vyborg districts, who has not visited his friend in Pesky or by the Moscow Gate for some time, may be sure of meeting him. No directory or enquiry bureau will furnish such accurate information as Nevsky Prospect.

All-powerful Nevsky Prospect! It provides the one entertainment in a city starved of diversion. How cleanly its pavements are swept and—heavens!—how many feet have left their imprint here! The muddy, clumsy boot of the retired soldier, whose impact seems heavy enough to crack the granite itself, the tiny slipper, as light as a puff of smoke, of the young mademoiselle, who turns her pretty head to the sparkling shop windows as a sunflower to the sun, the clashing sabre of the ambitious ensign, which scores its surface as he walks—once on Nevsky they all display their special power, be it the power of strength or the power of weakness. It is a dizzying phantasmagoria! How often it changes in the course of a single day!

Let us begin with the very earliest hours of morning, when all St Petersburg smells of freshly baked bread and teems with old women in tattered dresses and coats, making forays to church and raids on compassionate passers-by. At that hour Nevsky Prospect lies empty awhile: the stout shopkeepers and salesmen are still slumbering in their holland nightshirts, or soaping their noble cheeks and sipping coffee; the beggars are gathering at the doors of the pastry shops, where a sleepy Ganymede, who the previous day had darted about like a fly bearing cups of chocolate, emerges tie-less and broom in hand, and throws them the stale pies and left-overs. Serving folk thread their way along the pavements: amongst them you sometimes see Russian peasants hurrying across the street on their way to work, shod in boots so caked with lime that not even the Yekaterininsky canal, so famed for its clean water, could wash them clean. At this hour it is unseemly for ladies to walk out, because the Russian populace is wont to employ the sort of strong language that they would be unlikely to hear even in the theatre. Occasionally a sleepy functionary will trudge past with his briefcase thrust beneath his arm, if the route to his department* lies across Nevsky Prospect. We can state without fear of contradiction that at this time, before the stroke of noon, Nevsky Prospect is no one's destination, it is only the means to an end: it gradually fills with people going about their business and so burdened with their own worries and cares, that they pay it no heed whatsoever. The Russian peasant mutters something about ten copecks, or seven brass farthings, old men and women wave their arms, or talk to themselves, sometimes with expressive gestures, but no one pays attention or laughs at them, except for the urchins in dungaree smocks who hurtle down Nevsky Prospect clutching empty vodka bottles or freshly polished boots. At this time of day you can wear what you like, even a peaked cap instead of a hat,* or let your collar tips jut out too high above your cravat, and no one would so much as bat an eyelid.

At 12 o'clock tutors of all nationalities invade Nevsky Prospect with their charges buttoned into lawn collars. English Joneses and French Coques walk hand-in-hand with the young wards entrusted to their parental care and explain to them in a stolidly decorous way that signs are erected above shops as a means of indicating what may be found inside them. Governesses, pale English misses and rosy-cheeked Slav maidens, walk in stately fashion behind their lightsome, fidgety girls, commanding them to hold their heads high and backs straight; in other words, at this time Nevsky Prospect is a pedagogical thoroughfare. But as two o'clock draws near, the number of tutors, teachers, and children decreases as these are steadily displaced by their doting parents, fathers walking arm-in-arm with their brightly-plumaged and delicate ladies. Gradually they are joined by all those whose important domestic business for the day is done: they have conferred with their doctor about the weather or the small pimple that has sprung up on their nose, enquired after the health of their horses or children, both, incidentally, evincing remarkable talents, perused the theatre poster or an important article about arrivals and departures in the newspaper and, finally, drunk a cup of coffee or tea; their numbers are then swelled by those whom fate has blessed with the coveted title of officials on special commission. These are joined by their counterparts who serve in the Foreign Collegium* and are distinguished by the nobility of their occupations and habits. Goodness, what splendid offices and services there are! How they ennoble and delight the soul! But alas, I myself do not serve and so am deprived of the pleasure of being addressed in refined terms by departmental supervisors.

All that meets the eye on Nevsky Prospect is replete with decorum: on every side you will see men in long frock-coats with their hands in their pockets, ladies in pink, white, and pale blue satin redingotes and bonnets. Here you will encounter unique side-whiskers, admitted with extraordinary and remarkable skill to a point below the cravat, whiskers of velvet and satin, whiskers as black as sable or coal, but, alas, belonging only to the Foreign Collegium. Providence has denied the servants of the other departments black side-whiskers and they are forced, to their great displeasure, to wear ginger ones instead. Here you can see fantastical moustaches, which no pen nor brush can describe; moustaches to whose cultivation the greater part of a human life has been devoted—the object of watchful days and wakeful nights, moustaches which have been doused with the most ravishing perfumes and scents and anointed with the most expensive and rare pomades, moustaches which are encased at night in fine vellum, moustaches to which their proprietors are most tenderly attached and which are the envy of passers-by.

Anyone chancing on Nevsky Prospect will be dazzled by the infinite variety of hats, dresses, and scarves, wispy and brightly hued, which will sometimes retain the affections of their owners for two whole days on end. It is as though an entire sea of butterflies has suddenly taken off into the air, where they hover in a shimmering cloud above the black beetles of the male sex. Here you will encounter waists unlike any you have seen, even in your dreams: slender, narrow waists no thicker than the neck of a bottle, on beholding which you respectfully step aside lest inadvertently you should jostle them with an impolite elbow; your heart is seized with timidity and fear lest with a careless breath you might break in two this most exquisite work of nature and art. And as for the sleeves worn by the ladies on Nevsky Prospect! Sheer delight! They could be likened to twin aerostats, ready at any moment to hoist their wearer aloft into the air, were she not held down by her cavalier; indeed, to lift ladies into the air is as simple and agreeable a task as to raise a goblet of champagne to the lips.

Nowhere do people greet one another with bows so noble, so lacking in constraint, as they do on Nevsky Prospect. Here you can see a unique smile, a smile that is beyond art, that could make you melt with pleasure, or a smile that makes you feel so lowly that you involuntarily bend your head, or another that makes you feel taller than the Admiralty Spire;* so you raise your head up high. Here you will hear people discussing a concert or the weather in an extraordinarily genteel fashion and with remarkable dignity. Here you will encounter a thousand inscrutable characters and phenomena. Lord, what strange characters you see on Nevsky Prospect! Many of the people you meet will at once lower their eyes to your boots, and should you walk on past they will look back to observe the tails of your coat. To this day I am unable to comprehend why they should do this. At first I thought they must be shoemakers, but not a bit of it: for the most part they serve in various departments, many of them able to draft with superb skill a memorandum from one office to another; or they are people engaged in promenading and reading newspapers in pastry shops—in other words, they are, for the most part, highly respectable people.

It is during this hour from 2 to 3 p.m., the zenith of Nevsky's day, that we can enjoy the grand spectacle of all the best products of man's genius. One will exhibit a dandyish frock-coat with a collar of the finest beaver, another—a superb Grecian nose, a third sports excellent whiskers, a fourth—the prettiest pair of eyes and a remarkable hat, a fifth—a signet ring worn foppishly on the little finger, a sixth—a dainty little foot cased in the most charming slipper, a seventh—a cravat which provokes universal wonderment, an eighth—moustaches which astonish the beholder. But on the stroke of three the exhibition ends and the crowd begins to thin...

At three o'clock there is another change. Spring suddenly breaks on Nevsky Prospect: it is astir with functionaries in green uniforms. Titular, aulic, and other councillors* scurry along, propelled by pangs of hunger. Young collegiate registrars, gubernia and collegiate secretaries, anxious to make good use of their free time, stroll down Nevsky Prospect with dignified bearing, showing the world that they have not spent the last six hours sitting in an office. But the old collegiate secretaries and titular and aulic councillors walk swiftly with their heads bowed, for they cannot permit themselves to waste time studying the passers-by; they have not completely shed their daily cares and carry around in their heads an entire jumbled archive of files begun and unfinished; for a long time when they look at the shop signs they seem to see boxes full of documents or the fleshy face of their office supervisor.

From four o'clock onwards Nevsky Prospect is empty and you are unlikely to encounter on it a single functionary. You may see the odd seamstress run across bearing a box, or the wretched victim of some philanthropic court bailiff, with nothing left in the world but his coarse, frieze-cloth greatcoat,* or an eccentric wayfarer, who makes no distinction between the hours of day, or a gaunt English milady carrying a reticule and a little book, or a Russian porter with a thin beard and wearing a high-waisted, twilled cotton frock-coat, forever being patched, let out, taken in, hemmed and rehemmed, who constantly twitches in every part of his body as he gingerly picks his way along the pavement, or the occasional menial artisan; these are the only people you will encounter on Nevsky Prospect.

But as soon as dusk settles on the houses and streets and the night watchman, with a length of bast matting over his shoulders, clambers up a ladder to light the street lanterns, while in the low shop windows tableaux reveal themselves which dare not show themselves by daylight, then Nevsky Prospect once again comes

alive with movement. Now comes that mysterious time when the
street lamps bathe everything in an alluring, magical light. You will
encounter large numbers of young people, for the most part bach-
elors, in warm frock-coats and greatcoats. At this time the air is
vibrant with a sense of purpose, or something rather like purpose
but much harder to put your finger on. Everyone walks faster and
with rather jerky steps. Elongated shadows flit along the walls and
pavement, their heads almost reaching the Politseisky Bridge.* The
young gubernia registrars, and gubernia and collegiate secretaries
stroll up and down endlessly, but the old collegiate registrars and
titular and aulic counsellors for the most part remain at home,
either because they are married men, or because their live-in German maids are excellent cooks. Here you will meet those same
respectable old gentlemen who at two o'clock were promenading
along Nevsky Prospect with such staidness and remarkable nobility.
You will see them running, just like young collegiate registrars, to
peek under the bonnet of a lady espied from afar, a lady whose ripe
lips and rouged cheeks so entrance the promenaders, especially the
shop assistants, artisans, and merchants, who are invariably clad in
German frock-coats and stroll along in large groups, walking arm-
in-arm.

'Stop!' called out Lieutenant Pirogov, tugging at his young companion, attired in tailcoat and cloak. 'Did you see her?'

'I did indeed: what a beauty, the very image of Perugino's Bianca.'*

'Which one are you talking about?'

'That one there, the one with the dark hair. And those eyes! My
God, what eyes! the entire bearing and the lines, and the cast of the
face—unbelievable!'

'Well, I'm talking about the blonde who was walking behind her,
in that direction. Why don't you go after the dark one, if she so took
your fancy?'

'What a preposterous idea!' exclaimed the young man in the tails,
flushing. 'It's hardly as if she's one of those women who flaunt
themselves on Nevsky Prospect at night! She must be an extremely
distinguished lady,' he continued with a sigh, 'her cloak alone must
have cost eighty roubles!'

'Dunderhead!' shouted Pirogov, pushing him in the direction
taken by her billowing cloak: 'Get a move on, you dolt, or you'll
lose her! and I'll go for the blonde.'

The two friends parted.

'We know your kind,' mused Pirogov with a smug and self-assured smile, convinced that there was no beauty who could withstand his advances.

The young man in the tailcoat set off with a timid and hesitant gait in the direction of the colourful cape, which billowed in the distance, shining brightly as it approached the street-lights, and the next instant disappearing from sight as it was swallowed up in the gloom. His heart pounded as, involuntarily, he quickened his step. He dared not even entertain the possibility of attracting the attention of this elusive beauty, let alone admit such lewd thoughts as those Lieutenant Pirogov had been suggesting; he wished only to see the house, to discover the abode of this divine creature, who, it seemed, had descended directly from heaven on to Nevsky Prospect and was now floating away to some unknown destination. He himself dashed along so fast that he constantly collided with stolid, grey-whiskered old gentlemen and, one after other, knocked them from the pavement.

This young man belonged to that class which constitutes one of the stranger phenomena of our life and which has as little in common with the usual citizens of St Petersburg as a person seen in a dream has with the real world. This unique class is most remarkable in a city where everyone is a civil servant, a shopkeeper, or a German craftsman. Our young man was an artist. A strange phenomenon, do you not agree? A St Petersburg artist! An artist in the land of snow, an artist in the land of the Finns, where all is wet, smooth, flat, pale, grey, and misty. These artists bear little resemblance to their Italian counterparts, as proud and fiery as Italy and its skies; these, on the contrary, are for the most part kind and diffident creatures, shy and unworldly, people who are quietly devoted to painting, and fond of drinking tea with their two friends in a small room, modestly discussing the subject closest to their hearts and insensible of all other matters. The St Petersburg artist is forever bringing to his room some wretched old beggarwoman and making her sit for him for six full hours, in order to translate her blank and pitiable features on to canvas. He draws the perspective of his room, in which you will find all sorts of artist's clutter: plaster-of-Paris arms and legs, to which time and the accretions of dust have imparted the hue of coffee, dilapidated workbenches, an up-ended palette, a friend playing the guitar, paint-smeared walls and an open window, through which glint the pale Neva and the poor fishermen in their red shirts. In all their paintings you see the same drab colours—the ineradicable stamp of the North. Nevertheless they toil at their paints with true pleasure. They are frequently endowed with genuine talent, and were the fresh wind of Italy to blow on them this talent would probably blossom just as freely, generously, and brightly as a potted plant which has at last been brought outdoors into the fresh air.

On the whole they are very timid: a star and an imposing epaulette will reduce them to a state of such trepidation that they involuntarily lower the price of their pictures. They occasionally like to cut a dash but in them these attempts at flamboyance always stand out like an ill-sorted patch. At times they can be seen wearing a splendid tailcoat half-concealed by a scruffy old cloak, an expensive velvet waistcoat under a paint-stained frock-coat. The same is true of their art: superimposed on an unfinished landscape you may see a nymph standing on her head, whom the artist—for want of any more suitable canvas—has painted over an earlier picture, in its time executed with loving care. He will never look you straight in the eye, and if he does catch your eye his glance will be vague and distracted; he does not pierce you with the hawk-like stare of a supervisor or the falcon's gaze of a cavalry officer. This is because at one and the same time he will be seeing both your features, and those of the plaster-of-Paris Hercules standing in his room; or he will be contemplating some yet-to-be-painted picture. This will cause him to answer your questions incoherently, sometimes irrelevantly, and the objects jumbled up in his head will further increase his timidity.

Such a type was our young man, the artist Piskaryov, shy and retiring, but nourishing in his heart sparks of feeling, which, given the right opportunity, were ready to burst into flame. With a secret tremor he quickened his pace in pursuit of the quarry whose beauty had so enthralled him and, as he did so, marvelled at his own daring. Suddenly the unknown creature to whom his eyes, thoughts, and feelings were so firmly fastened turned her head and glanced at him. Good God, what divine features! Her exquisite brow, dazzling in its whiteness, was framed by a flounce of hair as beautiful as agate. The lustrous locks curled as they fell, and some escaped from

under her bonnet to brush against her cheeks, which were tinged a
fresh, delicate colour by the evening chill. The curve of her lips was
suggestive of a flock of the most enchanting reveries. It was as
though every cherished relic that survives of our childhood memories, the quiet inspiration of sweet day-dreams by the light of an
icon-lamp, was joined together and reflected in those lovely lips.

She glanced at Piskaryov, and on catching her eye his heart
missed a beat; it was a stern look and her face took on an expression
of displeasure that anyone should have the impudence thus to pursue her, but on this lovely face even anger was enchanting. Covered
with shame and confusion he halted and lowered his gaze; but how
could he bear to lose his goddess and not discover in what sanctum
she deigned to make her abode? Such were the thoughts that flocked
to our young dreamer's head, and he determined to continue his
pursuit. But to ensure that he would escape her notice he increased
the distance between them, casually looking about him and survey-
ing the shop signs, yet taking care not to miss a single step taken by
the lovely stranger.

The stream of passers-by thinned, the street grew quieter; his
unknown beauty looked back, and he fancied that the shadow of a
smile flitted across her lips. He shivered all over, unable to believe
his eyes. No, it was a trick of the light cast by the street-lamp that
had given her face the semblance of a smile—no, it was his own fancy
mocking him. But he suddenly caught his breath, and started to
tremble in every limb, as a burning sensation seized him and a mist
settled over his eyes. The pavement slipped away beneath him, and
the carriages with their galloping horses seemed motionless beside
him, the bridge stretched and snapped its arch, buildings turned
upside-down, a sentry-box rolled towards him, while the sentry's
halberd and the gold lettering and painted scissors of a shop sign
seemed to sparkle on one of his eyelashes. All this was caused by a
single glance, a single turn of that pretty head. Unseeing, unhearing,
and insensible to everything, he hurtled along in the tracks of those
dainty feet, vainly endeavouring to moderate the pace of his footsteps, which, willy-nilly, kept time with the beating of his heart. At
moments he would be seized by doubt: was he right to read encouragement in her eyes?—and he would pause for a moment; but the
pounding of his heart, the irresistible force and excitement of his
blood drove him onwards. He did not even notice the four-storey

building which suddenly loomed before him, or the four rows of
brightly lit windows which stared at him, or the metal railing at the
porch which barred his way. He saw the beautiful stranger fly up a
staircase, look round, put a finger to her lips and beckon him to
follow. His knees trembled; his heart and mind were afire; his breast
was seared by an unbearably sharp pang of joy. No, this was no
trick of his imagination! Heavens above! Such happiness contained
in a single instant! What bliss in a mere two minutes!

But was this perhaps not all a dream? Could it be true that this
creature, for one heavenly glance from whom he was prepared to
sacrifice his life, and to approach whose abode he felt to be an
unutterable joy, that this same creature was now so well disposed
and attentive towards him? He flew up the stairs. No earthly thought
passed through his head; he was not fired by the flame of earthly
passion—no, at this moment he was pure and chaste, like an innocent
youth who still harbours a spiritual need for love. And where a
more worldly man might have indulged certain lascivious thoughts,
his mind on the contrary only ascended to new heights of chaste-
ness. The trust placed in him by this frail and beautiful creature
committed him to a strict obligation of chivalry, a vow slavishly to
carry out her every behest. He wished only that these behests might
be as demanding and taxing as possible, so that he could the greater
exert himself to fulfil them. He had no doubt that something mysterious and significant had occurred to cause the stranger to put her
trust in him; that formidable services would be required of him, and
he already felt in himself the strength and determination to do
anything.

The staircase spiralled upwards, and with it soared the swift
flight of his fancy. The warning 'Mind your step!' rang in his ears
like the notes of a harp, and the sound of her voice caused him to
tremble anew in every nerve. High up on the dark fourth floor the
stranger knocked on a door which opened and they entered together. A woman of a not unpleasing appearance met them bearing
a candle, but she gave Piskaryov such a strange and brazen look that
he involuntarily lowered his eyes. They entered the room. His eyes
encountered three female forms in different corners of the room.
One was laying out cards; another, sitting at a piano, picked out
with two fingers a wretched imitation of an old polonaise; a third
sat before a mirror combing out her long hair, and showed no

inclination to abandon her toilet at the entrance of a strange person. Everywhere he saw the sort of unpleasant disorder you might find in the untidy room of a bachelor. The furniture, of fairly good quality, was covered in dust; a spider had spread its web over the moulded cornice; through the open door of an adjacent room could be seen a gleaming boot and spur and the red piping of a uniform; a loud male voice and female laughter rang out without the slightest inhibition.

Good God, where was he? At first he would not believe his eyes and he set about carefully studying the objects with which the room was filled: the bare walls and curtainless windows, however, displayed a lack of any housewifely care and the haggard faces of these wretched creatures, one of whom had plumped herself down in front of his nose and was quite calmly examining him as if he were a stain on another woman's dress, finally convinced him that he had strayed into one of those repulsive dens of iniquity, of that vice engendered and nourished by the tawdry sophistication and terrible overcrowding of the capital. For this was one of those establishments where man sacrilegiously suppresses and reviles everything pure and sacred, everything which adorns life, where woman, the beauty of this world, the pearl of creation, is degraded into something strange and equivocal, where she loses all purity of spirit and all femininity, where, in the most repellent way, she appropriates the manners and audacity of man and ceases to be the exquisite being that she once was, so different from the rest of us. Piskaryov measured her from head to toe with astonished eyes, as if to make absolutely sure that this was the same person that had so bewitched him and had borne him away on Nevsky Prospect. But as she stood there before him she was just as fair; her hair just as lustrous; and her eyes still appeared heavenly. She was a fresh flower, only 17 years old, whose descent into this terrible depravity must have been very recent; her cheeks had not yet been touched by it and still retained their freshness and rosy bloom: she was lovely.

He stood motionless before her and, in the simplicity of his soul, was about to be carried away again, as he had been before. But the girl grew tired of this long silence and gave a knowing smile, looking him straight in the eye. It was a smile full of shameless invitation, as unsuited to her face as an expression of piety to the countenance of a bribe-taker or an accounts ledger to the hand of a poet. He

shuddered. She opened her pretty mouth and started to say something, but it was all so stupid, so vulgar... It was as though the loss
of her virtue had also left her reft of all intelligence. He desired to
hear no more. Our hero was a ridiculous person, as naïve as a child.
Instead of availing himself of such a favourable opportunity, instead
of rejoicing at his good fortune, which would undoubtedly have
delighted anyone else in his place, he rushed headlong from the
room and out into the street, like a startled deer.

With lowered head and arms slumped at his sides he sat in his
room, feeling like a beggar who has found a priceless pearl and then
dropped it into the sea. 'What beauty, what divine features—but
in that place, that terrible place!...' These were the only words he
could utter.

For it is true that nothing evokes in us such sad regret as the
sight of beauty touched by the rotting breath of depravity. Far
better that ugliness should consort with debauchery, but not beauty,
tender beauty... In our thoughts beauty is associated only with
virtue and chastity. The belle who had so bewitched our poor
Piskaryov was indeed a wondrous and incomparable being. Her
presence in this despicable milieu was therefore all the more remarkable. All her features were so purely formed, her lovely face so
eloquent of an inner nobility, that it would seem quite impossible
for depravity ever to sink in her its terrible claws. She would have
been a priceless pearl, a universe, a Garden of Eden, an entire
fortune for an adoring husband; she would have been a radiant
silent star in an ordinary family constellation, issuing sweet commands with a single movement of her lovely lips. She would have
been a goddess in a crowded ballroom, on a shining parquet floor,
in the light of countless candles and surrounded by the speechless
devotion of a throng of admirers prostrate at her feet—but alas! by
the terrible will of some infernal spirit, hell-bent on destroying the
harmony of life, she had been cast with a mocking laugh into the
abyss.

Overwhelmed with unbearable, heartrending sorrow, he sat before a guttering candle. Midnight had long since passed, the tower
bell was striking half past twelve, but he sat motionless, not asleep
and yet not fully awake. A drowsiness crept over him, taking advantage of his stillness, and the room began to fade, until only the light
of the candle still penetrated the dream which had overtaken him.

A sudden knock on the door brought him rudely back to his senses. The door opened to admit a footman in rich livery. The walls of his coenobitic room had never before gazed on livery so rich, particularly at such a late hour... Nonplussed, he regarded the footman with impatient curiosity.

'The lady,' announced the footman with a respectful bow, 'in whose presence your honour happened to be a few hours previous, requests that you be invited to her and has sent you her carriage.'

Piskaryov was speechless with surprise: a carriage, a liveried footman... No, there must have been a mistake... 'Listen, my good man,' he said timidly, 'it would seem you've come to the wrong place. Your mistress must surely have sent you for someone else, not for me.'

'No sir, this is the right place. Because it was yourself that was so good as to escort the lady on foot to a house on Liteinaya, to a room on the fourth floor, was it not?'

'It was.'

'In that case if you don't mind we'll get moving, the lady is desirous to see you directly and requests you to go straight to her ladyship's house.'

Piskaryov flew down the stairs. Sure enough, there was a carriage in the street. He climbed in, the doors slammed shut, the cobblestones rattled beneath the wheels and hooves—and the illuminated façades of the buildings with their bright signs flashed past the carriage windows. As they drove along Piskaryov's mind raced ahead, endeavouring in vain to fathom the reason for this adventure. A house of her own, a carriage, a footman in rich livery... How could all this be reconciled with the room on the fourth floor, the dingy windows and untuned piano?

The carriage stopped at a brightly lit doorway and he was at once amazed by the row of coaches and cabriolets, the coachmen's voices, the illuminated windows, and the sounds of music. The liveried footman helped him down from the carriage and respectfully accompanied him through the brightly lit hall with its marble columns, a doorman covered in gold braid, and cloaks and fur coats strewn all around. A staircase with a gleaming balustrade, seemingly suspended in mid-air, led upwards through air heavy with perfume. He was already on the stairs, and entered the first hall, where he recoiled in fright at the sight of such a seething mass of people. The extraordinary variety of faces totally unmanned him; he had the impression that a demon had chopped the world up into hundreds of little pieces and jumbled them together quite at random. The radiant white shoulders of the ladies and the black tailcoats of the cavaliers, the chandeliers and lamps, the shimmering gauze, the ethereal ribbons and the fat double-bass visible through the railings of the magnificent gallery—this was all too dazzling for him. At a glance he could see entire multitudes of venerable ancients and elderly gentlemen with stars on their dress-coats, and ladies gliding so proudly and gracefully along the parquet floor, or sitting in rows; on all sides he heard so many French and English words, and, to cap it all, the young men in their black tailcoats had such noble bearing, conversed or remained silent with such dignity, manifested such dexterity at saying nothing superfluous, such finesse in the *bon mot*, smiled so respectfully, sported such magnificent side-whiskers, and displayed their superb hands with such adroitness whilst adjusting a cravat, while the ladies were so ethereal, so utterly ravishing and serene, and lowered their eyes so bewitchingly that... But a mere glance at Piskaryov, leaning timorously against a column, was sufficient to reveal his utter confusion.

At this moment the watchers formed a large circle around the dancers, the ladies draped in the latest diaphanous creations from Paris, in dresses woven from air itself: they carelessly tripped along the dance floor in their bejewelled feet, somehow looking even more ethereal and weightless than if they had not touched it at all. But there was one yet more ravishing, more glorious, and more exquisitely dressed than all the others. Her entire toilet displayed an ineffable and infinitely refined taste, and yet she appeared completely unconcerned about her appearance as if it had come about quite spontaneously. She looked at the surrounding crowd of spectators without appearing to see them, her lovely long eyelashes drooped with indifference and the gleaming whiteness of her face became even more dazzling when, as she bowed her head, a light shadow fell across her enchanting brow.

Piskaryov exerted himself to the utmost to keep her within view, but to his great annoyance an enormous head with dark curly hair kept obscuring her, then the crowd so hemmed him in that he was unable to move either forward or back for fear of bumping rudely into some privy councillor. When at last he did manage to push himself forward he glanced at his own clothes, intending to set his dress in order. Heavens above, what did he see! He was wearing a frock-coat entirely bespattered with paint; in his haste he had even forgotten to dress suitably. He flushed to the roots of his hair and, lowering his head, wished the ground would swallow him up, but there was simply no place to which he could vanish: Kammerjunkers* in brilliant uniforms closed together behind him to form a solid wall. Now he longed to be as far as possible from the beauty with the lovely brow and eyelashes. In fear and trepidation he raised his eyes to see whether she was looking at him and—Good God! she was standing right in front of him... But what was this? what was this? 'It's her!' he exclaimed, practically at the top of his voice. And indeed, it was her, the very one he had seen on Nevsky and had followed to her home.

Meanwhile she raised her eyelashes and cast a radiant look about her. Heavens above, how lovely!...' was all he could say, catching his breath. Her eyes swept round the entire circle, all of whom longed to draw her attention, but soon she turned away from them with a bored nonchalance, and her eyes met those of Piskaryov. Oh, how divine! What paradise! Give me strength, Lord, he prayed, to survive this! Life cannot accommodate such beauty, it will destroy and carry off my soul! She gave him a sign—but not with her hand, nor with a nod of her head: this sign was expressed in her bewitching eyes, expressed so subtly and imperceptibly that it was seen by no one but our hero, and he alone understood it. The dance went on for a long time; the weary music would appear to be dying away and then would burst into life once more, shrill and strident; until —at last!—it was over. She sat down, her bosom heaving beneath its fine gauze veil; her hand (Lord, what a lovely hand!) fell on her knees, crushing her gossamer dress, which seemed to tremble with the music, while its delicate lilac hue set off the dazzling whiteness of that exquisite hand. Oh, only to touch her, and no more! He wished for no more, it would be audacious to ask for more... He stood behind her chair, daring neither to speak nor breathe.

'Were you bored?' she asked. 'I was too. I observe that you hate me...' she added, lowering her long eyelashes.

'Hate you! Me? Why...' blurted poor, confused Piskaryov, and he would surely have spewed forth a stream of the most incoherent words, but at this moment a Kammerherr*, with his hair swept up

into a splendid cockscomb on top of his head, stepped forward with
a number of witty pleasantries. He smiled agreeably, displaying a
row of rather good teeth, and with each of his witticisms drove another sharp nail into Piskaryov's heart. Finally our artist was saved
by another guest, who turned to the chamberlain with a question.

'Oh, it's unbearable!' she said, raising her heavenly eyes to look
at him. 'I shall be sitting at the other end of the room: be there!' She
glided away and disappeared. He frantically elbowed his way through
the crowd and soon reached his destination.

And there she was, as regal and beautiful as a queen, searching
for him with her eyes.

'Here you are,' she said softly. 'I will be sincere with you: no
doubt the circumstances of our meeting struck you as strange. But
you surely do not think that I could belong to that despicable class
of humanity in whose company you encountered me? My actions
will strike you as strange, but I shall tell you a secret: are you
capable', she said, fixing him with her eyes, 'of never disclosing it?'

'Oh, I am, I am!...'

But at this moment a man, fairly well advanced in years, came up
and said something to her in a language unfamiliar to Piskaryov,
offering her his hand. She gave Piskaryov an imploring look, signalling him to stay where he was and wait for her to return, but he was
in such a fever of impatience that he was unable to obey any orders,
even from her own lips. He set off in pursuit, but the crowd sep-
arated them. He could no longer see the lilac dress: he wandered
in agitation from one room to another, mercilessly shoving people
out of his way, but everywhere important-looking guests sat at
whist, immersed in a deathly silence. In one corner, a small group
of elderly people debated the advantage of military over civilian
service; in another, gentlemen in superb tailcoats effortlessly exchanged pleasantries about the many-volumed *opus* of an industri-
ous poet. Piskaryov felt an elderly gentleman of a most respectable
appearance seize him by one of his coat buttons and submit for his
deliberation a very well-founded observation, but he rudely pushed
him aside, without even noticing the rather imposing order around
the aforesaid gentleman's neck.

Piskaryov hastened into another room—but she was not there.
Into a third—not there either. 'Where can she be? Oh give her back
to me! I shall die if I do not set eyes on her again! I must hear what

she was going to tell me.' Alas, all his searching was in vain. Exhausted and agitated he huddled in a corner and stared at the crowd; but the scene before his over-excited eyes started to grow dim. Finally he started to make out quite distinctly the walls of his own room. He lifted his eyes; before him he saw the candlestick, in which the candle had burnt down so low that its flame was almost extinguished, and its melted tallow had spilt on to the table.

So he had been asleep! Good God, what a dream! But why did he have to wake up? Why could he not have waited one more minute: she would surely have reappeared! The bleak, unwelcome face of dawn appeared at his windows, shedding its cold grey light over the disorder of his room... Oh, how repulsive was reality! How could he face it after his dream! He swiftly undressed and climbed into his bed, wrapping himself in a blanket and longing to recall his lost dream, if only for a moment. Sleep in fact wasted no time answering his call, but the visions it brought were very different from the ones Piskaryov wanted to see: first lieutenant Pirogov smoking his pipe, then the Academy watchman, then a dignitary with the rank of Actual State Councillor, the head of a Finnish woman who had once sat for him, and suchlike rubbish.

He lay on in bed until midday, longing for sleep, but his dream did not come to him. If he could only for one moment glimpse her lovely features, or hear her dainty footsteps, or see her naked arm, as dazzling white as driven snow, flash before his eyes!

Banishing all other thoughts from his mind he sat there feeling utterly dejected, entirely engrossed in his dream. He had no desire to do anything; his eyes stared dully and listlessly out of the window, which looked on to the yard where a grubby water-carrier was dispensing water which froze in the air, and a rag-and-bone man bleated in his tremulous, goat-like voice: 'Sell your old clothes!' These sounds of everyday reality rang strange in his ears. He sat on in this manner until evening and threw himself eagerly into his bed. For a long time he struggled against sleeplessness before finally dropping off to sleep. Once again he had some vile, banal dream. Dear God, have mercy: show me her, if only for a minute, for a single minute! Again he impatiently waited for evening to fall, and hurried to sleep, and once again he dreamt of some functionary, who was at one and the same time a functionary and a bassoon; no, this was unbearable! But at last she came! her lovely head and hair...

she was looking... Oh, how soon it was over! Again a mist settled over the scene and another stupid dream took its place.

In the end he started to live only for his dreams, and from this moment his existence took a strange turn: it was as though he slept during his waking life and was only awake when he slept. If he were seen by someone as he sat speechless at an empty table or wandered along the street they would be sure to think him a sleep-walker or a man ruined by heavy drinking; his gaze was completely vacant and his congenital absent-mindedness had developed to the point where it had banished all feeling and movement from his face. He came alive only as night fell.

This state of mind sapped all his strength, and the worst of it was that in the end sleep and, with it, his dream abandoned him altogether. In a bid to preserve this, the only thing he held dear, he did everything possible to repossess it. He had heard that there was only one sure way of overcoming insomnia: by taking opium. But where was he to get this opium? He recalled a Persian shopkeeper, a seller of scarves, who invariably asked Piskaryov, whenever he saw him, to paint him a pretty girl. Piskaryov decided to turn to him, on the assumption that he would surely have some opium.

The Persian received him sitting on a divan with his legs folded beneath him. 'What do you want opium for?' he asked.

Piskaryov told him about his insomnia.

'All right, I give you some opium, but you paint me pretty girl. And she must be very pretty. With black eyebrows and eyes big like olives, and with me lying next to her and smoking my pipe—you hear? she must be very, very beautiful girl!'

Piskaryov promised to do exactly as he said. The Persian went out and returned shortly with a small jar filled with a dark liquid, some of which he carefully poured into another jar and handed to Piskaryov with strict instructions not to use more than seven drops in water at a time. The artist eagerly seized this priceless jar, which he would not have exchanged for a crock of pure gold, and rushed home at full speed.

On arrival he poured a few drops into a glass of water, gulped it down and threw himself on his bed.

Lord God, what bliss! She came, she was back! But now he saw her in quite a different aspect. Oh, how pretty she looked, as she sat by the window of a bright wooden cottage! Her dress was simplicity itself, as simple as the weave of a poet's thought. And her coiffure... Heavens above, how simply her hair was dressed, and how well it suited her! A small kerchief was cast carelessly around her slender neck; everything about her was modest, her entire person bespoke a secret and exquisite taste. How sweetly and gracefully she moved! How musical the sound of her footsteps and the rustle of her simple dress! How lovely her arm, encircled by a hair bracelet!

She spoke to him with a tear in her eyes: 'Do not despise me: I assure you I'm not the person you take me for. Just look at me, look long and hard and tell me: could I really be capable of what you think?'

'Oh no, no, no! And if anyone should dare to think it I shall...'

But at that he awoke, deeply moved, tormented, with tears in his eyes. 'Better that you had never existed!' he thought. 'That you had never lived in this world, but had been the creation of some inspired artist! I would never have moved away from the canvas, I would have gazed upon you for ever and kissed you. I would have lived and breathed you, like a glorious dream, and I would have been happy. I would have asked for nothing more. I would have summoned you like my guardian angel on going to sleep and on awakening, and I would have waited for you whenever I wished to portray anything divine and sacred. But now... what a terrible life I am forced to live! What is the good of such a life? What pleasure can the life of a madman give those friends and relatives who once loved him? Lord, what a life we lead! Our dreams are constantly at war with reality!'

Thoughts like these occupied him constantly. He could think of nothing, ate almost nothing and waited for nightfall and his longed-for dream with impatience, with the passion of a lover. This obsession finally so captured his entire being and imagination that the image he coveted would appear to him almost every day, and always in a guise so contrary to reality, because his mind was so perfectly pure, like the mind of a child. Through the prism of these visions the object itself somehow became pure and transfigured.

The effects of the opium further inflamed his thoughts, and if ever there was a man driven by love to the final pitch of insanity, a man terribly, frantically, destructively, rebelliously in love, that unfortunate creature was Piskaryov.

There was one dream which brought him more joy than all the

rest: he saw his studio, and himself in it, so cheerful, and so contentedly wielding his palette! And she was beside him. She was by now his wife. She sat next to him, leaning her charming elbow on the back of his chair, and gazed at his work. Manifest in her eyes, so sultry, so weary, was the burden of bliss; everything in his room breathed paradise; it was so bright and orderly. Heavens above! She leant her lovely head on his chest... This was the best dream he had ever had. When it passed he felt somehow fresher and less distraught than before. Strange notions came into his head: 'Perhaps,' he thought, 'she was drawn into her depraved ways by some terrible incident not of her own devising; perhaps her soul is inclined towards repentance; perhaps she longs to break free from this terrible condition. And how can I stand by indifferently and let her perish when I need only hold out my hand to save her from drowning?'

This train of thought led him still further. 'No one knows me,' he said to himself, 'and why should they care about me—or me about them, for that matter? If she declares herself properly repentant and changes her life I will marry her. I must marry her and in doing so I will surely be doing far more good than many of those who marry their housekeepers and often even the most contemptible creatures. But my action will be utterly disinterested; it may even be a great deed. I will return to the world its most beautiful adornment.'

As he drew up this rather impractical plan he felt the colour flooding into his face and, as he stepped up to the mirror, he was alarmed to behold his sunken cheeks and sallow complexion. He painstakingly set about sprucing himself up; he washed, smoothed down his hair, put on a new dress coat, a stylish waistcoat, threw on his cloak and stepped out on to the street. As he inhaled the fresh air he felt a breath of freshness stir his heart, like a person who has just recovered from a lengthy illness and resolves for the first time to venture out of doors. His heart pounded as he drew nearer to the street on which he had not set foot since that fateful encounter.

He hunted for the house for a long time; it seemed that his memory had betrayed him. Twice he walked the entire length of the street, not knowing at which house to stop. At last one struck him as more likely than the others. He swiftly ascended the stairs and knocked at the door: it opened and who should come out to meet him? His ideal, his sacred image, the original of the pictures in his dreams, the person who had made his life so terrible, so full of suffering, and yet so sweet. She stood before him in the flesh. He began to tremble; he scarcely had the strength to stay on his feet, so overwhelmed was he by this sudden access of joy. She stood before him as lovely as he had imagined her, except that her eyes were sleepy, and a pallor crept over her face, which was not as fresh as he had seen it, but she was lovely just the same.

'Oh!' she exclaimed on seeing Piskaryov, and rubbed her eyes (it was already two o'clock). 'Why did you run away from us that time?'

He collapsed into a chair and stared at her.

'And I've only just woken up: they brought me back at seven o'clock this morning. I was completely drunk,' she added with a smile.

Oh, better you were dumb, with no tongue in your head, than that you should utter such words! With them she had revealed the full panorama of her life. Undeterred by this set-back, however, he steeled himself, determined to see whether his admonitions would have any effect on her. Mustering all his courage, he began describing to her in a trembling and at the same time ardent voice the full horror of her position. She listened with an attentive air and the surprised look of one whose eye has just lit upon something strange and unexpected. With a slight smile she glanced at her friend sitting in the corner, who had stopped cleaning her comb and was also listening with great interest to this new homilist.

'It's true that I'm poor,' Piskaryov concluded his long and edifying peroration, 'but we will work hard, we'll struggle together to improve our lot. There is nothing more gratifying than to owe nothing to anybody. I shall sit at my easel, and you, seated beside me, will inspire my work, as you embroider, or occupy yourself with other needlework, and we shall not lack for anything.'

'The very idea!' she interrupted, with an expression of contempt. 'I am no washerwoman or seamstress, to be putting myself to work.'

Dear God! How well these words conveyed all the despicable baseness of her life, a life of futility and indolence, the faithful companions of debauchery.

'Why don't you marry me?' interjected her friend with an impudent look, who, until now, had sat in silence in the corner. 'If you make me your wife I'll sit like this!' she said, whereupon her wretched face took on a stupid expression, which her lovely companion found extraordinarily funny.

No, this was too much! This was more than he could bear! He fled headlong, numbed in mind and senses. His head spun: he wandered about all day long in a stupor, seeing, hearing and feeling nothing. Where he slept—or whether he slept at all—no one knew; only on the following day did some blind instinct lead him to his lodgings, pale and ghastly to behold, with unkempt hair and the stamp of insanity on his face. He locked himself into his room, admitted no one, and sent out for nothing. Four days passed and never once did his door open; finally, a week elapsed and the room was still locked. The neighbours pounded on the door and called out to him, but to no avail; finally they broke the door down and found his lifeless body with its throat slashed. A bloody razor lay where it had fallen on the floor. From the twisted angle of his outflung arms and the terrible grimace on his face it could be concluded that his hand had been unsteady and that he had suffered a long agony before his sinner's soul had departed his body.

Thus perished poor Piskaryov, victim of an insane passion, a man so quiet, timid, modest, childishly naïve, and gifted with a spark of genius that in time might have flared up to dazzle all with its breadth and intensity. No one lamented his passing, no one stood beside his cold corpse other than the inevitable figures of the inspector of police and the impassive police physician. His coffin was quietly borne to the Okhta cemetery,* without benefit of any religious rite; only one person walked behind it, weeping; this was a sentry corporal, who wept because he had drunk a bottle of vodka too many. Even Lieutenant Pirogov did not come to look at the body of this unfortunate wretch, to whom when alive he had once extended his lofty patronage. Indeed, he had far better things to do with his time: he was caught up in a most unusual adventure. But we shall return to him shortly.

I do not like corpses and I find it extremely unpleasant when my path is crossed by a long funeral cortège accompanied by an invalid soldier, dressed like a Capuchin monk,* who takes snuff from his left hand, because his right is holding the funeral torch. I always feel vexed at the sight of a rich catafalque and a velvet coffin; but my vexation is tinged with sadness when I see a carter hauling along a pauper's undraped red coffin, behind which there trudges a solitary beggar-woman, who has met them at a crossroads and tags along behind, for want of anything better to do.

If I remember rightly, we left Lieutenant Pirogov taking his leave from poor Piskaryov and dashing in pursuit of his blonde. This blonde was a pretty but rather fickle creature. She paused before every shop and examined the objects in the window, the ribbons, headscarves, ear-rings, gloves, and other knick-knacks, fluttering this way and that, forever gazing about her and looking back the way she had come. 'Got you, my pretty!' crowed Pirogov exultantly, continuing his pursuit and turning up his collar to hide his face, lest he bump into any acquaintances. But it would not go amiss at this point to tell our readers more about this Lieutenant Pirogov.

But before we tell you what sort of man Lieutenant Pirogov was, it would be apposite to say something about the society to which Pirogov belonged. There is a category of officers in St Petersburg who constitute a middle class of their own. One of their number will invariably be found at a soirée or dinner given by an Actual State Councillor, who has received this rank in consideration of forty years of service. A handful of pallid daughters, as utterly devoid of colour as St Petersburg itself, some of whom are already past their prime, a table set for tea, a pianoforte, a *thé dansant*—this is all inseparably associated with the glittering epaulette, framed in the lamplight between a virtuous blonde on one side and the black dress coat of her brother, or a family friend, on the other. It is extremely hard to rouse these impassive maidens to a smile; to do this you have to be extremely artful, or, to be more precise, altogether artless. You have to make conversation in a way that is neither too clever, nor too funny, sticking to the sort of small talk of which women are so enamoured. This is an exercise in which the aforesaid gentlemen, to give them their due, excel. They have the gift of being able to make these insipid beauties laugh and listen. Exclamations stifled by laughter such as 'No, please desist! You shall make me die laughing!' are often their greatest reward.

In the very highest circles they are seldom, if ever encountered. They have been ousted by what in this society are called aristocrats; nevertheless they are regarded as scholars and educated people. They love to hold forth about literature; they praise Bulgarin, Pushkin, and Grech and talk with contempt and barbed witticisms about A. A. Orlov.* They never miss a public lecture, whether it be on bookkeeping, or even forestry. You can be sure to find one of them in the theatre, even at the performance of some *Filatka* vaudeville,* which he will find most offensive to his fastidious taste. As devoted patrons of the thespian arts, they are the theatre manager's ideal spectators. They are particularly fond of good verse in a play, and will loudly applaud their favourite actors; many of them, after long years of teaching in state institutions or cramming students for these institutions, can eventually splash out on a cabriolet and pair of horses. This leads to a widening of their circle: they finally achieve their ambition of marrying a merchant's daughter, who can play the piano, and has a tidy dowry of a hundred thousand or thereabouts, and large numbers of bearded relations. They cannot aspire to this honour, however, before they finally attain the rank of colonel, for the Russian bearded classes, notwithstanding the distinct smell of cabbage which emanates from their person, will on no account marry their daughter to anyone with a rank lower than general, or at the very least, colonel.

Such are the primary attributes of this class of young people. But Lieutenant Pirogov had a large number of talents, peculiar to himself. He could declaim with great effect lines from such classics as *Dmitry Donskoy* and *Woe from Wit*,* and was particularly skilful at releasing smoke-rings from his pipe, frequently achieving volleys of ten successive rings. He was adept at relating anecdotes like that concerning the difference between a cannon and a unicorn.* Indeed, it would be hard to list all the talents with which nature had endowed Pirogov. He liked to talk about actresses and dancers, but in a somewhat less outspoken manner than that in which young ensigns are wont to discuss this topic.

He was extremely content with his rank, to which he had been promoted quite recently, and although he would sometimes groan when lying down on his divan: 'Oh dear, oh dear! The vanity of life! What does it matter that I am a lieutenant?' he was secretly very flattered by his new position of merit; he would always try to steer a conversation round to the subject of rank, and once, when he encountered a clerk on the street who struck him as insufficiently deferential, he promptly stopped him and gave him to know in so many words that he was in the presence of a lieutenant and not just some run-of-the-mill officer. He took particular pains to express this in as eloquent a manner as possible because at that moment two extremely attractive ladies were walking past.

Pirogov in general nourished a passion for everything refined, and liked to patronize his artist friend Piskaryov; this, however, was perhaps prompted by his earnest desire to see his own manly visage grace one of the latter's canvases—but enough about Pirogov's qualities. Man is such a marvellous creation that it is quite impossible to list all his merits at a single attempt, for the closer you look the more excellent features you will discern, and their description could go on for ever.

Thus, Pirogov continued to pursue his fair stranger, from time to time addressing questions to her which she answered in sharp, curt and rather inarticulate terms. Passing through the dark Kazan Gates they entered Meshchanskaya Street, a street of tobacconists and bric-à-brac stalls, of German craftsmen and Finnish wenches. The blonde ran along faster and flitted through the entrance to a rather shabby building. Pirogov followed her. She flew up a dark, narrow staircase and passed through a doorway, which Pirogov also boldly traversed. He found himself in a large room with grimy walls and a soot-blackened ceiling. A pile of metal bolts and locksmith's tools, gleaming coffee-pots and candlesticks lay on the table; the floor was littered with brass and iron shavings. Pirogov saw at once that this was the workshop of a craftsman. His quarry flew on through a side door. Pirogov hesitated for a moment but, acting true to his Russian nature, resolved to press forward. He entered a room quite unlike the first and whose great neatness indicated that the master of the house was a German. Here he was brought up in his tracks by a most remarkable sight.

Before him sat Schiller—not the Schiller who wrote *Wilhelm Tell* and the *History of the Thirty Years' War*, but another Schiller, one tinsmith residing at Meshchanskaya Street. Beside Schiller stood Hoffmann—not Hoffmann the writer, but a rather good shoemaker from Offitserskaya Street, and a great friend of Schiller's. Schiller was drunk; he sat on a chair stamping his foot and heatedly making some point. None of this would have seemed particularly strange to Pirogov, had it not been for the extraordinary disposition of the figures. Schiller was seated, with his well-fleshed nose thrust forward and his head held high, while Hoffmann had seized this nose with two fingers and was wielding the blade of his shoemaker's knife in close proximity to its skin. Both of them were talking in the German language, which meant that Lieutenant Pirogov, who in German could only say 'Gut Morgen', was unable to understand precisely what was going on. The gist of Schiller's words was as follows:

'I don't want it, I don't need a nose!' he said, waving his arms... 'That nose costs me three pounds a month in snuff. And I have to buy it in a filthy Russian shop because the German shop does not keep Russian snuff; I pay forty copecks to the filthy Russian shop for every pound; that means one rouble twenty copecks, and twelve times one rouble twenty copecks makes fourteen roubles forty copecks. Do you hear, Hoffmann my friend? My nose alone costs me fourteen roubles forty copecks. And then on holidays I take *rapé** snuff because I don't want to take that filthy Russian snuff on holidays. In a year I use two pounds of *rapé* at two roubles a pound. Six and fourteen—twenty roubles forty copecks on snuff alone! That's robbery, now, isn't it, Hoffmann my friend?'

Hoffmann, who was also drunk, answered in the affirmative.

'Twenty roubles forty copecks! I am a German from Swabia, I have a king in Germany. I don't want my nose! Cut off my nose! Get rid of my nose!'

And had it not been for Lieutenant Pirogov's sudden entry there is no doubt but that Hoffmann would, without further ado, have severed Schiller's nose from his face, because he held the knife poised to cut, exactly as if he were about to slice out a new leather sole.

Schiller was most vexed that this sudden intrusion by a stranger, an uninvited guest, had thus upset his plan. Although his mind was clouded by an intoxicating haze of beer and wine, he was still aware that it is somewhat unseemly to show oneself to a complete outsider in such a state and performing such an action. Meanwhile Pirogov described a slight bow and pronounced in his customarily courteous manner: 'I do beg your pardon...'

'Get out!...' slurred Schiller in reply.

This retort left Lieutenant Pirogov quite nonplussed. It was for him an entirely unfamiliar form of address. The faint smile which had appeared on his face vanished at once. In a tone of offended dignity he continued: 'I beg your pardon, my good sir... perhaps you did not remark... that I am an officer...'

'Vot iss an officer! I am German from Swabia. Me too'—at which point Schiller pounded on the table with his fist—'vill be officer: one and half year cadet, two year lieutenant, now tomorrow I am officer. But I don't vant to serve. I make viz officer zo: poof!'

Here Schiller held out his palm and blew away an imaginary speck of dust.

Lieutenant Pirogov could see that he had no choice but to retreat. Yet this treatment, so unbefitting one of his station, was most displeasing to him. He paused several times on the staircase, endeavouring to recover his presence of mind and considering how to repay Schiller for his rudeness. Finally, he concluded that Schiller could be forgiven, as somewhat the worse for beer, and then he remembered the pretty blonde and decided to let the matter rest.

Early the following morning Lieutenant Pirogov reappeared in the locksmith's workshop. He was met in the front room by the comely blonde, who asked him in a severe voice, most becoming to her pretty face: 'What can I do for you?'

'Aha, good day my darling! Don't you recognize me! You little minx, what lovely eyes you have!'

At this Pirogov was about to chuck her under the chin in the most agreeable fashion with his finger, but the blonde recoiled in alarm and asked as sternly as before: 'What can I do for you?'

'Apart from you yourself, I require nothing,' replied Lieutenant Pirogov, with a pleasant smile, stepping a little closer; but observing that the timorous blonde was about to disappear through the door he added: 'I want to order some spurs, my darling. Can you make me some spurs? Although I need no spurs to love you, a bridle would be far more appropriate. My, what lovely hands!' Lieutenant Pirogov was always very generous with complimentary declarations of this sort.

'I shall call my husband right away,' exclaimed the German blonde and retreated from the room, which was entered a few minutes later by Schiller, eyes still heavy with sleep and the effects of his carousal. As he gazed blearily at the officer he vaguely remembered, as if in a dream, that something had happened the previous evening. The exact details he could not remember, but he felt that he had done something stupid, and he therefore received the officer with a most forbidding expression.

'I can't do spurs for less than fifteen roubles a pair,' he stated, wishing to get rid of Pirogov; as an honest German he found it extremely humiliating to have to face another man who had seen him in such an unseemly state. Schiller preferred to drink entirely without witnesses, in the company of only two or three friends, and at such times he would lock himself away even from his apprentices.

'Why so expensive?' asked Pirogov persuasively.

'German work,' replied Schiller coolly, stroking his chin. 'A Russian will do it for two roubles.'

'As a sign of my great affection for you and my wish to make your acquaintance, I am willing to pay fifteen roubles.'

Schiller hesitated: as an honest German he felt somewhat ashamed. Hoping to discourage his customer he announced that he could not complete the spurs in less than two weeks. But Pirogov declared himself entirely in agreement, without the least equivocation.

The German thought hard how best to do his work, to ensure that it would indeed be worth fifteen roubles. At this moment the blonde came into the workshop and started to rummage amongst the coffee-pots on the table. The lieutenant availed himself of Schiller's reverie to step across to her and squeeze her arm, which was bare to the shoulder. Schiller was most displeased by this.

'Mein Frau!' he shouted.

'Was wollen Sie doch?' answered the blonde.

'Gensie zum kitchen!'*—whereupon the blonde departed.

'So, they'll be ready in two weeks?' asked Pirogov.

'Yes, in two weeks,' answered Schiller pensively: 'I have very much work now.'

'Goodbye! I shall call for them.'

'Goodbye,' answered Schiller, locking the door after him.

Lieutenant Pirogov decided not to abandon his solicitations, even though the German blonde had given him such an unmistakable brush-off. He could not understand how anyone could be able to resist him; especially since his personal charms and exalted rank gave him every right to attention. We should point out at this junction, however, that Schiller's wife, for all her comeliness, was very stupid. All the same, stupidity is a great asset in a pretty wife. At any rate I have known many husbands who go into raptures about the stupidity of their wives and see in them all the attributes of childlike innocence. Beauty performs veritable miracles. In a beautiful woman all mental defects, instead of provoking revulsion, somehow become extraordinarily alluring; in such creatures vice itself strikes us as comely and harmless; but if she lacks beauty a woman must be fully twenty times as clever as a man in order to command at least respect, if not love. In addition, Schiller's wife, for all her stupidity, had always been true to her matrimonial vows, and thus Pirogov had many obstacles in the way of his intrepid undertaking; but the greater the obstacles to be overcome the sweeter the victory, and his quarry exercised increasing fascination for him with each successive day. He started to make frequent visits to enquire about his spurs, until Schiller finally lost patience. He redoubled his efforts to finish the spurs as soon as possible; and soon they were ready.

'Ah, what excellent work!' exclaimed Lieutenant Pirogov on seeing his new spurs. 'Heavens, what a fine job you've done! Even our general's spurs are no match for these.'

A warm glow of satisfaction spread through Schiller's heart. His eyes took on a merry sparkle and he felt quite well disposed towards Pirogov. 'This Russian officer's a smart fellow,' he thought to himself.

'In that case I suppose you could make a scabbard for a dagger?'

'Natürlich,' said Schiller with a smile.

'Well, I have a dagger which I'd like you to fix for me. I'll bring it in; it's a very nice Turkish dagger, but I'd like a different scabbard for it.'

Schiller was dumbfounded by this new request. His face darkened. 'Verdammt!' he thought, inwardly cursing himself for having invited the work. He felt it dishonourable to refuse, especially since the Russian officer had praised his work. With a slight shake of his head he expressed his agreement, but the kiss which Pirogov, on his way out, brazenly planted right on the pretty blonde's lips, left him completely aghast.

At this point I think it would not go amiss to acquaint the reader somewhat more closely with Schiller. Schiller was German to the marrow of his bones. Right from the age of 20, that happy age when the Russian lives in a devil-may-care manner, Schiller had planned out his entire life, and never made the least deviation, not on any account. He resolved to rise at seven, lunch at two, be punctual in everything, and get drunk on Sundays. He determined to earn himself a capital of 50,000 in the course of ten years, and this was as sure and incontrovertible as fate itself, for a lowly functionary is more likely to forget a summons to see his supervisor than a German is to go against his word. On no account would he ever increase his expenses, and if the price of potatoes rose above its usual level he would not increase his budget by a single copeck, but instead would reduce the quantity he purchased. Although at times he was forced to go hungry, he became accustomed to this.

His punctiliousness extended even to the point that he resolved to kiss his wife no more than twice a day and, to ensure that he would not give her an extra kiss, he was careful never to put more than one spoon of pepper in his soup. On Sundays this rule was not so strictly observed, however, because on these days Schiller would drink two bottles of beer and one bottle of caraway vodka, although he always used to fulminate against this latter beverage. In his drinking habits he was not at all like an Englishman, who will lock his door the moment he has done eating and tipple in solitude. On the contrary, as a German he always drank with inspiration, either in company with the shoemaker Hoffmann, or the carpenter Kunz, also a German and a great drunkard.

Such was the character of the worthy Schiller, who now found himself in such an unwelcome predicament. Phlegmatic though he was and a German to boot, Pirogov's antics none the less provoked in him something akin to jealousy. He pondered long and hard and was unable to decide how to rid himself of this Russian officer. In the mean time Pirogov, smoking his pipe in the company of his comrades—for thus is it ordered by Providence that where there are officers, there too will there be pipes—smoking his pipe and smiling pleasantly in the company of his comrades, made meaningful allusions to an intrigue with a pretty Fräulein, with whom, according to him, he was already on the closest possible terms, but whose favour he in actual fact almost despaired of winning.

One day he was strolling along Meshchanskaya, contemplating the building adorned by Schiller's sign with its coffee-pots and samovars, when, to his great delight, he espied the pretty head of his blonde, hanging out of a window, watching the passers-by. He stopped, waved and said: 'Gut Morgen!' The blonde nodded in answer, as to an acquaintance.

'Say, is your husband at home?'

'He is,' answered the blonde.

'And when is he not at home?'

'He's not at home on Sundays,' said the foolish blonde.

'Capital,' thought Pirogov: 'We must turn that to our advantage.'—And the following Sunday, like a bolt from the blue, he appeared before the object of his desire.

Sure enough, Schiller was not at home... The pretty mistress of the house was alarmed; but this time Pirogov proceeded with caution. He comported himself with great respect and described a deep bow, which displayed to great advantage the the elegance of his supple torso. He delivered himself of a few amusing and respectful witticisms, but the foolish Frau only answered in monosyllables. Finally, after deploying all his wiles and seeing that nothing availed, he invited her to dance. She agreed at once, because German ladies are always greatly enamoured of dancing. Pirogov had set great store by this ruse: first, it gave her a certain amount of pleasure, secondly, it would show off his graceful bearing and dexterity, and thirdly, as dancing allows one a great degree of proximity, he would be able to embrace his partner and lay the foundation for further intimacies. In short, he foresaw a complete triumph. He began with a gavotte, knowing that with German ladies you have to proceed in gradual stages. The comely Frau Schiller stepped out into the middle of the room and raised a pretty foot. This posture so delighted Pirogov that he rushed to embrace her. At this she cried out in protest, which only increased her charm in Pirogov's eyes; he smothered her with kisses. Suddenly the door opened and in walked Schiller with Hoffmann and Kunz the carpenter. All these worthy craftsmen were as drunk as lords.

But I will allow the reader to judge for himself Schiller's rage and indignation.

'Blackguard!' he shouted in furious indignation 'how dare you kiss my wife? You are a villain and not Russian officer. Dammit, Hoffmann my friend, I am a German and not Russian swine, is it not so?'

Hoffmann answered in the affirmative.

'Oh no, I don't want to grow horns! Grab him by the scruff of his neck, Hoffmann my friend—I don't want horns,' he continued, frantically waving his arms, the effort turning his face as red as the cloth of his waistcoat. 'I am living eight years in St Petersburg, I have my mother in Swabia and my uncle in Nuremberg, I am a

German and not a cattle mit horns. Away with him, Hoffmann my
friend! Hold him von his hand and foot, Kunz mein Kamerad!'

And the Germans seized Pirogov by his arms and legs.

In vain did he struggle to free himself: these three craftsmen
were the sturdiest of all the St Petersburg Germans. Had Pirogov
been in full uniform, respect for his rank and title would probably
have stayed the hands of these turbulent Teutons. But he had come
dressed like any other private citizen, in an ordinary frock-coat and
without his epaulettes. The Germans set about him in a wild frenzy
and rent the clothes from his body. Hoffmann sat on his legs,
pinning him down with all the weight of his hefty frame, while
Kunz seized his head and Schiller fetched a bundle of twigs, which
they used as a sweeping-brush. Here I am forced to disclose, to
my great regret, that Lieutenant Pirogov was given a very painful
thrashing.

We can be sure that the next day Schiller was in a proper fever
and that he trembled like a leaf, awaiting the arrival of the police,
and that he would have given his very last pfennig to turn the
events of the previous day into a dream. But we cannot alter what
has been. No words can describe Pirogov's indignation and rage.
The mere thought of this fearful humiliation threw him into a fury.
In his opinion Siberia and the whip were the very least punishment
Schiller deserved. He flew home to dress and to proceed forthwith
to his general; here he would paint in the most lurid colours the
unruly conduct of the German craftsmen. At the same time he
intended to deliver a written complaint to the General Staff. Should
the punishment prescribed not meet with his approval he would
take the matter still higher, to the State Council,* and thence to the
tsar himself.

But things turned out rather strangely: on the way he called in at
a pastry shop, ate two puff-pastries, read an article in the *Northern
Bee*,* and continued on his way feeling rather less angry. Moreover,
as it was a pleasant and cool evening he decided to take a stroll
along Nevsky; by nine o'clock he had recovered his composure and
realized the imprudence of disturbing generals on a Sunday; furthermore, his general would undoubtedly have been called away
somewhere. Accordingly, he set off to spend the evening at the
home of a director of the College of Inspectors,* where he could
always be sure to find a most agreeable gathering of civil servants

and officers. There he spent an enjoyable evening and so distinguished himself in the execution of the mazurka that he delighted not only the ladies but even their escorts.

'What an amazing world we live in!' I thought to myself the other day as I walked along Nevsky musing over these two stories: 'How strange, how inscrutable the games fate plays with us! Do we ever attain the object of our desires? Do we ever achieve that to which all our efforts seem to be directed? Everything happens the wrong way round. To one Providence has given a pair of splendid horses, and he rides along indifferently, oblivious of their beauty, while another, whose heart is fired with a passion for horses, is forced to go on foot and must content himself with clicking his tongue at the handsome beasts which gallop past. One fellow has an excellent cook, but, alas, is unlucky enough to possess such a small mouth that it cannot accommodate more than two pieces of meat, while another has a mouth as big as the arch of the General Staff but, alas, has to content himself with some sort of German concoction of potatoes. What strange games fate plays with us!'

But strangest of all are the things which happen on Nevsky Prospect. Oh, have no faith in this Nevsky Prospect! I always wrap my cloak tighter around me when I walk along it and endeavour not to look at the objects I pass. It is all deception, a dream, nothing is what it seems! You think that that gentleman promenading in a finely tailored frock-coat is very rich? Nothing of the sort: his entire fortune is in his frock-coat. You imagine that those two fat men, who have paused to watch builders at work on a church, are discussing its architecture?—Not a bit of it; they are remarking on the strange way two crows have alighted facing one another. You think that that excitable fellow waving his arms is describing how his wife threw a crumpled up piece of paper out of the window at some officer whom he did not know from Adam?—Not at all: he's demonstrating where Lafayette* went wrong. You think that those ladies... but trust the ladies least of all. Try to keep your eyes away from the shop windows: the knick-knacks displayed in them are fine to look at but they smack of large sums of money. Pray that the Lord keep you from peeking beneath the ladies' bonnets! However enticingly a lady's cloak may billow in the distance, I would never, not on any account, chase after it for a closer look. Keep your distance from the street-lamps, I implore you, and hurry past them quickly, as quickly as possible. Count yourself lucky if they only spill their malodorous oil on your fashionable frock-coat. But everything, not only the street-lamp, exudes deceit. Nevsky Prospect deceives at all hours of day, but the worst time of all is at night, when darkness descends upon it like a dense blanket and only the white and beige walls of the buildings can be discerned, when the entire city becomes a welter of noise and flashing lights, when myriads of carriages rattle down from the bridges, the postilions cry out and jig on their horses and when the devil himself is abroad, kindling the street-lamps with one purpose only: to show everything in a false light.

THE NOSE

I

On 25 March a most extraordinary occurrence took place in St Petersburg. The barber Ivan Yakovlevich, resident of Voznesensky Avenue* (his surname has been lost, and does not even appear on his shop sign, which depicts a gentleman with a well-soaped cheek and the legend: 'Blood-letting also performed')—the barber Ivan Yakovlevich awoke early one morning and caught the smell of hot bread. Raising himself slightly on his bed he saw that his wife, a most respectable lady, with a great partiality for coffee, was drawing freshly baked rolls from the oven.

'Today, Praskovya Osipovna, I shall not drink coffee,' announced Ivan Yakovlevich: 'instead I would like to eat a hot roll with onion.' (In fact, Ivan Yakovlevich would have liked coffee too, but he knew that it would be quite out of the question to insist on having both, for Praskovya Osipovna took a very dim view of such caprices).

'Let the old fool eat bread, all the better for me,' thought his wife: 'I'll get an extra cup of coffee.' And she tossed a roll on to the table.

For the sake of decency Ivan Yakovlevich put on his tailcoat on top of his nightshirt, and, seating himself at the table, poured out some salt, peeled two onions, took hold of a knife and, with an air of the utmost gravity, set about slicing his roll. Cutting it in half he glanced inside and, to his great surprise, saw something white. He cautiously prodded it with his knife and poked at it with his finger. 'Feels firm...' he thought, 'what on earth can it be?'

He stuck in his fingers and tugged—out came a nose!... At this his arms dropped to his sides; then he rubbed his eyes and felt the object: a nose, no doubt about it, a nose! And even, so it seemed, a familiar nose. An expression of horror crept over Ivan Yakovlevich's face. But this horror was nothing compared to the indignation that overtook his lady wife.

'Where did you cut off that nose, you butcher?' she shouted angrily. 'You villain! Drunkard! I'll report you to the police myself. Good-for-nothing criminal! I've already been told by three people that you tug their noses so hard while you're shaving them it's a wonder they stay on at all.'

But Ivan Yakovlevich was paralysed with fear. He had recognized the nose as belonging to none other than Collegiate Assessor* Kovalyov, whom he shaved every Wednesday and Sunday.

'Wait, Praskovya Osipovna! I'll wrap it up in a cloth and put it over there in the corner: let it sit there for a little while, then I'll take it away.'

'Not another word! Do you think that I would allow a cut-off nose to sit in my room?... You numskull! All you're good for is stropping razors, and soon you won't even be able to do your job at all, you stupid oaf! You scoundrel! Do you think I'm going to stick up for you with the police?... No fear, you good-for-nothing, you blockhead! Take it away! Away! I don't care where you put it, just so long as I never set eyes on it again!'

Ivan Yakovlevich stood there dumbfounded. He racked his brains, but came up with no answer.

'Devil knows how it happened,' he said finally, scratching behind his ear. 'Perhaps I came home drunk last night, or perhaps not, I can't say. But on the face of it this is quite unaccountable; I mean, bread is something you bake and a nose is nothing of the kind. It's a complete mystery!...'

Ivan Yakovlevich fell silent. The thought of the police finding him with the nose and arresting him terrified him. In his mind's eye he could already see the red collar, with its fine silver braiding, the sword... and he shuddered from head to toe. Finally he picked up his undershirt and boots, pulled them on and, to the accompaniment of Praskovya Osipovna's baleful injunctions, wrapped the nose in a cloth and stepped out on to the street.

He planned to secrete it away somewhere, perhaps stuffing it behind a curbstone by the gates or inadvertently dropping it as he walked along, and then popping down the nearest side street. But to his chagrin he kept on bumping into acquaintances, who importuned him: 'Where are you going?' or: 'Who are you planning to shave at this early hour?' leaving Ivan Yakovlevich no chance to carry out his scheme. Once he did manage to drop the nose, but a duty policeman called to him, pointing with his halberd: 'Hey, you there! You've dropped something!' And Ivan Yakovlevich had to pick the nose up and conceal it in his pocket. He began to despair, particularly since the street was filling with people as the shops and stalls opened for the day.

He decided to make for the Isakievsky Bridge,* where, with luck, he might be able to throw it into the Neva... But I have been rather amiss thus far to have told you nothing about Ivan Yakovlevich, a person commanding esteem in many respects.

Ivan Yakovlevich, like every self-respecting Russian tradesman, was an incorrigible drunkard. And although every day of the week he shaved the chins of other men, his own was permanently unshaven. Ivan Yakovlevich's tails (for Ivan Yakovlevich never wore a frock-coat) were pie-bald, that is they were black, but covered with yellowy-brown and grey blotches; the collar was shiny, and where there should have been three buttons there were only dangling threads. Ivan Yakovlevich was a great cynic, and when, as was his wont, Collegiate Assessor Kovalyov remarked to him during his shave: 'Ivan Yakovlevich, your hands always stink!' Ivan Yakovlevich would retort: 'How could they stink?'—'I don't know, old chap, but they do,' the collegiate assessor would say, and Ivan Yakovlevich, taking a pinch of snuff, would get even by plying lather to his cheeks, under his nose, behind his ears, and beneath his chin, in other words, wherever it pleased him to do so.

This worthy citizen had by now reached Isakievsky Bridge. First of all he looked round; then leaned over the railings as if to look at the water below, supposedly to check whether there were many fish that day, and stealthily dropped the cloth containing the nose. Ivan Yakovlevich felt as though a ton weight had been lifted from his shoulders; he even chuckled. Instead of heading back to shave the chins of officialdom he decided to make for an establishment fronted by the sign 'Victuals and Tea' to partake of a glass of rum punch, when he suddenly noticed at the other end of the bridge a police superintendent, of imposing appearance, complete with muttonchop whiskers, a tricorn hat, and a sword. He froze in his tracks; meanwhile the police superintendent crooked his finger at him and said: 'Step over here, my good man!'

Ivan Yakovlevich, knowing the correct procedure in such circumstances, took off his cap while still a good way off and, stepping up briskly, said:

'A very good day to you, Your Honour!'

'No, no, my friend, never mind the "Your Honour", but tell me now, what were you doing over there on the bridge?'

'Honest to God, Sir, I was on my way to shave a customer, and I thought I'd have a look and see how quickly the river was flowing.'

'You're lying! Don't think you'll get away with that. Now let's have the truth!'

'I would be happy to shave Your Honour twice a week, or even three times, without any further ado,' answered Ivan Yakovlevich.

'No, my friend, that won't get you anywhere. I already have three barbers to shave me, and they all consider it a great honour. But now let's hear what you were up to?'

Ivan Yakovlevich blanched... But at this point proceedings become enveloped in a fog, and we know absolutely nothing of what ensued.

II

Collegiate Assessor Kovalyov awoke fairly early and, pursing his lips, went: 'brrr!...' as he always did on awakening, for no reason that even he could discover. He stretched and called for the small mirror which stood on the dressing-table. He wanted to examine the pimple which had sprung up on his nose the previous night; but to his great astonishment he saw that where his nose should have been there was a flat space! Taking fright, he asked for some water and rubbed his eyes with a towel: it was true, there was no nose! He pinched himself, to make sure he was not still asleep. But it seemed he was not asleep. Collegiate Assessor Kovalyov leapt from his bed, and shook himself: no nose!... He at once called for his clothes and repaired at great speed directly to the Police Commissioner.

But in the mean time we must acquaint the reader with Kovalyov, so that he can see for himself the sort of man our collegiate assessor was. The collegiate assessors who earn this title with the attainment of various academic certificates are not on any account to be compared with those collegiate assessors who acquire their position in the Caucasus.* These are two altogether different species. Now, a learned collegiate assessor—but Russia is such an extraordinary place that if you say something about one collegiate assessor all its collegiate assessors, from Riga to Kamchatka, are sure to take it personally. The same holds true for all ranks and offices.—Kovalyov was a Caucasian collegiate assessor. He had only been a collegiate assessor for two years, and thus thought about it every minute of every day; to give himself greater weight and a sense of nobility he never called himself Collegiate Assessor, but always Major. 'Listen, my good woman,' he would say, encountering in the street a woman peddling shirt-fronts, 'come along to my place: my lodgings are on Sadovaya Street; ask anyone where Major Kovalyov lives and they'll show you.' And if the wench in question should be particularly comely he would give her an additional, secret commission, saying: 'Now, sweetheart, you just ask for Major Kovalyov's apartment.'—For this reason we too henceforth shall call our collegiate assessor Major.

Major Kovalyov was in the habit of taking a daily stroll along Nevsky Prospect. The collar of his shirt was always spotlessly clean and stiff with starch. His whiskers were of the sort which can still be seen on the cheeks of provincial and district surveyors, architects and regimental doctors, as well as on policemen of one sort and another, and, in general, all gentlemen endowed with full, ruddy cheeks and an aptitude for the game of boston: these whiskers travel down the very middle of the cheek and thence extend right across to the nose. Major Kovalyov had about him a number of cornelian seals, some with crests and others with the inscription: Wednesday, Thursday, Monday, and so forth. The major had come to St Petersburg with a specific purpose, namely, to seek a position appropriate to his rank. If he succeeded, this would be at vice-governor level, and if not, he would settle for an administratorship in some important department. Nor was Major Kovalyov opposed to the idea of marrying; but only on condition that his bride possessed a capital of two hundred thousand. So the reader can now judge for himself the worthy major's state of mind when he descried, instead of a not unbecoming nose of moderate proportions, a ridiculous, empty, smooth space.

As ill luck would have it, not a single cab was to be seen on the street, and he was constrained to go on foot, wrapped in his cloak with a handkerchief over his face, like someone with a nosebleed. 'Perhaps, after all, it's only in my imagination,' he thought, 'a nose can't disappear just like that.' He went into a pastry shop with the express object of looking into a mirror. Luckily there was no one in the shop: the serving-boys were sweeping out the rooms and arranging the chairs; some of them, with bleary eyes, were bearing forth trays of hot pies; yesterday's coffee-stained newspapers lay about on the tables and chairs. 'Well, thank God for that, there's no one here,' he said, 'now I can take a look.' He approached the mirror timidly and looked in: 'What the devil is that supposed to be!' he exclaimed, spitting... 'If only there was something in the nose's place, but to have nothing at all!...'

Biting his lips with annoyance he left the pastry shop and, contrary to his custom, resolved not to look or smile at anyone. Suddenly he stopped dead in his tracks by a doorway, as an inexplicable phenomenon unfolded before his eyes: a carriage stopped at the entrance; the doors opened and, stooping, a gentleman in a uniform sprang out and ran up the stairs. Imagine Kovalyov's horror and amazement when he recognized this person as his very own nose! This extraordinary spectacle caused him to reel with astonishment, and he was barely able to retain his footing; but he resolved at all costs to await the nose's return to its carriage and stood there, shaking feverishly. Sure enough, two minutes later the nose emerged. He wore a gold-braided uniform, with a high stiff collar; he had on buckskin breeches, and by his side hung a sword. From his cockaded hat it was apparent that he pretended to the rank of state councillor. It was also clear from his demeanour that he was on his way to pay a call. He glanced to left and to right, shouted to the coachman: 'Let's be off!', climbed into the carriage and they galloped off.

Poor Kovalyov almost lost his mind. He did not know what to make of this most extraordinary occurrence. Indeed, how could one explain the fact that a nose, which only the previous day had still been attached to his face, unable to ride or walk, was now wearing a uniform! He set off in pursuit of the carriage, which, fortunately, did not go far before stopping in front of the Kazan Cathedral.*

He hastened into the cathedral, pushed his way through the row of old beggarwomen with their faces swathed in rags, leaving only two slits for the eyes, a sight which before had always caused him mirth, and entered the church. There were not many worshippers inside, and they were all clustered around the entrance. Kovalyov was so distraught that he was quite unable to pray, and instead he eagerly scanned the church, hoping for a glimpse of the uniformed gentleman. At last he saw him standing to one side. The nose had entirely concealed its face in its tall stiff collar, and was praying with an expression of utmost piety.

'How can I approach him?' thought Kovalyov. 'To judge by his uniform and hat he must be a state councillor. What the devil should I do?'

He sidled up to the nose, clearing his throat, but the nose paid no heed and continued its pious observances, describing deep bows in the direction of the altar.

'My good sir...' said Kovalyov, desperately plucking up the courage: 'my good sir...'

'What is it?' asked the nose, looking round.

'I'm somewhat surprised, sir... I do think... you should know your place. And just look where I've found you—in a church. You must agree...'

'Forgive me, but I find myself unable to make head or tail of what you are saying. Please explain yourself.'

'How can I explain?' thought Kovalyov, and steeling himself once again, began: 'Of course I... actually I'm a major. And, I'm sure you agree, it would be rather unseemly for me to walk around without a nose. It would be all right for some market woman, selling peeled oranges on the Voskresensky Bridge,* to sit there with no nose; but as I'm hoping for a promotion... and moreover being acquainted with the ladies of a number of distinguished houses: with State Councillor Chekhtaryov's wife, and others... Judge for yourself... I don't quite know how to put it, sir...' (Upon which Major Kovalyov shrugged his shoulders.) 'Forgive me, but if you look at this strictly from the point of view of duty and honour... you must surely agree...'

'Don't understand a thing,' answered the nose. 'Be so good as to make yourself clear.'

'My good sir...' said Kovalyov in a dignified tone, 'As a matter of fact I find your words hard to comprehend... It all seems quite plain to me... Or do you wish... The point is, you're my very own nose!'

The nose looked at the major and gathered its brows in a slight frown.

'You are mistaken, my good sir. I am a person in my own right. Furthermore there cannot be any close relations between us, for to judge by the buttons on your uniform you must serve in the Senate, or perhaps in the Department of Justice. Whereas I am in the Academy.'

Having said this the nose turned away and continued praying.

Kovalyov was now at a complete loss as to what to do and even what to think. Just then he heard the pleasant rustle of a lady's dress: an elderly lady walked up, festooned in a mass of lace, and accompanied by a slim creature, clad in a white dress which excellently suited her slender frame, and a pale yellow hat, as light as puff-pastry. Behind them stood a tall footman with massive whiskers and a coat which had at least a dozen collars, who proceeded to open a snuff-box.

Kovalyov moved a little closer, hitched up the cambric collar of his shirt, adjusted the fobs on his gold watch-chain, and, smiling to right and left, directed his attention to the slender lady, who bent slightly forward with the grace of a delicate spring flower as she raised the almost transparent fingers of her lily-white hand to her brow. Kovalyov's smile widened when beneath her hat he espied a round, perfectly white chin and a portion of cheek, lightly suffused with the blush of the first rose of spring. But suddenly he recoiled as if scalded. He had remembered that in place of a nose he had absolutely nothing, and tears issued from his eyes. He swung round in order to tell the uniformed gentleman in so many words that he was simply pretending to be a state councillor, that he was an impostor and a scoundrel and that he was nothing more or less than Kovalyov's very own nose... But the nose had vanished: in the interval it had galloped off, no doubt on its way to pay another call.

This plunged Kovalyov into despair. He walked out and stood a moment beneath the colonnade, peering all around him in the hope of spotting the nose. He remembered distinctly that it had been wearing a cockaded hat and a gold-braided uniform; but he had not noticed its overcoat, or the colour of its carriage, or its horses, or even whether a footman had stood behind it, and if so in what livery. Moreover there was such a multitude of carriages pressing to and fro and at such a speed that he could not distinguish one from the other, and even if he had spotted something he would have been powerless to stop any of them. It was a splendid sunny day. There were crowds of people on Nevsky; a floral cascade of ladies spilled over the pavements all the way from the Politseisky Bridge to the

Anichkov Bridge.* Over there was an acquaintance, an aulic councillor, whom he addressed as Lieutenant Colonel, especially in front
of strangers. Here he saw Yarygin, head of a desk in the Senate, a
great friend, who always used to render forfeit at boston when he
played an eight. Nearby another major, who had also gained his
assessorship in the Caucasus, beckoned to him...

'To the devil with them all!' said Kovalyov. 'Cabbie! Take me
straight to the Police Commissioner's!'

Kovalyov climbed into a droshky and sat there shouting at the
cabbie: 'Drive like the clappers!'

'Is the commissioner at home?' he shouted, looking into the
vestibule.

''Fraid not,' answered the porter, 'just gone out this moment.'

'Confound it!'

'Yes,' continued the porter, 'it weren't all that long ago, but he's
gone. A minute or so earlier and you'd have caught him in.'

Kovalyov, keeping his handkerchief to his face the whole time,
climbed back into the droshky and called out in a despairing voice:
'Drive on!'

'Where?' asked the cabbie.

'Straight ahead!'

'How can I? There's a fork: left or right?'

This question forced Kovalyov to stop and think. In his position
it would be best to make for the Board of Public Order,* not
because it was directly connected with the police, but because it got
things done far more quickly than did the other authorities; it
would obviously be imprudent to seek satisfaction from the authorities in the very place where the nose claimed to serve. It was
apparent from the nose's own statements that this character held
nothing sacred and would be just as likely to lie now as it had lied
before when claiming never to have set eyes on Major Kovalyov.
Thus Kovalyov was on the point of ordering the cabbie to proceed
to the Board of Public Order when another thought struck him,
namely, that this rogue and swindler, who at their very first encounter had behaved in such an unscrupulous manner, might by
now have made good his escape from town. In that case all attempts
to find him would either be quite futile or else might endure, which
God forbid, for an entire month.

Finally, almost as if divinely inspired, he resolved to make straight for the newspaper office and promptly place an advertisement giving a detailed description of all the nose's attributes, so that anyone who saw it might recover it for him, or at least inform him of its whereabouts. Having reached this decision, he ordered the cabbie to head for the newspaper office, and as they drove rained blows on his back, shouting: 'Faster, you rogue! Faster, you blackguard!'— 'Ouch, sir!' grunted the cabbie, shaking his head and flicking the reins to egg on his horse, which had a coat as shaggy as a poodle's.

At long last the droshky stopped, and Kovalyov ran breathless into the small reception room, where a grey-haired and bespectacled clerk in an old tailcoat sat behind a desk and, his quill pen clenched between his teeth, counted a pile of copper coins that had been put before him.

'Who takes advertisements here?' shouted Kovalyov. 'Ah—good day to you!'

'Morning,' said the grey-haired clerk, raising his eyes for a moment and then lowering them again to his neat piles of money.

'I would like to print...'

'Just a moment. If you wouldn't mind waiting,' said the clerk, writing down a number with his right hand, while moving two beads on an abacus with his left.

A footman in a gallooned coat, whose mien and bearing bespoke his position in an aristocratic house, stood beside the desk with a note in his hand, and feeling it incumbent upon himself to display a certain bonhomie, volunteered: 'Believe me, sir, the little mutt isn't worth eighty copecks—as for me, I wouldn't give you a brass button for it; but the countess loves it, she loves it something terrible, so she's offering one hundred roubles for whoever as finds it. If you want to know my honest opinion, just between you and me, there's no accounting for people's tastes: now take your hunter, he won't mind paying five hundred, even a thousand, for a pointer or a retriever, but then he's paying for a good dog.'

The worthy clerk listened gravely to this discourse and at the same time continued his calculations, counting the number of letters in the notice submitted for publication. Around him hovered a great number of old women, shop assistants, and doormen with notes. One sought employment for a coachman of sober habits; another advertised for sale a little-used calash, brought in 1814 from Paris; elsewhere a position was sought for a serf-girl, 19 years old and trained as a laundress, but suitable for other work; offers were invited for a sturdy droshky, missing one spring, a spirited young horse with grey dappled markings, a mere 17 years of age, new turnip and radish seeds imported from London, a country cottage with all amenities: stabling for two horses and land on which an excellent birch or fir grove could be planted; another notice drew the attention of all those anxious to purchase old boot soles, inviting them to visit the auction rooms any day, between 8 a.m. and 3 p.m. The room in which this company was assembled was of small dimensions and the air in it was extraordinarily dense; but Collegiate Assessor Kovalyov was unconscious of the atmosphere because he kept his handkerchief held over his face and because the whereabouts of his nose remained a complete mystery to him.

'My good sir, if I might interrupt... This is a matter of great importance,' he brought out impatiently.

'One moment! Two roubles forty-three copecks! Right away! One rouble sixty-four copecks!' commanded the grizzled scribe, tossing pieces of paper in the faces of the old women and doormen. 'What do you want?' he said at last, turning to Kovalyov.

'I'd like to...' said Kovalyov, 'a vile act of treachery has been committed, I still can't make it out. I want you merely to print that the person who brings this rogue to me will be handsomely rewarded.'

'Could I please have your name?'

'No, why do you need my name? I cannot divulge it. I have a great many acquaintances: Madame Chekhtaryova, wife of the State Councillor, Palageya Grigoryevna Podtochina, wife of a staff officer... They might see it, God forbid! You could simply write: "a Collegiate Assessor", or, better still, "a gentleman of the rank of Major".'

'And the person who has escaped was one of your serfs?'

'What, one of my serfs? Oh no, far worse than that! It's my... er—nose that's run away...'

'Hm! what a singular surname. And did this Mr Nosov swindle you out of a large sum?'

'No, no: this nose—that is... You've got it wrong! My nose, my very own nose, has vanished into thin air. It's playing some devilish trick on me!'

'But in what manner did it disappear? I'm afraid I can't quite follow all this.'

'Well I don't quite know myself; but the main thing is that it is now driving about the city, passing itself off as a state councillor. So I am asking you to place an announcement requesting that whoever catches it bring it to me forthwith and without the slightest delay. Judge for yourself: how am I to carry on without such a prominent part of my anatomy?—It is not as if I had lost a little toe, and could quickly slip my foot into my boot before anyone saw that it was missing. On Thursdays I call on State Councillor Chekhtaryov's wife; Palageya Grigoryevna Podtochina is the wife of a staff officer and she has a very pretty daughter, and they are both good friends of mine, so you can see for yourself what a predicament I am in... I simply cannot show myself to them now.'

The clerk fell to thinking for a moment, as was apparent from his tightly pursed lips.

'No, I cannot place such an announcement in the paper,' he said finally, after a long silence.

'What? Why not?'

'I cannot. The newspaper could lose its reputation. If everyone were to start writing that their noses had run away, just imagine... As it is people are saying that the paper publishes a lot of nonsense and false rumours.'

'But where's the nonsense in this? There's no nonsense here.'

'That's how it seems to you. But take this case which we had last week. An official came in just as you have today with a note, which came to two roubles seventy-three copecks, and all the announcement said was that a black-haired poodle had run away. On the face of it, nothing out of the ordinary. But it all ended in a libel suit, because this poodle was the treasurer of some institution, I don't recall which.'

'But I'm not making any announcement about a poodle, this is about my very own nose, which amounts to practically the same thing as myself.'

'Very sorry, I cannot place such an announcement.'

'Even when I really have lost my nose!'

'If that's so, then it's a job for the doctors. They say that there are people who can fit you out with any nose you like. I cannot help noting, however, that you are of a somewhat frivolous disposition and fond of practical jokes.'

'I swear to you, by all that's holy! Since things have come to this pass, I shall show you!'

'There's no need!' continued the clerk, taking a pinch of snuff. 'Actually, if it's not too much trouble,' he added, looking up in curiosity, 'perhaps I might take a look.'

Collegiate Assessor Kovalyov removed the handkerchief from his face.

'Well, that is most extraordinary!' said the clerk: 'That part of your face is completely smooth, like a freshly cooked pancake. Unnaturally smooth, in fact!'

'Now I hope that's put paid to your objections! You can see for yourself that the announcement has to go in. I will be extremely grateful to you, and I am very glad that this incident has brought me the pleasure of your acquaintance...'

The major, as we can see, had decided at this point to try a little ingratiation.

'Printing it would, of course, be a simple matter,' said the clerk: 'only I don't see what good this can do you. If you're so determined, you should find someone with a flair for words and get him to write it up as a rare occurrence of nature, then publish the article in the *Northern Bee*'* (here he took another pinch of snuff) 'for the edification of our young people' (here he wiped his nose) 'or just for the interest of the general public.'

This suggestion was the final blow. Collegiate Assessor Kovalyov lowered his eyes to the newspaper, where they alighted on the theatre column; his face was on the point of breaking into a smile as he caught the name of an attractive young actress, and his hand reached for his pocket to see whether he had on him a five-rouble note, for staff officers, in Kovalyov's opinion, must only have seats in the stalls—but then he remembered about his nose and his heart sank!

Even the clerk, it seemed, was moved by Kovalyov's plight. Wishing to offer some measure of consolation he deemed it fitting to express his sympathy in a few words: 'I am indeed most grieved that you have been the victim of such a peculiar accident. Perhaps you would care for a pinch of snuff? It dispels headaches and bouts of melancholy; it even has a beneficial effect on haemorrhoids.'

Whereupon the clerk offered Kovalyov his snuff-box, adroitly folding beneath it its lid, which displayed the portrait of a lady in a hat.

This thoughtless gesture was more than Kovalyov's patience could stand.

'I do not understand how you can think this a joking matter,' he said heatedly: 'surely you can see that I do not have the wherewithal to partake of snuff? The devil take your snuff! I can't even bring myself to look at snuff—and by that I mean the very best brand, to say nothing of that Berezinsky shag.'*

On saying this he stalked out of the newspaper office in high dudgeon and set off to see the superintendent of police, a man with an uncommonly sweet tooth. His entire front room, which was also his dining-room, was stacked high with loaves of sugar, which shopkeepers brought him as a token of friendship. At this moment his cook was engaged in divesting the superintendent of his jack-boots; his sword and all his military paraphernalia were already hanging peacefully in the comers of the room and his 3-year-old son was playing with his father's awe-inspiring tricorn hat, while the warrior himself, after his day in the throes of battle, prepared to savour the delights of peace.

Kovalyov was ushered in to him at just the right moment to hear him announce, after a good stretch and grunt: 'Ahhh, now for a good, two-hour nap!' Thus we can see that the collegiate assessor had timed his arrival extremely badly. I suspect that even if he had brought with him a few pounds of tea or a bolt of cloth he still would not have received a particularly effusive welcome. The superintendent was a great champion of all the arts and manufactories: but above all things he prized the State banknote. 'Now that's what I like,' he was wont to say: 'you can't beat one of these: it doesn't need feeding, takes up little space, there's always room for it in the pocket, and if you drop it, it won't break.'

The superintendent received Kovalyov rather coldly and remarked that after dinner was not the time to conduct an inquiry, that nature itself had ordained that after eating our fill we should rest a little (from which the collegiate assessor could see that the police superintendent was familiar with the utterances of the ancient sages), that if a man was respectable he would not thus be rudely parted from his nose, and that there were majors and majors in this world, some of whom did not even have a decent undershirt to their name and frequented the most disreputable places.

This, alas, was Kovalyov's Achilles' heel! We should note that the collegiate assessor was very quick to take offence. He could forgive anything that was said about his person but would brook no disrespect for his rank or title. He even argued that in theatrical performances you could permit any references to subalterns, but remarks about field officers definitely would not do. The superintendent's reception so took him aback that he shook his head and pronounced in a dignified tone, holding out his arms: 'I regret that after such offensive remarks on your part I am unable to make any further comment...' and departed.

He returned home, barely able to hold himself on his feet. Dusk had already fallen. After this long, futile search his apartments struck him as forlorn and totally uninviting. When he entered the hall he saw his footman Ivan lying on the grubby leather couch, aiming gobs of spit at a point on the ceiling, a target which he hit with some measure of success. The man's torpor enraged the collegiate assessor; whacking him over the head with his hat, he shouted: 'You're always loafing about, you swine!'

Ivan at once sprang to his feet and flew to his master's side to help him off with his cloak.

On entering his room the major sank exhausted and despondent into an armchair and, after heaving a few sighs, said at last:

'My God, oh my God! What have I done to deserve this? If only I had lost an arm or a leg—it would have been far better; or even my ears—that would have been hard, yet I could have borne it; but without his nose a man is nothing: neither man nor beast, but God knows what! Just some rubbish to be thrown out of the window! If at least it had been hacked off in the war or in a duel, or if I had lost it through some fault of my own; but it disappeared without rhyme or reason, just like that!... But no, it cannot be,' he added after a moment's thought. 'It's most unlikely that a nose should disappear; totally improbable. I'm either dreaming, or imagining it; perhaps instead of water I drank the vodka which I rub on my face after shaving. That fool Ivan didn't clear it away, and I must have picked it up by mistake.'

To make absolutely sure that he wasn't drunk the major pinched himself so painfully that he even cried out. The pain convinced him that he was quite fully awake. He stole up to the mirror and narrowed his eyes in the hope that his nose would reappear in its rightful place; but on seeing his reflection he leapt back, exclaiming, 'What a preposterous sight!'

It really was quite incomprehensible. This was not like losing a button, a silver spoon, a watch, or something of that sort—he had lost his own nose, and, to make matters worse, in his own home!... Major Kovalyov pondered all the circumstances, and decided that the most likely culprit was none other than staff officer Podtochin's wife, who wished him to marry her daughter. To be sure, he enjoyed flirting with the girl, but he carefully avoided any definite commitment. When one day the staff officer's wife had announced in so many words that she wished to marry her daughter to him he had cautiously extricated himself with a shower of compliments, saying that he was still too young, that he would have to serve another five years, when he would attain the requisite age of 42.

Thus the staff officer's wife, clearly spurred by a desire for revenge, had decided to ruin him and had hired for this purpose the services of witches, because it was quite inconceivable that his nose had been cut off: no one had entered his room; his barber Ivan Yakovlevich had last shaved him on Wednesday and throughout Wednesday and even all Thursday his nose had been intact—this he remembered and knew beyond any doubt; moreover, he would have felt the pain, and it was unthinkable that the wound would have healed so quickly and have become as smooth as a pancake. He started making plans: should he take the staff officer's wife to court through official channels or should he call on her in person and accuse her to her face? These reflections were interrupted by the light which appeared through the chinks of the door, telling him that Ivan had already lit the candle in the front room. Soon Ivan himself appeared, bearing the candle before him and lighting up the entire room. Kovalyov's first reaction was to seize his handkerchief and cover that empty space which only the day before had contained a nose, so that his idiot manservant would not stand there gawping.

No sooner had Ivan come into the room than an unfamiliar voice could be heard in the hall enquiring: 'Is this the residence of Collegiate Assessor Kovalyov?'

'Do come in. Major Kovalyov at your service,' said Kovalyov, leaping to his feet and opening the door.

Through it came a police officer of smart appearance, with whiskers neither a shade too light nor a shade too dark and fairly full cheeks—the very same officer whom we met at the beginning of the story on the Isakievsky Bridge.

'Did it please Your Honour to lose his nose?'

'Correct.'

'It has now been located.'

'What did you say?' shouted Major Kovalyov. Then, speechless with joy, he stared pop-eyed at the police officer standing before him, the flickering light of the candle dancing across his full lips and cheeks. 'How did you find it?'

'By pure chance: he was on the point of fleeing when we intercepted him. He had already mounted the stage-coach and was bound for Riga. His passport was an old one in the name of some official. Another odd thing is that at first I took him for a gentleman. But luckily I had my eye-glasses with me, and I saw at once that he was a nose. You see, I'm short-sighted, and if you were to stand right in front of me I would only see that you had a face, but I would be unable to make out anything like a nose, or a beard. My mother-in-law, the wife's mother, that is, can't see anything either.'

Kovalyov was beside himself with excitement.

'But where is it? Where? I shall go at once.'

'No need to bother. Knowing that you'd be needing it I brought it along with me. And the strange thing is that the main culprit in this business is that crooked barber on Voznesensky Avenue, who is now being held in the police station. I've had my eye on him for a long time, on suspicion of drunkenness and theft, and only two days ago he swiped a dozen buttons from a stall. Your nose is exactly as it left you.'

On saying this the policeman put his hand in his pocket and took out a nose wrapped in paper.

'That's it!' exclaimed Kovalyov. 'The very one! Won't you join me in a cup of tea today?'

'Greatly honoured, but I'm afraid I can't: I have to go on from here to the city gaol... Terrible the way prices are going up... The mother-in-law lives with us—the wife's mother, that is, and then there're the children; the oldest one is particularly promising: such a bright lad, but we haven't a brass copeck for his education.'

Kovalyov got the message, and taking up a ten-rouble note from his desk pressed it into the officer's hand; the latter went out through the door with a low bow, and the very next moment Kovalyov could hear him on the street outside, reading the riot act to some foolish peasant who had driven his cart right on to the footway.

When he had departed the collegiate assessor sat in a daze for a few moments, so overwhelmed by this sudden stroke of good fortune that it took him quite some time to return to his full senses. Finally, he gingerly lifted the newly recovered nose in his cupped hands and once again examined it closely.

'This is it, the very one!' he said. 'There on the left is the pimple which popped up yesterday.' He all but laughed for joy.

But nothing lasts long in this world, and in the second minute our transports of joy are never as vivid as in the first; by the third minute they subside altogether and our soul returns to its usual state, just as a ripple created by a falling stone eventually merges with the smooth surface of the water around it. Kovalyov fell to pondering and realized that the affair was not yet resolved: the nose had been found, but it still had to be attached, returned to its proper place.

'And what if it won't stick?'

As he put this question to himself, the major blanched.

In a panic he dashed across to the dressing-table and pulled the mirror closer, to be sure that he stuck the nose on straight. His hands trembled as, with minute care, he placed it in its former position. Horrors! The nose would not stick!... He held it to his mouth, warmed it a little with his breath, and once again placed it on the smooth expanse between his two cheeks; but the nose would not stay in place for a moment.

'Now, you... Stay put, you fool!' he commanded. But the nose was as stiff as wood and fell to the table with a strange noise, as if it were made of cork. The major's face twitched convulsively. 'How can it not stick?' he wondered in alarm. But however many times he set it in its place, all his efforts were in vain.

He called Ivan and sent him for the doctor, who lived in the same building, renting the best apartments on the first floor. This doctor was a distinguished-looking man, with splendid coal-black whiskers, and a bonny, fresh-complexioned wife; he ate fresh apples in the morning and kept his mouth remarkably clean, gargling for almost

three quarters of an hour every morning and polishing his teeth
with five different types of toothbrush.

The doctor came right away. After asking how long ago the
misfortune had occurred, he lifted Major Kovalyov's head by the
chin and flicked his thumb so hard against that part of his face
which had previously been home to a nose that the major recoiled
and banged his head against the wall. This, the doctor said, was
nothing, and advised him to move away from the wall. Thereupon
he bade him incline his head first to the right, and after feeling the
place where the nose had been, said 'Hm!' Then he told him to
incline his head to the left and, with another 'Hm!', gave him another flick with his thumb, causing Major Kovalyov to toss his head
like a horse having its teeth examined.

After this test the doctor shook his head and said: 'No, it cannot
be done. You would be better advised to leave it as it is, or you
might make it worse. It could of course be stuck on, and I could do
it right now; but I assure you that it would only be worse for you.'

'Now that's capital! How am I to carry on without a nose?'
protested Kovalyov. 'It can't be any worse than it is now. The devil
only knows what this is! Where can I show my face in such a
preposterous state? I move in the best circles, and even tonight I'm
expected at two houses. I have many acquaintances: Chekhtaryova,
wife of the State Councillor, Podtochina, whose late husband was a
staff officer... although after this exploit of hers my only dealings
with her shall be through the police. I implore you,' he pleaded:
'can it not be done? Stick it on any old how; even if it's not very
secure, just so long as it stays on; I could even prop it up with my
hand at dangerous moments. I should add that I never dance, and
so I shall not knock it off with any careless movement. You may be
assured that I shall certainly express my gratitude for your visit,
within the limits of my means...'

'Believe me,' said the doctor in a voice neither loud nor quiet but
extraordinarily compelling and magnetic: 'that I never treat people
out of a desire for personal gain. This is contrary to my code and
my art. I do admittedly accept a fee for visits, but only in order not
to offend my patients by my refusal. Of course, I could stick on
your nose, but I assure you on my honour, in case you don't trust
my word, that the result will be far worse. You would do better to
trust to the action of nature. Wash often with cold water, and I can

assure you that without a nose you will be just as healthy as if you still had one. As for the nose, I would advise you to preserve it in a jar of spirit, or, better still, to add two tablespoons of pepper vodka and warm vinegar—then you should get a reasonable price for it. I'll even take it myself, if your price isn't too steep.'

'No, no! I shan't sell it for any price!' shouted Major Kovalyov in despair: 'I'd sooner it rotted away!'

'So sorry,' said the doctor, bowing, 'I only wished to be of service... Well, there we are then! At any rate, you can't say I haven't tried.'

On saying this he stalked out of the room with a dignified air. Kovalyov had not even looked at his face, and in his trance-like state had seen only the cuffs of his shirt, as white and pure as driven snow, peeking forth from the sleeves of his black tailcoat.

The very next day he decided, before lodging an official complaint, to write to the staff officer's wife and ask whether she would not agree amicably to return to him what rightfully was his. The letter read as follows:

Dear Madame Alexandra Grigoryevna,

I find myself unable to understand the strangeness of your behaviour. You may be assured that by acting in this manner you stand to gain nothing and in no way will force me to marry your daughter. Believe me, I am perfectly well aware of the whole business behind my nose and also that you and you alone are the primary instigator of this affair. Its sudden separation from its proper place, its flight and disguise, first as a government official, then as itself, are no more nor less than the results of sorcerous actions performed by yourself or those engaged in similarly refined pursuits. For my part I regard it incumbent upon me to warn you that if today my above-mentioned nose is not back in its proper place I shall be forced to have recourse to the patronage and protection of the law.

None the less with my utmost respect, I have the honour to be

Your humble servant

Platon Kovalyov

My dear Platon Kuzmich,

I was most astounded by your letter. In all frankness it came as quite a shock, particularly with regard to the undeserved reproaches on your part. I can assure you that I have never received in my house the official you mention, neither in disguise, nor in his real aspect. Admittedly Filipp Ivanovich Potanchikov once used to call on us. And while it is true that he did seek the hand of my daughter, and is himself of a fine, sober disposition and a man of great learning, I have never given him any encouragement whatever. You also make mention of a nose. If by this you mean to say that I am, as it were, turning up my nose at you, that is, rejecting you out of hand, then I am surprised that you yourself should bring this up, since I, as you are aware, was of a directly contrary opinion, and if you were now to seek the hand of my daughter in the legitimate way I would be prepared forthwith to grant your request, for this has always been the object of my most earnest desire, in the hope of which

I am eternally at your service

Alexandra Podtochina

'No,' said Kovalyov, putting down the letter. 'She is definitely not guilty. She can't be! No one guilty of a crime could have written such a letter!'

The collegiate assessor was knowledgeable about these matters because once or twice while serving in the Caucasus he had conducted prosecutions. 'How on earth did this all happen? The devil only knows!' he exclaimed at last, dropping his hands.

Meanwhile rumours about this extraordinary occurrence were circulating around the capital, and, in the way of these things, not without certain embellishments. At that time people's minds were particularly receptive to all manner of extraordinary phenomena: shortly before this the public imagination had been preoccupied with experiments in the effects of magnetism. In addition a story had recently gone the rounds about dancing chairs in Konyushenny Street; thus it was hardly surprising that, before long, rumour had Collegiate Assessor Kovalyov's nose taking a daily stroll along Nevsky Prospect at three o'clock sharp. Every day a large crowd of inquisitive onlookers would gather. Someone said that the nose had been seen at Junker's emporium*, and such a crush of people collected around the shop that the police had to be called in. One entrepreneur, of respectable appearance, complete with whiskers, who sold various dry pastries at the entrance to the theatre, specially made some fine, sturdy benches on which he invited inquisitive members of the public to stand for a fee of eighty copecks per person. A certain distinguished colonel made a specially early start from home and forced his way through the crowd with great difficulty; but, to his great annoyance, in the shop window he saw no nose, but an ordinary woollen jersey and a lithograph which depicted a girl adjusting her stocking while a dandy wearing a cutaway waistcoat and a goatee beard observed her from a hiding-place behind a tree—a picture which had hung in the same spot for more than ten years. Stalking off he announced in an indignant tone: 'How can people be allowed to spread such ridiculous and far-fetched rumours?'

Then a rumour sprang up that Major Kovalyov's nose took its walk not on Nevsky Prospect but in the Tavrichesky Gardens, and that it had done so for a long time; and that when Persian envoy Khozrev Mirza* stayed there he had been most amazed by this strange freak of nature. Some of the students from the Surgical Academy set off to see for themselves. A certain respected lady of noble extraction wrote a special letter to the warden of the gardens asking him to show her children this rare phenomenon, and, if possible, to provide an edifying and admonitory elucidation for the young people's benefit.

To all those habitués of receptions and other men about town who so love to amuse the ladies these happenings were most welcome, as their own resources of entertainment were utterly depleted. A small number of respectable and law-abiding citizens were extremely displeased. One gentleman announced with annoyance that he failed to understand how in the present enlightened age such ridiculous fictions could gain currency, and that he was surprised by the government's failure to attend to the matter. As can be seen, this gentleman belonged to that class of citizenry who would like to involve the government in everything, even their everyday quarrels with their wives. After this... but at this point the incident is enshrouded in a mist, and what ensued is totally unknown.

III

The most absurd things happen in life. Sometimes they defy all the laws of verisimilitude: one day the very same nose which had been riding around with the rank of state councillor and which had created such a stir in the city reappeared, as if nothing had happened, in its rightful place—that is to say, mid-way between Major Kovalyov's two cheeks. This took place on 7 April. Waking up and accidentally glimpsing himself in the mirror what did he see but—

a nose! He seized hold of it—yes, his nose! 'Ha!' exclaimed Kovalyov, and in his delight would have danced a Cossack trepak barefoot in the room had he not been put off by Ivan's entry. He at once called for a basin of water, and after washing himself took another look in the mirror: there was the nose. Wiping himself with a towel he took yet another look: there it was, his nose!

'Ahem, Ivan, would you have a look, I think I have a pimple on my nose,' he said, thinking to himself: 'What a disaster if Ivan says: "Why no, sir, not only no pimple, but no nose either!"'

But Ivan said: 'No, no pimple, your nose is as clean as a whistle!'

'Capital, damn it!' said the Major to himself and clicked his fingers. At this moment the barber Ivan Yakovlevich peeked round the door, but as timidly as a cat which has just been thrashed for stealing the bacon.

'Tell me first, are your hands clean?' shouted Kovalyov while he was still some way off.

'They are.'

'Liar!'

'I swear they're clean, sir.'

'Well, they had better be.'

Kovalyov sat down. Ivan Yakovlevich swathed him in a towel and in a single instant, with the aid of a brush, transformed his entire beard and part of his cheeks into a mass of whipped cream, such as is served at nameday parties in merchant households.

'Well I never!' exclaimed Ivan Yakovlevich to himself on seeing the nose, then twisted the major's head round and looked at the nose from the side: 'Look at that! Who would have thought it!' he continued, gazing at length at the nose. Finally, with a movement more gentle and cautious than one could imagine, he raised two fingers and prepared to seize it by its tip. Such was Ivan Yakovlevich's method.

'Now now, careful!', shouted Kovalyov. At this Ivan Yakovlevich dropped his hand and for a time was totally nonplussed, even terror-stricken. Finally he started scratching gingerly away with the razor beneath the major's chin, and although he did not find it at all easy or convenient to shave without grasping his client's olfactory organ, he nevertheless managed, by somehow propping his coarse thumb against the major's cheek and lower jaw, to overcome all the obstacles and accomplished his tonsorial duties.

When the operation had been completed, Kovalyov made haste to dress, hailed a cab and drove straight to the pastry shop. While still in the doorway he shouted: 'Waiter, a cup of chocolate!' and repaired forthwith to the mirror: the nose was in place! He jauntily swung round and, narrowing his eyes, cast a supercilious glance at two officers, one of whom had a nose no bigger than a waistcoat button. After this he made for the office of the department in which he had been vying for the post of vice-governor, or, failing that, an administratorship. On his way through the reception room he glanced into the mirror: the nose was in place!

Then he went to call upon another collegiate assessor, a fellow major, and a great satirist, to whose caustic remarks he would usually answer: 'Tut, tut, you have such a sharp tongue!' As he drove he thought: 'If the major doesn't split his sides laughing when he sees me it will be a sure sign that all is as it should be and in its proper place.'

The collegiate assessor did not bat an eyelid. 'Capital, damn it!' thought Kovalyov to himself. On the road he met Madame Podtochina with her daughter, bowed to them and was greeted with cries of delight: clearly his appearance had not been adversely affected. He spoke with them at great length, making a point of bringing out his snuff-box, and with great deliberation plugged his nose in both orifices, thinking all the while: 'So much for you two, you pair of hens! And I shan't marry the daughter after all. A spot of *amour*—by all means!'

And from then onwards Major Kovalyov continued about his business as if nothing had ever happened, promenading along Nevsky Prospect, visiting the theatre, showing his face everywhere. And his nose, also as if nothing had ever happened, remained fixed to his face, and gave no sign of having once taken leave of absence. After this Major Kovalyov was forever in a good mood, smiling away, doggedly pursuing all the pretty ladies and once even stopping at a stall in the Gostiny Dvor* to buy a ribbon for a medal, although it is uncertain why, as he was not himself a cavalier of any order.

And such a thing happened in the northern capital of our vast country! Only now, when we ponder the entire story, do we see that it contains much that is highly implausible. Leaving aside the strange, supernatural detachment of the nose and its appearance in various places in the guise of a state councillor—how could Kovalyov fail to see that it is not done to place advertisements concerning missing noses in the newspaper? By which I do not mean that I regard newspaper advertisements as a pointless extravagance—that is nonsense, and I am in no way a tight-fisted person. But it is indecent, improper, incorrect! And then again: how did the nose turn up in a freshly-baked roll? And how in the first place did Ivan Yakovlevich... No, that I do not understand, I do not understand it at all! But stranger still, and hardest of all to understand, is how authors could take such incidents as their subject-matter. I am forced to admit I find this quite incomprehensible, I just... No, I simply do not understand. First, there is absolutely no benefit to the nation; secondly... no, and there's no benefit secondly either. I simply do not know what to make of it...

Yet all the same, all things considered, we could perhaps concede this and that, and the odd thing here and there, and maybe even... I mean, strange things happen all the time, do they not?... And you must admit, when you think about it, there is something in all this, isn't there? Whatever you might say, such things do happen—rarely perhaps, but they happen all the same.

THE PORTRAIT

PART I

You never saw such crowds anywhere as those in front of the picture stall on Shchukin Dvor,* for this stall displayed the most varied collection of curiosities: the pictures were for the most part painted in oils, covered with dark-green varnish and set in tawdry, dark-yellow frames. A winter scene with white trees, a bright-red sunset, glowing like a fire, a Flemish peasant with a pipe and a crooked arm, looking more like a turkeycock in shirt sleeves than a person—such was their usual subject-matter. Of course there were the etchings as well: a portrait of Khozrev-Mirza* in a sheepskin hat, portraits of generals in tricorn hats and with hooked noses. And, finally, the doors themselves on a shop like this are usually festooned with sheaves of those crude woodcut prints which bear witness to the remarkable native talents of the Russian. One portrayed the tsarevna Miliktrisa Kirbityevna,* another the city of Jerusalem, whose houses and churches were unceremoniously daubed with red streaks, and the same red colour was splashed across the ground and two Russian peasants, holding up their mittened hands in prayer.

There are usually few buyers for these works of art, but no shortage of observers. You are sure to see some truant lackey gaping at them, on his way back from the inn with a tray of covered dishes, containing dinner for his master, who in due course will find himself sipping lukewarm soup. In front of him you will see a soldier in a greatcoat, a stalwart of the flea-market, offering for sale two penknives, and a market-wife from Okhta* carrying a box full of shoes. Everyone reacts differently to what he sees: the peasants usually point; the pedlars carefully scrutinize the pictures; the serving boys and shop apprentices snigger and teasingly compare one another to the caricatures; the old servants in their frieze greatcoats only stop and look so as to sneak a quiet little yawn; as for the young Russian market-wives, they come scurrying across, guided by their instinct, to listen to what people are saying and to see what they are looking at.

At the time our story opens the young artist Chartkov had involuntarily stopped as he walked past the stall. His ancient topcoat and unfashionable clothes betrayed him as the sort of person who is so dedicated to his work that he has no time to attend to outward appearances, notwithstanding the mysterious attraction that apparel exercises over young people. He stopped before the stall and smiled inwardly at the hideous pictures on display. Then he found himself wondering: what sort of people could possibly want these pictures? He was not surprised that the Russian populace should gaze at pictures of Yeruslan Lazarevich, or 'He dined and drank aplenty', or Foma and Yeryoma:* the subjects were simple and comprehensible to plain folk; but who was going to buy these gaudy, dirty daubings in oils? Who wanted these Flemish peasants, these red-and-blue landscapes, with their hollow pretensions to some higher level of art, but which only expressed its utter debasement?

This, it appeared, was not the work of some self-taught child. Otherwise, the overall flatness and effect of caricature would have been partially redeemed by a youthful fervour. But here all one could see was obtusity, the stamp of ineffectual and flabby mediocrity, impudently styling itself art, when in fact its proper place was somewhere among the lower handicrafts, an inadequacy that, true to its nature, had degraded art itself to the level of a menial trade. All these pictures exhibited the same colours, the same style, the same stale hand, which seemed to belong more to a crude automaton than to a person!... He stood for a long time before these grubby paintings, until finally his thoughts strayed elsewhere, while the stallkeeper, a nondescript little man in a serge overcoat and with a growth of beard dating back at least to the previous Sunday, was importuning him, bargaining and naming prices without even finding out what he liked or what he wanted.

'Now I'll take twenty-five for these fine peasants and this little landscape. Just look at the brushwork! They're a delight to the eye; fresh from the salon, the varnish is still wet. Or take this winter scene! A snip at fifteen roubles! The frame's worth that alone. A gorgeous winter scene!' On saying this the merchant lightly tapped the canvas, as if to demonstrate the authenticity of its winter. 'Will you want them wrapped up and delivered to your home? Where should I have them sent? Hey, boy, bring some string.'

'Hold it, old man, not so fast,' said the artist, coming to his senses and seeing that the enterprising stallkeeper had already started tying the pictures together. He felt slightly guilty not to be buying anything, after spending so long in the shop, so he said: 'Just wait a moment, I'll see if there's something I like among these,' and, bending down, picked up from the floor some battered and dusty old pictures that had been piled together, obviously regarded as worthless. There were old family portraits, whose proper descendants were perhaps no longer to be found in this world, unidentifiable pictures with torn canvases, frames which had lost all their gilt, in a word, a heap of old rubbish. But the artist started sifting through them, thinking: 'Who knows, maybe I'll come across something here.' Many were the stories he had heard about people finding old masters amongst the junk of a bric-à-brac stall.

The merchant, seeing where he had turned his attention, lost interest in him and, resuming his air of self-importance, returned to his post in the doorway from which he importuned passers-by, beckoning them into his shop:

'This way, good sir; come and look at the pictures! Come in and see: they're fresh from the salon.' After shouting himself hoarse like this for upwards of an hour, entirely to no avail, and growing tired of talking to the rag dealer who stood across the way in the doorway of his own shop, he finally remembered that he had a customer, and turning his back on the passing world he went inside. 'Well, my friend, found anything?' But for some time the artist had been standing motionless before a portrait in a large and once magnificent frame, which retained barely a trace of its gilt.

It depicted an old man with a weather-bronzed face and sinewy, emaciated features; his face appeared to have been captured at a moment of feverish agitation and was redolent of some southern strength. The portrait bore the imprint of the fierce midday sun. Its subject was draped in a capacious Asiatic costume. Despite its dusty, dilapidated state, when Chartkov removed the grime from the area of the face he could see that the portrait was the work of an accomplished artist. It appeared to be unfinished; but the power of the author's brush was remarkable. The most unusual feature was the eyes: on them the artist had lavished all his zeal and considerable talent. They stared back at the observer with such lifelike intensity that they quite destroyed all the harmony of the composition. When he carried the portrait over to the doorway the eyes stared harder still. They had almost exactly the same effect on the public. A woman who had stopped behind him called out: 'He's looking, he's looking!' and recoiled. A strange feeling, something he himself could not explain, overwhelmed him and he put the painting down on the ground.

'Well, are you going to take the portrait?' said the stallkeeper.

'How much?' said the artist.

'Well, I wouldn't want much for that now, would I? I'll let it go for seventy-five copecks!'

'No.'

'Well, what'll you give for it?'

'Twenty,' said the artist, preparing to leave.

'Huh, call that money? you couldn't even get the frame for twenty copecks. Are you planning to buy it tomorrow, then? Wait, sir, come back! Another ten copecks and it's yours. All right, all right, take it for twenty. To get things started, seeing as you're my first customer.'

He gave a dismissive wave, as if to say: 'Let him have it, to hell with the picture!'

In this way Chartkov quite unexpectedly bought the old portrait and found himself thinking as he did so: 'Why did I buy it? What do I want it for?' But it was done now. He took twenty copecks out of his pocket, handed it to the stallkeeper, tucked the portrait under his arm and set forth. On his way he remembered that the twenty copecks he had paid out were his last. His mind suddenly clouded over, and a feeling of irritation combined with total apathy swept over him. 'To hell with it! It's a stinking life!' he said, with the despondency of a Russian down on his luck. And he stepped on at a brisk and almost mechanical pace, oblivious to everything. The red glow of eventide still lingered across half the sky; the buildings facing that direction remained flushed with its warm hue, while the cold, bluish light of the moon gained in brightness. The semi-translucent evening shadows cast by the buildings and passers-by lay across the ground in long bars. The artist gazed at the sky with its shimmering, evanescent light and exclaimed, almost in the same breath: 'What a subtle tone!' and 'How damnably annoying!' And, tucking the portrait more firmly under his arm, he quickened his step.

Exhausted and drenched with sweat, he dragged himself back to his home in the Fifteenth Line on Vasilyevsky Island.* Panting heavily, he hauled himself up the filthy staircase, covered with pools of slop and decorated with the leavings of cats and dogs. There was no answer to his knocking: no one at home. He leant against the window, patiently preparing for a long wait, when suddenly he heard footsteps behind him as a young lad in a blue shirt arrived. This was his combined factotum, model, paint-mixer, and sweeper, who was in fact better at muddying the floors with his dirty boots than at sweeping them. The lad was called Nikita, and whenever his master was out he would take to the street and stay there until he returned. Nikita fumbled for a long time with the key before he could get it into the key-hole, practically invisible in the dark. Finally the door swung open. Chartkov stepped into his front room, which, like every artist's home, was unbearably cold, since cold is something to which artists are quite oblivious. Without removing his coat and handing it to Nikita, he went straight into his studio, a large square room with a low ceiling and frosted windows, filled with all sorts of artist's rubbish: sections of plaster arms, canvases stretching on frames, sketches begun and abandoned, sheets of cloth draped over the chairs. He felt a rush of fatigue, threw off his coat, stood the portrait, which he had by now almost forgotten, between two small canvases and collapsed on to the narrow divan, of which it could no longer truthfully be said that it was upholstered in leather, for the row of brass tacks which had once held the leather in place had long since been divested of this function, and the leather covering, similarly unattached, now lay loosely on top of the divan, providing Nikita with something beneath which he could stuff socks, shirts, and other dirty laundry. After sitting briefly and then lying down for as long as was possible on such a narrow divan he finally called for a candle.

'There ain't none,' said Nikita.

'How come?'

'Well, there weren't none yesterday neither,' said Nikita. The artist recalled that indeed there hadn't been any the day before either, calmed down and fell silent. He let himself be undressed and put on his threadbare dressing-gown.

'And another thing, the landlord called,' said Nikita.

'He came for the money, I know,' commented the artist, with a shrug.

'And he didn't come on his own,' said Nikita.

'Who with?'

'I don't know... a policeman I think.'

'What did the policeman want?'

'I don't know; he said something about your rent being overdue.'

'So, what can they do about it?'

'I don't know what they can do about it, but he said that if he don't want to pay, then he can clear out of the flat; they said they'd come again tomorrow, both of them.'

'Let them come,' said Chartkov with morose indifference. After this he sank into a state of dejection.

Young Chartkov was a talented artist, who promised great things: his work sporadically demonstrated fine observation, perspicacity, and an eagerness to get closer to nature. 'Now listen, *mon frère*,' his professor often used to say to him, 'you have talent and it would be a shame for you to waste it. But you're impatient. You get an idea into your head, something takes your fancy, and that's it: you have no time for anything else, it's all rubbish to you, and you don't even want to look at it. Take care that you don't turn into one of those fashionable painters. Already your colours are getting a bit clamorous. Your contours are not strict enough: sometimes they're so weak the line cannot be seen at all. You're too eager to achieve fashionable effects of light, to paint in an eye-catching way—if you're not careful you'll wind up painting in the English style. Take care: you're developing a great fondness for society; now and again I see you wearing a foppish scarf, a glossy hat... It's tempting, I know, and you could easily find yourself painting fashionable pictures and society portraits for handsome fees. But this is the way to destroy your talent, not to develop it. Be patient. Think about each picture properly, and forget about stylish effects: let other people make money that way. You'll reap your reward in the fullness of time.'

In some ways the professor was right. It is true that our artist occasionally longed to get himself spruced up and go out on the town—in other words, to give free rein to his young spirit. But he was able to control these impulses. At times he would become utterly absorbed when he picked up his brush, and would put it down like someone rudely awakened in the middle of a wonderful dream. His taste had broadened. He had not yet grasped the full depth of Raphael, but was already drawn by the sweeping brush of Guido Reni, lingered over Titian's portraits, and admired the Flemish masters. Though unable altogether to penetrate the veil which had previously obscured his view of these old pictures, he could now discern something in them, although inwardly he did not share the professor's view that the old masters were so far ahead of us; he even felt that the nineteenth century in some respects had made significant advances on them, and that our imitation of nature was much more vivid, alive, and immediate; in other words, on this score he thought as do all young people who have achieved something new and are proudly aware of it. It would vex him when occasionally he saw some painter from abroad, a Frenchman or German, often not a painter at all by vocation, create a sensation by an act of pure legerdemain, a nimble brush-stroke and vivid colours, and in no time amass vast sums of money. This feeling of annoyance would not bother him at those times of total absorption in his work, when he would even forget to eat and drink; it only came when his own circumstances became so straitened that there was no money for brushes and paints, and his importunate landlord called ten times a day demanding the rent. Then his hungry imagination would dwell with envy on the lot of the rich artist; then would come the impulse that so often takes possession of Russians: to throw everything to the four winds and go on a mad, desperate fling. This, more or less, was how he felt at the moment.

'Pah! be patient, be patient!' he exclaimed in annoyance. 'There's a limit to patience, too. Be patient! And how am I going to buy my dinner tomorrow? No one will give me a loan. And it's no use trying to sell my pictures and drawings: I'd get twenty copecks for the lot. They have some value, I suppose: each one of them has helped me in some way, has taught me something. But what use are they really?—they're all studies and sketches, and they'll never be completed. And who would buy them, when they don't know my name; who wants my art school studies, or my unfinished Psyche, or views of my room, or a portrait of my Nikita, although it is a lot better than the portraits by some fashionable painter? Why do I bother? Why should I suffer, and slave away at the rudiments of art like a schoolboy when I could enjoy success as brilliant as theirs and have money?'

Having said this the artist suddenly shuddered and went pale: from a canvas propped up on the floor a feverishly distorted face stared back at him. Two terrible eyes bored into him as if preparing to devour him alive; the lips were framed to utter a grim command to be silent. Taking fright, he wanted to call for Nikita, whose Herculean snores could be heard from the front room; but suddenly he stopped and laughed. In an instant his fear vanished. This was the portrait he had bought earlier and since forgotten. In the glow of the moon, with which the room was suffused, the picture had taken on an uncannily lifelike quality. He set about examining it and cleaning it of dust. He soaked a sponge in water and wiped the picture a few times, removing almost the entire layer of accumulated dust and grime. Then he hung it before him on the wall and stared in even greater amazement at this remarkable work: the whole face had practically come to life and the eyes stared at him so piercingly that finally he shuddered, stepped back, and said in an astonished voice: 'It's looking at me, looking with eyes that are human!'

He then remembered a story he had heard long before from his professor about a portrait by Leonardo da Vinci, on which the great master had worked for a number of years and still regarded as unfinished but which, in Vasari's* description, was regarded by everyone else as a most perfect and accomplished work of art. Its most remarkable feature had been the eyes, which amazed the artist's contemporaries; even the tiniest veins had not been forgotten and were reproduced on the canvas.

There was, however, something very strange about this portrait before him. This went beyond art: it violated the harmony of the portrait itself. These were living, human eyes! They seemed to have been cut out of someone's head and inserted in the picture. Contemplation of the portrait did not uplift the soul in the way a true work of art should, however terrible the subject matter; this picture provoked an unhealthy, morbid reaction.

'What can it be?' the artist found himself asking. 'This is nature, after all, real, live nature: so why should I have this strange and unpleasant feeling? Is it that such slavish, literal copying of nature is wrong, and strikes one as harsh and discordant? Or does it mean that, if you depict an object with cold detachment, without compassion, it will appear before you only in its own terrible reality, reft of the illumination that would be imparted by the artist who painted with a deep, unfathomable feeling for his subject? Such is the reality which would be revealed if, in an endeavour to reveal the essence of some noble person, you were to take up a scalpel, cut him open and expose his entrails and all that is most revolting within him. How is it that simple, base nature can be represented by one artist in a kind of bright radiance, so that the impression of baseness is completely absent and, on the contrary, you feel exhilarated and afterwards everything around you seems to flow more smoothly and calmly? And then how can another artist take the same subject-matter and make it appear base and sordid, while in fact remaining just as true to life? The truth is that it has no inner light. It is like a fine view in nature: however magnificent, it will still seem to lack something if the sun is not shining.'

He went up to the portrait again to examine its remarkable eyes and realized to his horror that they were unmistakably staring back at him. This was no copy from nature, this was that strange semblance of life which you would expect to see on the face of a corpse risen from the grave. Perhaps his delirious state had been caused by the moonlight, which bathed everything in its phantasmagoric light and falsified the images of daylight, or perhaps the cause lay elsewhere, but for some reason he was suddenly afraid to sit alone in the room. He quietly walked away from the portrait, turned aside, and tried to ignore it, but his eyes kept turning back against his will. Finally he was even afraid to walk about the room; he felt as though someone was about to walk up behind him and he cast nervous glances over his shoulder. His was not a timorous disposition, yet his imagination and nerves were sensitive and he could not account for the involuntary fear which overcame him that evening. He sat in the corner, but at once had the feeling that someone was about to lean over his shoulder and look into his face. Even Nikita's snoring, which reverberated from the front room, could not dispel his fear. Finally he rose timidly, careful not to lift his eyes, withdrew behind his screen and lay down on the bed. Through a gap in the screen he could see his room bathed in moonlight and the portrait hanging on the wall. The eyes bored into him even more terribly, more fixedly, seeming to scorn everything else. With a heavy sense of foreboding he forced himself to rise from the bed and, taking up his sheet, walked across the room and draped it over the entire portrait.

After this he lay down feeling calmer and gave himself up to thoughts of the poverty and wretched lot of the artist, of the thorny path he has to tread in life; all the while his eyes were constantly drawn to the gap in the screen, through which they could see the draped portrait. The moonlight accentuated the whiteness of the sheet and he even fancied that he could make out the terrible eyes through the cloth. In horror he stared harder still, to assure himself that this was nonsense! But instead he saw that it was true... he could see quite clearly: the sheet was no longer there... The portrait was fully exposed and stared past everything else straight at him, its gaze penetrating deep inside him... His heart froze. He saw the old man move and take hold of the frame with both hands. Then he pulled himself up and, thrusting out both legs, leapt from the frame... Now through the gap in the screen he could see only an empty frame. The room echoed with the sound of footsteps, drawing closer and closer to the screen.

The poor artist's heart started to pound. More dead than alive he waited for the old man's face to appear round the screen. Which in due course it did, the very same weather-bronzed face with its large eyes now roving about the room. Chartkov tried to cry out but he had lost his voice; he tried to move, but his limbs were paralysed. Mouth agape, he stared at the tall, terrible phantom, draped in its capacious Asiatic robes, and waited to see what it would do next. The old man seated himself at his feet and proceeded to remove something from beneath the folds of his robe. It was a bag. He untied it and, holding it by its two corners, shook out the contents: several long, heavy, cylindrical packages fell with a thud to the floor; each was wrapped in blue paper and bore the legend: '1,000 pieces of gold.' Thrusting his long, bony hands out from his wide sleeves the old man started to unwrap the packages, revealing the glint of gold.

Despite the artist's foreboding and incapacitating fear, he could not tear his eyes away from this gold, and he watched spell-bound as it was unwrapped, glinted and clinked with a thin dull ring in the old man's bony hands, and was then wrapped up again. At this point he noticed one package which had rolled along the floor to the head of his bed. He made a desperate lunge for it, then looked round in terror, lest he had been observed. But the old man appeared completely engrossed. He gathered together all his packages, replaced them in the bag and, without a glance at the artist, disappeared round the screen. Chartkov's heart beat harder still as he listened to his retreating footsteps. He clenched his package harder,

trembling in every limb as suddenly he heard the footsteps returning to the screen—the old man must have realized that one package
was missing. The next instant his face reappeared round the screen.
Filled with despair, the artist clutched the package with all his
strength and did his utmost to move, to cry out—and awoke.

He was in a cold sweat; his heart pounded violently: his chest
contracted as tightly as if his last breath were about to escape. 'Was
that really a dream?' he said, gripping his head with both hands; but
the terrible lifelike quality of the scene he had beheld made it unlike
any dream. As he woke he saw the old man returning into the
frame, even glimpsing the hem of his ample robe, and his hand
distinctly felt the impression of some weighty object it had been
holding a minute before. Moonlight flooded the room, reaching
into its dark corners, where it lit up a canvas, a plaster-of-Paris arm,
cloth draped over a chair, a pair of trousers and muddy boots. Only
at this point did he realize he was no longer lying on his bed but
standing upright in front of the portrait. How he had got there he
was quite unable to explain. He was even more amazed to observe
that the portrait was uncovered and there was in fact no sheet over
it. Transfixed with fear he stared before him and saw the old man's
living, human eyes literally bore into him. A cold sweat broke out
on his face; he wanted to move away but felt that his feet were
rooted to the ground. And then he saw—and this was now no
dream—the old man's features move and his lips start to purse as if
he wanted to suck him into the picture... He leapt up with a wail of
terror and awoke.

So was that also a dream? His heart pounding furiously, he
reached out and felt around him. Yes, he was lying on his bed in the
very same position in which he had gone to sleep. Before him stood
the screen: the room was filled with moonlight. Through the gap in
the screen he could see the portrait, covered as it should be with the
sheet—just as he had left it. So that had also been a dream! But
even now he could still feel the impression of something in his
clenched fist. His heart was beating at a fearful rate; there was an
unbearable heaviness in his chest. He stared through the gap at the
sheet. At this point he clearly saw the sheet move as if there were
hands flailing beneath it trying to throw it off. 'Lord God above,
what is it!' he exclaimed, crossing himself in terror, and awoke.

That, too, was a dream! He leapt from his bed, half out of his mind and quite unable to comprehend what was going on: was this the influence of some nightmare, or a demon, was it the delirium of a fever or real life? In an attempt to calm his agitation and slow the frantic pounding of his blood, he went over to the window and opened its small ventilation pane. The cold gust of wind revived him. The roofs and white walls of the houses were still bathed in moonlight, although small dark clouds scudded across the sky. Silence reigned: his ear could catch only the occasional distant clatter of a droshky in some unseen alley, its driver dozing on his seat, lulled to sleep by the lazy motion of his nag as they waited for a tardy fare. He stood there for a long time, his head thrust out of the window. The first glimmer of the approaching dawn had already appeared in the sky; at last, feeling a drowsiness steal over him, he closed the window, walked away, lay down on the bed and was soon fast asleep.

He awoke very late, feeling that severe discomfort which overtakes a man after a night's carousing: his head throbbed with pain. His room was gloomy and unpleasantly humid with the dampness of the outside air, which seeped through the chinks in his windows, blocked with pictures and primed canvases. As glum and out of sorts as a rain-drenched cockerel, he sat down on his tattered divan wondering what to do next, and finally recalled his entire dream. As the dream came back to him, it seemed so hideously vivid that he even started to suspect that it had not been a dream at all, it had not been mere delirium, but a vision. Pulling off the sheet he examined the ghastly portrait in the daylight. It was true, the eyes were amazingly lifelike, but he could see nothing particularly frightening about them; their only effect was to give him a strange and unpleasant sensation in his stomach. Even so he could not totally convince himself that it had been a dream. He fancied that some terrible shred of reality was mixed up with the dream. Something in the old man's look and expression seemed to say that he had been with him that night; his hand felt as though it had just been holding some heavy object which the moment before had been snatched away from him. He felt that if only he had held on to the package a little harder it would still have been in his hand when he woke up.

'Lord God, if only I could put my hands on a little of that money!' he sighed deeply, and in his imagination he saw all the packages being emptied out of their bag, each with its alluring inscription: '1,000 pieces of gold'. The packages were unwrapped, there was a flash of gold, and they were wrapped up again; all the while he sat motionless, staring blankly into space, unable to tear himself away from this vision, like a child sitting before a plate of sweetmeats and hungrily watching as they are eaten by others. Finally he was brought rudely to his senses by a knock on the door. In came the landlord with a police sergeant, whose appearance is even less welcome to poor people than the face of a petitioner is to the rich. The landlord of the small house in which Chartkov lived was a member of that species commonly encountered amongst land-lords in the Fifteenth Line on Vasilyevsky Island, on the Petersburg Side, or in some distant corner like Kolomna*—a species which is very widespread in Russia and whose character is as hard to define as the colour of a threadbare frock-coat.

In his youth he had been a loud-mouthed captain, who also performed certain civil duties, was a great one for flogging, a busy-body, dandy, and dunderhead; but in his old age all these pro-nounced traits had blended into a murky vagueness of character. He was by now a widower, already retired, no longer a dandy, or a braggart, or a dare-devil, interested only in drinking tea and natter-ing away; he would walk about his room trimming the wick of his tallow candle; promptly at the end of every month he would do the rounds of his tenants collecting the rent; he would hold the key in his hand if he stepped out into the street to inspect the roof; would repeatedly chase the janitor out of his cubbyhole whenever he slunk inside it for a nap; in other words, he was the sort of retired person who, after a reckless youth and bumpy carriage-ride of a life, is left with nothing but boorish habits.

'Please see for yourself, Varukh Kuzmich,' he addressed the police sergeant, spreading wide his hands: 'he won't pay for his flat, he just won't pay.'

'How can I when I have no money? Wait a little while and I'll pay up.'

'I can't afford to wait, my good man,' said the landlord angrily, wagging a key at him; 'I have an officer amongst my tenants, Lieutenant-Colonel Potogonkin, he's been renting from me for seven years; and then there's Anna Petrovna Bukhmisterova who rents a shed and two stalls in the stables, she has three servants—those are the sort of tenants I have. To be quite honest with you, I don't run the kind of establishment where you can live without paying. Be so good as to pay me the rent now and then vacate the premises.'

'Yes, seeing as you've agreed you'd better pay,' said the sergeant with a slight shake of the head, tucking one finger inside the front of his tunic.

'That's all very well, but what am I supposed to pay with? I haven't a brass copeck to my name.'

'In that case you shall have to repay Ivan Ivanovich in kind, with the products of your trade,' said the sergeant: 'he might agree to receive the rent in pictures.'

'Oh no, sergeant, thank you very much, but not in pictures. I might agree if they were pictures with a decent subject, the sort of thing you could hang on your wall, some general with a star at least, or a portrait of Prince Kutuzov,* but look at the peasants he paints— that peasant there in the long shirt: that's his servant, the one who grinds his paints. To think of that rascal having his portrait painted— I'd like to wring his neck: he's pulled all the nails out of my bolts, the thief. Just have a look at the stuff he paints: here he's painted the room. It would be all very well if he'd taken some tidy, well-ordered room, but he's gone and painted it just as it is with all its rubbish and filth lying around. Just look how he's fouled up my room, please have a good look for yourself. And some of my tenants have been living here for seven years, decent tenants, colonels, Anna Petrovna Bukhmisterova... No, let me tell you: there's nothing worse than an artist for a tenant; he turns his room into a pigsty, God save us from the likes of him.'

Meanwhile the poor artist was expected to stand by and listen to all this. The sergeant started examining the paintings and sketches, showing as he did so that his mind was much more animated than the landlord's and was even not entirely invulnerable to artistic influence.

'A-ha,' he said, prodding one canvas which depicted a nude woman, 'this one's rather... how shall I put it?—naughty. But why does that one have a black smudge under his nose? Has he spilt snuff on his lip, it that it?'

'It's the shadow,' answered Chartkov curtly, without looking in his direction.

'Well, I think you should have put it somewhere else, and not right under the nose—too prominent,' said the sergeant; 'and who is this a portrait of?' he continued, coming to the portrait of the old man: 'what an ugly mug. Was he this ugly in life? The way he's looking at you—it's enough to frighten the daylights out of you! Who's it meant to be?'

'Oh that's just a...' said Chartkov, but he was brought short by the noise of splintering wood. The sergeant must have been leaning too hard against the picture frame, and the weight of his spade-like policeman's hands had caused the side boards to break inwards. One of these fell to the floor releasing a blue paper package, which clunked loudly as it landed. Chartkov's eyes lit on the inscription: '1,000 pieces of gold.' He hurled himself at the package and clutched it feverishly in his fist, which sagged under the weight.

'Sounded just like money dropping,' said the sergeant, who had heard something fall but had been unable to see what it was because Chartkov had moved so swiftly.

'What business is it of yours?'

'This is what: you have to pay your landlord your rent right away, you have the money but you don't want to pay—that's what it's got to do with me.'

'Well, I'll pay him today.'

'Why would you not pay him before, causing all this trouble for your landlord, and even for the police?'

'Because I didn't want to touch this money; I'll pay him everything I owe this evening and I'll vacate the flat tomorrow, because I have no wish to remain with a landlord like him.'

'So, Ivan Ivanovich, he'll pay you,' said the sergeant to the landlord. 'And if it should happen that he doesn't give you proper satisfaction this evening, then we'll have to apply tougher measures, will we not, mister painter?'

Saying this he donned his tricorn hat and went out through the door, followed by the landlord, his head bent, apparently lost in thought.

'Thank God I've got rid of them!' said Chartkov, hearing the door in the hall close behind him.

He looked into the hall, dispatched Nikita on an errand so as to be completely alone, locked the door behind him and, coming back into the room, set about undoing the package, his heart pounding. It contained pieces of gold, each mint-new and glowing like fire. Wild with excitement he sat next to his pile of gold and marvelled, wondering whether it was all a dream. The bundle contained exactly a thousand pieces; on the outside, it was identical to those he had seen in his dream. For a while he fingered the coins, examining them carefully, lost in his reverie. His imagination lingered over all those stories about hidden treasure, coffers with secret drawers, left by ancestors for posterity, in the firm conviction that their descendants would be driven by dissipation to their eventual ruin.

He wondered if this was perhaps the case with his own lucky find: had some aged patriarch, wishing to leave his descendant a present, hidden it in the frame of a family portrait? Full of romantic delusions he even began to wonder whether there might not be some secret link here with his own fate, whether the existence of the portrait might not be linked with his own, and his acquisition of it a pre-ordained act. He eagerly set about examining the frame. On one side a cavity had been carved into the wood, and so skilfully concealed by a board that if the frame had not been cracked open by the ham-fisted police sergeant the money would have remained undiscovered until the end of time. As he examined the portrait he was amazed anew by the artistry, the extraordinary execution of the eyes: they no longer seemed so terrible to him, but an unpleasant feeling still lingered in his heart.

'No,' he said to himself, 'I do not care whose ancestor you were: I'm going to put you behind glass and give you a gold frame.'

Thereupon he reached out for the pile of gold before him and he felt a rush of blood as he touched it.

'What should I do with it?' he mused, staring intently at his lucky find. 'I am now set up for at least three years; I can shut myself in my room and work. I now have funds for paints, for food, for tea, my daily needs, my rent; now no one will be able to get in my way or annoy me: I can buy myself a first-class mannequin, order a plaster-of-Paris torso, model the legs, get myself a Venus, buy up prints of the old masters. And if I work three years for myself, taking my time, not worrying about sales, I'll surpass them all, I can be a great artist.'

This is what the voice of reason told him, but deep down inside him he could hear another voice, louder and more persuasive. He looked again at the gold and felt more strongly the force of his 22 years and ardent youth. He now had in his power all he had always admired and feverishly craved from afar. He felt his pulse quicken at the very thought of it! To don a fashionable tailcoat, to break his never-ending fast, to rent a splendid new apartment, to be able to frequent the theatre, the pastry shop, the... and so on and so forth. The money clenched in his hand, he headed out through the door.

First of all he called on a tailor, had himself fitted out from head to foot, and gazed at the new Chartkov in child-like wonder; he bought an array of perfumes and pomades and rented the very first apartments he found on Nevsky Prospect without haggling over the price, a splendid abode, with mirrors and French windows; he absent-mindedly bought himself an expensive lorgnette, just as absent-mindedly bought a mass of cravats, far more than he needed, had his hair curled in a hairdresser's, drove twice around the city in a carriage for no real reason, gorged himself on sticky confections in a pastry shop and called in at a French restaurant about which he knew only from hearsay, as vague and remote as if it was situated in distant Cathay. He took his dinner sprawled in a casual way across his chair and as he ate he cast arrogant looks at his fellow diners and constantly stared into the mirror, adjusting his newly curled locks. Then he downed a bottle of champagne, hitherto known to him only by repute. The wine went to his head a little and he stepped jauntily out on to the street, ready to take on the devil himself. He strutted along the pavement as smug and spruce as a golden-eye drake,* peering at all and sundry through his lorgnette. On the bridge he espied his former professor and swept blithely past him, leaving the astounded pedagogue standing motionless on the bridge, his face contorted into the shape of a question mark.

He arranged for all his belongings and assorted effects—easel, canvas, pictures—to be transferred that same evening to his splendid new residence. His best pictures he displayed in prominent places, and the worst he pushed away into a corner, and then he busied himself by striding up and down his grand and spacious rooms, his eyes constantly drawn to the mirrors. His heart strained with an uncontrollable desire to seize fame by the scruff of its neck that very moment and to flaunt himself before the world! He could already hear the shouts of acclaim: 'Chartkov, Chartkov! Have you seen Chartkov's picture? How nimbly that Chartkov wields his brush! What talent!'

He walked about his room in great excitement, his head on fire with such thoughts. The very next day he took ten of the gold pieces and set off to see the publisher of a popular newspaper in the hope of securing his magnanimous assistance; the latter gave him a most cordial reception, immediately addressing him as 'most respected sir', shaking Chartkov's hand with both of his own, making detailed enquiries about such details as his name, patronymic, and place of residence. The following day, beneath an advertisement for a new type of tallow candle, there appeared an article with the heading: 'Chartkov and his Remarkable Gifts'.

'We hasten to inform the city's educated inhabitants,' it read, 'of a delightful and splendid new acquisition. No one would deny that our society boasts many excellent physiognomies and marvellous faces, but hitherto we have lacked the means of committing them to the miracle of canvas for the benefit of posterity; now this deficiency has been filled: an artist who combines all the necessary qualities has emerged in our midst. Now the society belle may rest assured that she will be portrayed with all the grace of her ethereal beauty, with her lovely, enchanting radiance, like butterflies fluttering amongst the flowers of spring. The venerable paterfamilias will be able to behold himself in the bosom of his family. The merchant, warrior, patrician, man of state—they can all apply themselves to their noble professions with renewed zeal. Hurry, hurry, leave your promenading, abandon your visit to a friend, or cousin, or to that glittering shop—stop what you are doing, wherever you are, and hasten hither. The artist's splendid studio (Nevsky Prospect, number such-and-such) is hung about with *chefs-d'œuvre* of his brush, an instrument worthy of a Van Dyke or a Titian. You will not know what is more impressive, the *vraisemblance* and similarity to the original, or the extraordinarily fresh and vivid brushwork. Praise to you, artist, you have drawn a lucky ticket in life's lottery. Bravo, Andrei Petrovich!'—(The newspaperman, as we can see, liked the personal touch.) 'Glorify yourself and us. We will show proper appreciation. May the crowds of people who descend on you, and the money they will bring—for all that certain of our fellow journalists may be opposed to this—be your reward.'

Our artist read this notice with secret satisfaction; his face positively beamed. His name had appeared in print: this was a great occasion for him, and he reread the lines several times. He found the comparison with Van Dyke and Titian particularly flattering. The phrase 'Bravo, Andrei Petrovich!' also pleased him greatly; to

be referred to in the newspaper by his forename and patronymic*
was an honour such as he had never before experienced. He started
to pace briskly about his room, running his hands through his hair,
by turns sitting down in his armchair, then leaping up and sitting
on the divan, imagining to himself how he would receive his visitors, gentlemen and ladies alike. He practised walking up to his
canvas and making a sweeping stroke with his brush to impart a
graceful movement to the arm. The next day his doorbell rang; he
ran to open it, admitting a lady, who was preceded by a footman in
a livery coat with a fur collar, and accompanied by her daughter, an
18-year-old girl.

'Monsieur Chartkov?' enquired the lady.

The artist bowed.

'So much is written about you; your portraits, they say, are the
height of perfection.'

Saying this, the lady perched a lorgnette on her nose and marched
off to peruse the walls—which, as it happened, were bare.

'But where are your portraits?'

'With the movers,' said the artist, a little confused: 'I've only just
moved to this apartment, so they are still on their way... they
haven't arrived yet.'

'You were in Italy?' asked the lady, directing her lorgnette at
him, for want of anything else at which to direct it.

'No, I wasn't but... I would like to go there... in fact for the time
being I have had to postpone my trip... Please, take this chair, you
must be tired...'

'Thank you, I have been sitting for a long time in our carriage.
Ah there, at last I see your work!' she exclaimed, running to the
opposite wall and directing her lorgnette at the studies, sketches,
perspective drawings and portraits stacked on the floor.

'*C'est charmant*, Lise, Lise, *venez ici*! A Teniers room, look: see
the disorder, the untidiness, the table with its bust, the arm, the
palette; look at all the dust, see how he's painted the dust! *C'est
charmant*! And look at the woman washing her face in this picture—
quelle jolie figure! Ah, un moujik! Lise, Lise, a *moujik* in a Russian
tunic! Look: a *moujik*! So you do not paint portraits exclusively?"

'Oh, that's just some nonsense... A little frivolity, studies...'

'Tell me, what is your opinion of today's portrait painters? Is it
not true that there are none who have the stature of Titian? They

don't have the strength in their colours, or the... What a pity that I cannot express myself to you in Russian' (the lady was a devotee of the fine arts and she and her lorgnette had coursed through all the galleries in Italy).

'However, monsieur Nolle... now there's a superb painter! An extraordinary talent! I observe that he has even more expression in his faces than you will find in Titian. You do not know monsieur Nolle?'

'Who is this Nolle?' asked the artist.

'Monsieur Nolle. Ah, such talent! He painted her portrait when she was only 12. You absolutely must pay us a visit. Lise, show the monsieur your album. I should tell you that we have come here so that you may begin work on her portrait at once.'

'Why of course, I am ready to commence.'

Without further ado he moved up an easel with a prepared canvas, took up his palette and focused his gaze on the girl's pallid face. Had he been a connoisseur of human nature he should at once have been able to read in her features the stirrings of a young girl's passion for the ballroom, an awakening ennui and impatience about the unbearably slow passage of time before dinner and after dinner, a desire to run about at carnivals in a new dress, the deep traces of an unwilling application to various arts forced upon her by her *maman* to improve her mind and sensibilities. But all the painter could see in this delicate little face was an artistically intriguing transparency, like that of fine porcelain, an appealing gentle languor, a slender, fair neck and aristocratic frailty. He was already anticipating his triumph, determined to demonstrate the delicacy and brilliance of his brushwork, whose only outlet hitherto had been the coarse features of his uncouth models, the austere visages of antiquity and copies of classical masters. He could already see in his mind's eye how the finished portrait of this pretty little face would look.

'Do you know,' said the lady with a note of pathos in her voice: 'I would rather... She is wearing a dress at the moment; to be honest, I would rather she wasn't wearing such a commonplace dress: I would like her to be dressed in something simple and sitting in the shade of a tree, with fields in the background, with animals grazing in the distance, or a grove... so that you wouldn't think she was on her way to a ball, or a fashionable soirée. Our balls, I must confess, are so destructive to the soul, they deaden the feelings so...

Simplicity, more simplicity, that's what we need.' (Alas! it was apparent from the wax-like countenances of both mother and daughter that they had danced away too many a night at precisely such balls.)

Chartkov resumed his work, arranged his model, and composed a mental picture of the scene. He waved his brush in the air, marking out imaginary points, narrowed one eye, stepped backwards, studied the scene from afar—and in the course of a single hour commenced and completed the sketch. Content with the result he at once started painting, becoming quite carried away by his work. He had already forgotten everything else, forgotten that he was in the company of aristocratic ladies, and even started to give vent to certain artistic eccentricities, muttering strange noises and humming snatches of melody, as artists do when totally absorbed in their work. Unceremoniously, with a brusque motion of his brush, he got his model to raise her head, before she finally started to fidget and complain of fatigue.

'That will do, enough for the first time,' declared the lady.

'Just a little longer,' said the artist, forgetting whom he was addressing.

'No, time to stop! Lise, it's three o'clock!' she said, producing a miniature watch which hung by a gold chain from her belt, and exclaimed: 'Dear me, look at the time!'

'Just another minute,' pleaded Chartkov in the ingenuous and imploring voice of a child.

The lady was apparently not in the least inclined to indulge his artistic whims on this occasion, but promised to allow him a longer session the next time.

'It's annoying, all the same,' thought Chartkov, 'I was just getting into my stride.' And he recalled that no one had ever interrupted him or stopped him when he worked in his studio on Vasilyevsky Island; Nikita would sit stock-still in one position and you could paint him for as long as you liked; he even used to fall asleep in the pose he had been put in. Filled with vexation, Chartkov set his brush and palette down on the chair and stood gloomily before the canvas. A compliment paid him by his lady visitor brought him to his senses. He rushed to the door to show them out, and on the staircase received from them an invitation to dine with them one evening the following week. He returned to his room looking very cheerful. This aristocratic lady had quite enchanted him. Hitherto he had regarded such creatures as something outside his orbit, brought into this world for the express purpose of driving about in splendid carriages with liveried footmen and popinjay coachmen, from which vantage point they cast indifferent looks at the wretched pedestrian, trudging along in his drab overcoat. And now one of these creatures had actually entered his own room; he was painting her portrait and had been invited to dinner in an aristocratic house. He was seized with a feeling of extraordinary contentment; such was his elation that he rewarded himself with a magnificent dinner, followed by a visit to the theatre. The remainder of the evening he spent once again driving aimlessly about the city.

Over the next few days he could not get his mind on to his usual work. He was constantly on tenterhooks, waiting for the doorbell to ring. At length the aristocratic lady returned with her pale daughter. He seated them, pulled up his canvas with an adroit flourish which he hoped would show him to be a man of the world, and started to paint. The sunny day and bright light greatly assisted him. He could see in his spindly model much that, if he could capture it on the canvas, would give the portrait considerable merit; he saw that, if he could convey his subject fully and in every detail, he would achieve something outstanding. His heartbeat quickened when he realized that he could give expression to something which others had failed to observe. His work took complete possession of him, and he immersed himself entirely in the activity of his brush, allowing himself once again to forget that his model was a creature of fine breeding. Breathlessly he watched the delicate features and almost translucent skin of the 17-year-old girl appear on the canvas. He caught every nuance, her slightly sallow complexion, the bluish shades beneath her eyes, and he was on the point of adding the little pimple which had appeared on her forehead when he suddenly heard above him the voice of her mother. 'Oh, but why paint that? that's not necessary,' the lady said. 'And look here too, here, in several places... why, it's even a little yellow, and here there are some dark patches.' The painter started to explain that in combination these patches and yellow streaks were effective, bringing out the attractive, delicate tones of the face. But he was informed that they did not bring out any tones and were not in the least effective; and that he was imagining all this.

'Let me just dab on a touch of yellow in one place, I beg you,' said the artist good-naturedly. But he was not permitted this either. It was announced that Lise was a little out of sorts that day, and that her face was never sallow; quite the contrary, it was in fact striking for its freshness of complexion. Sadly he began painting out the details his brush had succeeded in imparting on canvas. Many barely perceptible nuances disappeared, and with them disappeared much of the the likeness he had captured. Working without feeling, he spread on those conventional tones which an artist can apply quite mechanically and which turn even a portrait painted from life into something cold and academic, as in a painting manual. But the lady was content that the offensive colours had been banished, and only expressed her surprise at the length of time the portrait was taking, adding that she had heard Chartkov could do an entire portrait from start to finish in two sittings. The artist was lost for a reply to this.

The ladies gathered themselves up and prepared to leave. He put down his brush, saw them to the door, and after they had gone remained motionless before his portrait for a long time, staring at it gloomily, stupidly even, as he recalled those fine feminine features, the subtle shades and ethereal tones which he had succeeded in capturing, and had then ruthlessly destroyed. While these memories filled his mind he put the portrait aside and sought out a head he had long ago sketched of Psyche. The face had been skilfully executed, but it remained quite cold and academic, consisting exclusively of abstract features and altogether lacking in life. For want of anything better to do he now set to work on it, imparting to it all the nuances he had observed in the face of his aristocratic young model. The features, shades and tones he had captured were here transmitted in the purified form that an artist can only achieve when, after staring lengthily at nature, he withdraws from it to create an artistic work of equal perfection. Psyche gradually came to life, and what had been born as a barely discernible idea now started to take on material form. The facial features of the fashionable young girl were miraculously imparted to the countenance of Psyche, giving it a unique appearance which entitled the portrait to be described as an original work. It seemed as if he had used everything his model offered, piece by piece and in combination; he became totally immersed in his work. For several days on end he remained absorbed in this painting, and it was while thus engaged that he was discovered by his lady acquaintances. He had no time to remove the canvas from his easel. The two ladies emitted shrieks of delight and clapped their hands.

'Lise, Lise! Look, what a likeness! *C'est superbe, superbe!* What an inspired idea to clothe her in Greek costume. Oh, what a wonderful surprise!'

The artist was unsure how to disabuse his ladies of this misconception that pleased them so. Somewhat shamefaced and lowering his eyes, he said in a quiet voice:

'That's Psyche.'

'Portrayed as Psyche? Why, *c'est charmant!*' said the mother with a smile, and her daughter smiled too. 'Just look, Lise, how well it becomes you to be portrayed as Psyche. *Quelle idée délicieuse!* But what fine work! It is Correggio. I must confess that, although I have read and heard about you, I did not know that you were possessed of such talent. No, now you simply must paint my portrait too.'

The lady, it appeared, also wished to be portrayed as some kind of Psyche.

'What am I to do with them?' thought the artist. 'If this is their wish, then let Psyche be whatever they want her to be.' He said aloud:

'Be so kind as to be seated for a little time, and I will apply a few touches.'

'Oh, but I am afraid that you might somehow... the likeness is so good as it is.'

Realizing that the ladies were apprehensive about sallow shades, the artist reassured them that he would only make the eyes more sparkling and expressive. In all fairness, he felt thoroughly ashamed and desired to impart at least some similarity to the original, lest he be condemned as an out-and-out fraud. Sure enough, the pale girl's features gradually became discernible in the countenance of Psyche.

'Enough!' called the mother, afraid lest the similarity with her daughter become too great.

The artist was handsomely rewarded: smiles, money, compliments, warm handshakes, and invitations to dinner were pressed upon him; in other words, he received a thousand flattering rewards. The portrait created a sensation in the city. The lady showed it to her friends; they were all astounded by the skill with which the artist had managed to preserve a likeness and yet impart new beauty to his model. The latter observation was usually accompanied by a flush of envy on the cheek of the speaker.

Suddenly the artist was inundated with commissions. It seemed that the entire city wished to be painted by him. His doorbell rang incessantly. In one way this could have been a good thing, as it gave him the opportunity for infinite practice in variety, in painting different faces. But alas, these were all the sort of people who are difficult to please, people in a hurry, always busy, or members of high society—which meant that they were even busier than anyone else, and thus impossibly impatient. The first requirement, invariably, was that it should be done well and quickly. The artist saw that he would have to relinquish all thoughts of striving after perfection and would have to make do with artistic sleight of hand and nimble brushwork. He had to capture the general, the overall expression and not allow his brush to explore any finer detail; in other words, it was quite impossible to convey nature in all its exactitude.

To which we should add that all his sitters made many other demands on him. The ladies insisted that he depict their soul and character, and disregard the rest, rounding off all the sharp angles, glossing over—or even omitting altogether—all defects. In other words, the portrait had to be one the beholder could gaze on at length, perhaps even fall in love with. Consequently, when they sat for him, they sometimes adopted such expressions that the artist was quite taken aback: one endeavoured to arrange her features into an expression of melancholy, another sought that of dreaminess, a third was bent on reducing the size of her mouth, pursing it so tightly that it became a mere dot, no bigger than a pin-head. All this notwithstanding, they would demand that his portraits show a close likeness and natural ease.

The gentlemen were no better than the ladies. One insisted that he be portrayed with his head turned at a striking angle to look strong and resolute; another had his eyes turned upward in inspiration; a third, a lieutenant of the guards, demanded that Mars be visible in his eyes; a high-ranking official would have his face express greater forthrightness and nobility and his hand rest on a book emblazoned with the legend: 'Ever the champion of truth'.

At first the artist was not a little put out by such demands: he had to plan his work carefully and he was not given long to execute these commissions. Finally he grasped what was needed, and encountered no more problems. Two or three words were sufficient to tell him how the client wanted himself portrayed. To the would-be Mars he would give the visage of Mars; to those with Byronic aspirations he would give a Byronic posture and attitude. Should the ladies wish to be Corinna, Undine, or Aspasia,* he was only too happy to comply with their desires and, without even being asked, would enhance the beauty of their features, a little kindness which is never taken amiss, and for which an artist is sometimes even forgiven a poor likeness. Soon he himself began to marvel at the wondrous alacrity of his brush, while his sitters, it goes without saying, were in raptures, and proclaimed him a genius.

Chartkov became a fashionable painter in all respects. He started to dine out, to accompany ladies to galleries and even on promenades, to dress foppishly and assert loudly that the artist must belong to the beau monde, that he must keep up his reputation, that the common run of artists dress like bootblacks, are incapable of conducting themselves with decorum, do not maintain the *bon ton*, and are utterly lacking in refinement. He introduced a high standard of cleanliness and order in his home and studio, hired two splendid footmen, took on dandyish young students, changed his costume several times a day, curled his hair, assiduously studied the etiquette of receiving visitors, applied himself to beautifying his appearance in every possible way in order to produce the most agreeable effect on the ladies; in other words, it was soon quite impossible to recognize in him the modest artist who had once toiled, unremarked by the world, in his little garret on Vasilyevsky Island. He now expressed outspoken views on artists and their profession, maintaining that the old masters were far too highly rated, that before Raphael they all painted pickled herrings and not people; that the much-vaunted holy aura of sanctity which is said to surround their work is purely a figment of the popular imagination; that even Raphael himself did not paint all that well and the popularity of many of his pictures is due largely to the persuasion of fame; that Michelangelo was a braggart, because he wished only to parade his knowledge of anatomy, and there is nothing gracious about his work, and that true brilliance, artistic power, and sense of colour can only be found today, in the present century. This line of discourse would inadvertently, as it were, bring him round to the subject of himself.

'Something I cannot understand,' he would say, 'is how people can force themselves to sit and slog at their work. The fellow who toils away for several months at a single picture is, in my view, a plodder and not an artist. I do not consider him to have any talent. The genius creates swiftly and boldly. Now this portrait,' he would remark, turning to his visitors, 'I painted in two days, this head in a day, this in several hours, this in just over an hour. No, I... I must confess, I don't accept that something which has been laboriously painted stroke by stroke is art; it's the work of a tradesman, not art.'

Thus did he regale his visitors, and they in their turn were amazed at the power and agility of his brush, even uttering little gasps of surprise to hear how quickly his works were executed and then informing one another: 'Now this is talent, real talent! Just listen to him, see how his eyes sparkle! *Il y a quelque chose d'extraordinaire dans toute sa figure!*'

The artist was very flattered to hear such comments. When he read favourable reviews of his work in the journals he was as thrilled as a small child, although this praise was paid for with his own money. He would carry these reviews about with him everywhere, and would create pretexts to show them around to his friends and acquaintances. He was sufficiently naïve to derive great satisfaction from this exercise. His fame grew, and he received more and more commissions. He began to tire of the same old poses and portraits, which he now knew by heart. He felt increasingly loath to paint them, and would endeavour to do no more than the initial sketch of the head, leaving the rest to his pupils. Where previously he had tried to find new poses, to achieve a striking and forceful effect, he began to find this tedious too. His mind grew weary of the constant effort of conjuring up new ideas. He lacked both the energy and the time for it: the social whirl into which he had been swept, and where he tried to play the role of a man of fashion carried him further and further away from work and thought. His style grew cold and uninspired and, without his being aware of it, his work gradually became limited to stale and monotonous forms. The austere and dreary visages of civil and military officials, invariably spruced up and, so to speak, tightly laced, offered little scope for his brush: it began to forget the splendid draperies, the striking poses, and the passions, not to mention the grouping, the artistic drama, and its exalted tension. All he ever had to do with was a uniform, or a corset, or a tailcoat, objects which chill an artist's brain and stifle his imagination. His pictures now lacked even the most ordinary merits, yet for the time being they continued to enjoy renown, although true connoisseurs and artists would dismiss his latest work with a telling shrug of the shoulders. Some of them, who had known Chartkov in the old days, could not understand how he had managed to forfeit that talent which had been so obvious even at the very beginning of his career, and wondered in vain how a person could lose a gift at the very moment when he had achieved the full development of all his powers.

But our self-intoxicated artist was deaf to these criticisms. He was approaching the age of staidness, both in body and in spirit; he was putting on weight and visibly expanding in girth. His name was now accompanied by honorifics in the newspapers and journals: 'our distinguished Andrei Petrovich', 'our worthy Andrei Petrovich'. He was offered honorary positions, invited to join boards of examiners and to sit on committees. He now started, as is the rule with those of a distinguished age, to lean towards Raphael and the old masters—not because he was entirely convinced of their great merit but in order to use them as a stick with which to beat young artists. For he was beginning, like all men entering his station of life, to inveigh against all young people without exception for their lax morals and free-thinking ways. He was beginning to believe that there is a simple way to do everything in life, that there is no such thing as inspiration from above and that everything must be subjected to a single strict regime of decorum and uniformity. In other words, his life had reached the stage when all spontaneity of spirit withers, when emotional impulses carry more feebly to the soul and do not stir the heart with penetrating sounds, when contact with beauty no longer sparks virgin strength into fire and flame, and when the artist's burnt-out senses respond more willingly to the clink of gold coin, when he grows more attentive to its alluring music, and gradually, unwittingly, allows himself to be lulled insensible by its sweet melody.

Fame can give no pleasure to him who has come by it dishonestly, undeservedly; it will produce a constant tremor of excitement only in the person who is worthy of it. Therefore did all his feelings and impulses become directed towards gold. Gold became his passion, his ideal, his fear, his pleasure, his purpose. The bundles of banknotes grew in his coffers, and like all those on whom fate bestows this terrible gift, he became dull and unreceptive to everything save gold, and started to hoard without reason, to collect without purpose. He was on the point of turning into one of those creatures who have become so numerous in our insensitive world, regarded with horror by those still full of life and feeling, to whom they appear like walking coffins of stone with dead matter in place of a heart. But then something occurred which gave him such a jolt it brought him back to life.

One day he saw on his desk a note in which the Academy of Arts invited him, as one of its distinguished fellows, to come and state his opinion of a new picture, sent from Italy by a Russian artist working there. This artist was one of his former friends, who since an early age had nourished a passion for art, immersing himself in it heart and soul with all the zeal of a devoted acolyte, cutting himself off from family, friends, and favourite pastimes to hasten to that vineyard of the arts which basks beneath glorious skies, the wondrous city of Rome, whose name alone sends a quiver through the ardent heart of every artist. There he immersed himself in toil, like a hermit, and allowed nothing to distract him. It mattered nothing to him what people thought of his character, of his gaucherie, his ignorance of social etiquette, or the disrepute into which he brought the artistic profession by his wretched and shabby dress. It mattered nothing to him that his colleagues might be annoyed with him. He gave himself up entirely to art, spurning all else. He haunted the galleries, standing rapt for hours on end before the canvases of the great masters, studying and analysing their wonderful brushwork. He would never complete any work without checking what he had done against the achievements of these great teachers and without finding in their immortal creations unspoken yet eloquent advice for himself. He never entered into loud debates and arguments; he neither sided with nor condemned the purists. He gave every side its due, extracting only that which was beautiful, and finally retained as his teacher only one painter, the godlike Raphael, just as once the great poet-painter himself, after perusing many great works full of splendour and beauty, had finally retained by his side only one book, the *Iliad* of Homer, having discovered that it contained all one might possibly require, and that there was nothing in any other work which was not reflected here in exquisite perfection. In similar fashion did the Russian artist come away from his studies with an awareness of the sublime idea of creation, the magnificent beauty of thought and the sublime enchantment of the master's heavenly brush.

Entering the hall Chartkov found that a great throng of visitors had already gathered before the picture. They stood in profound silence, a rare phenomenon with such crowds of connoisseurs. He quickly composed his features into the self-important expression of an expert and stepped up close to the picture—and heavens! what a picture it was!

Before him hung a painting as pure, beautiful, and chaste as a bride. The artist's creation soared above all else with the humility, divinity, innocence, and simplicity of pure genius. It was as though the celestial figures on the canvas were startled by the great number of eyes staring at them, and had diffidently lowered their beautiful eyelashes. The connoisseurs were astounded by the phenomenal power of the artist's brush. The picture appeared to contain everything: a reflection of Raphael, discernible in the noble poses; a reflection of Correggio, in the accomplished brushwork. But most striking of all was the picture's revelation of the artist's creative power. It suffused every detail in the picture, and everywhere there was symmetry and inner strength. He had caught that melting roundness of line that is descried in nature only by the eye of the true artist and which the crude imitator renders as harsh angles. It was obvious that what the artist had drawn from the outer world he had first absorbed into his soul, whence it surged forth as from a spiritual fount, in harmonious and triumphant song. It was at once apparent, even to the laymen, how great a gulf divides the true artistic creation from the mere copy of nature.

An extraordinary silence hung over all those who stared at the picture, not a rustle, not a murmur could be heard, while with every minute the picture appeared to soar upwards; it seemed to detach itself from its surroundings and, growing steadily more radiant and marvellous, was suddenly transformed into an instant of time, that moment of divine inspiration, that instant for which the entire life of a human being is but a preparation. The observers felt tears welling up in their eyes. It was as though all likes and affinities, all brash and aberrant deviations from good taste had fused together into an unspoken hymn to this divine work of art.

Chartkov stood before the picture stock-still, his mouth agape, and finally, when the other viewers and connoisseurs gradually recovered their composure and began to discuss the merits of the painting, and when he was requested to express his own views, he returned to his senses; he strove to compose his features into an indifferent, matter-of-fact expression, and utter one of those trite and dismissive comments in which stale and mediocre artists excel, along the following lines: 'Yes of course, we certainly cannot deny that the artist has talent; he does have something; you can see he wishes to express something; however, as to the fundamental thing...' and to add, of course, the sort of faint praise which would damn any artist. He wanted to say something to this effect but words failed him, and in lieu of an answer he started sobbing uncontrolledly and hurtled from the room like a madman.

Once back home, he stood motionless and insensible in his magnificent studio. In an instant his whole being, his life had been reawakened as if youth had suddenly returned to him, as if the dying sparks of his talent were blazing forth again. Suddenly the scales fell from his eyes. Lord! To think he had relentlessly squandered the best years of his youth; had destroyed, extinguished the spark which had perhaps glowed in his breast, the spark which could perhaps by now have flared up in all its glory and splendour, and which might also have caused others to weep with astonishment and gratitude! To have destroyed all this, and destroyed it utterly without remorse! At that moment he felt again the surge of excitement and zeal that he had once known so well. He seized hold of a brush and stepped up to a canvas. Beads of perspiration formed on his brow with the strain; his whole being was aflame with one idea: to paint a fallen angel. This idea seemed to conform most closely to his state of mind. But, alas! Once on canvas his figures, poses, groups, and thoughts looked forced and disjointed. His technique and imagination had been caught in a rut for too long and this urge to break through the limits and cast off his self-imposed fetters proved impotent, ringing false and untrue. He had disdained the long and tortuous uphill path of acquiring preliminary knowledge and learning the primary laws that are the foundation of future greatness. Vexation overcame him. He ordered all his recent works to be removed from his studio, all his lifeless, fashionable pictures, all his portraits of hussars, ladies, and state councillors. He then locked himself in his room, leaving word that no one was to be admitted, and immersed himself in work. He sat at his easel like a patient youth, like a young apprentice. But all the results of his labour were ruthlessly unrewarding. He was halted at every step by his ignorance of the most fundamental elements; his enthusiasm was dashed against the simple and hollow mechanical skills he had evolved, which formed an impassable barrier to the imagination. His brush involuntarily turned to stale forms, the angel's arms were folded in the same stilted way, its head proved unable to make an unaccustomed turn, even the very folds of its robes were wooden and refused to submit to his will, refused to drape themselves over the unfamiliar pose of the body. And all this he could see and sense for himself!

'But was I ever really talented?' he finally asked himself. 'Was I not deluding myself?' Having uttered these words he sought out his early works, which at one time he had worked on with such pure dedication, so unselfishly, in his poor garret on the isolated Vasilyevsky Island, far from the crowds, from the abundance and caprices of life. He now went up to them and started to examine each with care, while images of his old impoverished life returned to his memory. 'Yes,' he pronounced in despair; 'I did have talent. Signs of it are visible everywhere...'

As he stood there he suddenly shuddered from head to toe: his eyes had encountered another pair of eyes which stared fixedly back at him. This was that strange portrait which he had bought in Shchukin Dvor. All this time it had been covered up and obscured by other pictures and had completely faded from his memory. Now, as if by design, when he had removed all the fashionable portraits and paintings which cluttered up his studio, it re-emerged to stand alongside the works of his youth. Remembering its strange history he recalled that in a sense it was this bizarre portrait which had been the cause of his metamorphosis, that the fortune which he had come by in so miraculous a fashion had sent him on all his vain pursuits and thereby destroyed his talent, and he felt his soul fill with rage. He at once called for the removal of the loathsome portrait. Yet this did not bring his agitated soul any peace: all his emotions—his entire being—had been shaken to the core, and he experienced that fearful torment that is sometimes and exceptionally manifested in nature when feeble talent outreaches itself and cannot find expression, that torment which can lead a young man to great things, but which, in one who has already reached the limits of his dreams, can only become a barren thirst; that unbearable torment which can lead a man to commit hideous crimes.

He was possessed by a terrible envy, an envy which bordered on madness. The bile rose in his gullet when he saw a picture which bore the stamp of talent. He would grind his teeth and fix his eyes on it with the searing stare of a basilisk. In his soul there was born an infernal design, the most despicable plot ever hatched by man, and he threw himself into its fulfilment with the energy of one possessed. He set about buying up all artistic works of any merit. Having purchased a picture at a high price he would carefully carry it back to his room and throw himself at it with the fury of a tiger, tearing it asunder, ripping it into pieces and stamping on it, accompanying all these actions with gales of delighted laughter. The countless riches he had amassed enabled him to satisfy this diabolical longing. He untied all his bags of gold and opened up his caskets of treasure. Never before had any monster of ignorance destroyed so many works of beauty as were destroyed by him in his maddened pursuit of vengeance. Should he appear at an auction all the other buyers despaired of purchasing any work of art. It was as if the enraged heavens themselves had sent this terrible scourge down to earth to wrest from it all harmony. This terrible passion stained his whole countenance: his face became permanently jaundiced. Hatred of the world and negation of life itself were stamped on his very features. He was an embodiment of the terrible demon which Pushkin portrays in his verse.* His lips uttered nothing but words of venom and eternal condemnation. He stalked the streets like a ghastly ogre and even his friends, when they espied him from afar, hastened to turn back and avoid meeting him, asserting that such an encounter would suffice to poison the rest of their day.

Fortunately for art and the world at large a life led amid such violence and under such unnatural strain could not endure long: the scope of his passion was too massive and unbalanced for his feeble strength. Fits of rage and madness attacked him with increasing frequency until they finally turned into a terrible sickness. He succumbed to a combination of high fever and galloping consumption so fierce that after a mere three days he was reduced to a shadow of his former self. To this were added all the symptoms of hopeless insanity. At times several men together had not the strength to hold him down. In his mind's eye he started to see the long forgotten, but still living eyes of that extraordinary portrait, and at such moments his rage was terrible. All the people standing around his bed looked to him like hideous portraits. He started to see double, quadruple, and the fearful portrait multiplied before his eyes; his walls seemed to be hung with portraits whose fixed, living eyes bored into him. Diabolical portraits stared down at him from the ceiling and stared up from the floor, the room expanded and stretched away into infinity, in order to accommodate ever more of these fixed, staring eyes. The doctor who had undertaken to treat him and had already heard some of his strange history, made every endeavour to discover the underlying relation between his hallucinations and the events of his life, but without success. The sick man comprehended nothing and felt nothing apart from his torments, uttering only horrible wails and incomprehensible jabbering. At last his life was cut short in a final, silent paroxysm of suffering. His corpse was gruesome to behold. No trace could be found of his untold wealth; but when people saw the torn fragments of the great works of art which he had bought for amounts totalling millions they understood to what terrible purpose this wealth had been put.

PART II

A great number of chaises, droshkies, and carriages stood before the gates to a house in which an auction was being held. Up for sale was the property of one of those wealthy art lovers who spend their lives in blissful indolence, surrounded by their zephyrs and cupids, and unsuspectingly earn themselves the reputation of patrons of the arts, by blithely expending on paintings the millions accumulated by their prudent fathers and sometimes even by their own earlier labours. Alas, these patrons are an extinct breed, and our nineteenth century has taken on the dull visage of a banker who can only enjoy his wealth when he sees it spelt out in figures on the paper before him.

The long hall was filled with the motliest crowd of visitors, drawn like vultures to carrion. Among them was an entire flotilla of Russian merchants from the Gostiny Dvor arcade* and even the flea market, attired in their dark blue German coats. In these surroundings their appearance and expression became somehow more at ease and self-possessed, and they shed that unctuous servility which is so characteristic of the Russian merchant in his natural element, as he attends to a customer in his shop. Here they behaved entirely without ceremony, despite the fact that gathered in this very room were many of those aristocrats before whom they were usually only too willing to bow and scrape. Here they were quite uninhibited, unceremoniously prodding and fingering the books and pictures, to see how sturdy they were, and boldly bidding against their titled opponents. Here there were great numbers of those ubiquitous sale-goers, who attend an auction daily before eating breakfast; there were aristocratic connoisseurs, who felt duty-bound never to miss an opportunity of augmenting their collections and with nothing better to do between the hours of twelve and one; and finally there were those noble gentlefolk, with threadbare clothes and pockets, who make their daily appearance unmotivated by any thought of material gain, but with the sole purpose of seeing how it all ends, who pays the most, who the least, who outbids whom and who gets what.

A great number of pictures were scattered about higgledy-piggledy; mixed in amongst them were pieces of furniture and books with the ex libris plates of previous owners, who, it seemed, had none of that laudable curiosity which might have induced them to investigate their contents. Chinese vases, marble slabs for tables, old and new furniture with round contours and embellished with gryphons, sphinxes and ball-and-claw feet, gilt and ungilt, chandeliers, oil lamps—all this lay about in untidy heaps not arranged in any order, as it would have been in a shop. The visitor beheld a chaos of the arts. In general, auctions give us disagreeable feelings: everything in them seems to recall a funeral cortège. The halls in which they are held are always gloomy; the windows, obscured by piles of furniture and pictures, admit only a meagre trickle of light, the hushed faces, and the sepulchral voice of the auctioneer, beating down sales with his hammer and calling out the funeral dirge of the wretched arts, here brought together in this bizarre way. All this combines to heighten the already strange and unpleasant effect created by such occasions.

The auction appeared to be in full swing. A great number of highly decorous people had surged forward and were bidding excitedly. On all sides calls of 'rouble, rouble, rouble' could be heard, and before the auctioneer had time to repeat the bids from the crowd, they had increased fourfold. The crowd was bidding for a portrait which could not but impress anyone who had the least understanding of painting. In it the brush of a master was clearly visible. The portrait had apparently been restored on several occasions and depicted the swarthy features of an Asiatic in flowing robes, with a strange and most unusual expression, but what struck the observers most of all was the extraordinarily lifelike quality of the eyes. The longer the beholder gazed at them the deeper they seemed to bore into him. This strange quality, this extraordinary *trompe-l'œil* captivated almost all those present. Many had already withdrawn from the bidding, which had reached fantastic heights. There remained only two well-known aristocrats and collectors, each determined at all costs to make this picture his own. They grew heated and would have raised the price beyond all reason, had not an onlooker suddenly announced:

'Allow me to interrupt the bidding for a moment. For I have perhaps greater entitlement than any other person to this portrait.'

At once all attention was focused on the speaker of these words. He was a slender man of about 35, with long curly black hair. His pleasant face, which wore a bright and carefree air, was evidence of a soul alien to the vanity of this world; his attire displayed no pretensions to fashion: everything about him was eloquent of the true artist. And indeed this was the artist B., known personally to many of those present.

'You may think what I say very strange,' he said, observing the general attention focused on him, 'but if you deign to hear out my story you may perhaps see that I was quite justified in saying what I did. From all the signs I am sure that this is the very portrait I have been searching for.'

The faces of all his listeners lit up with a natural curiosity, and the auctioneer himself, his mouth agape, froze with his hammer in mid-air, and prepared to listen. At the beginning of the story many kept turning to look at the portrait, but as his story became increasingly engrossing all eyes focused on the narrator.

'You all know that part of town which is called Kolomna.' Thus did he begin his account. 'Here everything is different from the other parts of St Petersburg; it is neither metropolitan nor provincial; you seem to feel, as you enter the streets of Kolomna, that all your youthful desires and aspirations are leaving you. Here the future does not intrude, here quiet and retirement reign, and here refuge can be sought from the bustle of the streets.

'Amongst those who settle here you find retired civil servants, widows, people of modest means who have acquaintances in the Senate,* and have therefore condemned themselves to pass practically their entire lives here; cooks who have retired from service and spend their whole day bustling about the market, gossiping with the porter in their grocery stall and buying a daily ration of five copecks' worth of coffee and four copecks' worth of sugar, and, finally, that entire class of people who can best be described as ash-grey, people whose attire, faces, hair, eyes have the same dull-grey appearance as one of those days when there are neither storm clouds nor sun in the sky, but something quite indeterminate: a mist settles and blurs the outlines of all objects. To these we can add retired theatre commissionaires, retired titular councillors, retired officers— old warhorses with a gouged out eye and a scarred lip. These people are utterly impassive: they walk along looking neither to right nor to left, saying nothing and thinking nothing. In their rooms you will not find much in the way of belongings; at most, there may be a bottle of pure Russian vodka, which they mechanically sip away at all day without ever experiencing that rush of blood to the head induced by a more vigorous intake of liquor, such as young German craftsmen, the cavaliers of Meshchanskaya Street,* enjoy when they lord it alone over the pavements in the small hours of the morning after their Sunday binge.

'Life in Kolomna is terribly quiet: a carriage is a rare sight except for the odd one conveying actors and shattering the general peace and quiet with its rattling and clanking. This is the domain of the pedestrian; if you do see a cab it is probably plodding along passengerless, carrying hay to feed its bearded nag. A flat can be rented for five roubles a month even inclusive of morning coffee. The widows who live here on their pensions constitute the most aristocratic stratum; they conduct themselves in a refined manner, often sweep out their rooms, and like to converse with their lady-friends about the terrible price of beef and cabbage; their possessions usually include a young daughter, a quiet, self-effacing creature, often of pleasing aspect, a nasty little dog, and a wall clock whose pendulum emits a melancholy ticking. After them come the actors, whose finances do not permit them to move out of Kolomna, a freedom-loving race, like all stage folk, living only for pleasure. You will find them sitting about in their dressing-gowns, cleaning a pistol, gluing together some useful household contraption out of pieces of card-board, or playing a game of draughts or cards with a visiting friend, and spending their evenings in exactly the same manner as their mornings, only with the occasional addition of a glass of rum punch.

'After these, the grand folk and aristocrats of Kolomna, come the rank and file. They are as hard to enumerate as the infinite variety of insects which breed in old vinegar. You will find old ladies who pray; old ladies who drink; old ladies who both pray and drink; old ladies who subsist by mysterious means, dragging old rags and linen like ants from the Kalinkin Bridge* to the flea market, where they hope to sell them for fifteen copecks; in other words, the very dregs of humanity, whose lot even the most philanthropic politician would be hard put to improve.

'I mention them here in order to demonstrate how often people of this kind are constrained to hunt for some sudden source of temporary aid, to have recourse to loans, and this leads to the emergence in their midst of a particular genus of extortionist, who on security will lend them small sums of money at high rates of interest. These petty usurers are often even more callous than their more exalted colleagues, because they proliferate in a milieu more ragged and poverty-stricken than any the wealthy money-lender will ever encounter, his dealings being confined to people who drive about in carriages. Thus any lingering spark of human feelings is soon extinguished in their hearts.

'Among these money-lenders there was one... but I should point out here that the incident I am about to relate belongs to the last century, namely to the reign of our late sovereign Empress Catherine II. As you will realize, both the outward look of Kolomna as well as its inner life must have changed considerably since then. So, among these money-lenders there was one who was a remarkable character in every respect, and a resident of long standing in these parts. He went about in flowing Asiatic robes; his swarthy complexion be-trayed his southern provenance, but precisely to which nationality he belonged, whether Hindu, Greek, or Persian, no one was able to say for sure. His height, his unusually large frame, his swarthy, sunken, and haggard features with their hideous hue, his large eyes with their unnatural gleam and his pendulous, bushy eyebrows, set him strikingly apart from the city's ashen inhabitants. Even his abode was quite unlike the little wooden houses around it. It was a stone structure of the sort once built in great numbers by Genoese merchants, with irregular and unmatching windows, iron shutters, and bolts.

This money-lender differed from the other representatives of his profession in that he was able to provide absolutely anyone with whatever sum they required, from the poorest of beggar-women to spendthrift habitués of the imperial court. Before his house the most dazzling carriages often pulled up, and through their windows you could glimpse the exquisite head of a society lady. Rumour had it that he possessed iron trunks full of countless riches, jewels, and all manner of valuables left as pledges, but that he somehow had none of the greed so characteristic of other money-lenders. He lent money quite willingly, giving what were regarded as very favourable terms of repayment. But by some strange machinations of arithmetic he always made his loans attain exorbitant interest. Or thus, at any rate, was it rumoured. Yet the strangest thing of all and a source of general wonderment was the fate that befell his debtors: they all, without exception, met unhappy ends. It remains uncertain whether this was merely public opinion, absurd and superstitious gossip, or deliberate slander. There were, however, one or two vivid and unmistakable examples which took place in the space of a short time before the eyes of all.

A young man from one of the finest aristocratic families of the time had come to public attention, having already earned considerable distinction in the state service, proving to be an ardent champion of everything true and noble, a zealot of all the fruits of art and human genius, showing all the signs of a future Maecenas. Soon he earned the approval of the sovereign herself, who appointed him to a high position that fully answered his own requirements, a position in which he was able to do great things for learning and for the common weal. The young nobleman surrounded himself with artists, poets, and scholars. He longed to provide them all with work and inspiration. He undertook personally to finance a great number of useful publications, commissioned a mass of works, sponsored competitions as a form of encouragement, expending huge sums of money on all these projects and driving himself into straitened circumstances. But, driven by the force of his magnanimity, he was loath to renounce these activities, explored every available avenue for loans and finally turned to the money-lender I have described.

'No sooner had he received from the latter a substantial loan than the young nobleman underwent a complete transformation: he became a scourge of talent and a persecutor of developing minds. He started to see something bad in all literary works and twisted the meaning of every word he read. Then, as ill luck would have it, the French Revolution took place, and this gave him the ammunition for all sorts of malicious attacks. He saw revolutionary tendencies in everything and detected suspicious innuendoes wherever he looked. He became so suspicious of everything that he eventually started to suspect himself, composing terrible and unjust denunciations and wreaking unhappiness all about him. Naturally enough, news of these activities could not fail to reach the throne. Our benevolent sovereign was horrified, and, inspired with that nobility of soul which graces potentates, delivered an address the exact words of which have not, alas, come down to us, but whose profound meaning has remained imprinted in the hearts of many.

'Her Majesty remarked that it is not under monarchic rule that the exalted and noble impulses of the soul are suppressed, and creations of genius, poetry, and the fine arts despised and persecuted, but, on the contrary, that monarchs have been their only true patrons; that the Shakespeares and Molières of this world have flourished under their magnanimous protection, whereas Dante was unable to find himself a niche in his republican state; that true geniuses are born when nations and their lords are at the pinnacle of their power and glory, and not when they are dogged by disgraceful political agitation and republican terrorism, which to this day have not brought the world a single poet; that we should exalt poets and artists, for they are able to instil in the souls of others peace and serene tranquillity, and not tumult and perturbation; that scholars, poets, and all exponents of the arts are pearls and diamonds in the imperial crown; they cannot but enhance the beauty and increase the brilliance of the epoch of a great sovereign.

'As she uttered those words, Her Majesty was nothing less than divine in her splendour. I recall that old men were unable to discuss the Empress's words without tears. Everyone became caught up in the matter. It stands to our credit as a nation that the Russian heart is always inclined to take the side of the underdog. The nobleman who had betrayed the trust put in him was accordingly punished and removed from his position. But a far more terrible punishment could be read in the faces of his fellow countrymen: the utter and universal contempt in which they held him. Words cannot describe the suffering which this inflicted on his conceited soul; his injured pride and shattered hopes combined together to cut short his life in fits of terrible insanity and delirium.

'There was another striking case, observed by all involving a lady of great beauty—of whom our northern metropolis could at that time boast a good number—but this one far outshone all the others. She embodied a marvellous fusion of our northern beauty with that of southern climes, a jewel of rare brilliance. My father used to maintain that he had never in all his life seen another woman who could compare with her. She seemed to be a happy combination of everything: wealth, intelligence, and lovely disposition. She had hosts of suitors, and the most notable of them was Prince R., the best and the most noble of young men, extremely handsome and filled with the most magnanimous and chivalrous impulses. He was like a woman's ideal taken from a novel, a Grandison* in every respect. Prince R. was passionately and madly in love; this love was reciprocated with equal ardour.

'But the relatives regarded the match as an unequal one. The prince had long since lost his birthright, his family had gone down in the world, and the sorry state of his affairs was common knowledge. Suddenly the prince left the capital for a while, putting it about that he wished to attend to his affairs, and returned in fabulous wealth and splendour. He threw magnificent balls and fêtes and became known at court. The father of the beautiful girl began to look on him with favour, and the city played host to a most exciting wedding. Whence this change in the bridegroom's fortunes, this fabulous wealth had come no one could say for sure; but it was rumoured that he had entered into some contract with the mysterious money-lender and received a loan from him. Be this as it may, the marriage was the talk of the town. Both bridegroom and

bride were the object of universal envy. Their ardent and constant
love for one another was known to all, as well as the long wait that
had been forced on them and the high merits of both partners.
Ardent ladies anticipated the heavenly bliss that the young couple
would enjoy. Things were fated to take a quite different course,
however. In the course of a single year a terrible change took place
in the husband. His character, hitherto noble and gracious, became
poisoned with the venom of suspicion and jealousy, intolerance and
captiousness. He became a tyrant and tormentor of his wife, and—
something that no one would have predicted—had recourse to the
most unspeakable deeds, even beating her with a whip. At the end
of a year no one would have recognized the woman who but a short
time before had radiated such joy and had had shoals of rapt admirers following in her wake. Finally, no longer able to endure her
miserable lot, she was the first to broach the question of divorce.
The very mention of the word threw her husband into a terrible
rage. Propelled by his fury he burst into her room, brandishing a
knife, and would undoubtedly have stabbed her had he not been
forcibly restrained. In a paroxysm of despair he turned the knife on
himself—and ended his life in terrible agony.

'In addition to these two cases, which unfolded before the eyes of
all, tales were told of a great many others concerning members of
the lower classes, almost all of whom met terrible ends. Honest and
sober men took to the bottle; a shop assistant robbed his employer;
a cab-driver, who for years had earned an honest living, murdered
a passenger for a few copecks. Such occurrences, which were never
related without embellishments, could not fail to strike terror into
the hearts of the simple inhabitants of Kolomna. No one had any
doubt but that the money-lender was possessed of some dark power.
It was rumoured that the conditions he prescribed were so horrific
that the unfortunate victim could never dare pass them on to anyone else; that his money had a magnetic property, the coins would
become red-hot and bore certain strange marks... in other words, all
sorts of ridiculous stories were told.

'But the remarkable thing was that the entire population of
Kolomna, this whole world of impoverished old women, lowly functionaries, walk-on actors and, in a word, all the rank and file we
were talking about before, chose to endure the worst of hardships
rather than turn to this evil money-lender; cases were even reported

of old women starving to death, preferring thus to mortify their flesh rather than to destroy their souls. People felt an instinctive fear on meeting him on the street. Passers-by carefully stepped back and stared after him for a long time, watching his striking, tall frame disappear into the distance. His outward appearance was in itself so extraordinary that people were bound to conclude that beneath it lurked supernatural powers. Those striking features, hewn so deeply into his face, as in no other person, his burnished bronze complexion, the inordinate shagginess of his eyebrows, his burning, intolerable eyes, even the very folds of his flowing Asiatic robes— all these seemed to proclaim that the passions of ordinary human beings paled in comparison with the passions that burned in this breast. On encountering him my father would invariably stand stock still and exclaim: "The devil, the devil himself!" But I should quickly acquaint you here with my father, who is in fact the main hero of this story.

'My father was a remarkable man in many respects. He was one of those rare artists, one of those marvels which only the chaste loins of mother Russia can produce: a self-taught painter, who sought guidance only in his own soul, without teachers or schools, rules or guide-lines, driven purely by the desire for perfection and proceeding along principles perhaps unknown to himself, following the path to which his soul pointed him; one of those prodigies of nature often dismissed contemptuously as ignoramuses by their contemporaries, yet who are not deterred by criticism and failure, instead deriving from them new zeal and strength and leaving far behind those works which had brought such contempt on them in the first place. He had a deep instinct for the essential meaning of every object; he was able to grasp the true significance of the term "historical painting"; understood how a simple head, a simple portrait by Raphael, Leonardo, Titian, or Correggio could be called historical painting, and why an enormous painting on a historical subject would never be anything more than a *tableau de genre*, despite the artist's pretensions to historical painting. Both inner feeling and personal conviction guided his brush to Christian subjects, to the supreme and ultimate degree of the sublime in art. He altogether lacked the conceit and irritability that vitiated the character of so many artists. He was a man of firm character, honest and straightforward, coarse even, with a tough exterior yet not without a certain inner pride, accustomed to state his opinion of people in terms that were at once indulgent and harsh.

' "Why listen to them," he would say, "after all, they are not the ones I work for. I do not paint my pictures for their drawing rooms, they are placed in churches. Those who understand me will be grateful, those who do not will pray to God just the same. A man of the world cannot be blamed for not comprehending art;—if he plays a good hand of cards, knows a thing or two about wine and horses—what more need he know? Indeed, should he get it into his head to dabble in the arts, and start giving himself intellectual airs he would only make a terrible nuisance of himself. Each unto his own; may each of us follow his own concerns.

' "For myself I have greater respect for a man who says straight out that he does not understand a thing than for one who puts on hypocritical airs, claiming to know what he does not and only confounding matters still further." He worked for modest fees, asking only the money he required for the upkeep of his family and to provide himself with the wherewithal for his work. Furthermore, he never, on any account, refused to help others and to hold out a helping hand to a fellow artist; he professed the simple, pious faith of his forefathers and it was perhaps for this reason that he was able to impart to his portrayal of the saints a truly sublime air which eluded the most brilliant and talented painters. Finally, through the consistent merit of his work and his unflinching adherence to the path he had chosen, he began to win the respect even of those who had dismissed him as an ignoramus and home-spun amateur. He received a constant stream of commissions for churches and was never short of work. One of these orders in particular absorbed him. I no longer remember exactly what its subject was, I know only that he was required somewhere in the picture to portray the spirit of darkness. For a long time he deliberated what image to give it: he wanted to embody in it all that was oppressive, all that weighed down on man. During such reflections the image of the mysterious money-lender would sometimes enter his mind, and he found himself thinking: "Now there's the man I should take as the model for my devil." Imagine his surprise when one day, as he worked in his studio, he heard a knock on the door, which opened to admit the terrible money-lender. He shuddered inwardly and the convulsion shook his entire body.

'"Are you an artist?" the visitor asked my father without any preliminaries.

'"I am," said my father in bewilderment, wondering what would follow.

'"Good. Paint my portrait. I will probably die soon, and I have no children; but I do not wish to die altogether, I wish to live. Can you paint a portrait so good that it seems to breathe?"

'My father thought to himself: "What could be better? He has come and offered himself as a devil for my picture." He gave his word. They agreed on a time and a fee and the very next day, palette and brush in hand, my father arrived at his client's house. The fenced-in courtyard, the dogs, the iron gates and shutters, the arched windows, the chests draped in exotic carpets and finally the extraordinary master of the house himself, seated motionless before him, all made a strange impression on him. The window-sills were so cluttered, as if by design, that the windows only admitted light from a slit at the top. "Damnation, this is the ideal lighting for his face!" exclaimed my father to himself, and he threw himself eagerly into his task, as if afraid that this favourable light would not last. "What power!" he repeated to himself, "if my portrait can be even half as striking as he is in life he will destroy all my saints and angels; they will pale next to him. What diabolical power! If I can achieve the merest shadow of a likeness he will leap from the canvas. What extraordinary features!" he repeated constantly, his enthusiasm for his subject mounting as he began to see certain of the features taking shape on his canvas.

'But the closer he drew to those features the more acutely he sensed an oppressive anxiety, for which there was no apparent cause. Nevertheless, despite this anxiety, he prevailed upon himself to record with literal accuracy every nuance of feature and expression. He gave closest attention to the eyes. These eyes contained so much power that it might have seemed impossible to capture them on his canvas. Undeterred, he resolved, however, to seek out their every trait and shade of expression, to fathom their mystery... But no sooner had he begun to explore them with his brush than his soul filled with such revulsion, such strange oppression, that for a while he would have to set aside his task. Finally he could endure it no longer, he felt that the eyes were searing his soul and filling him with incomprehensible fears. The next day this alarm mounted, and on the third it was stronger still. He became afraid, threw down his brush and declared outright that he could not continue. Upon hearing these words the sinister money-lender reacted in the most extraordinary way. He flung himself at my father's feet and implored him to finish the portrait, declaring that his whole destiny and existence in the world depended on it, that my father had already caught his living features with his brush and that, if he succeeded in conveying them fully, his life would be preserved through a supernatural force in the portrait, that thanks to this he would not die altogether, but would live on in the world. My father was overcome with horror on hearing these words: they sounded so strange and terrible to his ears that he threw down his brushes and his palette and dashed headlong from the room.

'All day and all night he remained deeply agitated about what had occurred, and the next morning he received the portrait from the money-lender, delivered by a woman, the only person who remained in his service, who declared then and there that her employer did not want the portrait, would pay nothing for it, and was sending it back. That same evening he learnt that the money-lender had died and that preparations were already being made to bury him according to the rites of his religion. All this was most unsettling to him. At the same time a perceptible transformation took place in his own character: he was haunted by an uneasy feeling, the reason for which he could not fathom, and a little later he did a thing which no one would have expected of him. For some time the work of one of his pupils had been attracting the attention of a small group of connoisseurs and art-lovers. My father had always been aware of this pupil's talent, and had consequently accorded him special attention. Suddenly he started to feel envious of him. The universal interest and discussion which surrounded this painter became intolerable to him. Finally, to cap it all, he learnt that his pupil had been invited to paint a picture for a recently restored and richly appointed church. This was more than he could stand. "No, I shall not let that young pup get away with his triumph!" he announced. "Don't be in too great a hurry, my lad, to grind the faces of your elders in the dirt. I still have some strength in me, thank God. Now we shall see who ends up in the dirt first."

'And this upright and honest man stooped to every type of intrigue and to machinations of the sort that he had always abhorred;

through his scheming he managed to have a contest arranged for the picture, as a stratagem to get other artists to put forward their entries. He thereupon locked himself in his room and set feverishly to work. It was as though he wished to muster all his strength, to put his whole being into his work, and he did indeed produce one of his best paintings. No one had any doubt but that the prize would go to him.

The pictures were entered and, beside his own creation, all the others were as night to day. Then one of the members of the jury, a man in holy orders, if I am not mistaken, came out with an unexpected criticism which took everyone by surprise. "There is certainly a great deal of talent in the artist's picture," he said, "but there is no holiness in his faces; on the contrary, there is even something demonic in their eyes, as if the artist's hand had been guided by some evil influence." On looking closely at the picture all those present were forced to agree with the speaker. My father dashed forward to his picture, as if to check for himself the truth of this most offensive remark, and realized with horror that he had rendered nearly all the figures with the eyes of the money-lender. They stared back at him with such a demonic and destructive force that he gave an involuntary shudder. The picture was rejected, and to his unutterable vexation he saw the prize go to his pupil.

Words cannot describe the rage in which he returned home. He almost attacked my mother, chased us children away, broke his brushes and smashed his easel, pulled the portrait of the money-lender from the wall, called for a knife and had a fire lit in the hearth, intending to cut the picture into pieces and burn them. He was busy with the execution of this plan when an acquaintance entered the room, a painter like himself, a cheerful man, who was always content, never troubled by any distant longings, happily worked away at whatever chanced his way, and was even happier to sit down to a good meal or to carouse with his friends.

'"What are you doing? What are you planning to burn?" he asked, stepping up to the portrait. "My dear fellow, that is one of your very best works. That's the money-lender who died recently; why, it's a perfect likeness. It's a spitting image, it's more than lifelike. Even in life eyes do not stare like that."

'"Well, now we shall see what they look like in the fire," said my father, preparing to toss it on to the flames.

' "Stop, for pity's sake!" cried his friend, restraining him. "Rather give the picture to me, if you find it so offensive."

'At first my father was loath to agree, but eventually submitted and his jovial friend took the portrait off with him, delighted with this new acquisition.

'No sooner had he taken his leave than my father felt much more at ease. It was as though the removal of the portrait had lifted a great weight from his soul. He himself was amazed at the malice and envy he had displayed and at the change in his character. As he recalled his actions he grew sad and declared remorsefully:

' "No, this must be a punishment from God; I deserved to be thus shamed with my picture. I painted it with the express aim of destroying a fellow painter. My brush was guided by a satanic longing for envy, and this demonic influence was bound to be manifested in the picture."

'He at once set off in search of his former pupil, embraced him warmly and begged his forgiveness, doing his utmost to make amends for his wrongdoing. His work returned to its former untroubled path; but his face took on a pensive look. He turned more often to prayer, was more taciturn than usual and no longer so outspoken in his opinions of people; the harsh exterior of his character appeared to soften. Shortly thereafter he received another rude shock. For a long time he had not seen the friend who had asked to take the portrait. He was planning to pay him a visit when suddenly the friend appeared in his room. After a brief exchange of pleasantries his visitor announced:

' "Well, brother, you had good reason to want to burn that portrait. The devil take me if there isn't something strange about it... I don't believe in sorcery, but there's no getting away from it: it has an evil force lurking within..."

' "What do you mean?" asked my father.

' "Well, from the moment I hung it in my room I had an oppressive feeling... just as if I were planning to murder someone. Never in my life have I experienced insomnia, but now I not only had difficulty sleeping, I also had such nightmares that... To this day I do not know whether they were dreams or something else: I felt as though I was suffocated by an evil spirit, and I kept on seeing the image of that accursed old man. I really cannot describe my state of mind. I've never known anything like it. All those days I wandered about like a madman, feeling some fear, an unpleasant sense of foreboding. I felt unable to say a cheerful or sincere word to anyone; it was as though someone was constantly spying on me. And the moment I gave the portrait to a nephew who had begged me for it I felt as though a weight had been lifted from my shoulders: I at once recovered my high spirits, as you can see. Yes, my friend, you brought the devil to life!"

'My father heard him out with rapt attention and finally asked:
'"So the portrait is now in the hands of your nephew?"

'"I should think not! He couldn't stand it either," replied his jovial friend, "it seems the old money-lender's soul has taken possession of the portrait: he leaps out of the frame and strides up and down the room; and the things my nephew tells me are simply incomprehensible. I would have thought him insane if I had not experienced it myself. He sold the picture to a collector, who also could not keep it for long and quickly passed it on to someone else."

'This account had a powerful effect on my father. He became seriously preoccupied, lapsed into melancholy, and at last was convinced that his brush had served as a tool for the devil, that some portion of the money-lender's life-force had in fact entered the portrait and was now preying on people, provoking diabolical delusions, leading artists astray, afflicting them with terrible torments of envy, and so on and so forth. The three tragedies which then befell his family—the sudden deaths of his wife, daughter, and infant son—he took to be a divine judgement on him and resolved to withdraw from the world forthwith.

'As soon as I turned 9 years old he placed me in the Academy of Fine Arts, and, after settling all his debts, departed for a distant monastery, where in due course he took the monastic vows. There he amazed all his brethren by the strictness of his life and his rigorous observance of all the monastic rules. Upon learning that he had been a skilled painter, the abbot commissioned him to paint the main icon in the church. But the humble brother protested that he was unworthy to take up his brush, that it had been besmirched, that he must first purify his soul through toil and great self-sacrifice, in order that he might once again be worthy to undertake such work. No pressure was put on him, and of his own volition he increased to the utmost the severity of his monastic regime. Finally even this

seemed too little to him and insufficient in its rigour. He received
the abbot's blessing to depart for the wilderness, that he might be
entirely alone. There he built himself a hut of branches, subsisted
on a diet of raw roots, hauled stones from place to place, stood
motionless on one spot, his hands raised heavenwards as he recited
his prayers, from sunrise to sunset. In brief, it was as though he
wished to subject himself to every known test of endurance and to
attain that ultimate pitch of self-denial which we expect only to find
in the lives of the saints.

'Thus for a period of several years did he mortify his flesh,
sustaining it only with the life-giving strength of prayer. Finally he
returned one day to the monastery and firmly announced to the
abbot: "Now I am ready. If God is willing I shall perform my
appointed task." The subject he took for his picture was the Nativ-
ity of Christ. For a whole year he worked at it, never leaving the
confines of his cell, hardly partaking of the frugal monastic fare and
engaging in constant prayer. At the end of the year the picture was
finished. It was, without question, a miracle of art. Although neither
the brethren nor their abbot were particularly versed in the fine
arts, they were all astounded by the remarkable sanctity of the
figures. The aura of divine humility and meekness in the face of
the Mother of God, as she bent over her child, the deep wisdom in
the eyes of the Christchild, which seemed to see far into the distance, the solemn silence of the Magi, awed by the divine miracle
and kneeling at His feet, and finally the holy, ineffable quiet which
pervaded the entire picture—all this was represented with such
harmonious force and powerful colour that its effect was no less
than magical. All the brethren sank to their knees before the new
icon, and their awe-struck abbot declared: "No, such a painting
cannot have been painted by man with the help of human art alone:
a higher, holy force has guided your brush, and the blessing of
Heaven rests on your work."

'At this time I completed my studies in the Academy, winning
the gold medal and together with this prize the wonderful prospect
of a voyage to Italy—the dream of every 20-year-old painter. It only
remained for me to take my leave of my father, whom I had last
seen twelve years before. I confess that even his image had long
since faded from my memory. I had heard something of the auster-
ity and holiness of his life and I prepared to meet someone with the

desiccated look of a hermit, estranged to everything in the world
save his cell and his prayers, worn out and withered from eternal
fasting and vigil. Imagine my surprise when before my eyes I saw
a resplendent, beatific patriarch! His face bore no traces of self-
mortification, and glowed with the radiance of heavenly joy. His
snow-white beard, and his fine, almost ethereal hair of the same
silvery hue flowed splendidly down his chest and over the folds of
his black cassock, falling almost to the cord tied around the waist of
his austere monastic habit. But for me the most remarkable thing
was to hear what he had to say about art, words and thoughts which
I know I shall retain long in my soul, and I sincerely wish that they
would be similarly heeded by all my fellow artists.

'"I have been waiting for you, my son," he said, when I came up
to receive his blessing. "You are about to set off on the path which
your life shall henceforth follow. Your chosen path is a pure one,
do not be led astray from that path. You have talent; talent is God's
most valuable gift—do not squander it. Examine and study everything that you see, submit all to your brush, but learn to seek the
inner meaning to everything, and above all endeavour to fathom the
great mystery of creation. Blessed are the chosen few who hold this
secret. To them no object of nature is base. The creator and artist
is just as strongly evident in things insignificant as he is in things
great; in his work the contemptible shows no trace of contempt, for
the beautiful soul of the creator permeates it invisibly, and the
contemptible, having passed through the purgative of his soul, has
thereby been given elevated expression. For man all art contains a
hint of the divine, of heavenly paradise, and by virtue of this fact
alone it transcends all matter. A great work of art is higher than all
things on earth in the same way that heavenly repose is higher than
all earthly vanity, that creation is higher than destruction, that an
angel through the very innocence of his radiant soul is higher than
all the immeasurable powers and boundless vanity of Satan.

'"Bring forth all you have in sacrifice to art and love it with all
your heart. Love it not with the passion that is pervaded with earthly
lust, but with serene heavenly passion; without this man is powerless to raise himself aloft from earth and cannot utter those wondrous
notes that bring solace. For it is to bring solace and peace to all
living things that a great work of art comes down to earth. It cannot
cause the soul to murmur with discontent, but is a harmonious

prayer yearning eternally towards God. Yet there are moments in a man's life, moments of darkness..."

'He paused, and I observed his radiant countenance darken, as if crossed by a sudden cloud.

'"There was one such occasion in my life," he said. "To this day I am unable to comprehend what sort of creature was behind that strange image whose picture I painted. It was certainly some diabolical phenomenon. I know that the world rejects the existence of the devil, and thus I shall not speak of him. Let me say only that I painted him with repulsion, and did not feel the slightest affection for my work. I sought to subjugate my feelings and, by suppressing the repugnance in my soul, to paint him true to life. This was no work of art, and for this reason the emotions which stir all those who behold it are uneasy and turbulent, and not the emotions of an artist, for an artist breathes tranquillity even in his anxiety.

'"I am told that this portrait is being passed from hand to hand spreading disquiet, breeding in the artist a feeling of envy, of dark hatred for his neighbour and an evil desire to persecute and oppress. May the Almighty preserve you from such terrible passions! There is no thing worse than them. Better yourself to suffer the pain of the worst possible persecution than to inflict the merest shadow of persecution on anyone else. Preserve the purity of your soul. He who is blessed with talent must be purest in soul. Much which can be forgiven his fellows will not be forgiven him. The man who steps forth from his home attired in bright festive clothing need only be splashed with a single spot of mud from a passing carriage for everyone to surround him, pointing at him, and discussing his slovenly aspect while these same people would not even notice a multitude of far worse stains on the ordinary everyday attire of other passers-by. For stains do not show on workaday clothes."

'"He gave me his blessing and embraced me. Never in my life have I been so uplifted and moved. With a reverence that surpasses filial affection I clung to his breast and pressed my lips to his flowing silver locks. Tears glistened in his eyes.

'"I ask you to fulfil one request, my son," he said as we were about to take our leave of each other. "It may pass that one day you see somewhere the portrait of which I have spoken. You will recognize it at once by its remarkable eyes and their unnatural expression. I ask you, at whatever cost, to destroy it..."

'As you can see for yourselves it was only natural that I gave my oath to carry out this request. Over the past fifteen years I have not come across anything even remotely resembling the portrait described by my father, until I saw this at the auction today...'

Here, without completing his sentence, the artist turned his eyes to the wall, to have another look at the portrait. His motion was copied by the entire crowd of listeners, who turned as one man to behold the extraordinary portrait. But to their great astonishment the picture was no longer on the wall. An excited murmur at once ran through the entire crowd, and the word 'stolen' could clearly be discerned. While the listeners' attention had been distracted by the narrative someone had made off with the portrait. For a long time after this all those present at the auction could not be sure if they had really seen these extraordinary eyes, or if it had merely been a vision which had appeared momentarily before their eyes, wearied as they were by long contemplation of antique pictures.

THE OVERCOAT

In the department* of... but we'd do better not to say in which department exactly. For all these departments, regiments, chancelleries —in a word, all estates of government service—are the most bad-tempered lot. Nowadays private citizens take any personal criticism of themselves as an insult against society as a whole. There is a story that recently a complaint was received from the police inspector of some town or other, I don't recall its name, in which he declared in no uncertain terms that all the government decrees were being flouted left, right, and centre and that his own sacred name was most decidedly being taken in vain. As proof he appended to his petition an immense tome containing a romantic *œuvre*, in which on every ten pages a police inspector appeared, sometimes in a state of complete inebriation. So, to avoid any such unpleasantnesses we had best call the department with which we are concerned *a certain department*.

Thus, *in a certain department* there served *a certain official*; the official cannot be described as very remarkable; he was shortish, somewhat pockmarked, with somewhat reddish hair, apparently with somewhat less than perfect eyesight, with a somewhat baldish pate, wrinkles on both sides of his cheeks and endowed with what might be called a haemorrhoidal complexion... Well, it can't be helped! St Petersburg's climate is to blame. As for his rank (and with us rank is the first thing that has to be declared), he was of the genus eternal Titular Councillor,* who, as the reader will know, are the butt of the jokes and mockery of many a writer, given to the commendable habit of hitting out at those who cannot hit back.

The official's surname was Bashmachkin. It is at once clear that the name originates from *bashmak*, a shoe; but when, at what time, and in what manner this derivation from a shoe came about we cannot say. Both his father and his grandfather, and even his brother-in-law, indeed absolutely all the Bashmachkins went about in boots, only having them resoled three times a year. His first name and patronymic were Akaky Akakievich. This may strike the reader as somewhat strange and contrived, but I can assure him that there was no contrivance in its selection, and that the very circumstances of his naming were such that no other name was possible. It all happened like this.

Akaky Akakievich was born just before nightfall on—if my memory serves me right—22 March. His late mother, herself the wife of an official and a very fine woman, resolved to christen the child in due and proper manner. The mother was still lying in her bed opposite the door, with the godfather standing on her left, an excellent gentleman, Ivan Ivanovich Yeroshkin, head of a desk in the Senate, and the godmother, wife of a police officer, a woman of rare virtues, Arina Semyonovna Belobryushkova.* The new mother was given the choice of three names: Mokkey, Sossy, or Khozdazat, after the martyr.

'No,' thought the mother, 'those aren't the right sort of names.'

To appease her the calendar was opened at another page, and once again three names were proposed: Trifilly, Dula, and Varakhasy.

'Lord! What have I done to deserve this?' exclaimed the mother, 'all such odd names, I can't say I've ever heard the like before. Varadat or even Varukh would be one thing, but not Trifilly and Varakhasy.'

They turned to yet another page and were confronted by Pavsikakhy and Vakhtisy.

'No, it is clear to me now,' said the mother, 'that this is the hand of destiny. Better let him take his father's name. His father was Akaky, so let the son be Akaky too.'

Thus did he acquire the name Akaky Akakievich.* The boy was duly christened, and in the process he started crying and pulled an awful face as if he were having premonitions that one day he might become a titular councillor.

So now you know how all this came to pass. We have made this digression in order that the reader might see for himself that this was a matter of sheer necessity and it would have been quite impossible to give him any other name.

When and at what age he entered the department and who appointed him no one would now be able to say. Directors came and went, superintendents succeeded superintendents, but he remained in the very same spot, in the very same position, in the very same job, the very same copying clerk; so that afterwards people swore that he must have been born into the world in exactly that state, complete with uniform and bald pate. Absolutely no respect whatever was accorded him in the department. Not only did the porters not rise to their feet when he walked past, they even did not look at him; he might have been a fly flitting through the lobby. His superiors acted towards him in a cold and despotic manner. An assistant desk head would thrust papers under his nose, without even bothering to say 'Copy this lot' or: 'Here's a nice, interesting little job', or something friendly as is usual in more civilized establishments. He would take the work looking only at the papers, noticing neither who had given them to him, nor whether they had the right to do so. He would take them and at once set about copying them.

The young officials would mock him and make fun at his expense to the limits of their clerkish wit, in his presence relating all sorts of fanciful tales about him and about his landlady, a woman in her seventies, saying that she beat him, asking when their marriage was to take place, tearing up paper and throwing it over his head like confetti. Akaky Akakievich would not counter this with a single word and acted as if there were no one before him; it did not have any effect on his work: in the thick of all this horseplay he would not make a single error in his copying. Only if the fun got quite out of hand, when his arm was jogged, and he was prevented from continuing his work, would he protest: 'Leave me alone, why do you torment me?' And there was something strange about his words, and about the tone in which they were spoken. His voice contained something which inclined the listener to pity, which caused one young man of recent appointment, who followed the others' example in poking fun at him, suddenly to stop dead in his tracks, and thenceforth to see everything around him in a quite different light. Some unnatural force drew him away from his new friends, whom he had previously taken to be decent, cultivated people. For a long time after that, in times of great merriment, he would recall this downbent clerk with a baldish pate and his disturbing words: 'Leave me alone, why do you torment me?' and in these words he could hear quite another message: 'I am thy brother.' At these moments the poor young man would cover his face with his hands. Many a time during his life did he shudder at the sight of man's cruelty to man, at the violent and brutish nature concealed behind a refined, educated and civilized veneer and, heaven help us! to be found even in those whom society has recognized as noble and honest.

You would scarcely have found another who was so wedded to

his work. It would be an understatement to say that he served with diligence; nay, he served with love. In his work, his copying, he beheld a world that was colourful and attractive. His face would take on an expression of pleasure; there were certain letters of the alphabet which he particularly favoured and if he encountered them he would be quite transported: he would chuckle and wink and mouth sounds, so that it seemed possible to read in his face every letter described by his pen. Had he been suitably rewarded for his zeal he might well have become—to his great astonishment—a state councillor; but all his reward, as his witty workmates put it, was a badge on his frontside and piles on his backside.

It would not be true to say, however, that absolutely no attention was given him. One director, by nature a kind man, who wished to reward him for his long service, gave orders that he be given something more important to do than the usual copying; accordingly, he was instructed to write a report of a completed case for another office; all the task required was to change the heading and to shift the odd verb from the first to the third person. This was such hard work for him that he broke into a terrible sweat, mopped his brow and finally announced: 'No, rather give me something to copy.'

After that he was left as a simple copy-clerk. Beyond his copying the world seemed not to exist for him. He did not attend at all to his dress: his uniform was no longer green, but a kind of mottled rust colour. Its collar was low and narrow, so that his neck, although of medium length, stuck out and looked extraordinarily long, like the necks of these plaster-of-Paris kittens with nodding heads that foreign hawkers carry in baskets on their heads. And there would always be something sticking to his uniform: either a wisp of straw or a thread; furthermore he was particularly adept, when walking along the street, at passing under windows at the very moment when slops and rubbish were being thrown out of them, and thus he invariably carried on his hat watermelon and canteloupe rinds and suchlike refuse. Not once in his life had he paid any attention to the daily happenings and goings-on in the street, which are always so keenly observed by his young colleagues in the service, whose eyes have been so sharpened by careful practice that they will even notice someone on the other side of the street who has allowed the anklestrap on his trousers to come unstitched—a mishap that is sure to make them smile maliciously.

But when Akaky Akakievich ever looked at anything he only saw all about him the even lines scripted in his neat hand, and only if a horse should appear from nowhere and thrust its nose over his shoulder, emitting a blast of horsy breath through its nostrils on to his cheeks, might he realize that he was in the middle of the street and not the middle of a sentence. On his arrival home he would at once seat himself at the table, slurp down his cabbage soup, and eat a piece of beef with onions, quite oblivious to the taste of all this food, which he devoured complete with flies and whatever else the good Lord saw fit to provide. When he felt his stomach starting to bloat he would rise from the table, fetch an ink-well and set about copying the papers he had brought home. Should there be no such papers, he would make a copy for himself, for the sheer pleasure of it, which was all the greater when the document was one noteworthy not for the eloquence of its style, but for the unusual identity or importance of its addressee.

Even at that hour when the grey St Petersburg sky is shrouded in total darkness and all its tribe of functionaries have dined and sated themselves, each in his own way, in accordance with his means and culinary preferences, when the clerkdom of St Petersburg are resting from the departmental scratching of quills and from the fuss and bustle of their own and their colleagues' essential duties and from all the inessential and superfluous work voluntarily undertaken by all those of a restless disposition, at that hour when the officials are hastening to devote their remaining free time to the pursuit of pleasure: the more intrepid dashing to the theatre; some roaming the streets, peeking under the ladies' natty bonnets; some passing the evening addressing compliments to an attractive maiden, the star of a small constellation of clerks; some, and this is their most common occupation, simply setting off to a colleague's apartment on the third or fourth floor, where he occupies two small rooms and a hall or kitchen with one or two pretensions to fashion, a lamp or some other knick-knack, obtained at the cost of many a sacrificed dinner and night on the town; in other words, even at that hour when all officials disperse to the small apartments of their friends to play a stormy game of whist, sipping tea out of glasses and eating cheap rusks, smoking long churchwarden pipes, and, while the cards are being dealt, relaying some slander from the circles of high society, which the average Russian is always, irrespective of his state, quite powerless to resist, or even, when there is nothing else to talk about, retelling the age-old joke about the commandant who is informed that the tail of the horse on Falconet's* monument has been docked—that is to say, even at that hour when the rest of the world is avid for entertainment Akaky Akakievich would not permit himself any such frivolity. No one could say that they had ever seen him at a party. Having sated himself with the pleasures of copying, he would go to bed, smiling at the thought of the morrow, at the good things God would send him to copy.

Such was the peaceful life led by a man who, with a salary of four hundred roubles, could be content with his lot, and such would it have continued, perhaps, to hoary old age, were it not for the calamities which lie in store not only for titular, but even privy, state, aulic, and all other councillors and counsellors, and even for those who neither give nor take counsel of any sort.

All those in St Petersburg who receive a salary of four hundred or thereabouts have one implacable enemy. This enemy is none other than our northern frost, although you also hear it said that it is good for the health. At eight in the morning, the very hour when the streets fill with functionaries scurrying to their departments, it goes to work, administering sharp and stinging blows on their noses, which their wretched owners are quite unable to protect. At such times, when even those holding senior office feel the skin on their faces tighten with cold and tears spring to their eyes, the poor titular councillors are defenceless. Their only chance of survival is to dash four or five blocks at top speed in their thin, threadbare overcoats, until they reach the haven of the porter's lodge, where they stamp their feet until all their frostbitten talents and clerkly capabilities have thawed out.

For some time Akaky Akakievich had been feeling particularly sharp stabs of cold in his back and shoulders, despite the speed at which he endeavoured to scurry across the necessary distance. He finally wondered whether there might perhaps be some deficiencies in his overcoat. Examining it carefully at home, he discovered that in two or three places—namely, on the back and shoulders—it had worn as thin as sackcloth and let the cold through, while beneath it the lining had shredded away. We should observe here that Akaky Akakievich's coat also served as the butt of his fellow clerks' humour; they had even decided it was no longer fit to bear the noble name of overcoat and referred to it as his 'smock'. To be sure, it was rather a queer garment: its collar became smaller and smaller every year as bits of it were used as patches for other parts of the coat. These repairs did no great credit to the art of the tailor and were baggy and unsightly. Having thus identified the source of the problem, Akaky Akakievich resolved that the coat had to be taken to Petrovich the tailor, who resided somewhere on the fourth floor of a back staircase, and who, despite his squint and pockmarked visage, was rather deft at repairing the trousers and tailcoats of functionaries and other clients—deft, that is, when he was sober and his attention not taken up with some other undertaking.

We do not need to say much about this tailor, but as it is now customary in stories to give a full account of the character of each of the dramatis personae there is nothing for it: we shall have a close look at Petrovich too. Originally he was simply called Grigory and was the serf of some landowner; he started going by the name Petrovich after he had been granted his release* and had taken to imbibing rather liberally on saints' days, first on only the major holidays, but then indiscriminately, wherever the day was marked with a cross in the calendar. In this respect he was true to his ancestral habits, and in quarrels with his wife would call her a godless woman and a German. And since we have now brought his wife into the picture we must also say a couple of words about her: unfortunately not much was known about her. It was only known that Petrovich had a wife, who even wore a lace cap rather than a headscarf;* it appeared, however, that she could not boast of great beauty; at any rate, of the men who walked past her only guardsmen would peer beneath the brim of her cap, whereupon they would twitch their moustaches and utter a strange noise.

As he ascended the staircase leading to Petrovich's shop, a staircase which, to be perfectly truthful, was thoroughly steeped in dishwater and slops, and everywhere gave off that acrid smell which so stings the eyes and which, as the reader will know, is an inescapable adjunct of all back staircases in St Petersburg—as he ascended the staircase Akaky Akakievich was already speculating how much Petrovich would ask and had inwardly resolved to pay no more than two roubles. The door was open, because the tailor's good wife had been cooking some fish or other and in the process had produced so much smoke in the kitchen that even the cockroaches could no longer be seen. Akaky Akakievich walked through the kitchen, unobserved by the tailor's wife, and finally made his way into the workroom, where he saw Petrovich sitting on a big unpainted wooden table with his feet tucked beneath him like a Turkish pasha. His feet were bare, as is usual with tailors when they are seated at their work. The first thing to strike the visitor's eye was the tailor's big toe, which Akaky Akakievich had come to know so well, with its mangled nail, as thick and tough as tortoise shell. Round Petrovich's neck hung a skein of silk and cotton thread and on his knees lay some scraps of cloth. For the last three minutes he had been trying unsuccessfully to thread a needle and was consequently very angry at the darkness in the room and at the thread itself, at which he muttered threateningly: 'Go in, damn you! I've just about had it with you, you scoundrel!'

Akaky Akakievich was rather disquieted to find that he had come in at a moment when Petrovich was angry: he preferred to place his orders when Petrovich was slightly tipsy, or, as his wife would put it, when the old one-eyed devil had been hitting the bottle. In this state Petrovich would usually be quite amenable to his clients' requests, signalling his agreement with deep bows and expressions of gratitude. Later, admittedly, his wife would come complaining that her husband was drunk and had therefore agreed to do the work too cheaply; but it was usually sufficient to add another ten copecks and the job was in the bag. On this occasion, however, Petrovich appeared to be quite sober, and therefore abrupt, intractable, and likely to name a quite preposterous price. Akaky Akakievich quickly took stock of the situation and resolved to beat a hasty retreat, but it was too late. Petrovich directed his good eye at him with a fixed stare and Akaky Akakievich automatically pronounced: 'Goodday, Petrovich!' to which the latter replied, 'Goodday to you, sir!' redirecting his one-eyed gaze to Akaky Akakievich's hands to see what sort of booty he had brought.

'I er... just called in, Petrovich, to bring this here...'

At this stage we should point out that Akaky Akakievich expressed himself for the most part with the use of prepositions, adverbs, and all sorts of particles which have absolutely no meaning at all. If the situation was particularly awkward he would even not complete his phrases, and frequently, after venturing something like: 'Well, you see... it's actually...' the sentence would tail off, as he would be under the impression that he had said all he intended to say.

'What is it?' asked Petrovich, studying his client's uniform carefully with his good eye, starting from the collar and proceeding to the sleeves, the back, the skirts, and buttonholes, all of which were only too familiar to him, as it was his own handiwork. Such is the custom of tailors and the first thing they do on encountering a client.

'Well, it's like this, Petrovich... this coat of mine, the cloth... you see, it's quite strong in other places, it's just a bit dusty and looks sort of old, but it's actually new, only here in this one place it's a little sort of... on the back, and on one shoulder... it's a little worn, and here on this shoulder, too... there, you see, that's all. Not much work at all, really...'

Petrovich took the 'smock', spread it out on the table, examined it carefully, shook his head and leaned across to the windowsill for a round snuff-box decorated with the portrait of some general, although it is not clear exactly which, because someone had poked his finger through the place where the face had been painted and the hole had been patched with a square piece of paper. Taking a pinch of snuff Petrovich stretched the coat out in the air and held it up against the light. Once again he shook his head. Then he turned up its lining and shook his head again, and once again reached for the snuff-box, removed the portrait of the unknown general with its paper patch, conveyed a pinch of snuff to his nostril, replaced the lid, put away the box, and finally announced:

'No, it can't be fixed: the garment's worn out!'

Akaky Akakievich's heart sank at these words.

'But why not, Petrovich?' he said, in an almost childish, pleading voice: 'I mean, actually, it is a bit worn, but only on the shoulders, surely you have some sort of pieces of cloth...'

'I've got pieces of cloth all right, that's no problem,' said Petrovich. 'But I can't sew them on: the thing's completely rotten, put a needle through it and it'll just fall apart.'

'Let it come apart and then you can put a patch on straight away.'

'But there's nothing to put the patch on to, nothing to hold it fast, you've worn it terribly thin. You could hardly even call it cloth any more: put it in a strong wind and it'll fall to pieces.'

'But just fix it on somehow. I mean, it can't really...'

'No,' stated Petrovich decisively: 'there's nothing can be done about it. It's had it. You'd do better, when the cold winter days come, to cut it up into footcloths, because socks don't keep your feet warm. They were invented by the Germans, to squeeze more money out of people'—Petrovich never missed the chance to take a swipe at the Germans—'and it looks as though you'll have to get yourself a new coat made.'

On hearing the word 'new' Akaky Akakievich felt his eyes cloud over and the room swam before his eyes. The only thing he could see at all clearly was the general with a paper patch over his face on the lid of Petrovich's snuff-box. 'How do you mean a new one?' he asked, still feeling dazed, 'I haven't the money for it.'

'Yes, a new one,' replied Petrovich with brutal nonchalance.

'Well, just suppose I did have to have a new one, how much would it sort of, you know...'

'You mean, what would it cost?'

'Yes.'

'A hundred and fifty should about cover it,' said Petrovich with a significant pursing of his lips. He was very fond of strong effects, liked to say things which would shock, and then slyly watch the expression which these words brought to the face of his stunned listener.

'One hundred and fifty roubles for a coat!' exclaimed poor Akaky Akakievich, raising his voice for perhaps the first time in his whole life, being of an exceptionally soft-spoken disposition.

'Yes sir,' said Petrovich, 'but it'll be quite some coat. Put a marten collar on it, and a hood with a silk lining and it could set you back two hundred.'

'Please, Petrovich,' said Akaky Akakievich, in a beseeching tone, closing his ears to the tailor's words and all his effects: 'won't you just fix it up somehow or other, you know, so it lasts a bit longer at least?'

'No; that would be a waste of work and money,' said Petrovich. On hearing this final verdict Akaky Akakievich took his leave, a broken man.

After the departure of his customer Petrovich did not resume his work but sat without stirring for a long time, pursing his lips significantly, so pleased was he with himself for having stood his ground and having successfully upheld the tailor's art.

When he stepped out on to the street Akaky Akakievich felt as though he was dreaming. 'Well, there's a thing,' he said to himself, 'and to think it should turn out this way.' Then, after a short silence he added: 'Well, so there it is! So that's the way things have turned ont—and to think I would never have imagined that they could have turned out like this.' This was followed by another silence, a long one, after which he said: 'Well there! Now, who would have... what a... well, I mean... that is... what a turn of events!'

Having said this he did not repair home but set off in quite the opposite direction without even realizing what he was doing. On the way a grimy chimney-sweep bumped into him and completely blackened his shoulder; an entire hodful of lime was dumped on him from the top storey of a building under construction. He remained quite oblivious to all this, and only when he collided with a constable on his beat, who had put down his halberd in order to shake snuff out of his tobacco horn into the calloused palm of his hand, did he return somewhat to his senses, and then only because the policeman said to him: 'Where the devil do you think you're going—no room on the pavement or something?' This made him look round and turn back home. Here he was able to gather his thoughts and see his position in its proper light. He started talking to himself not in his usual jerky way, but coherently and openly, as if with a reasonable friend, with whom one could discuss the most intimate and delicate matter.

'Well no,' said Akaky Akakievich, 'there's no sense in arguing with Petrovich now: he's sort of... His wife must have sort of thumped him one. I would do better to go to him on Sunday morning: after the Saturday evening before he will be cockeyed and half asleep, and he'll need a drink for his head, but his wife won't give him any money, so at that point I'll slip him ten copecks so to speak and he'll listen to reason and then the coat will sort of...'

As he pursued this line of reasoning Akaky Akakievich felt his spirits lift and, come the following Sunday, he waited until he saw Petrovich's wife leave the house on some errand and he at once presented himself to the tailor. Petrovich was certainly groggy, his head drooped and his eyes were thick with sleep, but for all that, when the question of the coat was raised it was as if the devil had got into him. 'No,' he said, 'you'll have to order a new coat.' Whereupon Akaky Akakievich slipped him a ten-copeck piece. 'Thank you, kind sir, I'll fortify myself with a little something and drink your health,' said Petrovich, 'but it's no use asking me to mend your coat: it's no good for anything at all. I'll make you a new coat, a splendid overcoat, and let's leave it at that.'

Akaky Akakievich attempted to pursue the matter of repairs, but Petrovich would not hear him out and said: 'Now, I'll make you a new one by all means, you can depend on me there, I shall really do my best. We can even follow the latest fashion, and fasten the collar with silver clasps under little flaps.'

Akaky Akakievich saw that there was no getting away from it: he had to have a new coat. He completely lost heart. How, when all was said and done, was he going to pay for it—where would he find the money? Of course he could rely partly on the bonus he was due to receive for the holiday, but this money had long ago been accounted for and apportioned for other purposes. He needed new trousers, and had to pay the shoemaker a long outstanding bill for attaching new tops to his boots, he had to order three new shirts from the seamstress and two pairs of those undergarments which it is considered improper to mention on the printed page. In other words there would be nothing left of the money, and even if, in a fit of generosity, the director should give him not forty, but forty-five or fifty roubles he would still only be left with a trifling amount, a mere drop in the ocean of the price of an overcoat. Though he knew perfectly well that Petrovich had the habit of naming the most exorbitant prices, sometimes so high that even his wife would be unable to contain herself and would exclaim: 'What, are you out of your mind, you half-wit! Another time you'll take work on for nothing, and here you've taken some crazy notion to charge a price which you aren't even worth yourself.' He knew, of course, that Petrovich would eventually agree to make the coat for eighty roubles, but where was he going to get even eighty roubles? He might have been able to gather half that sum; maybe even a little more, but where would he get the other half?...

Before going any further we should explain to the reader where the first half would come from.

Akaky Akakievich had the habit of saving two copecks from every rouble he spent, putting it away in a little locked box with a slot in the top for coins. At the end of every six months he would count up the coppers and replace them with the equivalent in silver. He had maintained this practice for many years, and by this time had accumulated a sum in excess of forty roubles. Thus he had half the sum at hand, but where to find the other half? Where was he to get another forty roubles?

Akaky Akakievich racked his brains and decided that he would have to cut down on his day-to-day expenses, at the very least for one whole year: he would forgo his evening cup of tea, light no candles in the evening, and if he had any work to do, would go into his landlady's room and do it by the light of her candle; when he walked down the street he would tread more gently and carefully along the cobbles and flags, walking almost on tiptoes, so as to spare his shoeleather; he would have his laundry done as rarely as possible, and to prevent his clothes wearing out would undress as soon as he got home and go about in only his cheap cotton dressing-gown, an extremely elderly garment but spared even by the ravages of time.

To tell the truth, at first he found it rather hard to adapt to these austerities, but then he grew used to them and took them in his stride; he even became quite accustomed to going entirely without food in the evenings; but then he derived spiritual nourishment, feeding on the dream of his new coat. With this new regime his whole existence became somehow more fulfilled, as if he had got married, as if there were some other person with him, as if he were no longer alone but attended by some fair companion who had agreed to step down life's path with him—and this pleasant companion, this soul mate was none other than his heavy, padded overcoat, with its long-wearing and robust lining. He became somehow more alive, and stronger in character, like a man who has determined his goal in life. His face and behaviour lost their unsureness and indecision, in other words, all their vacillating and vague features. At times his eyes would light up and the boldest and most daring thoughts would flit through his head: perhaps he should have that marten collar after all? His deliberations on this subject made him quite absent-minded, and one day during his copying he so nearly made a mistake that he almost exclaimed 'Ooops!' out loud and at once crossed himself. At least once every month he would call on Petrovich to talk about the coat, asking where the best place was to buy cloth, which colour he should get and how much he should pay. After these visits he would come home happy, if a little troubled, but content with the thought that soon the time would come when he could actually make the purchase and the coat would be ready.

This moment arrived even sooner than he had expected. Contrary to all expectations, the director awarded Akaky Akakievich a bonus of not forty, nor forty-five, but sixty roubles! Perhaps he had a premonition that Akaky Akakievich needed the coat very badly, or perhaps it just happened this way, but the upshot was that Akaky Akakievich had an additional twenty roubles in hand. This unexpected development speeded up the course of events. After another two or three months of privation, Akaky Akakievich had the eighty roubles ready. His heart, normally so quiescent, started to pound. The very next day he set off with Petrovich to the shops. They bought a length of very fine cloth—and no wonder, for they had been planning this purchase for the last six months and hardly a month had passed without them going round the shops to compare prices. Petrovich himself declared that they would not find better cloth anywhere. They chose calico for the lining, but of such good quality and so firm that, in Petrovich's words, it was better than silk and even glossier and more impressive to look at. They decided against the marten because it was too dear, but instead chose the best cat fur they could find in the shops, cat fur that from afar would easily pass for marten. Petrovich toiled over the coat for a full two weeks because there was a lot of quilting work to be done; otherwise it would have been finished sooner. For the work Petrovich took twelve roubles—it could not have been done for a copeck less: everything was sturdily sewn with silk thread, with finely stitched double seams, and afterwards Petrovich worked over every seam with his teeth, leaving little patterns pressed into the cloth.

The day when Petrovich finally brought the overcoat... It's hard to say with any precision what day it was, but surely the most memorable and festive day in Akaky Akakievich's life was the day on which Petrovich finally brought the overcoat. He brought it in the morning, early enough for Akaky Akakievich to wear it to work. The coat could not have been finished at a more opportune moment, for the hard frosts had just set in and the weather was threatening to get colder still. Petrovich brought the coat himself, as befits a good tailor. The expression of solemnity on his face was such as Akaky Akakievich had never before seen. It would seem that, in his awareness of the auspicious nature of this undertaking, he had suddenly become conscious of the great chasm that divides tailors who merely stitch in linings and do repairs from those who create new garments. He took the coat out of the handkerchief in which he had carried it; even that was freshly laundered—he then folded the handkerchief up and put it in his pocket for future use. Holding up the coat he regarded it with great pride and with a deft sweep of his hands threw it over Akaky Akakievich's shoulders, straightened it out, pulled it down at the back and finally draped it round its new owner with its buttons undone. Akaky Akakievich, with the fussiness of an elderly man, was anxious to put it on properly, so Petrovich helped him put his arms in the sleeves—and it sat well like that too. In other words, the coat was a perfect fit.

Petrovich did not miss the opportunity to say that it was only because he lived on a small street and had no sign, and furthermore had known Akaky Akakievich for so long, that he had charged him so little; on Nevsky Prospect for the work alone he would have had to pay seventy-five roubles. Akaky Akakievich had no wish to discuss this point with Petrovich as he was afraid of the sound of the large sums with which Petrovich liked to alarm his clients. He settled up with him, expressed his thanks and at once repaired to the department in his new overcoat. Petrovich left with him and, for a long time, stood on the street watching the coat retreat. Then he made a deliberate detour down a crooked side-street which brought him out further down the same street: here he was able to take another look at his coat, but from a different angle, that is, *en face*.

Meanwhile Akaky Akakievich stepped along in as festive a mood as could be. Every fraction of every second he was aware that he bore on his shoulders his new raiment, and once or twice he even chuckled for sheer pleasure. In truth the coat offered two advantages: one that it was warm, and the other that it looked well. He did not notice the distance at all and suddenly found himself in the department; in the lobby he cast off the coat, examined it from all sides, and surrendered it for the skilled scrutiny of the porter.

Somehow or other everyone in the department had learnt that Akaky Akakievich had a new coat and that the old smock was no more. They all dashed out into the lobby to admire their colleague's latest acquisition, and started congratulating him and wishing him well, so that at first Akaky Akakievich only smiled, and then began to feel a little embarrassed. When they all set upon him demanding that the happy event should be celebrated and that the very least he could do was to give a party for them, Akaky Akakievich became thoroughly confused and did not know how on earth to talk his way out of this. After several minutes of this discomfiture he started naïvely assuring them, flushing deeply, that it was not a new coat at all, but in fact his old one.

Finally one of the officials, with the high rank of assistant head of desk, announced, with the probable intention of showing that he was not at all high and mighty and quite happy to associate even with his inferiors: 'Be that as it may; I shall give the party instead of Akaky Akakievich and invite you all to my place today for tea: by a lucky coincidence today is my birthday.' The officials at once congratulated the assistant desk head and accepted the invitation with alacrity. Akaky Akakievich attempted to make his excuses, but they all protested that this would be bad form, that he should be ashamed of himself, and there was nothing for it but to accept. Moreover he himself started to look forward to the party when he realized that it would give him an extra chance to show off his overcoat, this time in the evening light.

The whole of this day was for Akaky Akakievich the most exciting holiday imaginable. He returned home in the best possible frame of mind, threw off his coat and hung it carefully on a hook, gazed lovingly once again at the cloth and lining, and then fetched his old smock, by now completely ragged, to compare the two. As he looked he even laughed out loud: what an enormous difference! And for a long time after this, as he sat at his dinner, he chuckled whenever he thought of the appalling state of his old smock. He thoroughly enjoyed his dinner and afterwards did no copying, none at all, preferring instead to laze about on his bed until it grew dark. Then, without further ado, he dressed, donned his new coat, and sallied forth into the street.

Where exactly the official who was giving the party lived, I unfortunately cannot say: the old memory is starting to let us down badly and everything in St Petersburg, all its streets and buildings, has become so jumbled around in the head that it is very hard to retrieve anything from it in its proper shape. All that I do know for certain is that this official lived in the better part of town, that is, nowhere near Akaky Akakievich. At first Akaky Akakievich had to go down some deserted and dimly-lit streets but as he drew nearer to the official's apartments the streets became more alive, more populated and better lit. There were more and more pedestrians, including ladies in elegant costume, men with beaver collars, and fewer and fewer uncouth draymen with their wooden-slatted sleighs, decked out with cheap brass nails—their place was taken by jaunty cab-drivers in crimson velvet caps, careering down the street in gleaming, varnished sleighs draped in bearskins, and carriages with brightly painted coach-boxes, their wheels creaking over the snow.

Akaky Akakievich regarded all this with wonderment. It was several years since he had stepped out on to the street in the evening. He paused to examine with interest a picture in the brightly lit window of a shop, which depicted a beautiful woman removing a shoe, and in the process revealing her leg, and a most shapely leg it was too; behind her a man with whiskers and a dapper bodkin beard could be seen peeping through the doorway from another room. Akaky Akakievich shook his head and chuckled, then continued on his way. Perhaps he chuckled because he had beheld something quite unfamiliar, yet of the sort to which every man is intuitively drawn, or perhaps he was thinking, as would many another functionary in his place: 'These Frenchmen!... You have to hand it to them, once they sort of get their mind on a thing they really sort of...' Yet on the other hand, perhaps he was not thinking this at all—after all, you cannot see into the mind of another person and discover what he is thinking.

He finally reached the house in which the assistant desk head had his apartments. The assistant desk head lived in style: a lamp burned on the staircase, leading to the second-floor apartment. On entering the hall Akaky Akakievich saw rows of galoshes on the floor. In their midst, in the middle of the room, stood a samovar, which hissed and emitted puffs of steam. Hanging on the walls was a great mass of overcoats and cloaks, some of which were even fitted with beaver collars or velvet lapels. Through the wall he could hear a din of voices, which suddenly became clear and ringing when the door opened and out walked a footman bearing a tray laden with empty glasses, a cream-jug, and a basket of biscuits. It was apparent that the officials had been gathered for some time, and had already drunk their first glass of tea.

After hanging up his coat himself, Akaky Akakievich entered the room and was dazzled by the array of candles, officials, pipes, and card-tables, while his ears rang with the confused clamour of voices conversing on all sides and the noise of chairs being shifted. He stood in the centre of the room feeling quite at a loss, gazing around and trying to work out what he should do. But he had already been observed, and was received with shouts of welcome, which were followed by a general stampede into the hall for another look at his new coat. Akaky Akakievich was perhaps a little abashed, but— simple soul that he was—could not help delighting at the lavish praise heaped on his overcoat. Then, of course, the company abandoned both him and his coat and repaired, as was to be expected, to their tables, which were set out for whist.

All this: the noise, chatter, and numbers of people, was quite novel to Akaky Akakievich. He simply did not know what to do with himself, where to put his hands, feet, and all his person; finally he joined one of the tables, looked at the cards, stared at the faces of various of the players and after a little while started to yawn, feeling that all this was rather boring, especially since it was long past his bedtime. He tried to take his leave of his host, but the others would not let him go, protesting that they simply had to drink a glass of champagne to celebrate the new acquisition. An hour later dinner was served, consisting of *salade russe*, cold veal, pâté, pastries, and champagne. Akaky Akakievich was made to drink two glasses, after which he felt that it was altogether much jollier in the room, yet he still could not forget that it was past twelve and long since time for him to be going home. Lest his host attempt somehow to detain him still further he slipped out of the room surreptitiously, and hunted for his coat, which, to his distress, he observed lying on the floor. He shook it out, picked all the fluff off it, threw it across his shoulders, and descended the stairs into the street.

The street-lamps were still lit. A few small shops of the sort that everywhere serve as clubs for the servant classes and their kind, were still open, while others, which had by then closed, cast long slivers of light through the chinks in their doors, from which it was clear that they were not yet deserted, but probably harboured parlour maids or menservants, who would be finishing off their evening's gossip, while their masters and mistresses remained totally mystified as to their whereabouts. Akaky Akakievich stepped along feeling on top of the world, at one point almost breaking into a run, for no apparent reason, in pursuit of some lady who flitted past him like a flash of lightning, showing extraordinary mobility in every part of her body. He at once stopped, however, and walked on at his previous gentle pace, astounding himself with this quite unaccountable burst of speed. Soon he entered those deserted streets, which by day are bleak enough places to walk, let alone at night time. At that hour they were even more dismal and deserted: the street-lamps became fewer and farther between—oil was clearly in scarce supply; here the houses and fences were of wood; not a soul was in sight; the only light came from the snow glinting on the street while the low huts slept morosely behind their dark shutters. By now he was near the point where the street opened into a vast square, a terrible void, on the far side of which the buildings were barely visible.

In the far distance he could see shining the lamp of a sentry-booth, which appeared to stand on the very edge of the world. At this point Akaky Akakievich's good cheer faded perceptibly. He struck out across the square with an involuntary sense of dread, as if with inner premonitions that something bad was about to happen. He looked behind and about him: it was as though he were on the high seas. 'No, better not to look,' he thought and walked on with his eyes shut, only opening them to see how far he was from the edge of the square. Instead, there, standing right before his nose, were a couple of men with moustaches, although he still could not see them at all clearly. His head started to swim and his heart pounded.

'Hey—that's my coat you're wearing!' exclaimed one of them in a threatening voice and seized him by the collar. Akaky Akakievich was on the point of calling out for help when the other put his fist—the size of a civil servant's head—against his jaw and growled: 'Just you try and shout!' After this all Akaky Akakievich could recall was that they removed his coat, then one of them gave him a kick, whereupon he fell on his back in the snow and felt nothing more.

A few minutes later he came round and rose to his feet, but by this time there was no one to be seen. Feeling suddenly cold and exposed, he realized that his coat was gone and he started to call out, but his voice was too feeble to carry across the square. In a state of utter despair, and shouting frantically, he set off at a run across the square, heading directly for the booth. Next to the booth stood the duty constable, leaning on his halberd, and regarding Akaky Akakievich with curiosity, clearly wondering what the devil this was, running and shouting to him from afar. As he came up to the constable Akaky Akakievich, gasping for breath, started to rail at him for sleeping at his post and allowing people to be robbed beneath his very nose. The constable retorted that he had not seen anything untoward, that he had seen him being stopped by two people in the square and had assumed they were his friends; and that, instead of shouting and wasting his time, he should go and see the sergeant the next day and the sergeant would find out who had robbed him.

Akaky Akakievich ran home in a terrible state; his hair, of which small tufts still remained on his temples and the back of his head, was completely dishevelled, his side and chest and his trousers were covered in snow. On hearing a fearful banging on the door, his old landlady hastily sprang from her bed and—wearing only one slipper—ran to open the door, modestly clasping her nightshirt to her bosom. When she opened the door she stepped backwards in shock, seeing Akaky Akakievich in such a state. Once she had heard his story she clapped her hands and declared that he should go directly to the inspector, that the sergeant would tell all sorts of lies, make promises, and do nothing about it; and that he simply must go straight to the inspector, that the inspector was even an acquaintance of hers, because Anna, the Finnish girl who had once worked for her as a cook, was now in the inspector's employ as a nursemaid, that she often saw him passing their house, and also that he went to church every Sunday, cast cheerful looks about him while praying, and consequently must be a kind man. After listening to this advice Akaky Akakievich went forlornly to his room, and as for the way he passed the night there, we shall have to leave that to the imagination of those readers who can put themselves in other persons' shoes.

Early the following morning he set off to see the inspector; but there he was informed that the inspector was asleep; he came back at ten and once again was told that he was asleep; he came at eleven and was told that the inspector was not at home; he came at lunchtime but the clerks in the front room would not admit him until they had heard the nature of his business, what need he had of the inspector, and what exactly had taken place. For once in his life Akaky Akakievich showed some backbone and said straight out that he had to see the inspector in person, that they had no right to refuse him admission, that he had come from the department on official business, and that if they were not careful he would lodge a complaint against them. This the clerks did not dare counter, and one of them went to call the inspector.

The inspector's reaction to the account of the robbery was extremely odd, however. Instead of turning his attention to the main point at issue he started asking Akaky Akakievich why he had been coming home so late, and had he perhaps been visiting a house of ill-repute, with the result that Akaky Akakievich quite lost his composure and took his leave without even knowing whether the matter of the overcoat would be looked into or not.

The whole of that day he remained absent from the office—the first such absence in his life. The following day he turned up at work as pale as a ghost, wearing his old smock, which had acquired an even more pathetic aspect. Although some officials had no compunction about laughing at Akaky Akakievich even at this sad juncture, the tale of the robbery touched many of them to the quick. They resolved at once to organize a whip-round for him, but the sum collected was only trifling because the department staff had already been made to pay out a lot of money in contributions, first towards a portrait of the director, and then towards some new book, which their section head had recommended, being a friend of the author's. As a result they could only muster a paltry sum. One of their number, particularly moved with compassion, decided at least to help Akaky Akakievich with a piece of useful advice, and told him not to bother seeing the police sergeant, because even though the sergeant, anxious to win the approval of his superiors, might somehow or other recover the coat it would remain in the police station unless he could provide legal evidence of his ownership. Instead he should go and see a certain *important personage*, and this *important personage*, by sending notes and memorandums to the right people, would put things on the right track.

Akaky Akakievich decided there was nothing for it but to go and see the *important personage*. Exactly what office was held by the *important personage* and what this entailed remains a mystery to this day. All that we can say is that the *important personage* had only recently been made an important personage, and prior to that had been an unimportant personage. Besides, his new office was not regarded as particularly important in comparison with those of certain other even more important personages. But then you will always find people who regard as important things that are considered unimportant by others. Furthermore he endeavoured to augment his importance in all sorts of ways, in particular, by directing that junior officials meet him on the staircase when he came to work; that no one dare come straight to see him, but that the following strict order be observed: the collegiate registrar make a report to the gubernia secretary, the gubernia secretary to the titular councillor, or whoever came next in seniority, and thus the matter would eventually reach him. For such is the pass to which Holy Russia has come: imitation is the order of the day and each man spends his time aping and mimicking his superiors. The story is even told of some titular councillor who, on being put in charge of some minor department, at once partitioned off a room of his own, calling it 'Chambers' and posting beadles at the door in red collars and gold braid, who would step forward to open the door for any visitor, although the 'Chambers' were barely big enough to accommodate an ordinary desk.

The methods and procedures of the *important personage* were appropriately grand and imposing, but in no way complicated. The corner-stone of his system was strictness. 'Strictness, strictness and— strictness' he was wont to say, and on pronouncing the last word would look most significantly into the face of his listener. In fact there was no reason for this because the dozen officials who made up the entire administrative mechanism of the office abided in a state of permanent fear anyway: on seeing their principal approaching from afar they would abandon what they were doing and stand to attention until he had passed through the room. His conversation with subordinates was marked by its strictness and consisted almost exclusively of three phrases: 'How dare you? Are you aware who you're talking to? Do you realize who this is, standing before you?' For all that, he was a kind man at heart, companionable and obliging;

but his head had been completely turned by his promotion. On being promoted to the rank of general he went completely adrift and no longer knew how to conduct himself. When in the company of his equals he could be quite a decent fellow and in many respects even rather astute; but the moment he found himself surrounded by people even one rank below him he would be quite unable to cope: he would maintain a stony silence, and his position was all the more pitiable because he himself felt that he could be spending the time in a much more enjoyable fashion. Sometimes his eyes all too obviously betrayed a strong desire to join in some interesting conversation or group, but he would be held in check by the thought: would this not be rather beneath his dignity, would it not be over-familiar and detract from his importance? After such considerations he always preserved his silence, pronouncing only the occasional monosyllable, and in this way acquired the reputation of a crashing bore.

It was to this *important personage* that our Akaky Akakievich repaired, choosing a highly unpropitious time, most unfortunate for Akaky Akakievich but fortunate for the important personage. The important personage was sitting in his office and conversing in the most cheerful fashion with an old acquaintance and childhood friend who had recently arrived in the capital, whom he had not seen for several years. Whilst thus engaged he was informed that one Bashmachkin had come to see him. He snapped: 'Who is he?' and received the reply: 'Some official.'—'In that case let him wait, I've no time now,' he said.

At this point we should note that the important personage was telling a bare-faced lie: he had plenty of time, he and his friend had long since exhausted all topics of interest and their conversation had lapsed into lengthy silences punctuated by the occasional slap on each other's thigh and the exclamation: 'Well now, Ivan Abramovich!'—'Well there's a thing, Stepan Varlamovich!' Nevertheless he ordered the official to wait, in order to show his friend, a man who had long ago retired from service to his country home, how long officials were required to wait in his antechamber.

Finally, when they had had their fill of talking, and still more of long silences, and had finished smoking their cigars in their extremely comfortable chairs with reclining backs, he suddenly pretended to remember something and said to his secretary, who had stopped inside the door to take a report: 'By the way, there's some official out there, is there not? Tell him to come in.' Observing Akaky Akakievich's downcast look and shabby old uniform he briskly swung round to face him and enquired 'What is it?' in a hard, snappy voice, which he had carefully cultivated behind locked doors, rehearsing in solitude in front of a mirror for an entire week before receiving his promotion and his present position.

Akaky Akakievich, who had already been feeling suitably awe-struck, somewhat lost his composure, and, in so far as his tongue-tied state would allow, explained with even more than the usual admixture of 'sort-ofs' that he had a brand new overcoat, and he had been robbed in the most barbaric fashion, and that he was now turning to His Excellency, in order that through his intercession he might sort of get in touch with his honour the chief inspector of police, or someone else, and retrieve his coat. The general, for some obscure reason, regarded Akaky Akakievich's conduct as over-familiar.

'Do you mean, my good man,' he continued in the same sharp voice, 'that you don't know the form? Do you know where you are? Or how to conduct these matters properly? You should first have submitted a petition about this to the office, it would have been passed to the head of your desk, then to the department head, and then handed to the secretary and the secretary would have passed it on to myself...'

'But, Your Excellency,' said Akaky Akakievich, desperately striving to muster his scant presence of mind, and at the same time sweating profusely: 'I have made so bold as to trouble Your Excellency because you see your secretaries... are... er... an unreliable lot...'

'I beg your pardon?' said the important personage: 'how dare you be so impudent? Where on earth do you get such ideas from? What have the younger generation come to, treating their superiors with such mutinous insolence!'

The important personage apparently had not noticed that Akaky Akakievich was already on the wrong side of 50. Or perhaps he was assigning him to the younger generation in a relative sense, that is in relation to someone of 70. 'Are you aware who you're talking to? Do you realize who this is, standing before you? I'm asking you a question: do you hear me?'

At this point he stamped his foot, and raised his voice to such a pitch that anyone, not only Akaky Akakievich, would have been quite terrified. Akaky Akakievich was paralysed with terror, and lurched backwards, shaking like a leaf and quite unable to remain on his feet: if the two beadles had not run up at that point and supported him he would have fallen flat on his face. He was carried out almost unconscious. The important personage, delighted with the effect of his words, which had surpassed even his expectations, and quite entranced by the idea that his word alone was sufficient to scare the living daylights out of another person, gave his friend a sideways look to see how this was being received and noted, not without gratification, that his friend was in a most uneasy state and was even beginning to show visible signs of alarm.

How he got down the stairs and out into the street Akaky Akakievich was unable to recall. He could feel neither his legs nor his arms. In all his life he had never been given such a dressing-down by a general, let alone one from another department. Open-mouthed and constantly stumbling off the pavement he battled his way through the snowstorm which howled down the street. The wind, as is customary in St Petersburg, blew at him from all four directions at once, out of all the alley ways. In no time he caught a chest-cold and when he dragged himself home he had completely lost his voice, and took to his bed, aching all over. Such is the effect a good dressing-down can have!

The next day he was found to have a high fever. Thanks to the magnanimous assistance of the St Petersburg climate the sickness took its course even faster than was expected, and when eventually the doctor arrived and felt the patient's pulse he merely prescribed him a poultice, just to ensure that the sick man was not entirely deprived of the benefit of medicine, and thereupon declared that in a day and a half he would be 'kaputt'. After which he turned to the landlady and said: 'I'd advise you, my good woman, to waste no time, and order him a pinewood coffin right away, because he won't be able to afford an oak one.'

We do not know whether Akaky Akakievich heard these fatal words, and if he did, whether they made any impression on him, or whether he was sorry to depart this wretched life, because all this time he remained in a high fever and state of delirium. He had hallucinations, each one stranger than the last: he would see Petrovich and order a new coat from him fitted with special traps for thieves. He was forever seeing these thieves under the bed and kept calling for the landlady to remove a thief who had even got under the bedclothes; at times he would ask why his old smock was hanging in front of him, protesting that he had a new overcoat; or he would fancy he was standing in front of the general, receiving a severe reprimand, and muttering: 'Very sorry, Your Excellency', and finally he gave vent to such a torrent of foul and blasphemous curses that his good landlady even crossed herself, never before in her life having heard him utter anything like it, and all the more appalled because this stream of profanity had been immediately preceded by the words: 'Your Excellency'. Later on he started to rant; it was only apparent that his confused speech and thoughts were all centred on the ill-fated overcoat.

Finally poor Akaky Akakievich breathed his last. They did not bother to seal up either his room or his possessions, first because there were no heirs, and secondly because he left very little behind him, namely: a bunch of goose-quills, a quire of white office paper, three pairs of socks, two or three buttons which had come off his trousers, and the old smock already familiar to the reader. On whom all this finally devolved God only knows, and I must confess that the narrator of this story has made no attempt to find out. His corpse was carried out and laid in its grave, and St Petersburg continued its life without Akaky Akakievich just as if he had never existed. No trace remained of this creature defended by no one, dear to no one, of interest to no one, who failed even to attract the attention of the naturalist who will leap at the chance of putting a common housefly on a pin and studying it under a microscope; a creature who had endured with humility the jeers of his fellow clerks and had gone to his grave without any great achievement to his name, yet whose wretched life, for one brief moment so shortly before its end, had nevertheless been brightened by a radiant visitation in the form of a new overcoat, but who had then been crushed by an intolerable blow of misfortune, as crushing as those which befall the potentates and sovereigns of this world...

A few days after his death the watchman from his department was sent to his lodgings with instructions that he should come to work forthwith: such was the director's command; but the watchman was forced to return without him, reporting that he would not come to work any more. When asked: 'Why not?' he replied: 'Well he's dead, see, and they buried him three days ago.' Thus did they find out in the department about Akaky Akakievich's death and the very next day his place was occupied by another clerk, much taller than his late predecessor, and copying his letters in a hand quite unlike Akaky Akakievich's upright ciphers, one which sloped heavily to one side.

But who could have predicted that this was not the end of Akaky Akakievich's story, that he was fated to live on after his death for a few dramatic days, as if in compensation for his lack lustre life? It so happens that our bleak story has an unexpected and fantastic ending.

Rumours suddenly started to circulate round St Petersburg that by Kalinkin Bridge* and far beyond it a ghost had been seen at night. This ghost had taken the guise of an official searching for a stolen overcoat and it went about accosting everyone in its path, regardless of rank and title, and rending the coats from their shoulders in order to replace its own: coats with cat-fur and beaver linings, quilted coats, marmot, fox, and bearskin coats; in other words coats of every manner of fur and skin ever employed by people to cover their own. One of the department officials saw the ghost with his own eyes and at once recognized Akaky Akakievich, but at this he took such fright that he turned tail and fled and thus failed to get a good look, only seeing the ghost wag a threatening finger at him from afar.

Complaints came pouring in that the backs and shoulders of citizens—and we're talking here not only of titular councillors but even privy councillors—had been severely chilled as a result of such nocturnal divestitures. The police put out an order to detain the ghost at whatever cost, alive or dead, and to punish him as an example for others, in the severest fashion, and they very nearly succeeded in carrying out this directive. A police constable on the beat in Kiryushkin Alley actually caught the deceased culprit by the scruff of his neck at the very scene of his crime, as he attempted to wrest a worsted overcoat from the back of some retired musician, who in his time had played the flute. Seizing him by the collar he summoned two colleagues, whom he instructed to hold the ghostly marauder while he swiftly reached into his boot for his snuff-box, intending to reanimate his frostbitten nose, which had suffered this fate six times in his life. The snuff was evidently so potent, however, that even a dead man could not take it. No sooner had the constable closed his right nostril with a finger, administered a liberal pinch of snuff to the left and inhaled deeply, than the dead man sneezed so violently that all three of them were temporarily blinded by the spray. In the space of time it took them to raise their hands and wipe their eyes, the dead man had vanished without trace, and they could not even say with certainty whether they had ever held him in their hands at all. After that the constables became so fearful of dead men that they were even wary of laying hands on the living, and would shout from a distance: 'Hey you, move along now!' The dead official even started to appear beyond Kalinkin Bridge, striking fear into the hearts of all timid people.

But we have quite forgotten about the *important personage*, who in a sense was the real cause of this fantastic twist to our story—a story which, I might say, is perfectly authentic. Our devotion to the truth requires us to say that this *important personage*, shortly after the departure of the wretched, thoroughly dressed-down Akaky Akakievich, experienced something in the nature of regret. Compassion was not an entirely alien emotion to him; his heart was stirred by many kindly impulses, although his rank usually prevented him from revealing them. As soon as his visiting friend had taken his leave his thoughts returned to poor Akaky Akakievich. Thereafter almost every day he would see in his mind's eye the pale countenance of Akaky Akakievich, crumbling under the onslaught of his censorious words. He became so disturbed by these visions that a week later he even dispatched an official to Akaky Akakievich to find out what the trouble was, and whether it would not after all be possible to help him. When they reported back that Akaky Akakievich had been carried off suddenly by a fever he was quite shocked, hearing the reproaches of his conscience, and remained out of sorts for the whole of that day. Wishing to distract himself somehow or other and to put this unpleasant news out of his mind he set off to spend the evening with a friend, in whose house he would be sure to find decent company, and best of all, where almost everyone held the same rank, so that he did not feel constrained in any way.

This had a remarkable effect on his state of mind. He became quite relaxed, conversed in the most agreeable manner, was amiable to all and, in a word, thoroughly enjoyed the evening. He drank a couple of glasses of champagne at dinner, a well-known means of restoring good humour. The champagne put him in the mood for adventure, so he decided not to go home right away but to call instead on a lady of his acquaintance called Karolina Ivanovna, of supposedly German extraction, with whom he entertained the friendliest relations. We should point out here that the important personage was no longer in the first flush of youth and that he was a good husband to his wife and father to his children. His two sons, one of whom was already in government service, and his attractive 16-year-old daughter with her slightly snub but pretty nose would come to him every day to kiss his hand, saying: 'Bonjour, papa.' His spouse, a lady still in her prime and by no means unattractive, would first give him her hand to kiss and then turn it over and kiss his hand. While thoroughly content with these domestic family endearments, the important personage still deemed it not unethical to cultivate a friendly relationship with a lady in another part of town. This lady acquaintance was no prettier or younger than his wife; but such puzzling things occur in this world and it is not our job to pass judgement on them.

Thus, the important personage descended the stairs, seated himself in his sleigh and ordered the coachman: 'To Karolina Ivanovnas', while he wrapped himself luxuriously in his warm overcoat, and lapsed into that state so cherished by the average Russian, when he no longer has to think for himself, for the thoughts come crowding into his head of their own will, each one more pleasing than the last, and require no exhausting pursuit. Replete with contentment, he cast his mind back over all the amusing moments of the dinner party, recalling all the witticisms which had occasioned mirth in his small circle, many of these he even repeated to himself *sotto voce* and discovered that they were quite as funny as before. It should come as no surprise, therefore, to learn that he even laughed out loud. His pleasure was occasionally marred, however, by a gust of wind, which would spring up God knows from where or for which reason, and whipped his face, lashing it with pellets of snow, making the collar of his coat billow like a canvas sail, or suddenly blowing the shoulder-flap with a quite unnatural force over his head and causing him no end of bother in his efforts to extricate himself.

Suddenly the important personage felt himself being seized firmly by the collar. Turning round he perceived a small man in an old, worn-out uniform, and was not a little horrified to recognize Akaky Akakievich. The wretched scrivener's face was as white as snow, and he looked exactly like a corpse. But the horror of the important personage passed all bounds when he saw the dead man's mouth contort, and, exhaling the hideous miasma of the grave, utter the following words: 'Aha! so there you are! At last I've got you by the scruff of the neck! It's your overcoat I'm after! You didn't want to help me and even gave me a severe reprimand so now you can hand over your coat!' The wretched *important personage* almost died of fright. For all his great strength of character in the office and in the world at large with those of inferior rank, and for all his manly figure and appearance, on beholding which people would exclaim: 'Goodness, what character!' at the present moment he, like many another with the outward look of a Titan, felt such terror that he even feared he might suffer a fatal seizure. He threw off his coat as quickly as he could and called to the driver in a trembling voice: 'Turn home, and make it fast!' Hearing that tone of voice that is so often employed at critical junctures and is usually accompanied by something far more emphatic, the driver took the precaution of hunching his shoulders to protect his head, cracked his whip and they shot forward like an arrow from a bow. In no more than six minutes the important personage was already at the entrance to his house.

Pale, in a state of shock and coatless, he had driven home, abandoning his plan of going to Karolina Ivanovna's. Somehow or other he staggered to his room and spent the night in a state of such great agitation, that the following morning his daughter told him flatly: 'Papa, today you are quite pale.' But papa held his tongue and said not a word to anyone about what had happened, where he had been or where he had been planning to go. This adventure had the most pronounced effect on him. He even stopped saying so often to his inferiors: 'How dare you—do you realize who you're speaking to?' and if he did say it, it was not without first listening to what the other had to say.

But most remarkable of all was the total disappearance of the scrivener's ghost after this date. Clearly, the general's overcoat had been just what he wanted: at any rate no more stories were told of people having their coats torn from their backs. None the less, many energetic and interfering people were unwilling to let matters rest there and claimed that the ghost was still appearing in outlying areas of the city. And it is quite true that with his own eyes a constable in the Kolomna district* saw a ghost appear from behind a building; but the constable was of such a feeble constitution that he had once been knocked off his feet by an ordinary, healthy young pig which came hurtling out of a private house, to the great hilarity of the cabbies standing nearby, for which insolence he fined them a copeck each, using the money to buy snuff. This same weakling of a constable lacked the courage to apprehend the ghost and instead followed it in the darkness until it suddenly stopped, swung round and asked: 'What do you want?' brandishing a fist such as you would see on no man living. The constable replied 'Nothing', and beat a hasty retreat. This ghost was much taller, however, and sported the most enormous moustaches. Heading off the direction of the Obukhov Bridge* it was soon lost in the darkness.

THE CARRIAGE

Life in the small town of B. perked up considerably when the ***
cavalry regiment rode in and set up its quarters there. Until then
things had been dreadfully dull. Any passing traveller coming across
the squat, crudely daubed little houses, which peered out at the
street with an unimaginably sour look, would... No, words cannot
convey the heavy feeling that pressed down on his soul: it was as if
he had just lost a game of cards, or committed some careless blun-
der; in short: a bad feeling. The clay with which the houses were
plastered had been washed away by the rain, and the once white
walls were now blotchy and piebald; most of the roofs had been
thatched with reeds, as is customary in our southern towns; as for
orchards and vegetable gardens, the mayor had long since decreed
that these be cut down, to enhance the look of the town. You would
not meet a soul on the street; only the odd cockerel scurried across
your path. The roadway was a cubit deep in dust as soft as a pillow,
which the lightest drizzle would turn into a quagmire. Then the
streets of the small town of B. filled with those portly beasts the
mayor liked to refer to as 'the Frenchmen'. Thrusting their haughty
snouts in the air as they wallowed in their mud-bath, they would
strike up such a chorus of grunts that the traveller was sure to crack
his whip and hurry on.

One was unlikely to meet a traveller in the small town of B.,
however. Once in a blue moon some landowner clad in a nankeen
frock-coat, master of eleven serfs, rattled over the cobblestones in
a contrivance that was half-britschka, half-cart, peering out from
behind a pile of sacks and urging on his bay mare, her foal hard
on her heels. Even the market-place was glum. For some stupid
reason, the tailor's house had been built not facing the street, but at
an angle, with one corner jutting out into the square; across the
square, a brick building with two windows had been under construction for the past fifteen years; further along stood an ostenta-
tious wooden fence, in splendid isolation, painted grey like the
mud. It had been erected by the mayor when he was still a young
man, as a model for other building projects. This was before he

took to falling asleep directly after luncheon and, last thing at night, drinking a strange concoction brewed with dried gooseberries. Elsewhere the fences were made of humble wattle; at the centre of the square stood diminutive stalls where you were sure to see strings of ring-shaped rolls, a market-wife in a red kerchief, a pood* of soap, several pounds of bitter almonds, gunshot for flintlocks, a bolt of demicoton, and two shop assistants who played at pitch-and-toss all day long in front of their stalls.

But no sooner did the cavalry regiment arrive to set up its quarters in the small town of B. than everything changed. The streets bustled with life and colour; indeed, it was an entirely new place. The squat little houses would often see a trim and debonair officer saunter by, in a smart cockaded hat, on his way to a fellow officer's quarters to discuss some business matter, or to debate the merits of this tobacco or that, or perhaps heading off to book the town droshky. It might just as well have been the regimental droshky, as it never left the regiment, making the rounds of all the officers: today the major rode out in it; tomorrow it turned up in the lieutenant's stables, and in a week's time—would you believe it?—it was back at the major's, having its axles greased by his batman.

The wooden fence between the houses was festooned with soldiers' caps, hanging in the sun; on a gate somewhere you were sure to see a dun-coloured greatcoat; soldiers with mustachios as bristly as bottle-brushes strolled by on the side-streets. These mustachios could be seen everywhere. Wherever market-wives gathered with their little scoops, mustachios popped up behind them. By the town scaffold another mustachioed soldier might be seen castigating some unfortunate bumpkin, whose only response would be to clear his throat and roll his eyes upwards.

The officers breathed new life into the local *haut monde*. Hitherto this had consisted only of the judge, who shared his apartments with a deacon's widow, and the mayor, who, though something of a *raisonneur*, was given to spending the whole day asleep: from luncheon until dinner, and from dinner until luncheon. Their social life became more hectic still when the brigadier general also moved his quarters to the town. The surrounding landowners, whose very existence had thus far passed quite unnoticed, started making frequent visits to their district town, to pay their respects to the gentlemen officers, and to play an occasional game of faro,* whose rules they could only dimly remember, so cluttered were their minds with harvests, hares, and errands for their lady wives.

To my great regret I no longer recall the particular occasion that prompted the brigadier general to throw a banquet. The preparations for this great event were prodigious; the clatter of chefs' knives in the general's kitchen could be heard from as far off as the town gates. For this one dinner the market was stripped of produce: the judge and his deaconess were forced to subsist on buckwheat rolls and potato-starch jelly. Droshkies and calashes* thronged the small courtyard outside the general's quarters. The company—all male—was made up of officers and a few local landowners. Prominent among the latter was Pifagor Pifagorovich Chertokutsky, a leading light of the district aristocracy and its most vocal member at election time, who paraded about in a hideous and gaudy carriage. He had served in a cavalry regiment, and had proved one of its most distinguished and conspicuous officers—at least, he had been seen at many balls and gatherings, wherever his regiment was stationed; corroboration thereof may be sought from the young ladies of Tambov and Simbirsk* provinces. He might very well have won such acclaim in other provinces too, had he not been compelled to retire from service by a disagreeable incident of the kind commonly described as an *histoire*: either he boxed someone's ears, or they boxed his, I cannot remember exactly—it was all so long ago. In any event, he was forced to hand in his resignation. In no way was his authority diminished, however: he took to gadding about in a tailcoat with its waist cut high in the style of a military uniform, wore spurs on his boots, and sported a moustache, lest the local gentry think he had served in the infantry, which he contemptuously referred to as the 'infantilery', or sometimes just the 'infancy'.

He frequented all the country fairs, where the heart and soul of Russia—consisting of its mothers and children, its daughters and fat landowners—would gather for entertainment, rolling up in an assortment of the most ridiculous and outlandish britschkas, gigs, tarantasses, and carriages. He sniffed out the quarters of the local cavalry regiment and paid his respects to the officers. With great adroitness he would spring from his spindly chaise or droshky and present himself to them, and in no time at all he would be on the friendliest footing. During the last election he had thrown a magnificent dinner for the local gentry, at which he proclaimed that if they elected him as their marshal he would greatly enhance their standing. All in all, he conducted himself—as country folk would say—like a proper squire, married a comely wife, who brought him a dowry of two hundred souls and several thousand roubles. This capital was instantly squandered on three handsome pairs of horses, gilt locks for the doors, a tame monkey for the house, and a French major-domo. He added the two hundred souls to two hundred of his own and mortgaged them all to finance various business ventures. In short, he was everything a landowner should be, an exemplar of the species.

There were, besides him, several other landowners at the dinner, but nothing special can be said about them. The other guests were all officers from the same regiment and two staff officers: a colonel and a fat major. The general himself was a big, beefy man, yet, according to his officers, a good commander. He spoke in a rather thick and ponderous bass voice.

The dinner was exceptional: from the abundance of sturgeon, beluga, sterlet, bustards, asparagus, quails, partridges, and mushrooms it was clear that the cook had not stopped to eat or sleep for two days on end. He was assisted by four soldiers who, knives in hand, had toiled the night through preparing *fricassées* and *gêlées*. The multitude of bottles—long, slender flagons of Château Lafite,* and tubby, short-necked carboys of Madeira—the splendid summer's day, windows thrown wide open, dishes of ice on the table, the nethermost button on the gentlemen's waistcoats left undone, the oversized tailcoats and crumpled shirt-fronts of the guests, the crossfire of conversation, drowned by the general's booming voice and washed down with champagne—a scene of perfect harmony. After dinner all the diners rose with an agreeable heaviness in their stomachs and, lighting long and short-stemmed pipes, stepped out on to the porch with cups of coffee in their hands.

The general, the colonel, and even the major had unbuttoned their tunics, revealing aristocratic suspenders of the best silk, but the gentlemen officers observed proper decorum and kept their tunics fastened, loosening only the bottom three buttons.

'Now I'll let you see her,' announced the general. 'I say, my good man,' he continued, turning to his adjutant, a sharp-witted young man with a pleasant mien, 'tell them to bring the bay mare! Then you shall see for yourselves.' Whereupon the general drew deeply on his pipe and released a plume of smoke: 'She's still not in proper fettle—this confounded backwater has no decent stable. But this beast of mine'—*puff, puff*—'you'll see, she's a fine specimen!'

'And, may it please Your Excellency'—*puff, puff*—'have you had her long?' asked Chertokutsky.

Puff, puff, puff, puff—'Well...'—*puff*—'not that long. It's only two years since I collected her from the stud farm!'

'And did Your Excellency take her already broken in, or did you have her broken in here?'

Puff, puff, puff, puh, puh...uh...uh...ff—'Here.' As he said this, the general disappeared in a cloud of smoke.

In the mean time a soldier came hurrying from the stable, the sound of hooves could be heard and then another soldier appeared. This one wore a white, tent-like cloak and sported enormous black moustaches; by its bridle he led forward a trembling, terrified horse, which suddenly jerked its head upwards and almost lifted the soldier, moustaches and all, clean off the ground. 'Now, now, Agrafena Ivanovna!' he scolded, coaxing the mare up to the porch.

The mare's name was Agrafena Ivanovna and she was as spirited and wild as a southern belle. Stepping on to the wooden porch she nervously drummed her hooves, then came to a sudden standstill.

Putting down his pipe, the general gazed contentedly at Agrafena Ivanovna. The colonel stepped down from the porch and took Agrafena Ivanovna by the muzzle. The major patted Agrafena Ivanovna's leg and the others clicked their tongues approvingly.

Chertokutsky also came down from the porch and walked behind the mare. Firmly grasping the bridle, the soldier drew himself to attention and stared fixedly into the guests' eyes.

'A very pretty beast!' said Chertokutsky: 'Excellent points! Permit me to ask, Your Excellency, how does she ride?'

'She has a good stride; only... confound him... that fool of a vet gave her some pills, and for the last two days she's done nothing but sneeze.'

'A fine horse, a very fine horse. And tell me, Your Excellency, do you have the right sort of carriage?'

'Carriage?.. But this is a riding horse.'

'Of course, of course; I was merely inquiring whether Your Excellency might have the right sort of carriage for your other horses.'

'Well now, I don't have all the carriages I need. I must confess, for some time now I've wanted a nice modern calash. I wrote to my brother about it—he's in St Petersburg now, you know—but I'm not sure whether he'll send one or not.'

'If you ask me, Your Excellency,' observed the colonel, 'you won't find a better calash than the ones they make in Vienna.'

'You're quite right there,' *puff, puff, puff*.

'Now I have a fine calash, Your Excellency, a genuine Viennese calash.'

'Which? The one you came in?'

'Oh, no. That one's just for getting about, I use it for daily visits, but you should see my other one... It's remarkable, as light as a feather and if Your Excellency were to sit in it, you would swear— if Your Excellency will pardon the expression—your nurse was rocking you in the cradle.'

'Comfortable, you mean?'

'Very, very comfortable; the cushions, the springs—all top-notch.'

'That's good.'

'And so roomy! To be honest, Your Excellency, I've never seen another like it. When I was still in service, I could fit ten bottles of rum and twenty pounds of tobacco into the carriage-boxes, and then about half a dozen uniforms, my linen and two tobacco pipes, Your Excellency, the long ones they call—if you'll pardon the expression—tapeworms, and the side pockets are so big you could stuff an ox into them whole.'

'That's good.'

'I paid four thousand for it, Your Excellency.'

'To judge by the price, it should be a good vehicle. Did you buy it yourself?'

'No, Your Excellency; it came to me by pure chance. A friend of mine bought it, a rare fellow, a childhood chum, a fellow you would get along with famously; he and I are the closest friends—we share everything. I won it from him at cards. Might Your Excellency do me the honour of being my guest at luncheon tomorrow, and we can inspect the calash together?'

'I find myself at something of a loss. It's rather difficult for me alone... Might I perhaps come with my fellow officers?'

'Your fellow officers are also most welcome. Gentlemen, I would deem it the greatest honour and pleasure to receive you in my home!'

The colonel, the major, and the other officers returned thanks with respectful bows.

'As for me, Your Excellency, I am of the opinion that if one is to buy something it should be of the very best, and if it's no good, it's not worth obtaining. Now tomorrow, when you honour me with your presence, I shall show you a few little items I've introduced about my estate.'

The general gazed at him and released a puff of smoke into the air.

Chertokutsky was delighted to have invited the gentlemen officers. He was already choosing the pâtés and gravies while he beamed happily at his future guests; furthermore, he could tell from the looks in their eyes, from their gestures and half-bows and so forth, that he had risen in the estimation of the gentlemen officers. Chertokutsky's manner became more familiar and his voice took on a tone of languor—the voice of a man agreeably burdened with pleasure.

'What's more, Your Excellency, you shall make the acquaintance of the lady of the house.'

'It will be my great pleasure,' said the general, stroking his moustaches.

At this point Chertokutsky resolved to return home without further delay, to make an early start on preparations for the forthcoming dinner; he was about to pick up his hat but somehow or other ended up staying a little longer. In the mean time card tables had been set out in the general's chambers; soon the entire company divided into foursomes for whist and took their seats here and there around the room.

Candles were borne in. For a long while Chertokutsky could not make up his mind to sit down and play. But since the gentlemen officers were urging him to join in, he decided it would be bad form to decline. He sat down. Mysteriously, there appeared before him a glass full of rum punch, which he promptly dispatched without a moment's thought. After playing two rubbers, he found another glass of punch by his elbow, and this too he downed absent-mindedly, after declaiming: 'It's time I was getting on home, gentlemen, it really is time.' Nevertheless, he sat down for a second game.

Meanwhile, private conversations had struck up in various corners of the room. The whist-players were taciturn by and large, but those who had elected not to play lounged on the sofas that lined the room, deep in conversation. In one corner, a captain of cavalry reclined on a cushion, a pipe clenched between his teeth, and thus ensconced regaled a circle of rapt listeners with a spicy, fluent account of his amorous exploits. A fat landowner, with short arms not unlike two overgrown potatoes, listened with a look of the utmost sweetness as he tried, now and then, to stretch one short, pudgy arm across his broad *derrière*, in the hope of reaching his snuff-box. Elsewhere a heated quarrel had flared up on the subject of cavalry drill, and from his own corner Chertokutsky, who had twice played a jack for a queen, kept butting into this conversation and shouting such questions as: 'What year was that?' or 'What regiment was he from?'—unaware that his questions were often at cross purposes.

Finally, a few minutes before supper, the whist game came to a stop, but it tarried in the guests' conversation. Everyone, it seemed, had whist on the mind. Chertokutsky distinctly recalled winning a great deal, yet there appeared to be no winnings for him to pick up from the table; when he rose to his feet, he stood for a long time in the attitude of a man who finds he has no handkerchief in his pocket. In the mean time supper was served. There was—it goes without saying—no shortage of wine; Chertokutsky was obliged to keep refilling his glass, more or less involuntarily, because to right and to left of his place at table stood a great number of bottles.

The conversation round the table seemed interminable; furthermore, it was conducted in a most peculiar manner. A landowner old enough to have served in the 1812 campaign* recounted a battle which had never taken place and then, for some unfathomable reason, removed the stopper from a decanter and plunged it into a cake. In short, when the party started to disperse it was already three o'clock, and the coachmen had to gather up some of the guests in their arms as a shopper might gather up an armful of parcels. For all his noble breeding, Chertokutsky bowed so low in his calash and swung his head about with such panache that he arrived home with two thistles in his moustache.

In the house everything and everyone was sound asleep; after much searching, the coachman rousted out the valet, who supported his master across the drawing-room and handed him over to a housemaid, behind whom Chertokutsky somehow managed to crawl to his bedroom. He flopped down next to his young, pretty wife, who looked so charming as she reclined in her snowy-white nightgown. The commotion created by her spouse as he collapsed on to the bed awoke her. She stretched, lifted her lashes and fluttered her eyelids three times in quick succession; finally she opened her eyes with a half-annoyed smile, but when she observed that her companion was definitely not going to vouchsafe her any marks of his affection, she peevishly turned her back to him and, resting her fresh cheek on her hand, soon joined him in sleep.

When the young mistress finally awoke beside her snoring spouse, the clock had reached an hour no longer deemed early by country-folk. Recalling that it had been past three o'clock when he returned home the previous night, she decided to spare him and let him sleep. She put on the bedroom slippers specially ordered by her husband from St Petersburg, and, the soft folds of her white dressing-gown flowing like water over her limbs, closeted herself in the bathroom, washed her face with water as fresh as herself and sat down at her dressing-table. Glancing once or twice into the mirror, she concluded that she was looking rather well that day. This apparently insignificant circumstance was sufficient for her to sit before the mirror precisely two hours longer than usual. At last she rose and dressed, and, looking quite lovely, stepped out into the garden for some air.

As if by design, the day was as splendid as only a summer day in the south can be. The heat of the sun, which was at the meridian, beat down with its full force, but the dense foliage protected the garden paths and offered cool shade in which to stroll, and the flowers, warmed by the sun's rays, were triply fragrant.

The pretty young mistress of the house had quite forgotten that it was already twelve o'clock and her husband was still asleep. The post-prandial snores of two coachmen and one postilion, who lay fast asleep in the stable behind the garden, carried to her ears. But she remained seated on the shady garden path, from where she could watch the open road below. As she gazed absently at its deserted, unpeopled surface, a cloud of dust rising in the far distance suddenly caught her attention. Peering closer, she soon made out several carriages. Out in front came a light, two-seater cabriolet, with an open canopy; in it rode a general, whose bulging epaulettes glinted in the sun, and next to him a colonel. Behind the cabriolet came a four-seater chaise; in it sat a major with the general's adjutant and, facing them, two other officers; behind the chaise came the by-now familiar regimental droshky, which had passed into the possession of the fat major; behind the droshky, a four-seater *bonvoyage*, conveying four officers on the seats, with a fifth squeezed in between them; behind the *bon-voyage* she could make out three officers on handsome bay horses with dark, dapple markings.

'Surely they're not coming to see us?' she wondered. 'Oh my God! They've turned on to the bridge—they are!'

She shrieked, wrung her hands and flew over the flower-beds and through the shrubbery right into the room where her husband lay abed. He was still sleeping like a log.

'Get up! Get up! Quickly, get up!' she cried, tugging at his arm.

'Huh?' mumbled Chertokutsky and stretched, his eyes still closed.

'Get up, pumpkin! We have visitors! Do you hear? Visitors!'

'Visitors? What visitors?' This said, he made a little moan, like a calf mooing as it nuzzles around its mother's udder in search of a teat. 'Mmm,' he mumbled, 'come, my lambkin, let me have your slender neck: I want to give you a kiss.'

'Sweetheart, for heaven's sake, get up, get up at once. It's the general and his officers! Oh my God, you've got thistles in your moustache.'

'The general? You mean, he's on his way here already? Why in damnation did no one wake me? And what about the luncheon, the luncheon, has it been prepared? Is everything ready?'

'What luncheon?'

'What—did I not give orders?'

'You? Orders? You arrived home at four in the morning and wouldn't answer any of my questions. I didn't wake you, my pumpkin, because I felt sorry for you: you had had no sleep...' These last words she spoke in a particularly languid and suppliant tone.

Chertokutsky lay for a minute on his bed, his eyes staring wildly, as if jolted awake by a bolt of thunder. Finally he sprang from the bed clad only in his night-shirt, forgetting that this was most indecorous.

'God, I'm such an ass!' he exclaimed, beating his brow. 'I invited them to luncheon. What shall we do? Are they far off?'

'I'm afraid not... They're likely to arrive any minute.'

'Sweetheart... Go and hide!... Hoy, who's out there? You, girl!

Quickly come here, on the double—what are you scared of, you dolt? The officers will be here any moment now. Tell them the master's not at home, that he won't be coming back, that he left early this morning, do you hear? And tell all the other servants, quickly, get moving!'

This said, he snatched up his dressing-gown and ran to the carriage shed, hoping to find safe concealment somewhere inside. But when he stood in the corner of the shed he realized that even here he could be spotted.

'Ha! The very spot,' he declared in a flash of inspiration, and quickly pulled down the steps of the calash that stood right before him, leapt inside, slammed the door shut and, just to be on the safe side, pulled the carriage apron and sheepskin coverlet over him. He lay very, very still, curled up in his dressing-gown.

In the mean time the visitors' carriages had driven up to the front porch.

The general alighted and gave himself a good shake; the colonel followed, adjusting the plume on his helmet. Then the fat major thudded down from the droshky, clutching his sabre beneath his arm. After him the slender subalterns sprang nimbly from the *bon-voyage*; then the ensign, who had been squeezed in between them, alighted; last of all, the mounted officers, who had looked so dashing as they rode along, leapt from their saddles.

'The master's not at home,' said the footman, coming out on to the porch.

'What do you mean: not at home? He will be back for lunch, I presume?'

''Fraid not. The master's gone out for the day. He won't be back until about this hour tomorrow.'

'Well I'll be damned!' said the general. 'What the devil's going on?..'

'I imagine it's a little joke,' said the colonel, with a little laugh.

'I should hardly think so—what sort of joke is this?' continued the general, by now visibly displeased. 'Damnation... Damn and blast... Well, if he wasn't going to be in, why did he bother inviting us?'

'I agree, Your Excellency; I don't see how anyone could do such a thing,' said one young officer.

'What's that?' said the general, who habitually used this interrogative form when addressing a subaltern.

'I was saying, Your Excellency: I ask myself how anyone could behave in such a fashion.'

'Indeed... Well, perhaps something cropped up—still, he could at least have let us know, or not asked us over in the first place.'

'Well, Your Excellency, there's nothing for it, let's go back!' said the colonel.

'You're quite right, there's nothing more to be done. Mind you, we could have a look at the calash even if he's not here. I doubt he took it with him. I say, you there, step over here, my good man!'

'Yes Sir; what can I do for you?'

'Are you the stable-hand?'

'That's me, Your Excellency.'

'Show us the new calash, the one your master acquired the other day.'

'Yes sir! Follow me into the shed!'

The general and his officers betook themselves to the shed.

'First let me pull it out for you, it's dark in here.'

'Never mind, it'll do where it is!'

The general and his officers walked round the calash, carefully examining wheels and springs.

'Well, I don't see what all the fuss is about,' said the general, 'it's a perfectly ordinary calash.'

'Nothing much to look at, even,' said the colonel, 'nothing special about it at all.'

'If you ask me, Your Excellency, it's surely not worth four thousand,' said one of the young officers.

'What's that?'

'I was saying, Your Excellency, that I don't think it's worth four thousand.'

'Four thousand, my foot! It's not worth two. There's nothing to it, nothing at all. Perhaps there's something special about the inside?.. I say, my good man, unfasten the coverlet...'

And there, before the eyes of the officers, lay Chertokutsky, hunched in a preposterous position and wrapped in his dressing-gown.

'Ah, here you are!...' said the general in surprise.

And with that he slammed the door shut, pulled the apron back over Chertokutsky and drove off, together with the gentlemen officers.

DIARY OF A MADMAN

Today the most extraordinary thing happened to me. I rose rather late this morning, and when Mavra brought me my polished boots I asked her the time. Learning that ten o'clock had long since struck I dressed with great haste. I must confess I almost did not bother to go to the department* at all, knowing in advance what a sour face our section head would make. As it is, for ages he has been saying to me: 'What's the matter with you, man, are you completely addled? Sometimes you dash around so wildly and get your work into such a tangle that Satan himself couldn't sort it out, with small letters where there should be capitals, and no date or number at the top of the page.' Damn him, the old crow! I expect he envies me sitting in the director's study and sharpening HE's quills.

As I was saying, I wouldn't have gone to work if it hadn't been for the chance of seeing the paymaster and squeezing an advance on my salary out of the old Jew. There's another one for you! You won't catch him giving you your wages a month in advance—good God no, not until kingdom come. You can beg until you're blue in the face, but he won't give in, the old pinchfist, not even if you're starving. Yet at home his own kitchenmaid slaps his face. Everyone knows that. I don't see the advantage of serving in our department. The job has nothing to offer. Now it's quite a different story in the *gubernia* administration and the civil and treasury chambers:* take one of those chaps hunched in his corner and scribbling away. He may wear the filthiest old tailcoat and have a mug ugly enough to make you spit, but just look at the country villa he rents! Don't try buttering him up with a gilt porcelain tea-cup: 'That,' he will say, 'is a present for a doctor.' He won't accept anything less than a pair of coach-horses, or a droshky or a three-hundred-rouble beaver coat. He may look the retiring type, with such a courteous turn of phrase: 'Could I trouble you for the loan of your knife to sharpen a quill?' he'll ask, and the next moment he'll fleece some petitioner so ruthlessly that the wretched fellow is left with nothing but the clothes on his back. Admittedly, in our department we perform a noble service, and the place is kept spick and span in a way the gubernia administration could never imagine possible, with mahogany desks and courteous treatment from our superiors. Yes, I must say that if it weren't for the nobility of the job I would have left the department long ago.

I put on my old coat and took an umbrella, because it was pouring with rain. There was no one on the streets, except for a few old women sheltering beneath the skirts of their coats, Russian merchants bearing umbrellas, and here and there the odd coachman. Of the noble elements of the human race I could see only one specimen, a fellow official weaving along. I saw him at the crossroads, and at once said to myself: 'Aha! Oh no, my good man, I know you, you're not on your way to the department, you're chasing after that young lady tripping along there, and looking at her pretty little ankles.' What a creature he is, our fellow civil servant! Honest to God, he's a match for any officer: just let some pretty young miss walk past in her bonnet and he will be sure to latch on to her.

While occupied by these thoughts I saw a carriage drive up to the shop I was walking past at that moment. I at once recognized it: it was our director's carriage. But he has no reason to be calling at a shop, I thought, 'it must be his daughter, not him.' I pressed up against the wall. A footman opened the carriage door and she flitted forth like a little bird. She glanced right and left, her eyebrows trembled, her eyelashes fluttered... Dear God above! That's it, I thought, I've had it now, I've really had it. But why did she have to drive out in such heavy rain? Don't try and tell me that women aren't a little crazy when it comes to clothes. She did not recognize me, and I tried to conceal myself deeper in the folds of my coat, because the coat was covered with stains and, to make matters worse, quite out of fashion. Nowadays people wear cloaks with tall collars, while mine had several collars one on top of the other, and all of them short, and the cloth was of very inferior quality.

Her little dog was not quick enough to slip through the shop door and remained on the pavement. I know this little dog: she's called Madgie. I had not waited there a full minute before I suddenly heard a squeaky little voice say: 'Why, hello Madgie!' So fancy that! Who could it be? I peeked round and glimpsed two ladies walking beneath an umbrella: one old, the other young; but as soon as they passed I heard a voice beside me say: 'Shame on you, Madgie!' What the devil was going on? And then I saw Madgie exchanging sniffs with another little dog, which was trotting along behind the ladies. 'Well!' I said to myself, 'enough of this nonsense, surely I'm not drunk?' But it's a rare thing for me to get drunk. 'No, Fidèle, you're wrong to think that,' I could see Madgie saying, 'I was,'—*woof, woof*!—'I was'—*woof, woof*!—'very sick.' Fancy a little dog talking like that! I must confess I was very surprised to hear it.

But afterwards, when I had thought it all out properly, I stopped being surprised. There have been many similar cases in the world already. They say that somewhere in England a fish swam to the surface and said two words in such a strange language that scholars have been racking their brains for the last three years and still can't fathom what they mean. I also read in the papers about two cows which went into a shop and asked for a pound of tea. But I must admit I was much more surprised when I heard Madgie say: 'I wrote to you, Fidèle; Polkan* obviously didn't deliver my letter!' I swear—I'd stake my salary on it!—never in my life have I heard of a dog that could write. Only a gentleman knows how to write properly. There are of course a few shopkeepers and even the occasional serf who can copy things, but their writing is largely mechanical: without commas, full-stops, or any sort of style.

Now I was truly amazed. I must confess that of late I have started to hear and see things that no one before has ever seen or heard. 'I know what,' I said to myself, 'I'll follow this dog and find out who she is and what she's up to.'

I unfurled my umbrella and set off in pursuit of the two ladies. We crossed over to Gorokhovaya Street, turned on to Meshchanskaya, from there made our way to Stolyarnaya, and finally came out at the Kokushkin Bridge* and halted in front of a large house. 'I know this house,' I said to myself. 'It's the Zverkov house.'* What an establishment! The number of people living in that place; all those kitchenmaids, all those Poles!—And as for our fellow clerks, they're packed in there like dogs. I even have a friend amongst them, who plays the trumpet rather well. The ladies ascended to the fifth floor. Very well, I thought: I shall go no further now, but make a note of the place and will be sure at the first opportunity to avail myself of it.

Today is Wednesday, and consequently I was called to the director's house, to his study. I intentionally arrived a little early and sitting down to work soon sharpened all his quills. Our director must be a very wise man. All the walls of his study are covered with bookcases. I read a few of the titles: such erudition, such learning, way above the head of your average civil servant. They were all either in French or in German. Take one look at him: you'll be amazed at the glow of importance shining from his eyes! I've never yet heard him pronounce a superfluous word. Except perhaps when you're handing in some document he might ask: 'What's it like outside?' 'Damp, Your Excellency!' Yes, he's a cut above the average clerk all right! A man of state. I've noticed, however, that he is particularly fond of me. If only the same were true of his daughter... Phew! what a thought...

Never mind, my lips are sealed!—Been reading the *Bee*.* Stupid lot, these French. What do they want anyway? If you ask me the whole lot of them should be flogged! I read an extremely pleasing description of a ball, rendered by a Kursk landowner, in the same issue. Kursk landowners have a way with words. At this point I noticed that it was already half past twelve, and his lordship had not yet emerged from his bedroom. But at around half past one an event took place which no pen could describe. The door opened and I thought it was the director, so I leapt to my feet with my papers; but it was her, her young ladyship! Holy fathers, you should have seen how she was dressed! She wore a dress as white as a swan: such a splendid dress! And her eyes sparkled like the sun, I swear, just like the sun! She bowed and said: 'Papa hasn't been in, has he?' Heavens, what a voice! As sweet as a canary's. 'Your Ladyship,' I was on the point of saying, 'do not have me put to death, but if it is your will, let me be executed by your imperial little hand.' But, confound it, my tongue stuck to my palate and all I could blurt out was: 'No ma'am.' She looked at me, then at the books and dropped her handkerchief. I dashed to pick it up, slipped on the cursed parquet floor and almost squashed my nose. Somehow I managed to keep my footing and recovered her handkerchief. Saints above, what a handkerchief! The finest cambric—the very shadow of cloth! And so redolent of generalship. She thanked me, with a slight smile barely touching her honeyed lips, and after this was gone.

I sat there for another hour, until suddenly a footman came in and said: 'You may go home, Aksenty Ivanovich, the master has already left the house.' I can't stand the footman type: always slouching about in the hallway and never bothering so much as to nod their heads. And that's not the worst of it: once one of these rascals had the presumption to offer me some of his snuff, without even rising from his seat. I will have you know, you stupid peasant, that I am an official, I am of noble extraction. Still, I took my hat and put on my coat myself, because these characters will never hold it for you, and departed. Most of the day I spent at home lying on my bed. Then I copied down some very good verses:

> My sweetheart an hour I saw not,
> And thought a whole year had gone by;
> And thus was my life made sheer torment,
> 'No more shall I live,' I did sigh.*

By Pushkin, I should think. Towards evening, wrapping myself up in my coat I went to HE's gateway and hung about for a long time in the hope that she might come out and get into her carriage, so that I might have another look at her—but no, she did not emerge.

6 November

The section head really made me mad. When I came to work he summoned me and started speaking to me like this: 'Well, what exactly do you think you're playing at?'—'What do you mean? I'm not playing at anything,' I answered.—'Now listen here: after all, you're over 40 now—time you had your wits about you. What do you think you're up to? Do you imagine I don't know about all your goings-on? Fancy chasing around after the director's daughter! Now just take a look at yourself, and ask yourself who you think you are? You're nothing, less than nothing. You haven't a brass copeck to your name. Take a look in the mirror at your face—how can you even think of such things!' Confound him, just because he has a face like an apothecary's alembic with his hair twisted up into a little cockscomb and held in place with scented pomade, he thinks he can get away with murder. I know, I know why he's angry with me. He's envious; he probably saw the signs of favour manifested in my direction. Well I spit on him! It's no great shakes to be an aulic councillor.* Fix a gold chain to your watch, order a thirty-rouble pair of boots—who the devil does he think he is? Am I descended from a line of half-educated peasants, or tailors, or under-officers? I'm a born gentleman. I may yet rise high in the service. I'm only 42—that's the age at which your career really only begins. Just you wait, my friend! We'll be a colonel yet, and who knows, God willing, perhaps something even a little higher, and we'll earn ourselves a better reputation than yours. What on earth gave you the idea that you're such a paragon? Just give me a dress coat tailored in the latest fashion by Rutsch* and a cravat like yours and you won't be able to hold a candle to me. I just don't have the funds, that's the trouble.

8 November

Went to the theatre. Saw a play about the Russian fool Filatka.* I had a good laugh. There was also some farce with comic poems about scriveners and pettifoggers in general, and a certain collegiate registrar in particular. Such free language that I was surprised it got past the censor: it said about merchants that they cheat people, that their sons are debauched and try to worm their way into the upper classes. There was a very witty couplet about journalists too: that they like to abuse everything and everyone, and the author seeks the audience's protection. These modern authors write some devilish amusing plays. I do love a good play. As soon as I have a few copecks in my pocket, off I go to the theatre, and nothing will stop me. But as a whole civil servants are ignorant pigs: nothing will drag them to the theatre, unless you give them free tickets. There was some very nice singing by an actress. It reminded me of you know... oh, rats!... never mind, my lips are sealed.

9 November

At eight o'clock I set off for the department. The section head pretended he had not seen me come in at all. I also behaved as though nothing had passed between us. I looked over and checked some papers. Knocked off at four. Walked past the director's residence, but could not see anyone. Spent most of the time after dinner lying on my bed.

11 November

Today I sat in our director's study, sharpened twenty-three quills for him and four quills for her—Oh, bliss!... for her Ladyship. He always likes to have a lot of quills standing ready. Heavens! What a mind that man must have! Doesn't say a thing, but I reckon he's sifting through it all in his head. If only I knew what he was thinking about, what was brewing in that skull of his. I'd like to have a closer look at the way these gentlefolk live, to watch all their little niceties and courtly goings-on, and to see how they behave when they're by themselves—that's what I'd like to know! On several occasions I've tried to strike up a conversation on the subject with HE, but, confound it, my tongue simply will not obey: I can only get it to say that it's warm or cold outside and nothing more. I'd like to peek into their drawing-room, where sometimes you can see an open door leading into yet another room. Lord, the richness, the finery! The mirrors and the fine china! I'd like to have a look in there, in her Ladyship's half of the house, that's what I'd like! I'd sneak into the boudoir, where she has all her little pots and phials, and such exquisite flowers that you wouldn't dare breathe on them, I'd see her dress lying there, so ethereal it is more like air than a dress. Oh, for a look into the bedroom.... In there I reckon you would see something truly wondrous, you would find a paradise to surpass even that in heaven. You would see the little stool on which she places her dainty foot as she alights from her bed, and see her drawing on her snow-white stocking... Oh, rats! Never mind... my lips are sealed.

Today, in a sudden flash of inspiration, I remembered the conversation between those two dogs which I heard on Nevsky Prospect. 'Very well,' I thought to myself, 'now I'll find out everything. I must get my hands on the letters which those good-for-nothing dogs are writing to each other. I'm bound to learn something from them.' I must confess, once I even called Madgie over and said to her: 'Listen Madgie, we're on our own now, and if you like I'll lock the door so no one will be able to see us, so why don't you tell me everything you know about your mistress, what she's like and so on? I give you my word that I'll not let anyone in.' But the sly little creature put her tail between her legs, cringed, and slunk out of the room as if she had heard nothing. I've long suspected that dogs are far more intelligent than people; I was even convinced that they are able to speak but are only prevented from doing so by their great stubbornness. Dogs are remarkable politicians: they notice everything, every move a person makes. No, I don't care what happens, tomorrow I'm going to the Zverkov house to ask Fidèle a few questions and, if I can, I'll get hold of all the letters she's received from Madgie.

12 November

Set off at two in the afternoon to see Fidèle and put a few questions to her. I cannot abide cabbage, and there's a stink of cabbage wafting from all the shops along Meshchanskaya; to make matters worse there's such an infernal stench seeping from under the door of every house that I had to hold my nose and run at full speed. Added to which the uncouth craftsmen generate such a mass of soot and smoke in their workshops that it is quite impossible for any person of noble birth to promenade here. When I climbed to the sixth floor and rang the doorbell a young girl came out, quite pretty, and with little freckles. I recognized her. She was the girl who had been walking with the old lady. She blushed slightly and I caught on at once: 'Aha, my darling,' I thought, 'you want a husband.' 'What can I do for you?' she asked. 'I wish to talk to your dog.' Such a stupid girl! I could see at once that she was stupid.

At that moment the dog ran up barking; I tried to grab it but the evil little beast almost sank its teeth in my nose. But then I espied its bed in the corner. That, I thought, is just what I'm looking for. I stepped over to it, rummaged in the straw and to my great delight pulled out a small bundle of little pieces of paper. On seeing this the nasty little brute first bit me on the calf and then, when it sniffed that I had taken the letters, started whining and fawning, but I said: 'Oh no, my beauty, goodbye!' and took to my heels. I'm sure the girl must have thought me quite mad because she was extremely alarmed.

When I got home I set to work right away and started studying these letters, because I don't see too well by candle-light. But as ill luck would have it, Mavra had decided to scrub the floor. These stupid Finnish women are such a nuisance with their cleanliness. So instead I went for a stroll to ponder over all these events. Now, at long last, I will find out about everything, all they do and think, what makes them tick, I'll get to the very bottom of things. These letters will tell me everything. Dogs are a smart crowd, they know all the political ins and outs and so everything's sure to be there, including a true picture of this man and of all his doings. They'll also contain something about her, the one who... Never mind, my lips are sealed! I got home towards evening. Spent most of the time lying on my bed.

13 November

Well now, let's have a look: the letters are fairly clearly written. There is something rather doggy in the handwriting, however. I'll read it out:

Dear Fidèle! I simply cannot get used to your pretentious name. You'd think they could have given you something a bit better! Fidèle, Rosa—such *mauvais ton*, but that is neither here nor there. I am very glad that we had the idea of writing to each other.

The letter's written most correctly. All the spelling and punctuation are correct, and even our section head couldn't write like that, despite his claims to have been to some university or other. Let's read on:

It seems to me that it is one of life's greatest blessings to share one's thoughts, feelings and impressions with another soul.

Hmm! An idea lifted from a book; something translated from the German. Don't remember the title.

I say this from experience, although I've seen no more of the world than the gates of our house. But do not think that my life does not brim with joy. My mistress, called Sophie by her papa, loves me to distraction.

Oh, rats!... Never mind, my lips are sealed.

Papa also often pets me. I drink tea and coffee with cream. Ah, *ma chère*, I must confess to you that I simply cannot see the attraction of the big, gnawed bones which our Polkan slavers over in the kitchen. Bones are only nice if they come from game-birds, and then only if no one has already sucked out the marrow. Another thing I like is a mixture of several sauces, but without capers and parsley; but I cannot think of anything worse than the stupid custom of giving dogs little pellets of bread. Sometimes we have a visitor who's been holding all sorts of rubbish in his hands, and he rolls these little balls of bread, then calls you over and thrusts them between your teeth. It seems impolite to refuse, so you have to eat them; revolting they may be, but eat them you must...

What the devil is all this? What a lot of tripe! As if she had nothing better to write about. Let's look at another page. Maybe it'll be more to the point.

I'm only too happy to let you know about everything happening in our house. I have already told you something about the main gentleman, whom Sophie calls papa. He is an extremely strange man.

Aha! Here we are at last! I knew it: they have a political outlook on everything. Let's see what she has to say about papa:

...an extremely strange man. Most of the time he remains silent. He rarely speaks; but last week he kept talking to himself, asking: 'Will I get it or not?' He would pick up a piece of paper in one hand, clench the other one and ask: 'Will I get it or not?' Once he turned to me and asked: 'What do you think, Madgie? Will I get it or not?' I could not understand a thing, so I merely sniffed his boot and walked away. Then, *ma chère*, papa came home a week later overjoyed about something. All that morning gentlemen in uniforms came to see him and congratulated him on something. At table papa was in better spirits than I've ever seen him before, telling jokes, and after dinner he lifted me up to his neck and said: 'Look at that, Madgie, what do you think that is?' I saw some ribbon. I sniffed it, but could not discern any interesting smell at all. So then, stealthily, I licked it: it was slightly salty.

Hm! If you ask me this dog has got out of hand, it should be whipped! And talk about vanity! It should be reported!

Farewell, *ma chère*! I must run and so on... and so forth. I'll finish this letter tomorrow. Well, hello again! I'm back with you once more. Today my mistress Sophie...

Aha! now we'll find out about Sophie. Oh, rats!... Never mind... let's carry on.

...my mistress Sophie was in a fearful flap. She was getting ready to go to a ball and I was delighted that I would have the chance to write to you while she was out. My Sophie is always terribly eager to go to balls, although she almost always gets angry while she's dressing. I can never understand the pleasure, *ma chère*, in going to these balls. Sophie returns from them at six in the morning, and I can always tell from her pale and haggard look that the poor thing hasn't had a bite to eat. I must admit I would never be able to live like that myself. Now if I had to go without my grouse in wine sauce, or roast chicken wings, I... well, I don't know what I would do. I also like gravy and wheatmeal. But I could never stomach carrots, or turnips, or artichokes...

Extraordinarily uneven style. You can see at once that it's not the work of a human being. She begins properly but ends with all this dog rubbish. Let's take a look at another letter. A bit on the long side. Huh—with no date.

Ah! my dear, how one can feel the approach of spring. My heart is already beating in expectation of something. There is a merry ringing in my ears. So I often just stand for minutes on end with one paw raised, looking at the door. I'll tell you a secret: I have many admirers. I often sit on the window-sill and watch them. Goodness, if you could see what gargoyles some of them are. There is one terribly coarse mongrel, a fearfully stupid beast, with stupidity written all over his face, who struts pompously along the street and imagines that he's some kind of noble being and that is how everyone else sees him. Not a bit of it. I didn't pay any attention to him, acting as if I hadn't seen him. And you should see the hideous mastiff that stopped in front of my window! If he had stood on his hind legs—mind you, I doubt whether he knows how, the oaf—he would have towered head and shoulders above my Sophie's papa, who's pretty tall himself, and fat with it. This great lump of a dog is dreadfully impudent. I growled at him, but did he turn a hair? Didn't even bat an eyelid! Instead he stuck out his tongue, drooped his enormous ears, and looked into the window—what a country bumpkin! But I hope you don't think, *ma chère*, that my heart is indifferent to all assailants—oh no ... I wish you could have seen one cavalier called Trésor, who climbed through the fence of the house next door. Ah, *ma chère*, you should have seen his handsome muzzle!

Pshaw!... What rubbish!... How can you fill a letter with such idiocy? Give me a human being any day! I want a human being before my eyes; I want sustenance to nourish and delight my soul and instead I must feed it such nonsense. Let's skip a page and maybe we'll turn up something better:

...Sophie was sitting at the little table and sewing something. I looked out of the window because I like watching the passers-by. Suddenly the foot-man came in and announced: 'Mr Teplov!' Ask him in,' called Sophie and rushed to embrace me. 'Oooh Madgie. Madgie! If only you knew who this is: dark-haired, a courtier—a Kammerjunker*—and such gorgeous eyes! Black and flashing, like fire.' And Sophie ran off into her room. A minute later the young Kammerjunker entered, with black whiskers: he stepped up to the mirror, smoothed down his hair, and examined the room. I gave a little growl and went back to the window. Sophie soon emerged and dropped a merry curtsey as he clicked his heels and bowed, while I behaved as if I noticed nothing, and continued to stare out of the window; I kept my head tilted a little to one side, however, and tried to listen to their conversation. And, *ma chère*, if you could have heard the rubbish they were talking! They were discussing some lady at a dance, and saying how, instead of dancing one figure, she danced another; and also that some fellow called Bobov looked just like a stork in his frilly shirt, and almost fell on his nose; that some Lidina fancies that she has blue eyes, when in actual fact her eyes are green—and so on. Lord, I thought to myself, imagine if you compared the Kammerjunker with Trésor. Heavens above! What a difference! For a start the Kammerjunker has a completely smooth, broad face, framed by whiskers, as if he had tied a black cloth around his mug, while Trésor has a slender nose, with a white flash on his brow. Nor is there any comparison between the courtier's figure and Trésor's. His eyes, habits, and manners are also all wrong. Dear me, what a difference! I can't imagine what she sees in her Kammerjunker. How can she admire him so?...

I also think there's something wrong here. This Kammerjunker cannot have turned her head like that. Let's read on:

I'm afraid that if she likes the Kammerjunker she'll soon start liking that clerk who sits in papa's office. Oh, *ma chère*, if only you could see that gargoyle. Just like a tortoise in an old sack . . .

Which clerk could that be?

He has the strangest name. He's always sitting there sharpening quills. The hair on his head is just like straw. Papa always sends him instead of his servant . . .

I have a feeling that guttersnipe dog is referring to me. What does she mean, my hair looks like straw?

Sophie simply cannot stop herself laughing when she looks at him.

You're lying, you horrible little dog! What a foul tongue! As if I can't tell that it's all spoken out of pure envy. As if I didn't know whose work all this is. It's the doing of the section head. That man has sworn his undying hatred of me and he does his damnedest to spite me at every step. Still, let's take a look at one more letter. Maybe it'll reveal what he's up to.

Ma chère Fidèle, you must forgive me for not having written for so long. I was in a state of sheer bliss. It's perfectly true what some writer said, that love is like a second lease of life. In addition, there are big changes taking place in our house. The Kammerjunker calls every day. Sophie is madly in love with him. Papa is in top spirits. Even our Grigory, you know, the sweeper who talks to himself, I even heard him say that there would be a wedding soon, because papa is determined to see Sophie marry either a general, or a Kammerjunker, or an army colonel...

What the devil! I can't read on... You have all the luck if you're a Kammerjunker or a general. All the best things in life, they all go to Kammerjunkers or generals. You find yourself a miserable piece of good fortune, and as soon as you stretch out your hand—along comes a Kammerjunker or a general to snatch it away. Damn it all! I would like to be a general myself, and not just so that I could marry her and all those other things. No; I would like to be a general merely in order to see how they would fawn on me with all their la-di-da airs and graces, and then I'd tell them that I spit on the pair of them. Damnation. How vexing! I tore the stupid pug's letters into tiny pieces.

3 December

It can't be true! They're lying! There can't be a wedding! So what if he is a Kammerjunker? After all, that's only a rank; it isn't something you can see, or you can hold in your hand. Just because you're a Kammerjunker it doesn't mean you get a third eye in the middle of your forehead. It's not as if his nose is made of gold: it's no different from mine or anyone else's; like anyone else he uses it for sniffing, and not eating, for sneezing and not coughing. I've already tried to work out the cause of these distinctions on several previous occasions. Why am I a titular councillor and what is the point of my being a titular councillor? Perhaps I'm really a count or general, and only appear to be a titular councillor? Perhaps I myself do not know who I am. After all, there are so many examples in history: you get some simple fellow, not by any means of gentle birth, but a simple working man, even a peasant—and suddenly it turns out that he's some sort of big shot, and sometimes even a king. If that can happen to a peasant, just imagine what a gentleman could turn out to be? Suddenly, for example, I could be walking around in a general's uniform, epaulette on my left shoulder, epaulette on my right shoulder, blue sash across my chest—how about that? Our little beauty will sing a different tune then, won't she? And what about papa—our director—what will he say? Of course, he's such a snob! He's a Mason, definitely a Mason,* although he gives himself such airs and graces, but I spotted at once that he's a Mason: when he shakes hands with someone he only holds out two fingers. And who's to say that at this very moment I won't be appointed governor general, or quartermaster or something else? I would really like to know why I should be a titular councillor? Why exactly a titular councillor?

5 December

Today I spent the whole morning reading the papers. There are strange things afoot in Spain. I can't even make them out properly. They write that the throne is empty and the grandees are in difficulties about electing an heir, which is leading to widespread perturbation. This strikes me as extremely strange. How can a throne be empty? They say that some doña* is supposed to accede to the throne. No doña can accede to a throne. It's quite impossible. There can only be a king on a throne. So, they say there's no king. It cannot happen that there's no king. No state can exist without a king. There is a king, but no one knows who he is. He's lying low somewhere, incognito, perhaps because of family reasons, or because of fears of attack from neighbouring powers, like France and other countries, which are forcing him into hiding, or perhaps there are some other reasons.

8 December

I was just on the point of going to work but various reasons and considerations prevented me. I simply cannot get this Spanish business out of my head. How can they possibly have some doña as their queen? Surely this won't be allowed. For a start England won't allow it. And then there are those political goings-on all over Europe: the Emperor of Austria, our own Tsar... I must admit, all these events have left me so completely devastated that I simply haven't been able to get down to anything all day. Mavra remarked that I was extremely distracted at the table. It's true, I appear to have thrown two plates on to the floor, and they both smashed. After dinner I walked around by the mountains. Couldn't discover anything instructive. Most of the time I lay on my bed and reflected on this business in Spain.

Today we celebrate a most illustrious event! Spain has a king. He
has been found. I am this king. And it was only today that I
discovered this. I must admit it suddenly dawned on me, in a flash.
I can't understand how I could ever have thought I was a titular
councillor. How could I have got this absurd idea into my head? It's
a lucky thing no one put me in a madhouse. Now everything has
been revealed to me. I see it all as clearly as my own hand. But
before this, I don't know why, before I seemed to see everything
through some sort of fog. I think this all can be explained by the
ridiculous idea people have that the brain is in the head. Nothing of
the kind: it is carried by the wind from the direction of the Caspian
Sea. First I informed Mavra who I am. When she heard that the
King of Spain was standing before her she clapped her hands and
almost died of fright. The silly girl—she's never seen a Spanish
king before. Nevertheless I endeavoured to calm her, assuring her
in benign words of my good favour, and insisting that I am not at
all angry if occasionally my boots are not cleaned too well. She's
just an ignorant peasant, after all. You can't talk to people like that
about higher things. She took fright because she was convinced that
all the kings in Spain looked like Philip II.* But I explained to her
that there is absolutely no resemblance between Philip and myself
and that I do not have a single Capuchin monk* in my entourage...
I did not go to work. To hell with the department! No, my friends,
you won't entice me back there; you won't catch me copying any
more of your detestable documents!

*Marchober the 86th.
Somewhere between day and night.*

Today our divisional manager came to say that I should come to the
department, that I hadn't been at work for more than three weeks.
So, just for a joke, I went. The section head obviously expected me
to bow to him and to start apologizing, but I gave him a nonchalant
look, not too angry and not too benevolent, and sat at my place as
if nothing had happened. I looked around at all the office rabble and
thought: 'If you only knew that amongst you sits... Lord God
above! The uproar you would create, and the section head himself

would start bowing and scraping before me, as he now does before the director.' They stuck some papers in front of me for me to make a summary. But I didn't lift a finger.

A few minutes later the place flew into a hubbub. Apparently the director was on his way. Many of the officials dashed forward jostling one another, hoping to be seen by the director. But I didn't budge. When he walked through our section everyone buttoned up their coats, but I didn't do a thing. Who do they think the director is? Am I to rise to my feet before him?—Not on your life! Director —I ask you! He's a cork, not a director. An ordinary, common-or-garden cork, no more. The sort you use to stop bottles. But what I found most amusing was the way they thrust some papers under my nose for me to sign. They thought that I would write at the very bottom of the sheet: 'desk head such-and-such,' what else? But I chose the most important place, where the department director signs his name, and wrote with a flourish: 'Ferdinand VIII.' You wouldn't believe the reverent silence that filled the room; but I merely nodded my head and said: 'There's no need for any signs of homage!' and departed.

From there I went straight to the director's apartments. He was not at home. The footman did not want to let me in, but I gave him such a mouthful he was quite stupefied. I went straight to the boudoir. She was sitting before her mirror, and on seeing me she leapt to her feet and retreated. I didn't tell her I was the king of Spain, however. I merely said that a happiness beyond her wildest dreams awaited her, and that, despite the ploys of our enemies, we would be united. I did not wish to say more and took my leave.

Women! Such deceitful creatures! Only now have I understood what they are. Until now no one has discovered who it is that women really love, but I can now reveal the truth: women are in love with the devil. I swear. Physicists write all sorts of nonsense, that women are one thing and another—but they love only the devil. You see that one over there, in the first circle, adjusting her lorgnette? You think she's looking at that fat gentleman with the star? Not a bit of it, she's looking at the devil standing behind his back. Now he's hidden behind the fat man's star. But look, he's beckoning to her from there with his finger. And she'll marry him. She will, I tell you. And all this lot, their high-ranking fathers, smarming around and oiling their way into the court, and putting it about that they are patriots and so on and so forth: all they're after, these patriots, is rent and more rent! They'd sell their own mother, father, their God for money, they're nothing but opportunists and Judases! All this vainglory and opportunism is caused by a little blister under their tongues containing a tiny worm the size of a pinhead, and this is all the handwork of a barber living on Gorokhovaya Street. I don't recall his name. But the whole conspiracy has been concocted by the Turkish sultan, who is bribing the barber and wants to spread Muhammadanism throughout the world. They say that the majority of the population in France have already adopted the faith of Muhammad.

> *The nothingth. There was no*
> *date today.*

I walked incognito along Nevsky Prospect. His Majesty the Emperor rode past. The entire town doffed their hats and I did likewise, although I gave no sign that I was the king of Spain. I thought it improper to reveal myself then and there to all; first one must be presented at court. The only thing that has prevented me from appearing at court is that I do not have any legal garb. If only I could get hold of a decent mantle. I would have ordered one from a tailor but these people are such asses and, to make matters worse, they totally neglect their work, as they are up to their ears in all sorts of shady business and spend most of the time paving the roads. I decided to make a mantle out of my new uniform, which I've only worn twice. But as these scoundrels would only spoil it, I decided to sew it myself, first locking the door so no one could watch. I cut it up into pieces with scissors, because it has to have quite a different pattern.

> *Don't remember the date. There*
> *was no month either. Devil knows*
> *what's going on.*

The mantle is quite ready and sewn now. Mavra cried out when I put it on. All the same, I haven't yet made up my mind to present myself at court. I still haven't received a deputation from Spain. It's not the right thing to go without deputies. It wouldn't be consistent with my rank and dignity. I'm expecting them at any minute.

I'm most surprised by the extreme tardiness of the deputies. What on earth can be detaining them? Surely not France? Yes, France is the most animadvertent of all the powers. I went to make enquiries at the post office, in case the Spanish deputies had arrived. But the postmaster is extremely stupid and does not know anything—'No,' he says, 'we have no Spanish deputies here, but if you wish to write a letter we will accept carriage for the appropriate payment.'—To the devil with him! What's a letter? It's rubbish. Apothecaries write letters...

Madrid. Februarius the Thirtieth

Well, here I am in Spain, and it all happened so quickly that I have not yet regained my senses. This morning the Spanish deputies came to see me and I got into a carriage together with them. I was astonished by its extraordinary speed. We moved at such velocity that in half an hour we had reached the Spanish frontier. Actually they have these iron roads all over Europe now and the ships travel at a tremendous speed. It's a strange place, Spain: when we went into the first room I saw a large number of people with shaved heads. I soon guessed that they must be Dominicans or Capuchins, however, because they shave their heads. I found the behaviour of the Chancellor of State extremely odd: he took me by the hand, pushed me into a small room and said: 'You sit here, and if you carry on calling yourself King Ferdinand I'll come and King Ferdinand you.' But I knew that he was only putting me to the test so I answered in the negative. For this the Chancellor whacked me so hard across the back with a stick that I almost cried out, but restrained myself, recalling that this is a chivalric custom on acceding to a higher office, because such customs survive to this day in Spain.

Once left alone I decided to get down to affairs of state. I discovered that Spain and China are one and the same and that it is only through sheer ignorance that they are regarded as two different countries. I advise everyone carefully to write on a piece of paper Spain and they will see the word China. I was extremely dismayed, however, by the event which is to take place tomorrow. Tomorrow at seven o'clock a strange phenomenon will be observed: the earth will sit on the moon. The famous English chemist Wellington has also written about this. I must admit, I experienced grave misgivings when I thought about the moon, how flimsy and tender it is. For the moon is usually made in Hamburg, and made extremely badly, I might add. I'm surprised that England hasn't turned her attention to this. The moon is made by a one-legged cooper, and you can see the idiot has no idea about moons at all. He put in a creosoted rope and some wood oil; and this has caused such a terrible stink all over the earth that you have to plug your nose. Another reason the moon is such a tender globe is that people cannot live on it any more, and only noses live on it now. This is also why we cannot see our own noses—they're all on the moon. And when I thought that the earth is a heavy object and could grind all our noses to a pulp once it sits on the moon I was overcome by such anxiety that I put on my stockings and shoes and hastened to the chamber of the State Council to direct the police not to allow the earth to sit on the moon. The Capuchins, of whom I found a great number in the chamber of the State Council, are extremely intelligent folk, and when I told them: 'Gentlemen, we must save the moon, because the earth wants to sit on it', they all dashed off at once to carry out my monarchical bidding. Many of them climbed up the wall in order to grab hold of the moon, but at that moment the Lord Chancellor came in. On seeing him everyone fled. As the king, I alone stayed behind. But the Chancellor, to my great surprise, hit me with a stick and chased me back to my room. It's astonishing what power popular customs have in Spain!

January of the same year, occurring after February

I still cannot understand what sort of a place this Spain is. The popular customs and court etiquette are quite extraordinary. I do not understand, I quite simply do not understand a thing. Today they shaved my head, although I screamed at the top of my voice that I had no desire to be a monk. But I can no longer remember what happened to me when they started dripping cold water on my head. I've never experienced such hell before in my life. I very nearly threw a fit, and they had difficulty holding me down. I simply cannot understand the point of this ridiculous custom. A stupid, pointless custom! Nor can I understand the irrational behaviour of the kings who through all the ages have done nothing to stamp it out. I'm starting to wonder, from all the signs, whether I haven't perhaps fallen into the hands of the Inquisition, and the chap I took to be the Chancellor isn't in fact the Grand Inquisitor. The only thing I can't quite understand is how a king could be subjected to the Inquisition. Of course, the whole thing might have been planned in France, by Polignac. Oh, that scoundrel Polignac!* He has sworn to hound me to death. And he persecutes me night and day, but I know, my friend, that you are being led by the English. The English are great schemers. They worm their way in everywhere. All the world knows that when England takes a pinch of snuff France sneezes.

25th day

Today the Grand Inquisitor came into my room, but I heard his footsteps from afar and hid under the chair. When he saw that I wasn't there he started to call me. First he shouted: 'Poprishchin!'— I didn't say a word. Then: 'Aksenty Ivanov! Titular Councillor! Gentleman!' I still held my tongue. 'Ferdinand VIII, King of Spain!' I was on the point of sticking out my head, but then I thought: 'Oh no, brother, you won't get me that easily! We know your tricks: you'll start pouring cold water on my head again.' He spotted me, however, and drove me out from under the chair with his stick. That cursed stick really hurts when it hits you! But I was compensated for all this by a discovery I have now made: I learnt that every cockerel has its own Spain, but it is under its feathers. The Grand Inquisitor stormed off in a rage, threatening some punishment. But I totally ignored his impotent fury, knowing that he functions like a automaton, that he is the tool of the English.

The th34 of yrae Λιυπιqɔɟ 349

No, I cannot stand any more of it. God! the things they are doing to me! They pour cold water on my head. They won't hear me, they won't see me, they won't listen to me. What have I done to them? Why do they torment me? What do they want from me, wretch that I am? What can I give them? I have nothing. I have no more strength, I cannot take all their torture, my head is burning and everything's spinning before my eyes. Save me! Take me away! Give me a troika with three horses as fast as the wind! Climb aboard, coachman, ring, my bells, fly up and away, horses, and bear me hence from this world! Further, further, where nothing more can be seen, nothing! Look at the sky unfurling there before me; a star twinkles in the distance; the forest streaks by with its dark trees and silver moon; a grey mist wreathes beneath the horses' hooves; a musical note rings out in the mist; on the one side lies the sea, on the other Italy; yonder Russian cottages come into sight. Is that not my house I can dimly see in the distance? Is that my mother sitting by the window? Mother, save your poor son! Shed a tear on his aching head and look how they torment him! Press your poor orphan child to your breast! There is no place for him on earth! He is persecuted!—Mother! have pity on your sick little child!... But did you know that the king of France has a wart right under his nose?

PLAYS

MARRIAGE

An utterly improbable occurrence in two acts

(written in 1833)*

CHARACTERS

AGAFYA TIKHONOVNA, a merchant's daughter, the marriageable
  girl
ARINA PANTELEIMONOVNA, her aunt
FYOKLA IVANOVNA, a matchmaker
PODKOLYOSIN, a functionary, by rank a court councillor*
KOCHKARYOV, his friend
PANCAKE,* a manager
ANUCHKIN, a retired infantry officer
ZHEVAKIN, a naval man
DUNYASHKA, a serving girl
STARIKOV, a shopkeeper
STEPAN, Podkolyosin's manservant

ACT ONE

SCENE I

[A bachelor's room.]

[PODKOLYOSIN alone, lying on a divan smoking his pipe.]

When you start thinking things through like this, at your leisure, you realize that there's nothing for it: marriage is the only way. What else is there, after all? You live and you live, and in the end you just can't take it any longer. Now I've gone and missed the marrying season again. When everything seemed to be ready, too, and the matchmaker has been calling to see me for the last three months. I should be ashamed of myself! Hey, Stepan!

SCENE II

[PODKOLYOSIN, STEPAN.]

PODKOLYOSIN. Hasn't the matchmaker come yet?

STEPAN. Not as yet.

PODKOLYOSIN. And did you go to the tailor?

STEPAN. I did.

PODKOLYOSIN. Well, is he working on my tailcoat?

STEPAN. He is.

PODKOLYOSIN. So, how far has he got?

STEPAN. Quite far. He's already doing the buttonholes.

PODKOLYOSIN. Come again?

STEPAN. I said: he's already doing the buttonholes.

PODKOLYOSIN. And didn't he ask: 'What does your master need a tailcoat for?'

STEPAN. No, he didn't.

PODKOLYOSIN. Perhaps he wondered whether your master was thinking of getting married?

STEPAN. No, he didn't wonder anything.

PODKOLYOSIN. All the same, you must have seen other tailcoats in his workshop? He sews for other people too.

STEPAN. It's true, he has a lot of tailcoats.

PODKOLYOSIN. Still, their cloth wouldn't be quite as good as mine would it?

STEPAN. It's true, I'd say yours was a bit smarter looking than theirs.

PODKOLYOSIN. Come again?

STEPAN. I said your cloth is smarter looking than theirs.

PODKOLYOSIN. Good. So, didn't he ask you why the master was having a tailcoat made from such fine cloth?

STEPAN. No.

PODKOLYOSIN. Didn't he say anything like, er, 'Is your master thinking of getting married?'

STEPAN. No, he didn't say anything like that.

PODKOLYOSIN. But I presume you told him what my rank is and which department I'm in?

STEPAN. I did.

PODKOLYOSIN. And what did he say to that?

STEPAN. He said: 'I'll see what I can do.'

PODKOLYOSIN. Good. Off you go, now.

[*Exit* STEPAN.]

SCENE III

[PODKOLYOSIN *alone*.]

The way I see it, a black tailcoat is somehow more imposing. Coloured ones are more for secretaries, titular secretaries, and other small fry, for underlings and the like. Those of us with a rather higher rank must try and look a little more, how do you say, er... damn, I've gone and forgotten the word! Such a good word, too, and I've forgotten it. Yes, by God, you can say what you like but a court councillor is just the same as a colonel, even if his uniform doesn't have epaulettes. Hey, Stepan!

SCENE IV

[PODKOLYOSIN, STEPAN.]

PODKOLYOSIN. Well, did you buy the polish?

STEPAN. I did.

PODKOLYOSIN. Where did you buy it? In that little shop I told you about, the one on Voznesensky Avenue?

STEPAN. The very one.

PODKOLYOSIN. So, is it good polish?

STEPAN. It's good.

PODKOLYOSIN. Have you tried cleaning my boots with it?

STEPAN. I have.

PODKOLYOSIN. Well, is it shiny?

STEPAN. Shiny, yes, it's good and shiny.

PODKOLYOSIN. And when he gave you the polish, didn't he ask anything? Didn't he say: 'What does the master need this polish for?'

STEPAN. Nope.

PODKOLYOSIN. Or maybe he said something like: 'Perhaps the master's thinking of getting married?'

STEPAN. No, he didn't say anything.

PODKOLYOSIN. Very well, off you go.

SCENE V

[PODKOLYOSIN *alone*.]

You would think that boots are nothing really, and yet if they're badly made and the polish is a bit on the red side, you won't get the same respect in good company. It's just not the same... But it's even worse if they give you corns. I can put up with anything, but not corns. Hey, Stepan!

SCENE VI

[PODKOLYOSIN, STEPAN.]

STEPAN. You called?

PODKOLYOSIN. Did you tell the shoemaker that I don't want any corns?

STEPAN. I did.

PODKOLYOSIN. And what did he say?

STEPAN. He said: 'Fine'.

[*Exit* STEPAN.]

SCENE VII

[PODKOLYOSIN, *then* STEPAN.]

PODKOLYOSIN. But it's a confounded rigmarole, all the same, this marriage business! First this, then that. And you have to make sure that everything's just so—no, God damn it, it's not as easy as they say. Hey, Stepan! [*Enter* STEPAN.] There was something else I wanted to tell you...

STEPAN. The old woman's here.

PODKOLYOSIN. Ah, she's come, has she? Ask her to come in. [*Exit* STEPAN.] Yes, it's such a business... it's not at all, er... it's a tough business.

SCENE VIII

[PODKOLYOSIN *and* FYOKLA.]

PODKOLYOSIN. Ah, good day, good day, Fyokla Ivanovna! Well? How are things? Take a chair, sit down and tell me everything. So, how is everything? What did you say she was called? Melanya, was it?...

FYOKLA. Agafya Tikhonovna.

PODKOLYOSIN. Ah yes, Agafya Tikhonovna. I suppose this is one of your 40-year-old maids, isn't it?

FYOKLA. No, no, not a bit of it. Just you wait: when you're married, you'll never be done thanking me and singing my praises.

PODKOLYOSIN. Come now, Fyokla Ivanovna, don't talk rot.

FYOKLA. I'm too old for talking rot, my good sir; only dogs talk rot.

PODKOLYOSIN. And the dowry, what about the dowry? Tell me again.

FYOKLA. Ah yes, the dowry. A stone house in the Moscow quarter, double-storey, and so nicely appointed it's a pleasure to see. They have a grain-merchant renting a stall on the ground floor, he pays seven hundred for it. The beer cellar also pulls in a big crowd. There are two wooden wings: one wing is completely wooden but the other's on a stone foundation; they bring in four hundred apiece. There's an allotment too, on the Vyborg Side:* a merchant's been renting it for the past three years, and he has it under cabbage; such a nice, sober merchant he is too, never takes a drink and he has three sons: he's already married off two of them. 'As for number three,' he says, 'he's still a youngster, let him sit in the shop for a while, and take some of the load off me. I'm old now,' he says, 'but let the boy sit in the shop, to help with the business.'

PODKOLYOSIN. And her ladyship, what's she like to look at?

FYOKLA. So refined! Fair-skinned, with red cheeks—peaches and cream, too lovely to describe. You'll be so-so delighted [*showing him how delighted he'll be*] that you'll say to all and sundry, your friends and enemies alike: 'It's all Fyokla Ivanovna's work, I'm so grateful to her!'

PODKOLYOSIN. But you say she's not from officer stock?

FYOKLA. She's the daughter of a merchant of the third guild. And such a daughter, that she would do credit to a general. She doesn't want to hear about any merchants. 'I don't care', she says, 'what a man looks like, he can be nothing to write home about, just so long as he's from a good family.' Such refinement! And come Sunday, when she puts on her silk dress: Saints in heaven, you should hear how it rustles! A princess, pure and simple!

PODKOLYOSIN. But you see, the reason I ask is because I'm a court councillor, and for me—well, I'm sure you understand...

FYOKLA. It's an old story, of course I understand. We had a court councillor before, and they wouldn't take him: he wasn't to their liking. He had such a funny manner about him: he couldn't open his mouth without telling a lie, and such whoppers too. But what can you do: that's the way God made him. He didn't like it either, but he couldn't stop himself from telling lies. That's just the way God willed it.

PODKOLYOSIN. And apart from this one, are there any others?

FYOKLA. Why should you want any others? This is the best you'll find.

PODKOLYOSIN. The very best?

FYOKLA. You could search the world over and you'd not find another like her.

PODKOLYOSIN. Let me give it some thought. Come back the day after tomorrow, and then we'll go over it all again, like now: I'll have a little lie-down and you'll tell me all about it.

FYOKLA. Come now, sir, have a heart! I've been calling on you for nearly three months, and all to no avail. All you can do is sit there in your dressing-gown, sucking away on your pipe.

PODKOLYOSIN. I suppose you think getting married is as easy as shouting: 'Hey, Stepan, give me my boots!' I pull the boots on and off I go! No: I must give it some careful thought, I have to have a good look round.

FYOKLA. I agree, I agree. If you want to have a look round, then so you should. That's why the merchandise is there—for you to look at. So tell your man to fetch your coat and let's get going, while it's still good and early.

PODKOLYOSIN. Right now? But look how overcast it is. The moment we set off it could start raining.

FYOKLA. You wait: you'll be sorry later! You're already starting to get grey hairs, soon you won't be any good for the marriage business. Putting on such airs just because he's a court councillor! We can find really classy suitors, you know: you wouldn't even get a look in.

PODKOLYOSIN. What rubbish you talk! What gave you the idea that I've got grey hairs? Show me a grey hair! [*Feels his hair.*]

FYOKLA. Of course you've got grey hairs—that's life. So you should watch out! There's no pleasing him: he doesn't like this one, he doesn't like that one. Let me tell you: there's a captain I have my eye on, you couldn't hold a candle to him, and when he talks, his voice is like a trumpet; he works in that Admiralty place.

PODKOLYOSIN. You're lying, I'm going to look in the mirror—I challenge you to find a grey hair on my head! Hey, Stepan, bring the mirror! No, don't, I'll go and look myself. Grey hairs!—God only preserve us from that. It's worse than the pox. [*Exit to the next room.*]

SCENE IX

[FYOKLA *and* KOCHKARYOV, *running in.*]

KOCHKARYOV. Where's Podkolyosin?... [*Seeing* FYOKLA.] What are you doing here? Oh you, you...! Now listen here, you so-and-so, why the devil did you go and get me married?

FYOKLA. What's so bad about that? You did your duty as a man.

KOCHKARYOV. My duty as a man! And what reward do I get?—A wife! When I could have managed perfectly well without one!

FYOKLA. But you were always on at me: 'Please, granny, please find me a wife!'—You never let up.

KOCHKARYOV. Listen to you, you old hag!... But what business do you have here?... Don't tell me Podkolyosin's thinking of...

FYOKLA. And what if he is? It's only God's will, after all.

KOCHKARYOV. Never! And not so much as a word to me, the scoundrel! The old fox: thought you'd do it on the sly, did you?

SCENE X

[*The same, with* PODKOLYOSIN, *who enters carrying a mirror, into which he is peering attentively.*]

KOCHKARYOV [*creeping up from behind, gives him a fright*]. Boo!

PODKOLYOSIN [*exclaims and drops the mirror*]. You crazy fool! Why did you do that!... What a stupid thing to do: you gave me such a fright, my heart leapt into my mouth.

KOCHKARYOV. Calm down, it was only a joke.

PODKOLYOSIN. You call that a joke? You gave me such a shock I'm still shaking. And look: the mirror's smashed. It wasn't cheap, you know: I bought it in the English shop.

KOCHKARYOV. All right, all right: I'll find you another mirror.

PODKOLYOSIN. Yes, you'll find me one all right. I know your mirrors: they make you look years older, and your face is all twisted and crooked.

KOCHKARYOV. Listen here: I'm the one who should be angry. Here you are, keeping me completely in the dark, and I'm supposed to be your friend. So you've decided to get married?

PODKOLYOSIN. Nonsense! I've decided nothing of the sort.

KOCHKARYOV. But here's the proof. [*Points at* FYOKLA.] We all know our feathered friend over here, we know what kind of bird she is. Well, what of it. There's nothing untoward about it. It's a good Christian thing, even patriotic in its way. But leave it all to me: I shall take care of the whole business. [*To* FYOKLA.] Very well, tell us all about it—what's her background: aristocracy or civil service, or is she a merchant's daughter? And what's her name?

FYOKLA. Agafya Tikhonovna.

KOCHKARYOV. Not Agafya Tikhonovna Brandakhlystova?

FYOKLA. No, no—Agafya Tikhonovna Kuperdyagina.

KOCHKARYOV. Is she the one who lives in Shestilavochnaya?

FYOKLA. No, not her; her place is closer to Peski, on Mylny Lane.*

KOCHKARYOV. Oh yes, I know it: on Mylny Lane, right behind the little shop—the wooden house?

FYOKLA. No, not behind the shop—behind the beer cellar.

KOCHKARYOV. What do you mean, behind the beer cellar?—Then I don't know which one it is.

FYOKLA. When you turn into the side street, there's a sentry-box right before you, and just after you pass the sentry-box, look to your left and you can't miss it—right in front of you there's a wooden house where that dressmaker woman lives, the one who used to live with the Chief Secretary of the Senate. Now, don't go into the dressmaker's house, but right behind it you'll see another house, a stone one—and that's her house, I mean, that's the house she lives in, Agafya Tikhonovna, that is, the one who's for marrying.

KOCHKARYOV. Ah yes, I know. Now I shall take charge of everything, so you can run along—we have no further need of your services.

FYOKLA. You what? You're surely not thinking of fixing the marriage yourself?

KOCHKARYOV. I most certainly am; and we don't want you interfering.

FYOKLA. How could you—you should be ashamed of yourself! This is no business for a man. Take my advice and keep your nose out of this business—I mean it!

KOCHKARYOV. Go on, off you go! And don't start plotting anything, we don't want any of your interfering! The cobbler should stick to his last—so off with you, scram!

FYOKLA. Look at that—taking the bread out of people's mouths, the godless heathen! Fancy getting mixed up in this messy business! If only I'd known, I'd never have opened my mouth. [*Exit in annoyance.*]

SCENE XI

[PODKOLYOSIN *and* KOCHKARYOV.]

KOCHKARYOV. Well, brother, there's no time to be lost. Let's go.

PODKOLYOSIN. But I haven't decided anything yet. It was only a thought, really...

KOCHKARYOV. Rubbish! Fiddlesticks! No need to be bashful: I'll get you married so quickly you won't feel a thing. We'll go to the young lady right away and you'll see: in no time we'll have it all stitched up.

PODKOLYOSIN. What do you mean: 'right away'?

KOCHKARYOV. Well, why not? What's stopping you?... Just look for yourself: what's so good about this bachelor life of yours? Have a good look at your room! What do you see? A dirty boot over there, a wash-basin here, a big heap of tobacco on the table, and all you can do is lie around the whole day like a stuffed marmot.

PODKOLYOSIN. You're right. I admit, I am a bit disorderly.

KOCHKARYOV. Once you get yourself a wife you'll be a changed man: you won't recognize yourself, or anything else for that matter: over here there'll be a nice sofa, a little dog, some sort of a canary tweeting away in a cage, a piece of needlework... Just imagine, there you are sitting on your sofa, and suddenly this gorgeous creature plops down next to you, as pretty as a picture, and with her little hand she...

PODKOLYOSIN. Damnation, when you start to think about it, some of them have devilish pretty little hands. As soft and white as milk.

KOCHKARYOV. Now that's more like it! And it isn't only hands that they have!... Let me tell you brother, they also... But it's impossible to say! The things they have, brother, the devil only knows what they are...

PODKOLYOSIN. You know, to tell you the honest truth, I do enjoy it when a pretty young lady sits next to me.

KOCHKARYOV. There, you see: you've a taste for it already. All that remains to be done is to finalize the arrangements. You needn't

worry about a thing. The wedding banquet and the other things—
I'll take care of all that... Now, the champagne—you must have
at least a dozen bottles, I don't care what you say. And half a
dozen bottles of Madeira, definitely. The young lady will no
doubt have a host of aunts and cronies—and they take their
weddings seriously. But no hock—we shan't bother with that
rubbish, shall we? As for the meal itself—I know this steward
who works at the court: he'll stuff you so full, the dog, that you
won't be able to rise from your seat.

PODKOLYOSIN. Whoa, hold your horses, the way you're talking,
you'd think the wedding was on the cards.

KOCHKARYOV. And so it is! Why put it off? You've agreed, haven't
you?

PODKOLYOSIN. Have I? Well, no... I haven't fully agreed, not yet.

KOCHKARYOV. Just listen to that! And only a moment ago you
declared that you want to get married.

PODKOLYOSIN. I only said it wouldn't be a bad idea.

KOCHKARYOV. Hold on, hold on! And I thought we had the whole
thing stitched up... So what is it? Do you mean to say you don't
like the thought of married life?

PODKOLYOSIN. No... I do like it.

KOCHKARYOV. What is it then? Why the sudden cold feet?

PODKOLYOSIN. It's not cold feet. It just feels a little strange...

KOCHKARYOV. What's strange about it?

PODKOLYOSIN. It can't help feeling strange: when you've never
been married before, and then suddenly—you're married.

KOCHKARYOV. Come, come—you should be ashamed! I know what
needs to be done: I must speak firmly to you, heart-to-heart, like
a father to his son. I ask you: take a look, take a good look at
yourself, look at the expression on your face. What do you see? A
lump, a clod, something with no purpose or meaning. What are
you living for? Take a look in the mirror, and what do you see?
A stupid face and nothing more. Now, imagine: there are little
children running round you, and not just two or three, but six or
seven, and they all resemble their papa, like peas in a pod... As

things are, you're on your own, a court councillor, an office
manager, or even a supervisor—God knows what, but when
you're married, just imagine, you'll have all your baby managers
around you, such little scoundrels, and one naughty pup will
stick out his little paws and tug your whiskers and you'll answer
him in doggy language, *woof! woof! woof!* What could be better
than that, you tell me?

PODKOLYOSIN. But they're a confounded nuisance with their mis-
chief: they'll break everything and throw my papers all over the
place.

KOCHKARYOV. Agreed: they have their little pranks—but they'll all
be the spitting image of you, just think of that!

PODKOLYOSIN. I have to admit, it could even be rather entertaining: just imagine—there's this little dumpling running around, a
rascally little pup, and he's the spitting image of you.

KOCHKARYOV. It is entertaining, of course it's entertaining. Good,
now let's get going.

PODKOLYOSIN. Very well, I suppose we might.

KOCHKARYOV. Hey, Stepan! Come and get your master into his
clothes.

PODKOLYOSIN [*dressing before the mirror*]. I reckon, all the same,
that I should wear my white waistcoat.

KOCHKARYOV. Rubbish, it's all the same.

PODKOLYOSIN [*putting on his collar*]. That confounded laundress,
she starches my collars so badly I can't get them to stand up.
Stepan, next time you must tell her, the idiot, that if she irons
my things like this again I shall send my laundry elsewhere. I
expect she spends her time with her admirers, instead of ironing.

KOCHKARYOV. Come now, brother, shake a leg! What a fuss you
make!

PODKOLYOSIN. I'm coming, I'm coming! [*Puts on his tailcoat and
sits down.*] Listen, Ilya Fomich, I know what we should do. You
go on your own.

KOCHKARYOV. Whatever next! Have you quite taken leave of your
senses? Me, go on my own? Pray tell: which of us is getting
married, you or me?

PODKOLYOSIN. To be honest, I don't really feel like it; perhaps we should leave it until tomorrow.

KOCHKARYOV. Is there a whit of sense in that head of yours? Or are you a complete numskull? First he was rearing to go, and now, suddenly, he 'doesn't feel like it'! Tell me something: after this are you not an out-and-out scoundrel, a complete swine?

PODKOLYOSIN. Why are you insulting me? What have I done to deserve this?

KOCHKARYOV. You're a fool, a complete and utter fool, anyone will tell you that. Stupid, plain stupid, office manager or no office manager. Why do I bother? It's all for your good; if I didn't, they'd all beat you to the post. Look at him, lying there, the cursed bachelor! May I tell you what you look like? Like a heap of rubbish, a useless dolt, a jackass—I'd like to tell you what I really think, but decorum forbids... You're an old woman! Worse than an old woman!

PODKOLYOSIN. What's got into you all of a sudden? [*Sotto voce.*] Are you out of your mind? There are servants in the room, but you curse away, using such terrible words. Could you not find a more suitable place?

KOCHKARYOV. It's impossible not to curse you! No one could stand here and not curse you! No one would have the patience not to curse you. He decides to marry, like a decent person, follows the prompting of sound judgement and then suddenly— quite out of the blue, he takes complete leave of his senses, the dolt, the blockhead...

PODKOLYOSIN. That'll do, that'll do! I'll go—there's no need to shout like that.

KOCHKARYOV. 'I'll go' he says! Of course he'll go, what else could he do but go! [*To* STEPAN.] Give him his coat and hat.

PODKOLYOSIN [*in the doorway*]. Such a peculiar fellow! You never know where you are with him: all of a sudden he starts cursing and carrying on for no reason at all. He has no idea of good manners.

KOCHKARYOV. All right, all right; I've stopped cursing. [*Both go out.*]

SCENE XII

[*A room in* AGAFYA TIKHONOVNA'*s house.* AGAFYA TIKHO-
NOVNA *is setting out cards to tell a fortune; her aunt,* ARINA
PANTELEIMONOVNA, *is peeking over her shoulder.*]

AGAFYA TIKHONOVNA. It's another journey, Auntie! There seems
to be a king of diamonds here, showing some interest, tears, a
love letter; and on the left the king of clubs is quite smitten, but
there's some evil woman getting in the way.

ARINA PANTELEIMONOVNA. But who do you think the king of
clubs could be?

AGAFYA TIKHONOVNA. I don't know.

ARINA PANTELEIMONOVNA. Well I do.

AGAFYA TIKHONOVNA. Who?

ARINA PANTELEIMONOVNA. It's that handsome merchant, the one
with the cloth business, Aleksei Dmitrievich Starikov.

AGAFYA TIKHONOVNA. Oh no, not him, surely! I'll bet you anything it's not him.

ARINA PANTELEIMONOVNA. Don't argue, Agafya Tikhonovna. He's
the only one with red hair. No one else can be the king of clubs.

AGAFYA TIKHONOVNA. No, it can't be: the king of clubs means an
aristocrat. A merchant's a far cry from the king of clubs.

ARINA PANTELEIMONOVNA. Dear, dear: now you would never talk
like that, Agafya Tikhonovna, if your late father, our Tikhon of
blessed memory, our Panteleimonovich, was still alive. I remember how he used to thump the table with his fist and shout: 'I spit
in the face of any man,' he would shout, 'who's ashamed to be a
merchant; and I won't give my daughter's hand to any colonel.
Other men', he would say, 'can marry their daughters to colonels! And I won't let my son go into government service. Are you
telling me,' he would say, 'that a merchant doesn't serve the tsar
just as well as any other man?' And he would pound the table like
this with all his might. His fist was the size of a bucket—you
should have heard the noise! To tell the truth, he knocked your
old mother about quite a bit. If it wasn't for him, she might have
lived a few years longer.

AGAFYA TIKHONOVNA. So there: and you want me to have a husband like that too! No thank you, there's no way on earth I'll marry a merchant.

ARINA PANTELEIMONOVNA. But Aleksei Dmitrievich is not like that.

AGAFYA TIKHONOVNA. I shan't, I shan't! He has a beard: when he eats, the food all spills down his beard. No, no, I shan't!

ARINA PANTELEIMONOVNA. But where do you hope to find a nice aristocratic husband? They don't grow on trees, you know.

AGAFYA TIKHONOVNA. Fyokla Ivanovna will find me one. She promised to find me the best there is.

ARINA PANTELEIMONOVNA. But you can't believe a thing she says, my pet.

SCENE XIII

[The same, and FYOKLA.*]*

FYOKLA. Come now, Arina Panteleimonovna, you should be ashamed of yourself, spreading slander like that.

ARINA PANTELEIMONOVNA. Oh look, it's Fyokla Ivanovna! Well? Do you have someone for us, then?

FYOKLA. Oh, I do, I do, but first let me get my breath back—I had to rush about so! Just for you I went through every house in town, and every government office, I slogged round the ministries, stuck my nose in every officers' mess... And let me tell you, my dear, I almost got beaten up, honest to God! An old hag, the one who married off the Aferovs, came up to me and said: 'You so-and-so,' she says, 'you're trying to steal the bread from our mouths, find your own territory.'—'You can say what you like,' I told her, straight to her face, 'but I'm prepared to do anything for my young lady—and I don't care what you think!' But you should see the fine gentlemen I've rounded up for you! In all the years of my life I've never seen any to match them! Some will even be calling today, so I've hurried over to warn you.

AGAFYA TIKHONOVNA. What do you mean: today? But Fyokla Ivanovna, dear Fyokla Ivanovna, I'm so frightened!

FYOKLA. No need to be frightened, my dear! It's all part of life.
They'll drive over and take a look, nothing more than that. And
you can take a look at them; if you don't like them—well they'll
just drive off again.

ARINA PANTELEIMONOVNA. I hope you've found some decent ones
this time!

AGAFYA TIKHONOVNA. How many did you find? Are there many?

FYOKLA. There's six at least.

AGAFYA TIKHONOVNA [*shrieks*]. Ooh!

FYOKLA. Now there's no need to get all in a flutter, my dear. It's
always better to have a choice, you know: if one doesn't suit,
another will.

AGAFYA TIKHONOVNA. So what are they: aristocrats?

FYOKLA. The pick of the bunch. Aristocrats like you've never seen
before.

AGAFYA TIKHONOVNA. But what are they like, what sort of men
are they?

FYOKLA. They're the very best, top of their class. The first is
Baltazar Baltazarovich Zhevakin, such a fine fellow, served in the
navy—he'd be perfect for you. He says he wants his bride to be
on the full-bodied side, he doesn't go for the scrawny types.
Then there's Ivan Pavlovich—he's a top manager and he's such
a big wig it's impossible to get near him. And he's so imposing to
look at, so fat; you should hear how he shouts at me: 'Don't waste
my time with all that rubbish, telling me how you've got this
bride and that bride!' he says. 'Just give me a straight answer:
how much is she worth in movables and immovables?'—'This
much in movables and that much in immovables, honoured sir!'
I say.—'You're lying, you dog's spittle!' And he throws in another little word, my dear, decency forbids me to repeat it. I
could see it straight away: this gentleman is someone of real
importance.

AGAFYA TIKHONOVNA. And who else is there?

FYOKLA. Well, there's Nikanor Ivanovich Anuchkin. So refined!
And his lips: my dear, like raspberries, pure raspberries! Such a
fine specimen. 'I want my bride to be good-looking,' he says,

'well brought-up, and she must be able to speak French.' And he's so well-mannered himself, with such fine, slender little legs.

AGAFYA TIKHONOVNA. Oh no, I find all these polished types a bit too... I mean, for me they... I don't see anything in them.

FYOKLA. Well, if you want something with a bit more body, take Ivan Pavlovich. You couldn't find better than him. He's a real man of the house: he could hardly fit through this door, for example, he's such a fine figure of a man.

AGAFYA TIKHONOVNA. And how old would he be?

FYOKLA. He's still a youngster: about 50, maybe not even.

AGAFYA TIKHONOVNA. And what's his surname?

FYOKLA. His full name's Ivan Pavlovich Pancake.

AGAFYA TIKHONOVNA. That's his surname?

FYOKLA. That's his surname.

AGAFYA TIKHONOVNA. Oh my God, what a name! Just think, Feklusha, what if I married him?—I would have to go around being Agafya Tikhonovna Pancake! How awful!

FYOKLA. Now my dear, you know there are such b—— awful names in Russia that you want to spit* and cross yourself when you hear them. Well, if you don't like the name, then why not take Baltazar Baltazarovich Zhevakin?—He'd make a splendid husband.

AGAFYA TIKHONOVNA. What sort of hair does he have?

FYOKLA. A fine head of hair.

AGAFYA TIKHONOVNA. And nose?

FYOKLA. Mmm... his nose is good too. Everything's in the right place. And he's such a fine specimen. But there's one thing you mustn't get your hopes up about: all he has in his house is his tobacco pipe; there's nothing else—not a stick of furniture.

AGAFYA TIKHONOVNA. And who else is there?

FYOKLA. There's Akinf Stepanovich Panteleev, a civil servant, titular councillor by rank. He has a slight stammer, though; but then he's such a quiet, modest man.

ARINA PANTELEIMONOVNA. What is all this: 'civil servant, civil servant'! Does he drink?—that's what we really need to know!

FYOKLA. Well, yes, he does like his little tipple, I'll not deny it. What do you expect—he's a titular councillor, after all—but then he's as meek as a lamb.

AGAFYA TIKHONOVNA. No, I don't want a drunkard for a husband.

FYOKLA. As you wish, my dear! If you don't like one, take another. If you ask me, it hardly matters if he has the odd drink now and again—it's not as if he spends the whole week sozzled: some days you'll find he's even quite sober.

AGAFYA TIKHONOVNA. And who else is there?

FYOKLA. Well there is one more, but it's just that he's such a... No, to the devil with him! These others will suit you better.

AGAFYA TIKHONOVNA. But who is he, this other one?

FYOKLA. I wasn't going to bring him up. I do believe he's a court councillor, this one, and he wears those epaulette things, but he's such a lazy slug it's impossible to lure him out of his house.

AGAFYA TIKHONOVNA. So who else is there? You've only given me five, and you said there were six.

FYOKLA. Isn't that enough for you? Just look at you now, calling for more, and only a moment ago you said you were frightened.

ARINA PANTELEIMONOVNA. Anyway, what's so good about them, these aristocratic gentlemen of yours? I'd give you more for one merchant than for all six of your gentlemen.

FYOKLA. Oh no, Arina Panteleimonovna. A gentleman commands more respect.

ARINA PANTELEIMONOVNA. Who cares about respect? Now, take our Aleksei Dmitrievich, for example... With that sable hat of his, and the way he swooshes along in his sledge...

FYOKLA. Oh yes? And when a gentleman with his epaulettes comes walking up and says: 'Hey, you, grocer! Get out of my path!' Or: 'Now merchant, show me your very best velvet!' And the merchant will say: 'At your service, master!'—'Take your hat off when you talk to me, you numskull!'—that's what a gentleman will say.

ARINA PANTELEIMONOVNA. But the merchant doesn't have to show his cloth if he doesn't feel like it; then your gentleman will have to run around naked, he won't have anything to wear!

FYOKLA. A gentleman will whip the hide off your merchant.

ARINA PANTELEIMONOVNA. The merchant will go to the police and complain.

FYOKLA. And the gentleman will report the merchant to the senator.

ARINA PANTELEIMONOVNA. Then the merchant will go to the governor.

FYOKLA. Then the gentleman will go—

ARINA PANTELEIMONOVNA. You lie, you lie: the gentleman... A governor is higher up than a senator!* Your head's turned with these gentlemen of yours! There's many a time a gentleman also has to doff his hat, you know! [*The doorbell rings.*] Listen, someone's ringing.

FYOKLA. There you are! It's them!

ARINA PANTELEIMONOVNA. Who's 'them'?

FYOKLA. Them... it's one of the gentlemen.

AGAFYA TIKHONOVNA [*Shrieks*]. Oooh!

ARINA PANTELEIMONOVNA. Holy saints, have mercy on us sinners! The room is such a mess. [*Grabs everything on the table and runs around the room.*] And look at the table-cloth, the table-cloth's quite filthy. Dunyashka, Dunyashka! [DUNYASHKA *appears.*] A clean table-cloth! Quickly! [*Pulls off the table-cloth and scurries about the room.*]

AGAFYA TIKHONOVNA. Auntie, Auntie, what can I do? I'm still in my nightdress, almost!

ARINA PANTELEIMONOVNA. Quick, quick, my dear: run and get dressed! [*Scurries about the room;* DUNYASHKA *brings a table-cloth; the doorbell rings.*] Quickly run and tell him: 'Just a moment!'

[DUNYASHKA *shouts from far off:* 'Just a moment!']

AGAFYA TIKHONOVNA. Auntie, but my dress hasn't been pressed.

ARINA PANTELEIMONOVNA. Merciful God, please have pity on me! Put on another one.

FYOKLA [*comes running in*]. But why are you all still here? Quickly, Agafya Tikhonovna, hurry up, my dear! [*The doorbell rings.*] You see: he's still waiting!

ARINA PANTELEIMONOVNA. Dunyashka, show him in and ask him to sit and wait.

[DUNYASHKA *runs to the entrance-hall and opens the door. Voices are heard saying:* 'Is anyone at home?'—'They're at home, please step inside.' *In a frenzy of curiosity, they all try and peep through the keyhole.*]

AGAFYA TIKHONOVNA [*shrieks*]. Oh, he's so fat!

FYOKLA. He's coming, he's coming! [*All hurtle out of the room.*]

SCENE XIV

[IVAN PAVLOVICH PANCAKE *and* DUNYASHKA.]

DUNYASHKA. Wait here. [*Exit.*]

PANCAKE. Well, I suppose I can wait for a moment or two, provided it's not too long. I only slipped out of the office for a minute. At any moment the general might notice and ask: 'Where's the manager?'—'He's gone to view a wife.' He'll soon let me know what he thinks of wife-viewing!.. In the mean time, I might as well have another look at the inventory. [*Reads.*] 'Two-storey, stone house...' [*Looks up and surveys the room.*] Correct! [*Continues reading.*] 'Two wings: one on stone foundations, and one made of wood'... Hmm, the wooden one's a bit ropy. 'A droshky, a two-seater sleigh, with wooden carvings and two rugs, one large and one small.' I imagine those are ready for the scrap yard... Still, the old woman insists that it's all first-rate stuff, so we'll assume it's first-rate. 'Two dozen silver spoons...' Of course, one must have silver spoons in the home. 'Two fox-fur coats...' Hmm... 'Four large feather-beds, two small feather-beds.' [*Purses his lips significantly.*] 'Six silk dresses, six cotton dresses, two night-gowns, two...' Ha! Stupid fripperies! 'Linen, table napkins...' Let her have all that stuff, if she wants. All this must be carefully verified, however. Nowadays it can happen that they promise you houses and carriages, but once the noose is tied all you find are feather-beds and eiderdowns.

[*The doorbell rings.* DUNYASHKA *hurtles through the room to open the door. Voices are heard saying:* 'Anyone at home?'—'They're at home.']

SCENE XV

[PANCAKE *and* ANUCHKIN.]

DUNYASHKA. Wait here. They'll come through in a moment.

[*Exit.* ANUCHKIN *and* PANCAKE *exchange bows*].

PANCAKE. My respects!

ANUCHKIN. Do I have the honour of addressing the lucky papa of the charming lady of the house?

PANCAKE. By no means, certainly not the papa. I don't even have any children yet.

ANUCHKIN. Oh, I'm so sorry! I do beg your pardon!

PANCAKE [*aside*]. There's something suspicious about the look on this fellow's face: I wonder if he isn't here on the same business as me. [*Aloud.*] I presume that you have some business with the lady of the house?

ANUCHKIN. No, no... no business, that is; I just called in, as I was strolling by.

PANCAKE [*aside*]. The liar: 'strolling by', indeed! It's a wife he's after, the scoundrel! [*The doorbell rings.* DUNYASHKA *runs through the room to open the door. Voices can be heard in the entrance-hall, saying:* 'Anyone in?'—'They're in.']

SCENE XVI

[*The same, with* ZHEVAKIN, *accompanied by* DUNYASHKA.]

ZHEVAKIN [*to* DUNYASHKA]. I say, sweetheart, be a dear and brush my coat... There's so much dust blowing about outside, you know. And there, take off that piece of fluff. [*Turns round.*] That's it! Thank you, sweetheart. Look—what's that crawling on me?— It looks like a spider! And are you sure there's nothing in the folds at the back? Thank you, my treasure! There's another little speck, look. [*Strokes the sleeves of his tailcoat and looks at* ANUCHKIN *and* PANCAKE.] It's English cloth, of course! I bought it in '95, when our squadron was stationed in Sicily and I was still only a midshipman; I had a uniform made from it. I got my commission in 1801, when Pavel Petrovich was tsar*—the cloth was still like new. Then in 1814 I went on a round-the-world expedition and it got just a little frayed along the seams; I retired in 1815 and I only had the collars and cuffs turned: I've worn it ten years since then and it's still just like new. Thank you, sweetheart, mmm... what a pretty little thing you are! [*Kisses her hand and, stepping up to the mirror, slightly ruffles his hair.*]

ANUCHKIN. If I might make so bold, Sicily—did I hear you say Sicily?—Is it a nice place, this Sicily?

ZHEVAKIN. Ah, a gorgeous place! We spent thirty-four days there; the view, I might tell you, is ravishing! Such mountains, some kind of pomegranate tree, and everywhere you look, little Signorinas, such pretty bonbonitas, you want to kiss them all.

ANUCHKIN. And are they well brought up?

ZHEVAKIN. Excellently brought up! Here only countesses are that well brought up. Sometimes you'd be walking along the street—you know, a Russian lieutenant... As you know, in the navy we have epaulettes here [*shows place on shoulder*] and gold braid here... and such pretty little brown-skinned beauties—they have little balconies sticking out from every house and the roofs are completely flat, as flat as this floor here. Sometimes you'd look up and see such a pretty little rosebud... Of course, you don't want them to think you're completely uncouth, so you go... [*Describes a bow, with a wide flourish of his arm.*] And she goes like this [*makes a little movement with his hand*]. She's all dressed up, of course, over here she's wearing some sort of taffeta thing, with little ribbons, and those pretty little ear-rings that ladies like to wear... Take my word for it, a tasty little morsel...

ANUCHKIN. And, if I might make so bold as to ask, what language would it be that they use in Sicily?

ZHEVAKIN. Why, French, of course.

ANUCHKIN. And do all the young ladies really speak French?

ZHEVAKIN. They do indeed. You may find this hard to believe, but we stayed there for thirty-four days and in all that time I never heard them utter a single word in Russian.

ANUCHKIN. Not a single word?

ZHEVAKIN. Not a single word. And I'm not even talking about the
nobles and the Signori, about all those officers of theirs, but you
can take a simple peasant, a country fellow, hauling a load of
rubbish along on his back, and if you ask him: 'I say my man,
give me some bread,' he won't understand, honest to God he
won't understand; but say it in French: '*Dateci del pane*!' or
'*Portate vino*!'—he'll understand right away, and he'll bring it
just as you asked.

PANCAKE. Well, as I see it, this Sicily must be a most curious place.
You mentioned a country fellow, a peasant: what sort of a peasant would that be? Would he be like a Russian peasant, a chap
with broad shoulders, pushing his own plough, or is he not like
that?

ZHEVAKIN. That I couldn't tell you; I didn't observe whether they
plough the land or not, but I can tell you how they take snuff.
With them they don't just sniff the stuff, they even put it inside
their lip. Transport is also very cheap; there's water all over the
place and gondolas everwhere... And what do you see sitting in
those gondolas?—Pretty Signorinas, pretty as little rosebuds, and
all dressed up: a frilly blouse, a little kerchief... There were some
English officers with us, fellows just like us—you know, sailors,
that is—and at first, I must say, it was very odd. We just couldn't
understand one another—but after a while, when we made friends,
we found we understood one another without difficulty: you'd
just point at a bottle, say, or a glass—and they'd know right away
that you were saying: 'Let's drink'; or you clench your fist and
put it to your mouth like this: *puff, puff*—and they'd understand:
'smoking a pipe'. On the whole, I can tell you this foreign language business is a piece of cake; in about three days our sailors
were chatting away quite fluently.

PANCAKE. Indeed, I can see that life in foreign climes is most
interesting. I always enjoy meeting a man who has been about in
the world. If I might make so bold: with whom do I have the
honour?

ZHEVAKIN. Zhevakin, retired naval lieutenant. Allow me, for my
own part, to enquire: with whom is it my good fortune to hold
conference?

PANCAKE. Departmental manager by profession, Ivan Pavlovich Pancake.

ZHEVAKIN [*mishearing*]. Yes, I had a quick bite, too. I knew I had some way to drive, and there was a nip in the air: I had a little pickled herring with toast.

PANCAKE. No, I think you may have misheard—that's my surname: Pancake.

ZHEVAKIN [*bowing*]. I do beg your pardon! I'm a little hard of hearing. I confess I thought you were saying that you had eaten a pancake.

PANCAKE. It's such a nuisance. I even thought of asking the general if he would let me change my name to Pancakovitch, but my family dissuaded me: they said it would sound too much like 'son-of-a-bitch'.

ZHEVAKIN. You do get funny names, it's true. Our entire third squadron, officers and seamen alike, all have the oddest surnames: Dustbin, Sloshkin, and the lieutenant, Rottenov. There was one midshipman, a good midshipman too, whose surname was simply Hole.* The captain used to shout at him: 'Hey you, Hole, come here!' We always used to rib him: 'You're such a hole!' we would say to him. [*The doorbell rings.* FYOKLA *runs through the room to open the door.*]

PANCAKE. Ah, good day, my good woman!

ZHEVAKIN. Good day; how are you today, my dear?

ANUCHKIN. Good day, ma'am, good day, Fyokla Ivanovna!

FYOKLA [*breathless from running*]. Thank you, kind sirs! I'm well, thank you, I'm well. [*Opens the door; in the entrance-hall voices are heard saying:* 'Is she in?'—'She is.' *Then some more or less inaudible words, to which* FYOKLA *replies in a peevish voice:* 'Well, I like that! Who do you think you are!']

SCENE XVII

[*The same, with* KOCHKARYOV, PODKOLYOSIN *and* FYOKLA.]

KOCHKARYOV [*to* PODKOLYOSIN]. Now remember: all you need is courage, nothing else. [*Looks around and bows with some surprise; to himself*]: I say, what a crowd! What's going on? These aren't suitors, I hope? [*Nudges* FYOKLA *and speaks in a low voice:*] Where did you find all these old bustards?

FYOKLA. These, I'll have you know, are no bustards, as you call them, but all upstanding gentlemen.

KOCHKARYOV [*aside to her*]. I know your game: the more the sheep the more the fleece.

FYOKLA. That's pot calling kettle black—and your one is nothing to write home about!

KOCHKARYOV. I suppose yours are all rolling in money, with their pockets full—of holes. [*Aloud.*] But what is she up to now? This must be the door to her boudoir. [*Steps up to the door.*]

FYOKLA. Have you no shame! You know perfectly well she's still getting dressed.

KOCHKARYOV. Well, there's no harm in looking! I'll just have a little peek, nothing more. [*Peers through the keyhole.*]

ZHEVAKIN. If I might also make so bold as to have a little look...

PANCAKE. And with your kind permission I shall have a little look too.

KOCHKARYOV [*still looking*]. You can't see anything, gentlemen. There's something white, but it's impossible to say if it's a woman or a pillow. [*They all crowd round the door just the same, jostling for a position by the keyhole.*]

KOCHKARYOV. Shh!—someone's coming! [*All jump back.*]

SCENE XVIII

[*The same, with* ARINA PANTELEIMONOVNA *and* AGAFYA
TIKHONOVNA.]

[*All bow.*]

ARINA PANTELEIMONOVNA. Now to what, might I ask, do we owe
the pleasure of your visit?

PANCAKE. Well, madam, I learnt from the newspaper that you were
seeking contracts for the delivery of timber and firewood, and, in
my capacity as manager of a government office, I thought I
would pay a visit to ascertain the nature of the timber in question, the quantities available and how soon you would be able to
deliver it.

ARINA PANTELEIMONOVNA. We're not in the timber business, but
we thank you for your visit just the same. What would your name
be?...

PANCAKE. Collegiate Assessor Ivan Pavlovich Pancake.

ARINA PANTELEIMONOVNA. Please be so good as to be seated.
[*Turns and looks at* ZHEVAKIN.] Might I ask?...

ZHEVAKIN. I also saw a notice in the newspapers about something:
well, I thought, I'll go along and see. It turned out be a fine day,
with such nice green grass all along the road...

ARINA PANTELEIMONOVNA. And what would your name be, might
I ask?

ZHEVAKIN. Retired Naval Lieutenant Baltazar Baltazarovich
Zhevakin the Second. We had another Zhevakin, you see, but he
retired even before me: he was wounded, ma'am, just here below
the knee, and the funny thing is, the bullet didn't touch the knee
itself, but it caught the tendon and passed through it just like a
needle. When you stood next to him you'd swear he was always
about to stick his knee into your *derrière*.

ARINA PANTELEIMONOVNA. Please be so good as to take a seat.
[*Turning to* ANUCHKIN.] And what, might I ask, brings you here?...

ANUCHKIN. Just a neighbourly visit, ma'am.

ARINA PANTELEIMONOVNA. You wouldn't by any chance live in the house across the way, would you—I mean, the one which belongs to Tulubova, the merchant's wife?

ANUCHKIN. No, for the time being I'm still living in Peski, but it is my intention in time to move somewhere rather closer, to this part of town.

ARINA PANTELEIMONOVNA. Please be so good as to take a seat. [*Turning to* KOCHKARYOV.] And if I might make so bold?...

KOCHKARYOV. But surely you know who I am? [*Turning to* AGAFYA TIKHONOVNA.] Do you not recognize me either, miss?

AGAFYA TIKHONOVNA. As far as I know, I've never seen you before.

KOCHKARYOV. But try and cast your mind back. You must have seen me somewhere.

AGAFYA TIKHONOVNA. I really don't know. Was it at the Biryushkins', perhaps?

KOCHKARYOV. You've got it: at the Biryushkins'.

AGAFYA TIKHONOVNA. Oh dear, I expect you haven't heard what happened to her?

KOCHKARYOV. Why yes, she got married.

AGAFYA TIKHONOVNA. Oh no, that would be fine. It's much worse: she broke her leg.

ARINA PANTELEIMONOVNA. And she broke it badly. She was coming home rather late one night in a droshky, and the driver was drunk and tipped her out into the road.

KOCHKARYOV. Ah yes, now you come to mention it, I did hear something: either she got married, or she broke her leg.

ARINA PANTELEIMONOVNA. Might I ask your name?

KOCHKARYOV. Why of course: Ilya Fomich Kochkaryov, in fact we're relatives. My wife is forever talking about... But allow me, allow me. [*Takes* PODKOLYOSIN *by the arm and steers him forward.*] My friend, Ivan Kuzmich Podkolyosin, Court Councillor; he holds the position of senior manager and does everything on his own. He has his whole department running like clockwork.

ARINA PANTELEIMONOVNA. What's the name again?

KOCHKARYOV. Podkolyosin, Ivan Kuzmich Podkolyosin. They do have a director, of course, but it's purely for form's sake; Ivan Kuzmich here runs the whole show himself: he can do anything he turns his hand to, that's Ivan Kuzmich for you.

ARINA PANTELEIMONOVNA. Pleased to meet you. Pray be so good as to take a seat.

SCENE XIX

[The same, with STARIKOV.*]*

STARIKOV *[bowing vigorously and rapidly, in the merchant's manner, with his arms pressed lightly against his sides]*. Good day, Arina Panteleimonovna, ma'am. The fellows in Gostiny Dvor* tell me that you're selling wool, ma'am, so they do!

AGAFYA TIKHONOVNA *[turning aside with a supercilious look and speaking in a low voice, but loud enough for him to hear]*. This is not a trading store.

STARIKOV. Is that so? You mean, we've come at the wrong time, is that it? Or have you decided to do your business without us?

ARINA PANTELEIMONOVNA. Please, Aleksei Dmitrievich; although we're not selling wool we're still pleased to see you. Pray be seated.

[All are seated. Silence.]

PANCAKE. Odd weather these days: this morning it looked like rain, but now the rain seems to have passed.

AGAFYA TIKHONOVNA. Yes, the weather is quite peculiar: sometimes it's fine, and then later on it's very rainy. It's most disagreeable.

ZHEVAKIN. Now when our squadron was in Sicily, ma'am, it was the springtime—but if you work it out, it must have been our February. When you stepped out of the house it was bright and sunny, and before you knew it a spot of rain hit you; when you looked up, sure enough: rain was on its way.

PANCAKE. But the worst thing in weather like that is to be on your own. It's quite different for a married man—things are never dull for him. When you're on your own, however, that's worse than, er...

ZHEVAKIN. Death, it's worse than death.

ANUCHKIN. Well yes, you could say that...

KOCHKARYOV. It's abominable! Sheer torment! You can't enjoy life; may God spare us such a fate.

PANCAKE. Now tell me, miss, what if you had to make your choice? Allow me to discover your taste. Forgive me for being so direct, but which type of service, to your way of thinking, is most appropriate for a husband?

ZHEVAKIN. Tell me, miss, would you not wish your husband to be a man familiar with the tempests of the ocean?

KOCHKARYOV. No, no, no. To my mind, the best husband is a man capable of running an entire department single-handed.

ANUCHKIN. But why this prejudice? Why disparage a man who may have served in an infantry regiment, yet has proper regard for the etiquette of the highest society?

PANCAKE. Please, miss: state your preference!

[AGAFYA TIKHONOVNA *remains silent*.]

FYOKLA. Give them an answer, my dear. Tell them something.

PANCAKE. Well, miss?...

KOCHKARYOV. A penny for your thoughts, Agafya Tikhonovna?

FYOKLA [*aside to her*]. Just say to them: 'I thank you most humbly, with the greatest of pleasure.' It's not polite to sit there like that and say nothing.

AGAFYA TIKHONOVNA [*aside*]. I'm too embarrassed, really I am, I shall have to leave the room, I must, really. Auntie, please sit there for me.

FYOKLA. Oh no, you mustn't go, it'll be such a disgrace, you'll embarrass us all. God only knows what they'll think.

AGAFYA TIKHONOVNA [*aside*]. No, I must go, I must, I must!

[*Exit running.* FYOKLA *and* ARINA PANTELEIMONOVNA *follow her out.*]

SCENE XX

[The same, without the three women.]

PANCAKE. Well now, there's a thing: they've all gone! What can it all mean?

KOCHKARYOV. Something must have happened.

ZHEVAKIN. Something to do with the ladies' *toilette*... Something must be set right... a frill on the blouse... a little pin, perhaps.

[*Enter* FYOKLA. *All run towards her asking:* 'What is it? What is it?']

KOCHKARYOV. Is something wrong?

FYOKLA. How could anything be wrong? Honest to God, there's nothing wrong.

KOCHKARYOV. Then why did she leave the room?

FYOKLA. You embarrassed her, that's why; you made her all ashamed, so she couldn't take any more. She sends her apologies: you're invited to call round this evening for a cup of tea. [*Exit*.]

PANCAKE [*aside*]. These confounded cups of tea! That's why I don't like this courtship business—it's such a run-around: 'We can't do it today, so please won't you come tomorrow, and then again the day after tomorrow for a little cup of tea, and we'll have to give the matter a little thought.' And it's all such rubbish, there's nothing to think about. To the devil with it, I'm a busy man, I haven't the time for this nonsense!

KOCHKARYOV [*to* PODKOLYOSIN]. Our hostess is a good-looking lady, is she not?

PODKOLYOSIN. Yes, she's good-looking.

ZHEVAKIN. And the young hostess is pretty too.

KOCHKARYOV [*aside*.] Confound it! The fool's gone and fallen in love. That could get in the way. [*Aloud*.] Oh no, not at all pretty.

PANCAKE. Her nose is too big.

ZHEVAKIN: Why now, I didn't notice her nose. She's... such a perfect little rosebud.

ANUCHKIN. I think I share their view. There's something not quite right, not quite right... I even suspect she's not too well-versed in the etiquette of high society. And I wonder whether she knows any French?

ZHEVAKIN. Well now, if you don't mind my asking, why didn't you put her to the test, why didn't you talk to her in French? Perhaps she does know it.

ANUCHKIN. What makes you think I can speak French? No, I didn't have the good fortune to receive such an education. My father was a miserable swine. He never even thought of teaching me French. I was still a young child then, it would have been easy to teach me—a few good thrashings and I would have picked it up, I would have picked it up in no time.

ZHEVAKIN. In that case, seeing that you don't know it, what possible good would it be for her...

ANUCHKIN. Oh no, no. You're quite mistaken. For a woman it's quite a different matter. It's vital for a woman to know it, otherwise she would be like this and like that... [*gesticulates*]—it wouldn't be right at all.

PANCAKE [*aside*]. The others can worry all they like about her French, but I'm stepping outside to have a good look at the house and the two wings: if everything's up to scratch I shall have it in the bag by this evening. This miserable bunch doesn't bother me in the least—they're hardly the sort that appeal to the ladies.

ZHEVAKIN. I feel like smoking my pipe, so I think I'll be on my way. Are we going in the same direction, perhaps? Pray tell, where do you live?

ANUCHKIN. I'm in Peski, on Petrov Street.

ZHEVAKIN. It's a bit of a long way round as I'm on the island, on the Eighteenth Line;* never mind, I'll walk along with you. [*Exeunt.*]

STARIKOV. If you ask me, there's some hanky-panky going on here. Mark my words, you'll come looking for us one of these days, Agafya Tikhonovna. My respects, gentlemen! [*Exit with a bow.*]

SCENE XXI

PODKOLYOSIN. I suppose we should be on our way too.

KOCHKARYOV. I must say, the young lady is very charming, don't you think?

PODKOLYOSIN. Not at all! To be perfectly honest, I didn't take to her.

KOCHKARYOV. You don't say! How so? And yet you agreed that she's pretty.

PODKOLYOSIN. All the same, something's not quite right: her nose is too long and she doesn't know French.

KOCHKARYOV. What of it? What does she need French for?

PODKOLYOSIN. Say what you will, one's wife should know French.

KOCHKARYOV. Whatever for?

PODKOLYOSIN. Well, because... I can't explain: it's just not the same if she doesn't speak French.

KOCHKARYOV. Listen to that. He hears one fool say it, so he strikes up the same tune. She's a beauty, a real beauty; you won't find another filly like that anywhere.

PODKOLYOSIN. At first I did rather like the look of her, but later, when the others started pointing out how her nose is too long—well, I had a closer look and I could see for myself that her nose is too long.

KOCHKARYOV. You stupid oaf: they threw you a line and you swallowed it, hook, line, and sinker! They said all that specially to put you off; I didn't praise her either, but that's just the way you do these things. No, brother, this is a first-rate filly! Take a good look at her eyes: they're smashing, dammit, they talk and breathe! And her nose—I don't know how to do it justice. Pure white—like alabaster! Even alabaster's not a fair comparison. Take a good look at it.

PODKOLYOSIN [*smiling*]. Yes, now that you come to mention it, she is rather pretty, I must say.

KOCHKARYOV. Of course she's pretty! Listen, now that they've all gone, let's pop in and see her, we'll propose and put the lid on it.

PODKOLYOSIN. Oh no, I couldn't do that.

KOCHKARYOV. Why on earth not?

PODKOLYOSIN. How could we be so brazen? There are so many of us, let her choose for herself.

KOCHKARYOV. Why bother about them? Are you afraid of the competition, is that it? If you like, I'll send the whole lot packing.

PODKOLYOSIN. How could you do that?

KOCHKARYOV. That's my business. Just give me your word that you won't try and wriggle out of it afterwards.

PODKOLYOSIN. I can give you my word, I suppose. As you wish. I shan't try and get out of it: I want to get married.

KOCHKARYOV. Shake on it!

PODKOLYOSIN [*shaking his hand*]. Agreed!

KOCHKARYOV. Now we're getting somewhere.

[*Exeunt.*]

CURTAIN

ACT TWO

A room in AGAFYA TIKHONOVNA's *house.*

SCENE I

[AGAFYA TIKHONOVNA *alone; later* KOCHKARYOV.]

AGAFYA TIKHONOVNA. It's true, isn't it: there's nothing harder than having to choose! If there were only one or two, but there are four to choose from. I must decide which one I like best. Nikanor Ivanovich isn't bad-looking, although he's a bit on the thin side. Ivan Kuzmich isn't bad-looking either. And to tell the truth, nor is Ivan Pavlovich, although he's rather fat—but then at least he has presence. Oh dear, whom should I choose? Baltazar Baltazarovich is also a man of parts. It's so hard to decide, it's impossible! If you could take Nikanor Ivanovich's lips, and stick them on to Ivan Kuzmich's nose, and throw in some of Baltazar Baltazarovich's happy-go-lucky manner, and put all that on to Ivan Pavlovich's sturdy figure—then I should have no hesitation. But as things are I really don't know—it's such a headache! Perhaps I should draw lots to decide. I shall leave everything to the will of God: the one I choose will be the one I wed. I'll write their names down on pieces of paper, roll them into straws and what will be, will be. [*Walks over to the desk, takes some paper and scissors, cuts the paper into little pieces and rolls them up, speaking all the while.*] Such is the unhappy lot of a young woman, especially when she is in love. No man can grasp what that means, and they wouldn't even wish to understand. So here they all are, I can start! I just have to put them into my purse, and close my eyes; then what will be, will be. [*Places the twists of paper in her purse and shuffles them.*] I'm so afraid... I do hope God gives me Nikanor Ivanovich. But no, why him? Ivan Kuzmich would be better. But there again, why Ivan Kuzmich? Is he any better than the others?... No, no, I shall say no more... Whoever comes out first is the one it shall be. [*Gropes in the bag and, instead of one, takes them all out.*] Oh no! All of them! They all came out! No wonder my heart was pounding so! No: one only! One only! It must be one! [*Puts the pieces of paper back into the bag and shuffles them again. At this point* KOCHKARYOV *enters stealthily and stops behind her.*] Oh, if only I could pick Baltazar... What am I saying! I mean Nikanor Ivanovich...—No, no, not him either. I shall leave it to fate!

KOCHKARYOV. Listen, take Ivan Kuzmich, he's the best of the lot!

AGAFYA TIKHONOVNA. Oooh! [*Shrieks and covers her face with her hands, scared to look behind her.*]

KOCHKARYOV. What are you so afraid of? There's nothing to fear, it's only me. Seriously, you should take Ivan Kuzmich.

AGAFYA TIKHONOVNA. Oh, I'm so ashamed, you heard what I was saying.

KOCHKARYOV. Never mind, never mind! I'm one of the family, don't forget, so there's no reason to be ashamed in front of me; it's all right, you can show your face now.

AGAFYA TIKHONOVNA [*half-revealing her face*]. But I'm so ashamed.

KOCHKARYOV. You must take Ivan Kuzmich, really you must.

AGAFYA TIKHONOVNA. Oooh! [*Shrieks and hides her face again.*]

KOCHKARYOV. Seriously, he's a marvel, the way he transformed his entire department... a remarkable man.

AGAFYA TIKHONOVNA [*gradually revealing her face*]. But what about that other one? That Nikanor Ivanovich? He's a fine man, too.

KOCHKARYOV. I humbly beg your pardon, but compared to Ivan Kuzmich he's rubbish.

AGAFYA TIKHONOVNA. Why do you say so?

KOCHKARYOV. It's quite obvious. Ivan Kuzmich is a man... well, he's quite simply a man... a man unlike any other.

AGAFYA TIKHONOVNA. So what about Ivan Pavlovich?

KOCHKARYOV. He's rubbish too! They're all rubbish.

AGAFYA TIKHONOVNA. They're all rubbish?

KOCHKARYOV. Judge for yourself, just compare them: whichever way you look at it, Ivan Kuzmich is your man! As for the others, Ivan Pavlovich, Nikanor Ivanovich, and all the rest—all rubbish!

AGAFYA TIKHONOVNA. But I have to say, they're all very... quiet and modest.

KOCHKARYOV. Modest my foot! Brawlers and ruffians, the lot of them! How would you like to be beaten up the day after your wedding?

AGAFYA·TIKHONOVNA. Oh my God! That would be terrible, the worst possible thing that could happen!

KOCHKARYOV. Wouldn't it just! It's worse than you could even imagine.

AGAFYA TIKHONOVNA. So, in your opinion, I should take Ivan Kuzmich?

KOCHKARYOV. Ivan Kuzmich, it has to be Ivan Kuzmich. [*Aside.*] Things seem to be going according to plan. Podkolyosin's sitting in the pastry shop, I'd better run and fetch him.

AGAFYA TIKHONOVNA. So you really think: Ivan Kuzmich?

KOCHKARYOV. Ivan Kuzmich, most definitely.

AGAFYA TIKHONOVNA. And the others, should I turn them down?

KOCHKARYOV. Turn them down, of course.

AGAFYA TIKHONOVNA. But how can I? It's so embarrassing.

KOCHKARYOV. What's embarrassing about it? Tell them you're still too young and you don't want to get married.

AGAFYA TIKHONOVNA. But they won't believe me, they'll ask all sorts of questions.

KOCHKARYOV. Very well, if you really want to be rid of them once and for all, tell them: 'Clear off, you donkeys!'

AGAFYA TIKHONOVNA. How can I say that!

KOCHKARYOV. Just try it. Take it from me: when they hear that, they'll take to their heels.

AGAFYA TIKHONOVNA. But it seems rather insulting.

KOCHKARYOV. You'll get shot of them, so why should you care?

AGAFYA TIKHONOVNA. It doesn't seem right, somehow... They'll get angry, though.

KOCHKARYOV. So what if they do? If some harm were to come of all this, it would be a different matter; the worst that can happen is for one of them to spit in your eye—no more than that.

AGAFYA TIKHONOVNA. There, you see!

KOCHKARYOV. What's so bad about that? Some people get spat at all the time! I know a fellow like that: as handsome as can be, cheeks as red as apples; anyway, he gave his boss such a hard time, wheedling and pestering him for a rise, that finally the old man could stand it no longer—and fired a gob of spit full in his face, honest to God! 'There's your rise,' he said, 'now get the hell out of here!' In the end he gave him his rise, though. So what does it matter if they spit? If you had no handkerchief, it would be a different matter, but there it is right there, in your pocket— take it out and give your face a wipe. [*The doorbell rings.*] There's someone at the door: it must be one of them; I've no wish to see any of that lot now. There isn't another way out, by any chance?

AGAFYA TIKHONOVNA. Yes, of course, there's a back staircase. But look at me, I'm shaking all over.

KOCHKARYOV. Not to worry, presence of mind, that's all you need. Adieu! [*Aside.*] Now I must fetch Podkolyosin, post haste!

SCENE II

[AGAFYA TIKHONOVNA *and* PANCAKE.]

PANCAKE. I specially came a bit earlier, Mam'selle, so we could have a little tête-à-tête, at our leisure. Now, Mam'selle, as re- gards the question of rank, I believe you know my position: I hold the rank of collegiate assessor, I'm well thought of by my superiors, obeyed by my subordinates... There's only one thing I lack: a lady-companion on the path of life.

AGAFYA TIKHONOVNA. Ah yes.

PANCAKE. And now I've found just such a companion. This com- panion is you. Tell me straight: yes or no? [*Looks at her shoulders. Aside.*] Hah, this isn't one of those skinny German heifers—this one has meat on her!

AGAFYA TIKHONOVNA. But I'm still too young... I'm not ready for marriage yet.

PANCAKE. I beg your pardon, but what was all that business with the matchmaker? Or perhaps you meant to say something else? Please could you make yourself clear... [*The doorbell can be heard ringing.*] Damnation, just when I was getting down to business!

SCENE III

[*The same, with* ZHEVAKIN.]

ZHEVAKIN. Forgive me, Mam'selle, if perhaps I'm a little early. [*Turns and sees* PANCAKE.] Ah, you have company already... My respects to you, Ivan Pavlovich!

PANCAKE [*aside*]. To hell with you and your respects! [*Aloud.*] So what about it, Mam'selle?... Just say the word: yes or no?... [*The doorbell is heard ringing;* PANCAKE *spits angrily.*] That confounded bell again!

SCENE IV

[*The same, with* ANUCHKIN.]

ANUCHKIN. Perhaps I'm a little on the early side, Mam'selle, but I am impelled hither by my sense of duty... [*Sees the others, exclaims and bows.*] My respects!

PANCAKE [*aside*]. To hell with your respects! Why the devil do you have to come so soon—I wish you'd broken your scrawny legs in your haste! [*Aloud.*] So what about it, Mam'selle, please make your decision—I'm a busy man and my time is limited: yes or no?

AGAFYA TIKHONOVNA [*confused*]. Oh there's no need, no need... [*Aside.*] I haven't the faintest idea what I'm saying.

PANCAKE. What do you mean, no need? In what sense is there no need?

AGAFYA TIKHONOVNA. It's nothing, nothing at all... That is, I didn't mean... [*Plucks up courage.*] Clear off!... [*Aside, clasping her hands together.*] Oh my God, did I really say it?

PANCAKE. What do you mean: 'Clear off'? What's that supposed to mean: 'Clear off'? Might I make so bold as to enquire exactly what you mean? [*Putting his hands on his hips, steps up to her in a menacing way.*]

AGAFYA TIKHONOVNA [*staring into his face, shrieks*]. Aah! He's going to strike us! [*Flees.* PANCAKE *stands open-mouthed with astonishment. Hearing the scream,* ARINA PANTELEIMONOVNA *runs in and, seeing his face, also shrieks:* Aah! He's going to strike us! *and flees.*]

PANCAKE. What a carry-on! Heavens above, what a circus! [*There is a ring at the door and voices are heard.*]

VOICE OF KOCHKARYOV. Go on, go on, don't stop there!

VOICE OF PODKOLYOSIN. You go on ahead. I shall only be a moment: I must put my clothes in order; my stirrup-strap has come undone.

VOICE OF KOCHKARYOV. But you'll give me the slip.

VOICE OF PODKOLYOSIN. No, I shan't! I promise, I shan't!

SCENE V

[*Enter* KOCHKARYOV.]

KOCHKARYOV. Typical: trust him to have to fasten his stirrup-strap.

PANCAKE [*turning to* KOCHKARYOV]. Tell me, is the young lady of unsound mind, or something?

KOCHKARYOV. Why do you ask? Did something happen?

PANCAKE. It was quite extraordinary: she ran out of the room, screaming: 'He's going to strike me! He's going to strike me!' The devil only knows what's going on!

KOCHKARYOV. Well, yes, she does have these funny turns. She's not quite all there, you know.

PANCAKE. But tell me, are you not related to her?

KOCHKARYOV. I am, yes.

PANCAKE. How are you related, if I might ask?

KOCHKARYOV. To be honest, I'm not sure: either my mother's aunt is something to her father, or her father is something to my aunt—my wife knows all about it, women know about these things.

PANCAKE. And has she been having these turns for a long time?

KOCHKARYOV. Oh yes, since she was a small child.

PANCAKE. Of course, one would prefer her to be rather more intelligent, but the simple ones also have their advantages. Provided the other bits and pieces are all present and correct.

KOCHKARYOV. But surely you know there are no other bits and pieces?

PANCAKE. What do you mean? What about the stone house?

KOCHKARYOV. They only say that it's stone, but you should see how it's built: the walls are nothing but brick, and inside them there's all sorts of rubbish—woodchips, shavings, that kind of nonsense.

PANCAKE. You're not serious!

KOCHKARYOV. It's quite true. Don't you know how they build houses nowadays? Any old how—just so long as they can raise a mortgage.

PANCAKE. Well, it isn't mortgaged, at any rate.

KOCHKARYOV. Who told you that? That's the whole point: not only has it been mortgaged, they haven't even paid the interest for the last two years. Added to which, there's a brother in the Senate* who has his eye on the place; this fellow is as wily a crook as you're likely to meet: he would swindle the clothes off his own mother's back, the godless swine!

PANCAKE. But how could that old matchmaker woman... The cheating witch! Abomination! [*Aside.*] On the other hand, he might be lying. I'll give the old woman a proper grilling, and if what he says is all true... Well... I'll have her singing a tune she hasn't sung before.

ANUCHKIN. May I also trouble you with a question? I must confess, I'm not acquainted with the French tongue, and so I find it extremely hard to judge whether a woman knows French or not. With regard to the young lady of the house, does she, er...?

KOCHKARYOV. Not a syllable.

ANUCHKIN. You don't say!

KOCHKARYOV. Take it from me: I know it for a fact. She and my wife went to the same school and she was well known for being lazy; she was always the one in the dunce's cap. The French teacher used to whack her with a stick.

ANUCHKIN. It's a funny thing, from the moment I first saw her I had a sort of premonition that she didn't know French.

PANCAKE. To the devil with your French! How did that cursed matchmaker... Just you wait, you hag, you old witch! You should have heard how she described her—what a picture she painted! She's an artist, a genius with the palette! 'A house with two wings,' she says, 'on stone foundations, silver spoons, a sleigh'— you could see yourself settling down in it and sliding off!— Better than the stuff you read in novels! You old boot-sole! Wait till I get my hands on you...

SCENE VI

[*The same, with* FYOKLA. *Seeing her, they all start speaking to her.*]

PANCAKE. Ah! There she is! You come here, you lying toad! Step over here!

ANUCHKIN. To think how you deceived me, Fyokla Ivanovna!

KOCHKARYOV. Come over here, you evil witch, and let me thrash you!

FYOKLA. I don't understand a word: you're making me deaf with your shouting.

PANCAKE. The house is only made of brick, you old boot-sole, and you lied through your teeth: you said it had a mansard and God knows what besides.

FYOKLA. Well how should I know, I didn't build it. Perhaps it was supposed to be made of brick, so they built it like that.

PANCAKE. And to make matters worse, it's mortgaged! You should be eaten alive by devils, you old witch! [*Stamps his foot.*]

FYOKLA. Well I never! Listen to that language! Anyone else would thank me for the kindness and trouble I took over him.

ANUCHKIN. Come to think of it, Fyokla Ivanovna, you told me that she could speak French.

FYOKLA. She can, my dear, she speaks them all, German too, and any other language you care to mention; you name it, she can do it.

ANUCHKIN. That's not true: it seems she only knows Russian.

FYOKLA. Well what's so bad about that? You can understand her better in Russian, so she speaks Russian. Now, if she was to speak Blackamoor, yóu'd be far worse off—you wouldn't understand a word she said. So why all the fuss about speaking Russian! It's a perfectly good language: all the saints spoke Russian.

PANCAKE. Just come here, you damned she-ass! Step over here!

FYOKLA [*edging closer to the door*]. I shan't, I know what you're like. There's no telling what you'll do next, you could wallop someone for no reason.

PANCAKE. You mark my words, my little dove, you won't get away with this! One of these days I'll march you into the police station, then you'll find out what happens when you deceive honest people. You'll see! As for the young lady, tell her from me that she's a scoundrel! Do you hear? A scoundrel! [*Exit.*]

FYOKLA. Well I never! Listen to that! Just because he's fat, he thinks he can lord it over everyone else. Let me tell you: you're a scoundrel yourself, that's what you are!

ANUCHKIN. I must confess, my dear woman, I never imagined for a moment that you would deceive me like this. Had I known that the young lady's education was somewhat deficient, well... I would never have shown my face in this house. So there, you see. [*Exit.*]

FYOKLA. Have you all lost your wits, or perhaps you've had one too many? You're such a picky, finicky lot! It's that stupid education of yours, it's addled your brains!

SCENE VII

[FYOKLA, KOCHKARYOV, ZHEVAKIN.]

[KOCHKARYOV *laughs uproariously, looking at* FYOKLA *and pointing at her.*]

FYOKLA [*in a vexed voice*]. What are you laughing about?

[KOCHKARYOV *continues laughing.*]

FYOKLA. I'm glad you think it's so funny!

KOCHKARYOV. Matchmaker, you call yourself! Matchmaker! Mistress of the matrimonial art! Old hand at the marriage business! [*Continues laughing.*]

FYOKLA. Ha, ha, very funny! If you ask me, your late mother must have had bats in her belfry when she brought you into this world! [*Exit in annoyance.*]

SCENE VIII

[KOCHKARYOV, ZHEVAKIN.]

KOCHKARYOV [*still laughing*]. Oh, I can't bear it, it's too much! I'm laughing so much, my sides are going to split! [*Continues laughing.*]

[ZHEVAKIN *staring at him, also starts to laugh.*]

KOCHKARYOV [*collapses exhausted on to a chair*]. Oh dear, I'm quite exhausted. If I laugh any more, I'll burst every vein in my body.

ZHEVAKIN. I'm very pleased to see you have such a cheerful disposition. On our ship, in Captain Boldyrev's squadron we had a midshipman by the name of Petukhov, Anton Ivanovich: he also liked a good laugh. For example, you only had to show him one finger—that's all—and he'd start laughing, honest to God, he'd laugh all day long. Come to that, he was pretty funny to look at himself: when you looked at him, before you knew it you'd start laughing yourself.

KOCHKARYOV [*drawing a deep breath*]. Holy God, have mercy on us sinners! What did she think she was doing, the stupid goose? How did she imagine she was going to get anyone married? Now, when I fix a marriage, I do it right.

ZHEVAKIN. Really? Can you arrange marriages, seriously?

KOCHKARYOV. Certainly! I'll marry anyone to anyone.

ZHEVAKIN. In that case, would you marry me to the young lady here?

KOCHKARYOV. You? Why do you want to get married?

ZHEVAKIN. What do you mean, why do I want to get married? With respect, that's a rather peculiar question! It's obvious why.

KOCHKARYOV. But surely you know she has no dowry, none at all?

ZHEVAKIN. So much less to worry about. It's a pity, of course, but there again, she's such a delightful young lady, with such exquisite manners, you could get by without a dowry. A little room [*shows approximate size with his hands*], a little entrance-hall over here, with just a teensy little screen or a partition thingy...

KOCHKARYOV. What was it about her that you liked so much?

ZHEVAKIN. To tell you the truth, the thing I liked most was her plumpness. I'm very partial to plumpness in a woman.

KOCHKARYOV [*giving him a sidelong look, aside*]. And he's all skin and bones himself: like an old pouch, with all the tobacco shaken out of it. [*Aloud.*] No, you definitely shouldn't marry.

ZHEVAKIN. Why not?

KOCHKARYOV. You shouldn't, that's all. I mean, between you and me, what sort of figure do you have? Chicken legs...

ZHEVAKIN. Chicken legs?

KOCHKARYOV. Exactly! Take a look at yourself!

ZHEVAKIN. But what precisely do you mean, chicken legs?

KOCHKARYOV. Like a chicken, that's what.

ZHEVAKIN. I can't help feeling that there may be something rather personal about this...

KOCHKARYOV. I'm only telling you because I know you're a man of discernment; I wouldn't say it to anyone else. I will find you a wife—but not this one.

ZHEVAKIN. No thank you, I do not wish to marry anyone else. Please be so kind as to marry me to this one.

KOCHKARYOV. Very well, but on one condition: you must not interfere and on no account must you show your face, not even to your bride. I shall arrange everything in your absence.

ZHEVAKIN. But how can you do it all without me? Surely I'll have to show myself at some point?

KOCHKARYOV. No need. Go home and wait; it'll all be done by this evening.

ZHEVAKIN [*rubbing his hands*]. This is even better than expected! But don't you need some sort of a reference, or my service record?* The young lady might wish to satisfy her curiosity on some point? It'll only take a moment to fetch them.

KOCHKARYOV. I need nothing, just run along home. I'll give you the go-ahead before the day is done. [*Sees him to the door.*] Like hell I will, you stupid clodpate. What's going on? What's keeping that Podkolyosin? Something fishy, methinks. He can't still be adjusting his stirrup-strap! Perhaps I should nip round and fetch him?

SCENE IX

[KOCHKARYOV, AGAFYA TIKHONOVNA.]

AGAFYA TIKHONOVNA [*looking round*]. What, all gone? No one left?

KOCHKARYOV. They've all gone, there's no one.

AGAFYA TIKHONOVNA. Oh, if you only knew how I was shaking! I've never been so scared before. But that Pancake is so terrifying! He would be such a tyrant to any woman he married. I keep thinking he'll come back at any minute.

KOCHKARYOV. Don't worry, he won't come back. Not for anything in the world. I'll wager my own head that neither of those two shows his face here again.

AGAFYA TIKHONOVNA. And what about the third one?

KOCHKARYOV. Which third one?

ZHEVAKIN [*sticking his head round the door*]. I'm just dying to hear the sort of things she says about me with that little mouth of hers... my little rosebud!

AGAFYA TIKHONOVNA. Baltazar Baltazarovich?

ZHEVAKIN. Here we go, here we go! [*Rubs his hands.*]

KOCHKARYOV. Pah! Him! I wondered who you had in mind. A complete nonentity, a half-wit!

ZHEVAKIN. What's all this? I must confess, I don't altogether understand.

AGAFYA TIKHONOVNA. But to look at he seemed so nice.

KOCHKARYOV. A drunkard!

ZHEVAKIN. A what? I don't follow, honest to God, I don't follow.

AGAFYA TIKHONOVNA. Surely not a drunkard, not that too?

KOCHKARYOV. Believe you me, he's a rogue and reprobate!

ZHEVAKIN [*aloud*]. No, I must protest, that's not at all the kind of thing I wanted you to say. A word or two in my favour, a little praise—that would be another matter; but to speak of me in this manner, with these words—thank you most kindly, but you can save that for someone else!

KOCHKARYOV [*aside*]. Why the devil did he have to come back? [*To AGAFYA TIKHONOVNA, sotto voce.*] Just look, you can see for yourself: he can barely stay on his feet. You should see how he lurches about every day! You must send him packing, get shot of him! [*Aside.*] That Podkolyosin's still not here. The toad! I'll get even with him for this! [*Exit.*]

SCENE X

[AGAFYA TIKHONOVNA *and* ZHEVAKIN.]

ZHEVAKIN [*aside*]. He promised to sing my praises and instead he abuses me! What an extraordinary fellow. [*Aloud.*] Mam'selle, you must not believe...

AGAFYA TIKHONOVNA. Forgive me, I'm not well... I have a slight headache. [*Tries to leave.*]

ZHEVAKIN. But perhaps there's something about me that is not to your liking? [*Points to his head.*] You mustn't be put off by the little bald spot I have here. It's nothing, it's because I had a fever; the hair will grow back in no time.

AGAFYA TIKHONOVNA. Really, I couldn't care less what you have there.

ZHEVAKIN. And I must tell you, Mam'selle... When I put on a black tailcoat it gives me a lighter complexion.

AGAFYA TIKHONOVNA. I'm so glad to hear it. Goodbye! [*Exit.*]

SCENE XI

[ZHEVAKIN *alone, calls after her.*]

Mam'selle, I ask you, please tell me the truth: why? What is it? Do I have some major defect, is that it?... She's gone! How very extraordinary! It must be the seventeenth time this has happened to me, and always in almost exactly the same way: at first everything seems fine, then when we're about to put the seal on it— would you believe it?—They turn me down. [*Paces about the room, thinking.*] Hmm... this is bride number seventeen! What exactly does she want, I wonder? Why should she... I mean, what was the problem, exactly... [*Thinks some more.*] Baffling, quite baffling! I could understand it if there was something wrong with me. [*Looks himself up and down.*] But I don't think you could say that—thank the Lord, nature's dealt me a fair hand. Can't understand it. Perhaps I should go home and dig around in my jackdaw box for those little verses of mine. No young lady could possibly resist them... All the same, I cannot make head or tail of it! At first it seemed to be shaping up so well... Now it looks as though I'll have to swing my wagon round and head on home. Such a pity. [*Exit.*]

SCENE XII

[PODKOLYOSIN *and* KOCHKARYOV *enter and look round.*]

KOCHKARYOV. He didn't notice us! Did you see the long face on him as he left?

PODKOLYOSIN. You mean he got brushed off, just like the others?

KOCHKARYOV. Refused point-blank.

PODKOLYOSIN [*with a smug smile*]. It must be disconcerting, all the same, to be turned down like that.

KOCHKARYOV. You're telling me!

PODKOLYOSIN. I still can't believe it. Did she really say she prefers me to all the others, just like that?

KOCHKARYOV. What do you mean: 'prefers'? She's besotted with you. It's true love: you should have heard the sweet names she called you. Such passion—you can see it welling up inside her!

PODKOLYOSIN [*chuckles smugly*]. It's true though: women have a real way with words when they want. Words you and I could never think up: 'my little mugsy-wugsy, my cocksy-cockroach, blacksy-wacksy...'

KOCHKARYOV. Those are nothing! Just wait till you get married, and in the first two months you'll hear something really different. You'll hear words, brother, that will make you melt.

PODKOLYOSIN [*chuckles*]. You don't say!

KOCHKARYOV. As God's my witness! But listen, there's no time to waste. Make your declaration to her, open your heart, and ask for her hand with no further ado.

PODKOLYOSIN. What do you mean: 'with no further ado'? Don't be absurd!

KOCHKARYOV. Without further ado, do you hear?... Look, she's coming.

SCENE XIII

[*Same, with* AGAFYA TIKHONOVNA.]

KOCHKARYOV. I bring to you, Mam'selle, this mortal you see before you. Never before was a man so smitten by the mighty force of love—God help him, a fate I would not wish on my worst enemy...

PODKOLYOSIN [*nudging him, sotto voce*]. Come now, brother, don't overdo it.

KOCHKARYOV [*aside, to* PODKOLYOSIN]. Don't worry, don't worry. [*To* AGAFYA TIKHONOVNA, *sotto voce*.] You must be a little more forward: he's very shy; try and let yourself go with him. Twitch your eyebrows a little, like this, or flutter your eyelashes, then give him a sudden look and knock him out, the scoundrel! Or wave your shoulder under his nose, and make him see it, the good-for-nothing! What a pity you didn't put on a dress with short sleeves; still, this one's quite nice. [*Aloud.*] Well, I shall leave you in pleasant company! If might just have a little peek at your dining-room and kitchen, I must start making the arrangements: the steward will be here soon, to take the dinner order, and the wine may already have come... Farewell! [*To* PODKOLYOSIN.] Buck up, old man! [*Exit.*]

SCENE XIV

[PODKOLYOSIN *and* AGAFYA TIKHONOVNA.]

AGAFYA TIKHONOVNA. Please be so good as to take a seat.

[*They sit in silence.*]

PODKOLYOSIN. Tell me, Mam'selle, are you fond of boating?

AGAFYA TIKHONOVNA. How do you mean, boating?

PODKOLYOSIN. In the summer it's most agreeable to go boating in the country.

AGAFYA TIKHONOVNA. Yes, sometimes I go for boat-rides with friends.

PODKOLYOSIN. Who can say what sort of summer it'll be?

AGAFYA TIKHONOVNA. One hopes it will be a good one.

[*Both fall silent.*]

PODKOLYOSIN. Tell me, Mam'selle, what would be your favourite flower?

AGAFYA TIKHONOVNA. I like those with a strong scent; carnations, I would say.

PODKOLYOSIN. Flowers and ladies go well together.

AGAFYA TIKHONOVNA. Yes, it's a pleasant pastime.

[*Silence.*]

AGAFYA TIKHONOVNA. What church did you go to last Sunday?

PODKOLYOSIN. The Ascension. The week before I went to the Kazan Cathedral.* If you ask me, it doesn't matter which church you pray in. The Ascension is prettier inside, though.

[*They fall silent.* PODKOLYOSIN *drums his fingers on the table.*]

PODKÓLYOSIN. It'll be time for the Yekaterinhof* parade soon.

AGAFYA TIKHONOVNA. So it will, in a month, I think.

PODKOLYOSIN. Less than a month, even.

AGAFYA TIKHONOVNA. It's sure to be fun.

PODKOLYOSIN. Today's the eighth. [*Counts on his fingers.*] Ninth, tenth, eleventh... twenty-two days to go.

AGAFYA TIKHONOVNA. Fancy that, so soon!

PODKOLYOSIN. And I'm not even counting today.

[*Silence.*]

PODKOLYOSIN. Aren't the Russians a splendid nation!

AGAFYA TIKHONOVNA. How so?

PODKOLYOSIN. The workers, I mean. They tower above the world... I walked past a house, and the plasterer was at work, plastering away, quite fearless.

AGAFYA TIKHONOVNA. Is that so? Where was that, pray?

PODKOLYOSIN. On the street I take every day to the office. I have to report for duty every day, you know.

[*Silence.* PODKOLYOSIN *starts drumming his fingers again, then finally takes up his hat and bows.*]

AGAFYA TIKHONOVNA. Surely you're not?...

PODKOLYOSIN. I must. Forgive me if I bored you.

AGAFYA TIKHONOVNA. Oh no, not at all! On the contrary, I must thank you for allowing me to pass the time so agreeably.

PODKOLYOSIN [*smiling*]. I must confess, I thought I was boring you.

AGAFYA TIKHONOVNA. Not at all, I assure you.

PODKOLYOSIN. Well, in that case, perhaps you might permit me to call on you again, some evening perhaps...

AGAFYA TIKHONOVNA. Why, with great pleasure. [*They exchange bows. Exit* PODKOLYOSIN.]

SCENE XV

[AGAFYA TIKHONOVNA *alone.*]

What a fine, upstanding man! I can see it now that I've really got to know him; you couldn't fail to like a man like that—so modest and so understanding. Of course, what his friend said is quite true. It's a pity he left so soon—I would have liked to listen to him some more. It was such a delight to talk with him! The best thing about him is that he doesn't waste time on idle chatter. I would love to have said one or two things to him myself, but I have to confess the courage failed me, my heart started to flutter so... What an excellent man! I must go and tell Auntie. [*Exit.*]

SCENE XVI

[PODKOLYOSIN *and* KOCHKARYOV *enter.*]

KOCHKARYOV. Why do you want to go home? What nonsense! Why go home?

PODKOLYOSIN. But why should I stay here? Have I not said all that needs to be said?

KOCHKARYOV. You mean, you've already opened your heart to her?

PODKOLYOSIN. Well, not exactly; I haven't quite opened my heart yet.

KOCHKARYOV. Now he tells me! And why not, if I might ask?

PODKOLYOSIN. Well, what do you expect? We hadn't even broached the subject, so how was I supposed to say, quite out of the blue: 'Right, Miss, let's get married!'

KOCHKARYOV. In that case what did you say? What rubbish were you talking for the last half hour?

PODKOLYOSIN. Well, we discussed all sorts of things, and I must say I'm very happy with the way it went; the time passed in a most agreeable fashion.

KOCHKARYOV. But look, tell me this: when are you going to do your stuff? Do you realize we have to leave for the church, for the wedding service, in an hour's time?

PODKOLYOSIN. What, are you crazy? The wedding—today?

KOCHKARYOV. Why not?

PODKOLYOSIN. I'm to get married—today?

KOCHKARYOV. But you gave your word; you said you would be ready to get married as soon as we got rid of the other suitors.

PODKOLYOSIN. I'm not going back on my word—but we can't do it right away; we must give it a month, at least, as a breather.

KOCHKARYOV. A month!

PODKOLYOSIN. Of course.

KOCHKARYOV. Have you taken leave of your senses?

PODKOLYOSIN. Less than a month would be no good.

KOCHKARYOV. But I've already given the steward the dinner order, you dolt! Listen to me, Ivan Kuzmich, don't be pig-headed, my dear fellow: you must get married now.

PODKOLYOSIN. For heaven's sake, old chap. What are you saying? How can I get married now?

KOCHKARYOV. Please, Ivan Kuzmich, I beg you. If you won't do it for yourself, then do it for me.

PODKOLYOSIN. It can't be done, I assure you.

KOCHKARYOV. It can, my dear fellow, anything can be done. I beg you, please don't be difficult, my dear, dear fellow!

PODKOLYOSIN. It can't, and that's that. It wouldn't be right.

KOCHKARYOV. What do you mean, it wouldn't be right? Who told you that? Judge for yourself: you're an educated man. I'm not saying this to flatter you, I'm not saying it because you're an office manager, I'm saying it because you're so very dear to me... Enough of this nonsense, my dear friend, try and see things through the eyes of reason.

PODKOLYOSIN. I assure you, if it could be done, I—

KOCHKARYOV. Ivan Kuzmich! Dearest friend! Amigo! Cher ami! Would it help if I went down on my knees before you?

PODKOLYOSIN. What on earth for?

KOCHKARYOV [*falling to his knees*]. Look, I'm on my knees! I'm begging you, look. Do me this one favour and I shall never forget it, my dearest chap, please don't be so stubborn!

PODKOLYOSIN. But it can't be done, old boy, and that's the truth.

KOCHKARYOV [*leaping to his feet*]. Swine!

PODKOLYOSIN. Swear away, if you must.

KOCHKARYOV. You stupid ass! I've never known anyone so stupid.

PODKOLYOSIN. Go on, curse away.

KOCHKARYOV. Why did I try so hard for you, why did I go to such trouble? It was all for your good, you idiot. What's it to me? I give up with you now; I couldn't care less.

PODKOLYOSIN. Anyway, who asked you to go to all this trouble? Go ahead, drop the whole business.

KOCHKARYOV. But you'll perish, you'll be lost without me. If I don't marry you off, you'll remain a fool all the days of your life.

PODKOLYOSIN. So? What's that to you?

KOCHKARYOV. I'm concerned about your welfare, you blockhead.

PODKOLYOSIN. I don't need your concern.

KOCHKARYOV. Well then, go to hell!

PODKOLYOSIN. Very well, I shall.

KOCHKARYOV. Go that way, there!

PODKOLYOSIN. Thank you, I shall.

KOCHKARYOV. And while you're about it, I hope you break your leg! I wish, from the very bottom of my heart, that a drunken cab-driver rams his cab-shaft right into your throat! You're nothing but an old rag—you're no government official! Take it from me: it's all over between us; I hope I never set eyes on you again!

PODKOLYOSIN. Neither you shall. [*Exit.*]

KOCHKARYOV. Go rot in hell with your old friend the devil! [*Opens the door and shouts after him.*] Idiot!

SCENE XVII

[KOCHKARYOV *alone, pacing up and down in a state of considerable agitation.*]

Was there ever another like him on God's earth? What a prize idiot! To tell the truth, I'm a fine one to talk. I ask you, all of you, tell me what you think: am I not a dunderhead, a total cretin? Why do I go to all this trouble, shouting myself hoarse? You tell me: what's he to me? We're not even related! And what am I to him? His nursemaid, his auntie, his mother-in-law, his crony? Why in God's name do I even bother about him? Why tire myself out like this—may he rot in hell! The devil only knows! You wouldn't catch anyone else doing all this for him! The no-good, rotten scoundrel! What a revolting, common face he has! I'd like to take you, you stupid stubborn mule, and whack you on the nose, the ears, the mouth, the teeth—I'd beat you black and blue! [*In his anger he throws a few punches in the air.*] Then, to add insult to injury, he just trots off home without so much as a by-your-leave; it's all water off a duck's back to him—that's what makes it so unbearable! He'll go back home and lie on his divan smoking a pipe. A miscarriage of nature! There are some hideous mugs in the world, but his defies description; you couldn't make one as ugly as his if you tried! No, I shan't stand for it, I'll go and fetch him, the scoundrel! I shan't let him off the hook, I'll bring the villain back! [*Exit running.*]

SCENE XVIII

[*Enter* AGAFYA TIKHONOVNA.]

My heart is beating so fast, I can't imagine why. It seems wherever I look I see Ivan Kuzmich. It's true, though, you can't escape your fate. I keep trying to think about something quite different, but no matter what I set my mind to—I tried winding up some thread, I did some needlework—Ivan Kuzmich kept popping up in my head. [*Falls silent for a moment.*] And to think, at long last, I'm about to take the plunge! They'll take me from here and lead me into the church... then they'll leave me alone

with a man—ooh! It gives me cold shivers to think about it. I
must say farewell to my life as a single girl! [*Sobs.*] I've been
content for so many years. There I was, living away quite happily—and now I have to go and get married! There'll be no end
to my troubles: children, little boys, such mischievous little creatures; and there'll be little girls, they'll grow up—and they'll
have to find husbands too. Well and good if they found decent
husbands, but what if they marry drunkards or gamblers? Men
who blow their last copeck on a game of cards! [*Starts gently
sobbing again.*] I had no chance to enjoy life as a single girl, I'm
not even 27 and I'm getting married already... [*Changing the tone
of her voice.*] What's keeping that Ivan Kuzmich so long?

SCENE XIX

[AGAFYA TIKHONOVNA *and* PODKOLYOSIN, *thrust through the
door on to the stage by* KOCHKARYOV.]

PODKOLYOSIN [*stammering*]. I have come to see you, Mam'selle, to
explain a small matter... But I must first ask you one thing: you
won't think it a little odd, will you?

AGAFYA TIKHONOVNA [*fluttering her eyelids*]. What do you mean?

PODKOLYOSIN. Please, Mam'selle, tell me in all truth: will you not
think it rather odd?

AGAFYA TIKHONOVNA [*as before*]. I cannot imagine what you mean.

PODKOLYOSIN. Tell me the truth: you will think it odd, what I'm
about to tell you, won't you?

AGAFYA TIKHONOVNA. I beg your pardon, but how could I think
it odd? Everything you say is so agreeable to me.

PODKOLYOSIN. Ah, but you've never heard anything like this.
[AGAFYA TIKHONOVNA *lowers her eyes still further; at this moment*
KOCHKARYOV *steals in and stands behind* PODKOLYOSIN.] This is
what I wanted to say... But perhaps I should leave it until later.

AGAFYA TIKHONOVNA. But tell me, what is it, exactly?

PODKOLYOSIN. It's er... To be honest, I was going to declare
something to you, but I'm still not really sure.

KOCHKARYOV [*aside, clenching his arms*]. Dear God, the dunder-head! He's as much use as an old woman's shoe! He's no man—he's a travesty of a man, a disgrace to his sex!

AGAFYA TIKHONOVNA. But why aren't you sure?

PODKOLYOSIN. It just that I keep having doubts.

KOCHKARYOV [*aloud*]. This is so stupid, so utterly stupid! Please, Miss, listen to me: he's asking for your hand, he wants to declare his love for you, to tell you he cannot live, he cannot go another minute without you. All he needs to know is whether you are prepared to make him happy.

PODKOLYOSIN [*panic-stricken, pushes him back, saying sotto voce*]. For heaven's sake, man, what do you think you're doing!

KOCHKARYOV. Well, Miss, what of it? Will you make this humble mortal a happy man?

AGAFYA TIKHONOVNA. I'm not quite sure how I could make some-one a happy man... But yes, I will, all the same.

KOCHKARYOV. Of course, of course you will! We should have done this ages ago. Give me your hands!

PODKOLYOSIN. Just a moment! [*Tries to whisper something in his ear.* KOCHKARYOV *waves his fist at him, glowering fiercely;* PODKOLYOSIN *gives his hand.*]

KOCHKARYOV [*joining their hands together*]. There, may God give you His blessing! I give my consent and approval to your union. Matrimony is a wonderful thing which... It's not like hailing a cab and driving off into the blue; it's a commitment of quite another kind, it's an obligation... Only I'm a bit pressed for time at the moment, so I'll tell you the obligation stuff some other time. Come on, Ivan Kuzmich, give the bride a kiss. You're allowed to do so now. In fact, you have no choice. [AGAFYA TIKHONOVNA *bashfully lowers her eyes.*] It's all right, Miss, don't be shy; it has to be done, let him kiss you.

PODKOLYOSIN. With your permission, Mam'selle, if I might make so bold. [*Kisses her and holds her hand.*] What a charming little hand! How is possible, Mam'selle, to have such a delightful little hand?.. With your permission, Mam'selle, I would like us to marry here and now, without a moment's delay.

AGAFYA TIKHONOVNA. But how can we marry here and now? Isn't that perhaps a little hasty?

PODKOLYOSIN. Not another word! In fact, I wish it could be even sooner, I want us to get married this very minute!

KOCHKARYOV. Bravo! Well said! There speaks a true gentleman! To tell the truth, I always knew that one day you would be capable of great things! He's quite right, Miss, you must make haste and get dressed: I've already sent for the carriage and the invited guests. The guests are at the church already. And your wedding gown is ready, I know.

AGAFYA TIKHONOVNA. It is, of course, it's been ready for ages. I shall be dressed in a moment.

SCENE XX

[KOCHKARYOV *and* PODKOLYOSIN.]

PODKOLYOSIN. Well, old chap, I really am most grateful to you! Now I see what a good service you've done me. My own father wouldn't have done what you've done. I can see that you acted out of pure friendship. Thank you, brother, I shall remember your kindness all the days of my life. [*With emotion.*] This coming spring I shall pay a visit to the grave of your late father, I give you my word.

KOCHKARYOV. Why, don't mention it, old chap, the pleasure was mine. Hang on a moment: let me give you a kiss. [*Kisses him on both cheeks.*] May God grant that you live in happiness [*more kisses*], contentment, and prosperity; may He grant you a tribe of children...

PODKOLYOSIN. Thank you, thank you, old chap. At long last I have learned the true meaning of life. An entirely new world has opened up before me, a world in which all is alive with motion, living, pulsating, sort of fizzing and steaming away, it's hard to say exactly. But I couldn't see any of this before, I didn't understand a thing, in fact I was totally and utterly ignorant, I had no ideas of my own, I never thought about things and lived from day to day, just like the man in the street.

KOCHKARYOV. Delighted to hear it, old chap! Now let me run
along and check on the banquet preparations; I shall be back in
a jiff. [*Aside.*] I'd better hide his hat, though, just in case. [*Picks
up* PODKOLYOSIN's *hat and takes it with him.*]

SCENE XXI

[PODKOLYOSIN *alone.*]

It's true, though, what was I good for anyway? Did I understand
the purpose of life? I had no idea, no idea at all. Indeed, what sort
of life did I have as a bachelor? What purpose did I serve, what
good did I do? I lived my life, I did my job, I went to the office,
I ate and I slept—in short, I was the most empty and commonplace man on God's earth. Now I see how stupid all those people
are who don't get married; when you think of it, it's amazing how
many of them there are, all with their eyes closed tight against
the truth. If I were a dictator, I'd issue a decree that everyone
should get married, every single person without exception, so
there wasn't one unmarried person anywhere in my country!...
It's quite a thought, all the same: in a few minutes I'll be a
married man. You get married and suddenly you taste real bliss,
the sort of bliss you find only in fairy tales, bliss you can't
describe, there are no words for it. [*Falls silent for a few moments.*]
It's a funny thing, though, when you think about it carefully it
gets rather alarming. You tie yourself up, just like that, for the
rest of your life, for ever and ever, and once it's done there's no
getting out of it, no second thoughts, nothing: it's done and
cannot be undone. In fact, there's already no going back: any
minute now I'll be tying the knot. I can't get out of it now—the
carriage is waiting, and preparations have all been made. Is it
really too late, though?—Of course it is: the guests are standing
in the doorway and all over the place; they'll want to know what's
going on. It can't be done, it's not possible. But look: there's an
open window; why don't I pop through it? No, I couldn't—how
could I?—It wouldn't be right, and it's too high, anyway. [*Goes
up to the window.*] Actually, it's not all that high: we're only one
floor up, and the building's not that tall. But no, how could I? I

don't even have my hat and can't possibly go without my hat! It wouldn't feel right. Hmm, come to think about it, why shouldn't I go without my hat? Why don't I give it a try? [*Climbs on to the window-sill and, with the words* 'May the Lord have mercy!', *leaps to the ground below; sound of grunting and exclamations, off.*] Oof! That was a long drop! Ahoy there, cabbie!

VOICE OF CAB-DRIVER. Where to?

VOICE OF PODKOLYOSIN. Kanavka, near the Semyonov Bridge.*

VOICE OF CAB-DRIVER. That'll be ten copecks, give or take.

VOICE OF PODKOLYOSIN. Agreed! Let's get going!

[*Noise of cab driving off.*]

SCENE XXII

[AGAFYA TIKHONOVNA *enters timidly in her wedding gown, bashfully lowering her head.*]

AGAFYA TIKHONOVNA. I just can't think what's come over me! I feel so embarrassed, and I'm trembling all over. Oh, if only he could disappear for a moment from the room, if only he would slip out for something! [*Looks around timidly.*] Where is he? There's no one here. Where did he go? [*Opens door into hall and looks through it.*] Fyokla, where did Ivan Kuzmich go?

VOICE OF FYOKLA. He's there.

AGAFYA TIKHONOVNA. What do you mean: 'there'?

FYOKLA [*enters*]. But he was sitting here, in the room.

AGAFYA TIKHONOVNA. Well he's not here now, you can see for yourself.

FYOKLA. But he can't have left the room either; I was sitting in the hall.

AGAFYA TIKHONOVNA. Where is he then?

FYOKLA. I can't think; perhaps he left by another exit, down the back stairs, or maybe he's sitting in Arina Panteleimonovna's room?

AGAFYA TIKHONOVNA. Auntie! Auntie!

SCENE XXIII

[*Enter* ARINA PANTELEIMONOVNA.]

ARINA PANTELEIMONOVNA [*all dressed up*]. What's going on?

AGAFYA TIKHONOVNA. Is Ivan Kuzmich in your room?

ARINA PANTELEIMONOVNA. No, he must be in here; he hasn't been in to see me.

FYOKLA. He didn't go into the hall either, I was sitting there the whole time.

AGAFYA TIKHONOVNA. Well, he's not in here: you can see for yourselves.

SCENE XXIV

[*Enter* KOCHKARYOV.]

KOCHKARYOV. What's going on?

AGAFYA TIKHONOVNA. Ivan Kuzmich's not here.

KOCHKARYOV. What do you mean, 'Not here'? Has he gone?

AGAFYA TIKHONOVNA. No, he hasn't gone either.

KOCHKARYOV. What do you mean: he's not here, and he hasn't gone?

FYOKLA. I just can't imagine what's become of him. I was sitting in the hall the whole time and I never left my seat.

ARINA PANTELEIMONOVNA. Well, he couldn't possibly have left by the back staircase.

KOCHKARYOV. What the devil's going on? I mean, he couldn't just vanish into thin air, without even leaving the room. I wonder if he's hiding somewhere?.. Ivan Kuzmich! Where are you? Stop playing the fool, and come on out! This isn't funny, you know! You should have left for the church long ago! [*Looks behind the cupboard, and even peeks under the chairs.*] I can't understand it! No, he can't have left the room, it's impossible. He's still here somewhere; his hat's in the other room, I put it there deliberately.

ARINA PANTELEIMONOVNA. Perhaps we should ask the girl? She was outside the whole time, she might have seen something... Dunyashka! Dunyashka!...

SCENE XXV

[*The same, with* DUNYASHKA.]

ARINA PANTELEIMONOVNA. Where's Ivan Kuzmich, have you seen him?

DUNYASHKA. Yes, Ma'am; the gentleman hopped out of the window.

[AGAFYA TIKHONOVNA *shrieks and clasps her hands together.*]

ALL THREE. Out of the window?

DUNYASHKA. Yes Ma'am, and then, when he jumped out, he took a cab and drove off.

ARINA PANTELEIMONOVNA. Are you telling the truth?

KOCHKARYOV. You're lying, it can't be true!

DUNYASHKA. Honest to God, he jumped out! The stallkeeper over there saw him too. He offered the cabbie ten copecks and they drove off.

ARINA PANTELEIMONOVNA [*stepping up to* KOCHKARYOV]. I trust this isn't some kind of a practical joke! Hoping to have a little fun at our expense, were you? Thought you'd make fools of us, did you? In all my fifty and more years I've never known such disgrace. You may be an honest man, sir, but for this I should spit in your face! You may be an honest man, but after this you're nothing but an out-and-out rogue! Fancy humiliating a young girl in front of the whole world? I may only be a simple old woman, but I couldn't do a thing like that. And you're supposed to be a nobleman! I see your noble blood is only good for swinish tricks and swindling people! [*Exit angrily, taking her niece with her.* KOCHKARYOV *stands dumbfounded.*]

FYOKLA. Well? So look at you now, the one who knew how to do everything! Who could arrange weddings without a matchmaker! My suitors may be a peculiar lot, bustards, plucked hens, and the

like, but as for window-jumpers—no, I humbly beg your pardon,
I don't have any of those.

KOCHKARYOV. This is absurd, something must have gone wrong.
I'll run and get him, I'll bring him back! [*Exit.*]

FYOKLA. Yes, off you go, you bring him back! You don't know
much about the marriage business, do you? If the bridegroom
slips out through the door, that's one thing, but when he jumps
out of the window—I can only offer my heartfelt condolences!

THE GOVERNMENT INSPECTOR

It's no use blaming the mirror
if your face is skew.

(Popular saying)

CHARACTERS*

ANTON ANTONOVICH SKVOZNIK-DMUKHANOVSKY, Mayor
ANNA ANDREEVNA, his wife
MARIA ANTONOVNA, his daughter
LUKA LUKICH KHLOPOV, Inspector of Schools
HIS WIFE
AMMOS FYODOROVICH LYAPKIN-TYAPKIN, Judge
ARTEMY FILIPPOVICH ZEMLYANIKA, Warden of Charities
IVAN KUZMICH SHPYOKIN, Postmaster
PYOTR IVANOVICH DOBCHINSKY } local landowners
PYOTR IVANOVICH BOBCHINSKY
IVAN ALEXANDROVICH KHLESTAKOV, a clerk from St Petersburg
OSIP, his manservant
CHRISTIAN IVANOVICH HUEBNER, District Physician
FYODOR ANDREEVICH LYULYUKOV } retired civil servants,
IVAN LAZAREVICH RASTAKOVSKY } respected citizens
STEPAN IVANOVICH KOROBKIN
STEPAN ILYICH UKHOVYORTOV, Chief of Police
SVISTUNOV
PUGOVITSYN } police constables
DERZHIMORDA
ABDULIN, a shopkeeper
FEVRONYA PETROVNA POSHLYOPKINA, a locksmith's wife
SERGEANT'S WIDOW
MISHKA, Mayor's manservant
WAITER AT THE INN
GUESTS, SHOPKEEPERS, TOWNSFOLK, PETITIONERS

CHARACTERS AND COSTUMES

Notes for the Actors

The Mayor: a man who has been long in service and is, in his own way, quite shrewd. Although he does take bribes, he conducts himself with dignity; is fairly serious in mien, and even something of a moralizer; he speaks neither loudly nor softly, neither too much nor too little. Every word he utters is laden with meaning. His features are coarse and hard like those of any man who has begun his arduous career at the very bottom rung. He shifts easily from fear to joy, from servility to arrogance, like any man of coarse disposition. He customarily goes about in a uniform with collar tabs and top-boots with spurs. His hair is cropped short and greying.

Anna Andreevna, his wife: a provincial coquette, in early middle age, her education deriving partly from romantic novels and albums, partly from running the pantry and maids' room. Extremely curious with a proclivity to vanity. Occasionally exercises power over her husband, for the simple reason that the latter does not have a ready answer for her. But this power extends only to matters of trifling importance and consists of scolds and jeers. In the course of the play she changes her costume four times.

Khlestakov: a young man of about 23, of slight build; a little scatter-brained and, as they say, a bit weak in the top storey. One of those people who in government offices are described as 'hare-brains'. Speaks and acts without any forethought. Quite incapable of focusing his attention on any particular idea. His speech is jerky, and words spring from his lips quite unexpectedly. The more ingenuousness and naïvety the actor shows, the more effective his performance will be. Fashionably dressed.

Osip, his manservant: like all servants who are fairly advanced in years. Speaks in a serious tone; eyes mostly downcast, prone to moralize and fond of reciting to himself admonitions addressed to his master. His voice is nearly always level, and when talking to his master it takes on a harsh and curt expression, verging on rudeness. He is shrewder than his master and thus catches on before him, but does not talk much and keeps his own roguish counsel. Wears a shabby grey or dark-blue frock-coat.

Bobchinsky and *Dobchinsky*: both small and short and very inquisitive; extraordinarily alike. Both have little pot-bellies. Both gabble with furious gesticulations. Dobchinsky is a little taller and more serious than Bobchinsky, but Bobchinsky is more easy-going and lively than Dobchinsky.

Lyapkin-Tyapkin, the Judge: a man who has read five or six books and thus is something of a free-thinker. A great amateur of conjecture, he gives special weight to everything he says. The actor playing this part must always preserve a portentous look on his face. Talks in a bass voice, drawling his vowels and emitting wheezing and croaking noises, like an old clock hissing in preparation to strike the hour.

Zemlyanika, Warden of Charities: a very fat, sluggish, and clumsy man, but for all that a cunning rascal. Extremely servile and anxious to please.

Postmaster: a man simple-hearted to the point of naïvety.

The other roles do not require special explanation. Their prototypes can be seen almost anywhere.

The actors must pay particular attention to the last scene. The last word to be spoken must have an immediate, electrifying effect on everyone. The entire group must alter their positions in a split second. Cries of surprise must be emitted by all the ladies simultaneously, as if in one voice. The entire effect may be lost if these instructions are not followed.

ACT I

A room in the MAYOR's *house.*

SCENE I

[MAYOR, WARDEN OF CHARITIES, INSPECTOR OF SCHOOLS, JUDGE, CHIEF OF POLICE, DISTRICT PHYSICIAN, TWO POLICE CONSTABLES.]

MAYOR. Gentlemen, I have invited you here to convey to you some extremely unpleasant news. We are to be visited by a government Inspector.

JUDGE. Inspector?

WARDEN OF CHARITIES. What inspector?

MAYOR. A government inspector from St Petersburg. Incognito. And, what's more, with secret instructions.

JUDGE. Well there's a thing!

WARDEN OF CHARITIES. As if we hadn't enough on our plates already!

INSPECTOR OF SCHOOLS. Good Lord! And with secret instructions!

MAYOR. I had a sort of premonition of this: last night I dreamt the whole night about two extraordinary rats. I've never seen anything like them before, let me tell you: huge black brutes! They came in, sniffed around—and went away again. Now let me read you this letter from Andrei Ivanovich Chmykhov—you know him, Artemy Filippovich. Listen to this now: 'My dear friend, cousin and benefactor (*mutters under his breath, quickly skimming the lines with his eyes*)... to warn you...' Ah! Here it is: 'Amongst other things, I hasten to warn you that a government official has arrived here with instructions to inspect the entire province, and especially our district.' [*Raises his finger significantly.*] 'I have this from the most reliable sources, although I gather he poses as a private person. And since I know that, like everyone, you've committed the odd little sin, because you're a clever man and don't like to let things slip through your fingers...' [*Pauses.*] Well, we're all friends here... 'I would advise you to take precautions, as he could arrive at any time, if indeed he isn't already there, and staying somewhere incognito... Yesterday, I...' Well, this is all family stuff, 'my sister Anna Kirilovna is visiting us with her husband; Ivan Kirilovich has got extremely stout and is still playing the violin...' and so on and so forth. So now you know how things stand!

JUDGE. Yes, it's an extraordinary situation, quite extraordinary. There's something behind it all.

INSPECTOR OF SCHOOLS. But why, Anton Antonovich? What does it mean? Why are we getting an inspector?

MAYOR. Why! It's the vagaries of fate, I suppose! [*Sighs.*] Before this, thank God, they've always gone to other towns; it's our turn now.

JUDGE. It's my belief, Anton Antonovich, that there's a subtle, political reason for this. This is what it means: Russia... yes, Russia wants to go to war, and the ministry, you see, is sending an official to look for any traitors.

MAYOR. Well, now I've heard everything! And you a clever man! Traitors—in our backwater? You could gallop for three years without reaching a foreign country.

JUDGE. No, let me tell you, you're... er... it's not quite... There are no flies on those government fellows. We may be far away, but they keep tabs on us just the same.

MAYOR. Tabs or no tabs, you've been warned, gentlemen. Now, speaking for myself, I've given out a few instructions, and I advise you to do likewise. Particularly you, Artemy Filippovich. There's no doubt about it, the official will want to inspect the charitable institutions as soon as he arrives, and that's your department, so make sure everything is in order. Let's have clean nightcaps and tidy up the patients so they don't look like blacksmiths, the way they would if they were at home.

WARDEN OF CHARITIES. Well, that's no problem. We can easily put our hands on some clean nightcaps.

MAYOR. Do that. And another thing: put some inscription above each of the beds in Latin or some such language... That's really your department, Christian Ivanovich—the name of the illness, when the patient fell ill, date, day of the week. And for heaven's sake get them to stop smoking that foul tobacco—you almost choke when you get inside the door. And you'd better throw some of them out. There are too many of them: the Inspector will think the place is badly managed or the doctor's incompetent.

WARDEN OF CHARITIES. Oh no, Dr Huebner and I have worked out a system—we don't use costly medicines, we leave it all to nature. The common man is a simple creature. If he dies, he dies, if he recovers, he recovers. It's hard for Dr Huebner to discuss the patients' complaints with them, seeing as he can't speak a word of Russian.

[*The* DISTRICT PHYSICIAN *makes a sound somewhere in between 'ee' and 'eh'.*]

MAYOR. Now as for you, Ammos Fyodorovich, you'd better do something about that courthouse of yours. The watchmen are raising a family of geese in the waiting room, where the petitioners sit, and the goslings get under people's feet. I'm all for a bit of animal husbandry and why shouldn't watchmen try their hand at it too?—But the courtroom's not the place for it. I meant to say something about it to you before, but somehow it always slipped my mind.

JUDGE. I'll have them taken straight to the kitchen. Would you care to come to dinner tonight, Anton Antonovich?

MAYOR. I don't like the way you have all that stuff lying around in your own chambers, either. And that whip above the filing cabinet—it won't do. I know you're fond of hunting, but put it out of sight until after the Inspector's been, and then you can hang it up again, if you wish. And that assessor of yours... he's a learned man, I know, but he reeks like a distillery. It simply won't do. I wanted to mention it before but something put it out of my mind. There are things you can take for it nowadays, if it really is his natural smell, as he says. You could tell him to eat onions, or garlic or something. Or maybe Dr Huebner could give him something for it.

[DISTRICT PHYSICIAN *utters the same sound.*]

JUDGE. I'm afraid he can't get rid of it. He says the wet nurse dropped him when he was a baby and he's smelt of vodka ever since.

MAYOR. Well I just wanted to bring it to your attention. And as for my private arrangements, and what Chmykhov calls 'little sins' in his letter—I have nothing to say on that score. There's no such thing as a man with no sins on his conscience. That's the way God Himself has arranged things, despite what the Voltaireans say.*

JUDGE. But what do you consider to be 'little sins', Anton Antonovich? I mean, there are sins and sins. I'm quite prepared to admit that I take bribes—but what sort of bribes? Borzoi puppies. They don't really count.

MAYOR. Oh yes they do: puppies or whatever, they're still bribes.

JUDGE. Come now, Anton Antonovich. What about when someone accepts a 500-rouble fur coat, or a shawl for his wife?...

MAYOR. All right: so maybe you do only take borzoi puppies. But then you don't believe in God and you never go to church. At least I'm a devout, church-going man. But you... I know all about you: when you start talking about the creation of the world it's enough to make one's hair stand on end.

JUDGE. Well, that's the way I thought it out, for myself.

MAYOR. If you ask me, it would be better not to think at all than to think too much. Anyway, I just thought I'd mention the courthouse, but to tell the truth, no one's likely to go in there: you're in an enviable position, it must be under divine protection. As for you, Luka Lukich, as inspector of schools you really must do something about your teachers. I realize that they're learned men, and went to various colleges, but their behaviour is extremely odd, which I suppose is only to be expected with all that learning. But there's one of them now, the one with the fat face... I don't recall his name. He can't get up behind his desk without pulling the most frightful faces, like this (*pulls a face*) and then putting his hand under his cravat and stroking his beard. Of course, when he pulls these faces in front of his pupils it may not matter much, it may even be necessary, I'm no judge of these things, but just imagine what'll happen if he starts doing it in front of our visitor? The Government Inspector may take it as a personal affront. There could be one hell of a row.

INSPECTOR OF SCHOOLS. I ask you: what can I do with him? I've already spoken to him about it several times. Why, just the other day, when the Marshal* came into the classroom, he pulled a face the like of which I've never seen. I know he does it out of the kindness of his heart, but then I get choked off for filling the heads of the young with free-thinking ideas.

MAYOR. Then there's the history master. You can see he's a man of learning, and he knows his subject inside out, but he gets so carried away with it that he quite forgets himself. I listened to him once—so long as he was talking about the Assyrians and Babylonians he was fine, but the moment he got on to Alexander the Great—honest to God: I thought the place was on fire! He leapt out from behind his desk, picked up a chair and brought it crashing down on the floor. All right, Alexander was a great man, but that's no reason to smash the furniture. Those chairs cost money, you know. Government money.

INSPECTOR OF SCHOOLS. Yes, he's certainly an enthusiast! I've brought it to his attention before. His answer's always the same: 'You may say what you like, but I'll lay down my life in the cause of knowledge.'

MAYOR. It seems to be an inexplicable law of fate with clever men: either they have to be drunkards or they go about pulling faces so hideous they would make your icons crack.

INSPECTOR OF SCHOOLS. God help anyone who goes into education, you're never safe. Everyone pokes their noses in and interferes. They all want to prove they're just as learned as the next man.

MAYOR. Yes, well, all that wouldn't really matter, if it wasn't for this confounded incognito business! Any moment he'll poke his head round the corner: 'Ah! here you are, my little doves!' he'll say. 'And tell me, who's the Judge here?'—'Lyapkin-Tyapkin.' 'Fetch me Lyapkin-Tyapkin!—And who's the Warden of Charities?'—'Zemlyanika.'—'Then fetch me Zemlyanika!' That's the worst thing about it.

SCENE II

[The same, with the POSTMASTER.*]*

POSTMASTER. What's all this about some government official?

MAYOR. What, haven't you heard?

POSTMASTER. I heard something from Pyotr Ivanovich Bobchinsky. Just now, in the post office.

MAYOR. So? What do you think?

POSTMASTER. What do I think? I think we're going to war with Turkey.

JUDGE. Exactly! Just what I thought!

MAYOR. Now they're both barking up the wrong tree!

POSTMASTER. No, it's obvious! War with the Turks—it's the French up to their dirty tricks again.

MAYOR. War with the Turks, my foot! We're the ones who're going to suffer, not the Turks. That's a fact: I've had a letter.

POSTMASTER. Ah, a letter! Then it's not war with the Turks.

MAYOR. Now, what do you say to that, Ivan Kuzmich?

POSTMASTER. Me? More to the point, what do you say to it, Anton Antonovich?

MAYOR. Me? Oh, I'm not worried, not very much. It's true the shopkeepers and townsfolk bother me a bit, they complain I've been giving them a hard time, but let me tell you, if I do take the odd thing from them I do it without any malice. As a matter of fact, I have a sneaking feeling *[taking him by the arm, draws him to one side]* someone might have informed on me. Otherwise why should they send an inspector to us? Listen, Ivan Kuzmich, don't you think you might perhaps, for the benefit of us all, just take every letter which goes through your post office, and, you know, steam it open a little and see what it's about, if it's anyone informing, or just run of-the-mill correspondence? If it's harmless, seal it up again. Actually, you can even deliver it like that, unsealed.

POSTMASTER. Oh I know the way... No need to tell me, I do it anyway, but not to check up on people... more out of curiosity, really. I'm just devilish curious about what's going on in the world. And let me tell you, letters make fascinating reading... Some are such a delight to read—the way they describe things, and so edifying, too... Sometimes better than anything in the *Moscow Gazette*!*

MAYOR. Well, in that case tell me, didn't you read anything about some official from St Petersburg?

POSTMASTER. No, nothing about a St Petersburg official. Plenty about Kostroma and Saratov officials, though. Pity you don't read the letters, you don't know what you're missing. Just recently, in a letter to his friend, a lieutenant described a ball in quite the most audacious... really a fine description: 'My life, my dear friend, unfolds, as they say, in the Empyrean sphere: flags unfurling, bands playing, ladies aplenty.'... Yes, written with great, great feeling. I even kept it for myself. Shall I read it to you?

MAYOR. This is hardly the time. But do me a favour, Ivan Kuzmich, if you should happen to get one with any complaints or denunciations in it, then don't hesitate to intercept it, have no qualms about it.

POSTMASTER. Why, of course, with great pleasure.

JUDGE. You'd better be careful, you two, or you'll find yourselves in hot water.

POSTMASTER. God forbid!

MAYOR. Nonsense. It's not as if we're going to make them public knowledge; this is strictly confidential, you understand?

JUDGE. Yes, there's a nasty smell in the air. As a matter of fact, I was just coming to see you, Anton Antonovich, with a little treat: a puppy. From the same litter as that handsome hound of mine, you know the one I mean. You've heard, of course, that Cheptovich is suing Varkhovinsky, which is splendid for me: I can have free hunting on both their estates...

MAYOR. For heaven's sake! Don't talk to me about your hunting now: I can't get this damned incognito out of my head. Any minute I expect the door to open—and lo and behold...

SCENE III

[*The same, with* DOBCHINSKY *and* BOBCHINSKY; *both enter out of breath.*]

BOBCHINSKY. A most extraordinary thing!

DOBCHINSKY. A quite unexpected thing!

ALL. What? What is it?

DOBCHINSKY. Something quite unforeseen. We just popped into the inn...

BOBCHINSKY [*interrupting*]. Yes, I'd just popped into the inn with Pyotr Ivanovich.

DOBCHINSKY [*interrupting*]. Pray, allow me, Pyotr Ivanovich, I'll tell the story.

BOBCHINSKY. No, no, on the contrary, allow me... you can't tell stories properly.

DOBCHINSKY. But you'll get muddled and forget all the important things.

BOBCHINSKY. I most certainly will not. And I beg you not to interrupt; let me tell the story, and don't interrupt. Do me a favour, gentlemen, and tell Pyotr Ivanovich not to interrupt.

MAYOR. What is all this? For the love of God, get on with it—this is unbearable. Do sit down, gentlemen! Here, Pyotr Ivanovich, take this chair! [*They all sit round the two* PYOTR IVANOVICHES.] Well now, what is all this about?

BOBCHINSKY. Allow me: I'll get it all in the proper order. I'd just had the pleasure of leaving you right after you'd received that upsetting letter, yes, I'd just said goodbye to you and... now, please, Pyotr Ivanovich, don't interrupt! I can remember everything. So, as I was saying, I dropped in on Korobkin. But Korobkin wasn't at home, so I dropped in on Rastakovsky, but Rastakovsky was out, so then I called on Ivan Kuzmich to tell him your news, and when I left him I bumped into Pyotr Ivanovich.

DOBCHINSKY [*interrupting*]. Near the stall where they sell meat pies.

BOBCHINSKY. Near the stall where they sell meat pies. So when I saw Pyotr Ivanovich, I said to him: 'Have you heard the news Anton Antonovich got in his letter—from a reliable source?' But Pyotr Ivanovich had already heard about it from your house-keeper, Avdotya, who'd just been sent round to Filipp Antonovich Pochechuev's for something or other.

DOBCHINSKY [*interrupting*]. For a French brandy keg.

BOBCHINSKY [*pushing away* DOBCHINSKY*'s hands*]. For a French brandy keg. And then Pyotr Ivanovich and I went to Pochechuev's... Now please, Pyotr Ivanovich, really... I must ask you not to interrupt!... We were on our way to Pochechuev's when suddenly Pyotr Ivanovich says: 'Let's pop into the inn, I've had nothing to eat since this morning and my stomach's starting to rumble'—Pyotr Ivanovich's stomach, that is—'and they've just delivered some fresh salmon to the inn,' he says, 'we could have a bite to eat.' And no sooner do we enter the inn than this young man—

DOBCHINSKY. Not badly turned out, but in mufti.

BOBCHINSKY. Not badly turned out, but in mufti, starts strolling about the room with such a thoughtful look on his face... and such features... manners... and obviously with plenty up here. [*Waves his hand around his head.*] And suddenly it hits me, something like a premonition, and I turn to Pyotr Ivanovich and say: 'You know, there's something funny about all this.' And Pyotr Ivanovich just snaps his fingers for the innkeeper, you know, old Vlas: his wife had a baby three weeks ago, such a bright little chap, too, he'll be running an inn himself one of these days, just like his dad. So Pyotr Ivanovich whispers to old Vlas: 'Who is that young man?' he asks; and Vlas says: 'That,' he says... Look, don't interrupt, Pyotr Ivanovich, please stop interrupting. You can't tell a story properly, you've got a lisp; you know very well you have, one of your teeth whistles when you talk... Anyway, 'That young man,' he says, 'is an official, he is, come from St Petersburg. Name of Ivan Alexandrovich Khlestakov, and,' says old Vlas, 'he's on his way to Saratov province,* and there's something fishy', says old Vlas, 'about the way he's been carrying on: this is the second week he's been here, he never leaves the inn, has everything charged to his account, and won't part with a single copeck!' And when I heard this it suddenly dawned on me. 'Aha!' I said to Pyotr Ivanovich—

DOBCHINSKY. No, Pyotr Ivanovich, it was me that said 'Aha!'

BOBCHINSKY. Well, you said it first, then I said it. 'Aha!' we said, 'And just what might he be doing, staying put here when he's supposed to be going to Saratov?' Oh yes! It's him, the official, that's who it is.

MAYOR. Who? Which official?

BOBCHINSKY. The official you had news of, the inspector.

MAYOR [*in fright*]. Dear God, no! It can't be him.

BOBCHINSKY. It's him all right: he never pays for anything and never leaves the inn; who else could it be? And he's even got an order for horses to Saratov.

BOBCHINSKY. Oh, it's him, it must be him. He has eyes like a hawk, let me tell you. He doesn't miss a thing. He saw we were eating salmon—because of that business with Pyotr Ivanovich's stomach, you understand... Yes, and then he came over and glanced at our plates. Such a sharp look, too: I was scared stiff.

MAYOR. Lord have mercy on us sinners! What room is he in?

DOBCHINSKY. Number five, under the stairs.

BOBCHINSKY. The same room where those officers started a brawl last year.

MAYOR. And has he been here long?

DOBCHINSKY. About two weeks already. He arrived on St Basil's day, St Basil the Egyptian,* that is.

MAYOR. Two weeks! [*Aside.*] Holy saints and martyrs! In the last two weeks the sergeant's widow has been flogged! The convicts haven't had their rations! The streets are filthy, covered in rubbish! What disgrace! What infamy! [*Clutches his head.*]

WARDEN OF CHARITIES. Should we mount a deputation to the inn, Anton Antonovich?

JUDGE. No, no. First it should be the head of the community, then the clergy, then the tradesmen; let's do it all as it says in the *The Acts of John the Mason.**

MAYOR. No, no, I'll deal with this my way, thank you. We've had hard times before and we've pulled through, and even come out on top. With God's help we might pull through this one too. [*To* BOBCHINSKY.] You say he's a young man?

BOBCHINSKY. Oh yes, no more than 23 or 24.

MAYOR. So much the better. It's easier to get the measure of the young ones. We'd be in trouble if he was some old devil, but these youngsters are plain sailing. Now gentlemen, you go and polish up your doorsteps, and I'll just pop round with Dobchinsky, informally, to make sure the visitors are being looked after. Hey, Svistunov!

SVISTUNOV. Sir?

MAYOR. Run and get the chief of police.—No wait, I need you here. Go and tell someone else to fetch him, as quickly as possible, and then come back here. [SVISTUNOV *races off*.]

WARDEN OF CHARITIES. We'd better be off, Ammos Fyodorovich, we could be in for real trouble.

JUDGE. What are you worried about? Just stick clean nightcaps on your patients and no one will be any the wiser.

WARDEN OF CHARITIES. It's not the nightcaps I'm worried about. I'm supposed to be feeding them oatmeal porridge, and there's such a stench of cabbage wafting down all the corridors you have to hold your breath!

JUDGE. Well, I'm not going to lose any sleep about it. Who on earth would want to inspect the courthouse? If he does read any of the papers in there he'll bitterly regret it. I've sat fifteen years on the bench and every time I look at one of those legal documents I throw up my hands in despair: I can't make head or tail of it. Solomon himself couldn't sort out true from false in a law report. [*Exeunt* JUDGE, WARDEN OF CHARITIES, INSPECTOR OF SCHOOLS and POSTMASTER, *colliding in the doorway with* SVISTUNOV, *on his way back in.*]

SCENE IV

[MAYOR, BOBCHINSKY, DOBCHINSKY *and* SVISTUNOV.]

MAYOR. Well, is the droshky ready?

SVISTUNOV. It's ready.

MAYOR. Right: go outside—no, wait. Go and fetch me... where are all the others? Are you the only one? I thought I gave instructions that Prokhorov was to be here. Where's Prokhorov?

SVISTUNOV. Prokhorov's in the police station, only he's not really available for duty.

MAYOR. How come?

SVISTUNOV. It's like this you see: they had to carry him in this morning, dead drunk, Your Honour. We poured two tubs of water over him, but he still hasn't sobered up.

MAYOR [*clutching his head*]. Oh my God, oh my God! Quick, run outside and—no, wait, run up to my room, do you hear, and get my sword and my new hat. Right, Pyotr Ivanovich, let's go.

BOBCHINSKY. Me too—let me come too, Anton Antonovich!

MAYOR. No, no, Pyotr Ivanovich, you can't, you simply can't. It would be too awkward, and we wouldn't all fit in the droshky.

BOBCHINSKY. Never mind, I'll get there: I'll just scurry along behind the carriage like this—look. I only want to have a little peep through the chink in the door and get another look at this manner of his...

MAYOR [*taking his sword* to SVISTUNOV]. Now quickly round up the rest of the constables and tell them to... But look at that blade— all scratched to pieces! That confounded shopkeeper Abdulin— he can see the Mayor's sword is worn out and he doesn't send a new one. What a pack of rogues! Those swindlers—I bet they're already hard at it concocting petitions against me. Tell the constables to take brooms and start streeting the sweep—damn it! Sweeping the street, the one that leads to the inn, and make sure they sweep it clean. And listen, you, I know you, you get chatting and slip the silver spoons down your bootlegs, you needn't think you can pull the wool over my eyes... Remember how you cheated

Chernyaev, the draper? He gave you two yards of cloth for a uniform and you went and swiped the whole roll! You'd better watch out, constable, you're taking more than your rank permits. On the double!

SCENE V

[*The same, with* CHIEF OF POLICE.]

MAYOR. Ah! Stepan Ilyich, in God's name, where have you been? What the devil are you playing at?

CHIEF OF POLICE. I was here, at the gates.

MAYOR. Now listen here, Stepan Ilyich! This official from St Petersburg is in town already. What have you done about it?

CHIEF OF POLICE. As you directed: I got constable Pugovitsyn to go out with some of the men and sweep the pavements.

MAYOR. And where's Derzhimorda?

CHIEF OF POLICE. Derzhimorda's gone on the fire cart.

MAYOR. And Prokhorov's drunk?

CHIEF OF POLICE. 'Fraid so.

MAYOR. But how did you let that happen?

CHIEF OF POLICE. God knows. There was a brawl outside town yesterday—he went to instil order and came back drunk.

MAYOR. Now listen, this is what you must do: Constable Pugovitsyn, he's a tall chap, you should put him on the bridge for effect. And have them pull down that old fence by the shoemaker's and mark it out with posts, to make it look like a building site. The more things we pull down the better: it shows that the mayor is active. No, wait, good grief, I forgot about that rubbish behind the fence. Forty cartloads of it, at least. What a rotten, filthy town this is! The moment you put up a monument or even a fence they dump all sorts of refuse up against it, devil knows where they get it all from! [*Sighs.*] And another thing, if this inspector happens to ask any of your men if they've got any complaints, make sure they reply: 'No complaints at all, Your Excellency!' And if any of them do want to complain then I'll give them something to complain about afterwards... Oh dear God, I'm a sinner, I'm a wretched sinner! [*Picks up the hatbox instead of his hat.*] But if You pull us through this one I swear I'll light You the biggest candle You ever saw: I'll sting every swine of a tradesman for three poods of wax. Oh my God! Let's go, Pyotr Ivanovich! [*Puts on the cardboard hatbox instead of his hat.*]

CHIEF OF POLICE. Anton Antonovich, that's a box, not a hat.

MAYOR [*flinging it down*]. So it is, damn it! And if he asks why they haven't built a chapel for the hospital—the one we got funding for five years ago—don't forget: we started to build one, but it burnt down. I sent in a report about it. Some idiot might forget and say it was never even begun. And tell constable Derzhimorda to keep his fists under control: his way of keeping order is to give everyone a black eye, guilty and innocent alike. Let's go, Pyotr Ivanovich. [*Goes out and then comes back.*] And for God's sake don't let your soldiers run around outside in the altogether: those scoundrels only wear the top half of their uniforms, and nothing below. [*Exeunt all.*]

SCENE VI

[ANNA ANDREEVNA *and* MARIA ANTONOVNA *run on stage.*]

ANNA ANDREEVNA. Where are they? Oh my God... [*Opens door.*] Anton! Antosha! Antonchik! [*Speaks quickly.*] It's all because of you, it's all your fault. I've never seen such a performance: 'I must have a pin, I must have a ribbon.' [*Runs to window and calls out.*] Anton, where are you going? What? He's arrived? The Inspector? Has he got a moustache? What sort of moustache?

MAYOR [*off*]. Later, dear, later.

ANNA ANDREEVNA. Later? What do you mean, later? Don't give me your later!... Just tell me this: is he a colonel? What? [*With disdain.*] He's gone. You'll pay for this! You and your, 'Mama, mama, wait while I fasten my scarf, it won't take a second.' So much for your second! Because of you we've missed everything! Vain little upstart! Just because she hears the postmaster's here she starts preening herself in front of the mirror: first on this side and then on that side... You think he's set his cap at you, but he pulls a face every time your back is turned.

MARIA ANTONOVNA. Oh, do stop fussing, Mama! We'll know all about it in a couple of hours anyway.

ANNA ANDREEVNA. A couple of hours! Thank you most kindly! Much obliged, I'm sure. Why not say a month? We'd know even more by then! [*Leans out of window.*] Yoohoo, Avdotya! What? Hey, Avdotya, did you find anything out? You didn't? Silly girl! He shooed you away? Well, so what if he did, you could have asked him all the same. Couldn't find out indeed! No wonder: you think of nothing but men all the time. What? They drove off too quickly? Well, you should have run along behind the droshky! Get a move on now, do you hear, run and find out where they've gone, and make sure you find out who this visitor is, what he's like—you know! Have a peep through the keyhole and see what colour his eyes are, and come straight back, do you hear? Now run, faster, faster, faster! [*Still shouting as the curtain falls. Thus the curtain conceals them both, standing at the window.*]

ACT II

Small room at the inn: bed, table, suitcase, empty bottle, boots, clothes-brush, etc.

SCENE I

[OSIP, *lying on his master's bed.*]

Damn it all, I'm hungry! My stomach's clanking and rumbling so much it sounds like a regimental band. And we're not getting any nearer home, either! What a bind! Nearly two months since we left Petersburg. His lordship's been throwing his money about on the road and now he sits with his tail between his legs doing damn all about it. There would have been more than enough for the whole trip, but—oh no, he has to put on a big act every town we stop. [*Mocking him.*] 'I say, my man, scout around and find me the best room they have: I can't eat any old rubbish, you know, nothing but the best for me.' It'd be all right if he really was somebody, not just a measly clerk! Makes friends with some gadabout on the road, it's out with the cards—and here we are stuck in this dump without a sausage. I'm sick to death of it! Mind you, you can have a cushy time in the country—not too much excitement, I admit, but then it's an easy life. Get yourself a woman and lie about on the stove* all day eating pies. But let's face it, there's no two ways about it: Petersburg's the only place. All you need is a bit of cash and you can live the good life— theatres, dancing dogs, whatever takes your fancy. Everyone talks so refined and polite, they could all be nobles: wander along to Shchukin market,* the stallkeepers all call you Sir; take the ferry and find yourself sitting next to a government official; feel like a spot of company, drop round the shops: some brass hat will tell you about the camps, what the stars mean—simple as daylight. Madame the brigadier's missus drops in—and you should see some of them parlourmaids... Fuuah! [*Laughs and shakes his head.*] Genteel's not the word! You'll never hear a rude word and every-one calls you Sir. If you're tired of footing it—take a cab, just like your lordship, and if you don't feel like coughing up the fare?—No trouble, every house that has a front door has a back door too and you beat it so fast the devil himself wouldn't catch you. There's one problem with his lordship, mind: either you're stuffed to the eyeballs or you're starving to death. Like now, for instance. And does he learn? The old man sends him some funds, enough to keep going for a while—and before you know it he's out on the town again, riding around in cabs, sending for theatre tickets every night, and come the end of the week he packs you off to the flea market with his new tailcoat. He'll sell the lot, too, right down to his scruffiest jacket and overcoat. He spends a hundred and fifty on a tailcoat—finest English cloth—and blow me if he doesn't sell it for twenty. And his trousers just go for a song! And why? Because he won't work, that's why. You won't catch him in the office—oh no, he has to be swanning round the boulevards and playing cards. I wouldn't want to be in his shoes if the old man found out! Him being a civil servant won't cut any ice with the old man: it'll be up with his coat-tails and he'll get such a tanning he'll be smarting for days. Let's face it, if you've got a job to do, damn well do it. Now the landlord says no more food till we pay for what we've had—and what if we don't pay? [*Sighs.*] Holy God, what I wouldn't do right now for a bowl of cabbage soup! I'm that hungry I could eat a carthorse. Whoops—someone coming, must be his lordship. [*Quickly jumps off the bed.*]

SCENE II

[OSIP *and* KHLESTAKOV.]

KHLESTAKOV. Here—take this. [*Hands* OSIP *his hat and cane.*] What's this—loafing about on my bed again?

OSIP. Why should I loaf on your bed? Haven't I ever seen a bed before?

KHLESTAKOV. You've been loafing on it, you liar. Look—it's all rumpled.

OSIP. I don't need any bed. Don't I know what a bed is? I've got legs, I can stand on them, can't I? What do I want with your bed?

KHLESTAKOV [*walking up and down*]. Look in the bag and see if there's any tobacco left.

OSIP. Tobacco! What tobacco? You smoked the last scrap three days ago.

KHLESTAKOV [*paces up and down, twisting his mouth in different ways. Finally says in a loud and determined voice*]. Now listen here, Osip!

OSIP. Yes, what is it?

KHLESTAKOV [*loud, but not quite so determined*]. You go down.

OSIP. Down where?

KHLESTAKOV [*most undetermined, almost pleading*]. Down to the dining-room... and tell them... they're to give me some lunch.

OSIP. No chance. You won't catch me going down.

KHLESTAKOV. Don't you dare disobey me, you oaf!

OSIP. Even if I did go it wouldn't be any good. The landlord said he won't give us any more to eat.

KHLESTAKOV. What impertinence! I won't stand for it!

OSIP. And he also says he's going to the Mayor: 'You've been here two weeks without paying,' he says. 'You and your master,' he says, 'you're a right pair of crooks, and your master's a shyster. We've seen the likes of you before,' he says, 'spongers and scoundrels.'

KHLESTAKOV. And what are you so pleased about, you rat?

OSIP. And he says: 'If we just let everybody come along and set up house here we'd never get rid of them. I'm telling you straight,' he says, 'I'll be as good as my word, I'm going straight to the Mayor to have you two put in gaol.'

KHLESTAKOV. All right, you dolt, that'll do! Now go and tell him to send up my lunch. What an uncouth brute!

OSIP. I'd best call him up here to talk to you.

KHLESTAKOV. What do I want to see the landlord for? You tell him yourself...

OSIP. But it's no good...

KHLESTAKOV. Oh for God's sake, go and fetch the landlord then. [*Exit* OSIP.]

SCENE III

[KHLESTAKOV *alone.*]

It's terrible to be so hungry! I took a bit of a walk, thought it would help, make my appetite go away—but it made no difference, damn it. If only I hadn't gone on the razzle in Penza we'd have had enough money to get home. That infantry captain really rooked me at faro.* The hands he kept on dealing himself, the rogue! Sat down for quarter of an hour, and cleaned me out. All the same, I wouldn't half mind another bash at him. Never had a chance. What a dump this town is! Even the shopkeepers won't give you anything on tick. Skinflints! [*Walks up and down whistling air from* Robert le Diable,* *then a popular song, then any old thing.*] Why aren't they coming?

SCENE IV

[KHLESTAKOV, OSIP *and* WAITER.]

WAITER. The landlord sent me to see what you would be wanting.

KHLESTAKOV. Well, hello, my dear chap! How are you today?

WAITER. Very well, thanks be to God.

KHLESTAKOV. And how's business? Everything going all right?

WAITER. Yes, thanks be to God, everything's all right.

KHLESTAKOV. Plenty of guests?

WAITER. Plenty to be getting on with, yes.

KHLESTAKOV. Now look here, my dear chap. They haven't brought me my lunch yet, and I've got some urgent business to attend to, so run along and chivvy them a bit, there's a good fellow.

WAITER. The landlord says we're not to serve you any more. What's more, he says he's going to the Mayor to complain about you.

KHLESTAKOV. Complain? Really, my dear fellow, what about? I mean, a chap's got to eat, hasn't he? I'll waste away at this rate! I'm really hungry, I mean that seriously.

WAITER. Yes, sir. But the landlord said: 'He's not getting another bite till he's paid for what he's had.' Those were his very words.

KHLESTAKOV. But can't you reason with him, explain to him?

WAITER. What must I explain to him?

KHLESTAKOV. Make him understand, I've got to eat. Why worry about the money? The peasant, he thinks that if he can go the odd day without food, other people can too. I like that!

WAITER. Very well, I'll tell him.

SCENE V

[KHLESTAKOV *alone.*]

What'll I do if he says no? I've never been so hungry in my life! Maybe I could flog some clothes... my trousers perhaps? No: I'll hang on to my Petersburg suit if I have to starve to death in it. What a pity Jochim* wouldn't hire me that carriage in St Petersburg: it would have been devilish grand to ride home in a carriage—see me driving up like the devil himself to some neighbour's porch, lamps blazing away and Osip perched up behind in livery. I can just imagine all the excitement: 'Who is it?' 'What is it?' And the footman, all in gold livery, announces [*drawing himself up, playing the footman*]: 'Ivan Alexandrovich Khlestakov presents his card, is Your Lordship receiving?' The louts, they don't even know what 'receiving' means. If some cloddish landowner goes visiting round there he barges straight into the drawing-room, like a bear. I should step up to the pretty daughter: 'Mademoiselle, may I...' [*Rubs his hands and scrapes his foot.*] Pfui! [*Spits.*] I'm so hungry I feel sick!

SCENE VI

[KHLESTAKOV, OSIP, *then* WAITER.]

KHLESTAKOV. Well?

OSIP. They're bringing lunch.

KHLESTAKOV [*claps his hands and jigs up and down on his chair*]. They're bringing lunch! Hooray!

WAITER [*with plates and a napkin*]. The landlord says it's the last time.

KHLESTAKOV. The landlord can... I spit on the landlord! What's that you've got there?

WAITER. Soup and roast.

KHLESTAKOV. What—only two courses?

WAITER. That's it.

KHLESTAKOV. That's outrageous! I won't put up with that! You go and ask him what the devil he thinks he's doing!... It's not enough!

WAITER. The landlord says it's too much.

KHLESTAKOV. Why's there no gravy?

WAITER. There isn't any.

KHLESTAKOV. What d'you mean, there isn't any? I saw them making it when I went past the kitchen, oodles of it. And what about the salmon? There were two short little characters tucking into salmon and lots of other goodies this morning in the dining-room.

WAITER. Well, there is and there isn't, you might say.

KHLESTAKOV. What do you mean, there isn't?

WAITER. Just isn't any, that's all.

KHLESTAKOV. No salmon, no fish, no rissoles?

WAITER. Well, there is, but only for proper customers.

KHLESTAKOV. You stupid oaf!

WAITER. Yes, sir.

KHLESTAKOV. You horrible little pig... Why should they be given the food and not me? I'm a guest of the hotel too, you know.

WAITER. Well, that's because they're different.

KHLESTAKOV. What do you mean, different?

WAITER. It's simple: they pay their bills.

KHLESTAKOV. I'm not going to waste time talking to you, you idiot. [*Ladles out soup and eats.*] What's this? Call this soup? You've just poured dishwater into a cup: it's got no taste, it stinks. I don't want this, take it away.

WAITER. Certainly. The landlord says, if you don't like it you don't have to eat it.

KHLESTAKOV [*protecting the food with his hands*]. No, no, no, no, leave it there, you fool. You may be in the habit of treating your other guests like this, but I wouldn't advise you to try it with me, my friend, I'm a cut above them. [*Eats.*] God, what revolting soup! [*Continues eating.*] I doubt anyone else in the world has ever eaten such slop. Feathers floating in it instead of fat. [*Cuts chicken in soup.*] Good grief! You call that chicken? Let's try the roast. There's a bit of soup left, Osip, help yourself [*Carves roast.*] What in God's name is this? Not meat, that's for sure.

WAITER. Well, what is it then?

KHLESTAKOV. Devil only knows, but it's most definitely not meat. They must have cooked the kitchen cleaver. [*Eats.*] Look at the rubbish they're feeding me! The scoundrels, one mouthful's enough to make your jaws ache. [*Picks his teeth.*] Rogues! It's just like bits of bark: look!—won't come out. It'll probably turn my teeth black. The brigands! [*Wipes his mouth with napkin.*] Well, what else is there?

WAITER. That's the lot.

KHLESTAKOV. What! That's criminal! Not even any sauce or pastry. The scoundrels! Fleecing travellers, that's what it is!

[WAITER *clears up and exits with* OSIP.]

SCENE VII

[KHLESTAKOV, *then* OSIP.]

KHLESTAKOV. It's just as if I'd not eaten at all; it's only whetted my appetite. If only I had a bit of the ready I could send out for a bun.

OSIP [*enters*]. The Mayor's here. Making enquiries and asking about you.

KHLESTAKOV [*terrified*]. The Mayor? Oh my God! That swine of a landlord's complained already! Suppose he really does stick me in prison? Well, I suppose if they're not too rough about it... What am I saying? Prison? I might be seen. There are officers and people outside on the street and there's that pretty little shopkeeper's daughter I swapped a few winks with. I can't go to prison. What do they think I am? Some sort of tradesman or labourer? [*Drawing himself up, and gathering courage.*] I'll tell him straight to his face: 'How dare you?' I'll say, 'How dare—' [*Doorhandle turns,* KHLESTAKOV *goes pale and cringes.*]

SCENE VIII

[KHLESTAKOV, DOBCHINSKY, *and* MAYOR. *On entering,* MAYOR *stops dead.* MAYOR *and* KHLESTAKOV *stare at each other in terror for several minutes, goggle-eyed.*]

MAYOR [*recovering slightly and standing to attention*]. May I offer my salutations, sir!

KHLESTAKOV [*bowing*]. My honour, I'm sure.

MAYOR. Forgive my...

KHLESTAKOV. Not at all.

MAYOR. It is my duty, as the burgomaster of this town, to ensure that visitors and persons of rank are not in any way discommoded.

KHLESTAKOV [*stammering a bit at first, but speaking loudly by the end of his speech*]. But what am I to do! It's not my fault... I'll pay, I promise I will... They'll send me some money from home. [BOBCHINSKY *peeps round door.*] The landlord's more to blame: the meat he serves up is as tough as old boots, and as for the soup... God knows what he puts in the soup, I had to chuck it out of the window. The man lets me starve for days on end... And the tea! Such extraordinary tea! It smells of fish. And then why should I... I mean, fancy that!

MAYOR [*timidly*]. Please forgive me, I'm really not to blame. There's always fresh meat in the market, brought in by honest and sober tradesmen from Kholmogory.* I really don't know where he could have got meat like that. But if things aren't to your liking... Might I perhaps suggest that you come with me to other quarters?

KHLESTAKOV. No, I won't go! I know what you mean by other quarters, you mean gaol. You have no right, how dare you!... I'm—I'm a government official from St Petersburg! [*Blustering.*] I, I, I...

MAYOR [*aside*]. Oh my God, he's in a rage! He's found out everything! Those blasted shopkeepers must have beaten me to it!

KHLESTAKOV [*gathering courage*]. You can come here with a whole regiment, and I won't budge! I shall go straight to the Minister! [*Thumps table.*] What do you think... why should you...

MAYOR [*trembling all over, stands to attention*]. Please sir, have mercy, don't ruin me! I've a wife, small children... Don't ruin us all.

KHLESTAKOV. I won't go! What's that got to do with it? I have to go to gaol because you've got a wife and children? I like that! [BOBCHINSKY *peeps round door and shrinks back, terrified.*] No, thank you humbly, I won't go!

MAYOR [*trembling*]. It was my inexperience, honest to God, it was only my inexperience. And my miserable salary. You can judge for yourself: my official pay is not even enough for tea and sugar. And if there were a few bribes, they were nothing of any consequence: something for the table, or a piece of cloth for a coat. As for that business with the sergeant's widow—the one who keeps a stall at the market—that I'm supposed to have flogged, it's slander, pure slander! Fabricated by my enemies. Those people! You wouldn't believe it... I go in danger of my life.

KHLESTAKOV. So what? All that's got nothing to do with me. [*Pensively.*] Why are you giving me all this stuff about enemies and sergeant's widows? Sergeant's widows are one thing, but don't you try and flog me. The very idea! Who do you think you are? I'll pay my bill, I'll pay it all. It's just that at the moment I've got no money! That's why I'm stuck here like this, because I haven't got a bean on me.

MAYOR [*aside*]. My, this is a sly one! He's cast his line all right... but it's all so foggy you just don't know which way to take it. Well, we might as well take the plunge. What will be, will be. [*Aloud.*] Sir, if you happen to be in need of a temporary accommodation, allow me to be at your service. It's my duty to assist our visitors.

KHLESTAKOV. Yes, I could do with a loan! Then I could pay off the landlord at once... Two hundred roubles would do it, less, even.

MAYOR [*producing banknotes*]. Here you are, here's two hundred exactly. Please don't trouble to count it.

KHLESTAKOV. Much obliged. I'll send it back the moment I get to my estate. I always pay up on the nail... I can see you are a real gentleman. Things will be quite different now.

MAYOR [*aside*]. Well thank God for that! He took it. And I managed to slip him four hundred instead of two hundred.

KHLESTAKOV. Osip! [*Enter* OSIP.] Fetch that waiter back here. [*To* MAYOR *and* DOBCHINSKY.] But why are you standing? Please sit down, I implore you. [*To* DOBCHINSKY.] Pray sit, my dear sir.

MAYOR. Don't worry, we're quite happy to stand.

KIILESTAKOV. No, sir, I beg you, I see now what generous and sincere people you are; and to think that before I was under the impression that you had come to... [*To* DOBCHINSKY.] Please, sit down! [MAYOR *and* DOBCHINSKY *sit,* BOBCHINSKY *peeps round door, listening.*]

MAYOR [*aside*]. Have to be a bit bolder. He wants to stay incognito, I see. All right, we can play charades too: we'll pretend we really have no idea who he is. [*Aloud.*] We—that is, Pyotr Ivanovich Dobchinsky here, one of our local landowners, and myself—were just walking past on business, and we popped into the hotel to find out how they were treating our visitors, because, you see, I'm not the sort of mayor who leaves everything to look after itself. Not only in the line of duty, but as befits a Christian I like to ensure that a kind welcome is accorded to every passer-by, and in this case I have been rewarded by the pleasure of making such a distinguished acquaintance.

KHLESTAKOV. My pleasure too. To tell the truth, if it hadn't been for you I might have been stuck in this hole for quite a while. I really didn't know how I was going to foot the bill.

MAYOR [*aside*]. Just listen to that! Didn't know how he was going to foot the bill! [*Aloud.*] May I be so bold as to enquire in which direction you would be intending to travel?

KHLESTAKOV. I'm heading for Saratov, for my estate.

MAYOR [*aside, with ironic expression*]. Saratov, he says! And not a blush! Phew, you have to keep your wits about you with this one! [*Aloud.*] Ah yes, a fine occupation, travel. Of course, on the one hand, there's always the inconvenience of changing horses, but then they do say it exercises the mind. Do I presume you would be travelling more for the purposes of pleasure?

KHLESTAKOV. No, my father's sent for me. The old boy's got himself in a lather because I haven't earned myself a promotion or a St Vladimir.* He thinks decorations grow on trees in Petersburg. I'd just like to see him sweating in an office all day.

MAYOR [*aside*]. Talk about laying it on thick! Dragging in his old father—I ask you! [*Aloud*.] And would you be staying there for a while, sir?

KHLESTAKOV. I really don't know. The old duffer's as stubborn as a mule and twice as stupid. I shall tell him straight out: say what you like, I can't live anywhere except Petersburg. Why should I waste away my life among peasants, anyway? Nowadays one has different needs; my soul aspires to higher things.

MAYOR [*aside*]. A fine web he's spinning! One lie after the next and he never comes unstuck! And he's nothing to look at—so puny you could squash him with your thumbnail. I'll catch him out somehow, though. [*Aloud*.] Of course you're absolutely right. What can one do in these backwoods? Like here, for instance: I slave away all day for my country, work through the night, spare no effort—but where's the reward? [*Looks round the room.*] This room looks a little damp to me.

KHLESTAKOV. Damp? The room's a disgrace, and you should see the bedbugs: they bite like dogs.

MAYOR. Good God! Such a distinguished visitor and what is he subjected to? Bedbugs, which should never have been created in the first place. A little dark too, isn't it, I should think?

KHLESTAKOV. Black as night. The landlord has a policy of not issuing candles. Get an urge to read a book, or to do a bit of writing myself and I can't, it's too dark.

MAYOR. Might I be so bold... No, it's too presumptuous of me.

KHLESTAKOV. Well, what?

MAYOR. No really, I can't. I'm unworthy.

KHLESTAKOV. But unworthy of what?

MAYOR. You see... There is an excellent room for you in my house, very bright, quiet... But no, I can't, it would be too great an honour. Please don't be angry, I beg you, I was only trying to be of service.

KHLESTAKOV. But on the contrary, dear fellow, I should be delighted. I'd much rather be in a private home than remain in this doss-house.

MAYOR. The delight shall be mine! My wife will be quite overjoyed! That's the way I am, hospitable, always have been ever since I was a child—most especially when the guest is a man of learning like yourself. Please don't think I'm trying to flatter you. It's a weakness of mine: I always speak straight from the heart.

KHLESTAKOV. Sincere thanks. I'm just like you—can't abide two-faced people. I must say I really warm to your frankness and cordiality. When all's said and done, there's nothing better one can ask for in life than devotion and respect. Respect and devotion.

SCENE IX

[*The same, with* WAITER *accompanied by* OSIP. BOBCHINSKY *peeps round door.*]

WAITER. You called, sir?

KHLESTAKOV. Yes, give me the bill.

WAITER. I gave it to you the other day.

KHLESTAKOV. I can't keep track of all your stupid bills. Just tell me how much it is.

WAITER. Well, you had the full table d'hôte the first day, and then the next you had smoked salmon and after that everything was on tick.

KHLESTAKOV. Idiot! He thinks he has to itemize it. Just give me the total.

MAYOR. I beg you not to concern yourself about it, it can wait. [*To* WAITER.] You clear off, I'll see to it...

KHLESTAKOV. Yes, of course, that's a much better idea. [*Puts money away. Exit* WAITER. BOBCHINSKY *peeps round door.*]

SCENE X

[MAYOR, KHLESTAKOV, DOBCHINSKY.]

MAYOR. I wonder if you'd care to look over some of the public buildings in our town? The charitable institutions and so on?

KHLESTAKOV. What's there to see?

MAYOR. Well, you can see how we run the place, how we organize things...

KHLESTAKOV. Of course, with pleasure. [BOBCHINSKY's *head peeps round door.*]

MAYOR. And if you like, we can go from there to the district school, to see how we further the cause of science.

KHLESTAKOV. By all means.

MAYOR. And then you might take a look at the prison, visit the cells—just to see how we keep our criminals.

KHLESTAKOV. Why the prison? I'd much rather look over the charitable institutions.

MAYOR. Of course, of course, anything you say. Will you take your carriage, or will you ride with me in the droshky?

KHLESTAKOV. Oh, I might as well ride with you.

MAYOR [*to* DOBCHINSKY]. No room for you now, Pyotr Ivanovich.

DOBCHINSKY. Never mind, I'll be all right.

MAYOR [*aside to* DOBCHINSKY]. And listen, I want you to run, and I mean run at full speed, with two messages: one for my wife, and one for Zemlyanika at the charitable institutions. [*To* KHLESTAKOV.] May I take the liberty, sir, of writing a few lines to my wife so that she can start preparing for the arrival of our distinguished guest?

KHLESTAKOV. Oh, why should you bother?... In fact there's some ink here, but I don't know about paper... Will this bill do?

MAYOR. Perfectly. [*Writes, muttering to himself.*] We'll see how things work out after a good lunch and a fat bottle of wine! We'll give him some of that local Madeira: looks harmless enough but it'd floor an elephant. So long as I can find out what he's after and how much we have to be on our guard. [*Hands note to* DOBCHINSKY *who goes towards the door. At this moment the door flies off its hinges and* BOBCHINSKY, *who has been eavesdropping on the other side, lands on the stage on top of it. General exclamations of alarm.* BOBCHINSKY *picks himself up.*]

KHLESTAKOV. I say, have you hurt yourself?

BOBCHINSKY. No, no, it's nothing. Please don't trouble yourself, just a little scratch on my nose—here! I'll run over to Dr Huebner for one of his plasters—that'll fix it.

MAYOR [*gestures angrily to* BOBCHINSKY. *To* KHLESTAKOV]. Take no notice, it's nothing. Please allow me, Your Excellency. Your man can bring your luggage. [*To* OSIP.] Bring everything round to my house, will you, my dear fellow, anyone will show you the way. No, please sir, after you! [*Shows* KHLESTAKOV *out and follows him, but turns round to scold* BOBCHINSKY.] Trust you! Couldn't you find anywhere better to fall on your face? What a stupid thing to do! [*Exit followed by* BOBCHINSKY. *Curtain comes down.*]

ACT III

Same room as in Act I.

SCENE I

[ANNA ANDREEVNA, MARIA ANTONOVNA *standing by the window in the same positions.*]

ANNA ANDREEVNA. Just look at that, a whole hour we've waited, and all because of you and your stupid prinking and preening: you're dressed and ready to go, but no: you have to fuss away some more . . . I should never have listened to you in the first place. Ooh, it's maddening! There's not a soul to be seen in the streets—you'd think the whole town was dead.

MARIA ANTONOVNA. Really, Mama, we'll know everything in a minute! Avdotya's bound to come soon. [*Leans out of window and shrieks.*] Mama, look! Someone's coming, there, at the end of the street.

ANNA ANDREEVNA. Where? I can't see anyone. You're always imagining things. Oh yes, so there is. Who is it though? Short little man, in a frock-coat... Who can it be? It's simply infuriating! Who on earth is it?

MARIA ANTONOVNA. It's Dobchinsky, Mama.

ANNA ANDREEVNA. Dobchinsky, my foot! You and your imagination!... Of course it's not Dobchinsky. [*Waves her kerchief.*] Hey, you, come here, quickly!

MARIA ANTONOVNA. It is Dobchinsky, Mama.

ANNA ANDREEVNA. There you go again—you're only saying it to annoy me. I tell you it isn't Dobchinsky.

MARIA ANDREEVNA. There! Can't you see it's Dobchinsky?

ANNA ANDREEVNA. Well, so maybe it is Dobchinsky, I can see him now, so what are you arguing about? [*Shouting out of the window.*] Come on, hurry up! You're walking so slowly. Well, where are they all? What? No, tell me now. What? Very stern? What? My husband, what about my husband? [*Steps back from window, annoyed.*] The man's an idiot: he won't say anything till he gets indoors!

SCENE II

[*The same, with* DOBCHINSKY.]

ANNA ANDREEVNA. I hope you're thoroughly ashamed of yourself, Pyotr Ivanovich. I was relying on you in particular, as a decent person. But no: off they all go and you after them, and does anyone think of telling me what's going on? You should be ashamed! To think that I was godmother to your little Vanechka and Lizanka.

DOBCHINSKY. As God's my witness, ma'am, I've run myself out of breath to get here now. Goodday to you, Maria Antonovna!

MARIA ANDREEVNA. Goodday, Pyotr Ivanovich.

ANNA ANDREEVNA. Well? Now tell us all about it.

DOBCHINSKY. Anton Antonovich sent you a note.

ANNA ANDREEVNA. But what is he? A general?

DOBCHINSKY. Well no, not a general but he's every bit as impressive: so cultured, and such an imposing manner!

ANNA ANDREEVNA. Then it must be the man in the letter.

DOBCHINSKY. The very one. And it was me that discovered him— me and Pyotr Ivanovich!

ANNA ANDREEVNA. But tell me, what happened?

DOBCHINSKY. Well, praise God, so far everything's going smoothly. Mind you, he gave Anton Antonovich a hard time of it to start with. He got very angry, complained about the hotel, and he wasn't going with him and he wouldn't go to prison on his account. But then, when he realized it wasn't Anton Antonovich's fault and the two of them got chatting, he soon calmed down, thank God, and things started to look up. Now they've gone off to visit the hospital... To begin with, Anton Antonovich was even wondering if someone had informed on him, and I was a bit jittery myself.

ANNA ANDREEVNA. But what have you got to worry about, you're not in service?

DOBCHINSKY. Well, it's just that with a brass hat like him you can't help feeling scared.

ANNA ANDREEVNA. Now really!... But enough of that nonsense; tell me now, what's he like? Is he old or young?

DOBCHINSKY. Oh quite young, a young man, about 23, yet he talks just like an old man: 'Very well,' he says, 'we'll have a look at this, and that too' [*waving his arms*], all frightfully upper crust. 'I like to do a bit of reading and writing,' he says, 'but I can't here,' he says, 'because this room's a trifle dark.'

ANNA ANDREEVNA. But what's he like? I mean, is he fair or dark?

DOBCHINSKY. More sort of brown, but with such quick eyes, like a hawk's—they make you feel quite uneasy.

ANNA ANDREEVNA. What's this note all about? [*Reads.*] 'I hasten to inform you, my dear, that I appeared at first to be in great peril but trusting in God's mercy for two pickled cucumber specials and half a portion of caviar one rouble twenty-five...' [*Stops.*] I can't make head or tail of this: what's all this about pickled cucumbers and caviar?

DOBCHINSKY. He was in such a hurry he wrote it on a piece of used paper, it must have been a hotel bill.

ANNA ANDREEVNA. Oh, a bill, I see. [*Continues reading.*] 'But, trusting in God's mercy, all things will be well. Quickly prepare a room for our distinguished guest—the one with yellow wallpaper. Don't trouble about dinner, we'll eat at the hospital with Artemy Filippovich, but order plenty of first-rate wine; send down to Abdulin's for some of his best stuff and tell him that if he doesn't hand it over I'll ransack his cellar. I kiss your hand, my sweet, ever yours, Anton Skvoznik-Dmukhanovsky.' Oh my God! Now we really have to hurry! Hey, Mishka, are you there? Mishka!

DOBCHINSKY [*runs to door and shouts*]. Mishka! Mishka! Mishka! [*Enter* MISHKA.]

ANNA ANDREEVNA. Listen: run to Abdulin's... wait, I'll give you a list.　　　　　　　　　[*Sits at table, writes, talking all the while.*]

Give this list to Sidor and tell him to hurry along to Abdulin's and bring back some wine. And then I want you to go and get the spare room ready for a very special guest. Put in a bed, and a washbasin and all the rest of it.

DOBCHINSKY. I think I'd better run along now, Anna Andreevna, and see how the inspection's going, you know?

ANNA ANDREEVNA. Get along then, I'm not stopping you.

SCENE III

[ANNA ANDREEVNA *and* MARIA ANTONOVNA.]

ANNA ANDREEVNA. Now Masha, we must think about what we're going to wear. He's used to Petersburg fashions: we mustn't make ourselves a laughing stock. I think your pale-blue dress with the little flounces would be the most appropriate.

MARIA ANTONOVNA. Oh no, Mama, not the pale-blue one! I do hate it, and Mrs Lyapkin-Tyapkin goes about in pale-blue, and so does the Zemlyanika girl. I'd much rather wear my floral dress.

ANNA ANDREEVNA. Your floral dress! You know you're only saying that to be difficult. Your blue one will be best because I am going to wear my primrose; you know how I love my primrose dress.

MARIA ANTONOVNA. Oh no Mama! Not primrose. Primrose doesn't suit you at all!

ANNA ANDREEVNA. And why not, may I ask?

MARIA ANTONOVNA. Of course it doesn't. You have to have really dark eyes to wear primrose.

ANNA ANDREEVNA. Would you listen to that? As if I haven't got dark eyes! Very dark eyes! Whatever next—and she knows that I tell my fortune by the Queen of Clubs.

MARIA ANTONOVNA. But Mama, you're really much more like the Queen of Hearts.

ANNA ANDREEVNA. What utter rubbish! I was never the Queen of Hearts! [*Goes off hurriedly with* MARIA ANTONOVNA, *still talking. Offstage.*] Really! Me, the Queen of Hearts! What will she think of next?

[*Doors open as they go out and* MISHKA *sweeps out the rubbish.* OSIP *enters by another door carrying a trunk on his head.*]

SCENE IV

[MISHKA *and* OSIP.]

OSIP. Where d'you want this, then?

MISHKA. This way, old fellow, in here.

OSIP. Hang on a jiff while I get my breath back. What a dog's life! You can't go far on an empty stomach!

MISHKA. Well, tell us, old man, is the general coming soon?

OSIP. What general?

MISHKA. Why, your master, of course.

OSIP. My master? What do you call him, general?

MISHKA. Well, isn't he a general?

OSIP. Oh, he's a general all right, general and a half.

MISHKA. You mean he's more than a real general?

OSIP. You bet!

MISHKA. Well I'll be blowed! No wonder they're making such a fuss about him, then.

OSIP. Look here, son: I can see you've got a head on your shoulders, how about fixing me a spot of grub?

MISHKA. There won't be anything ready for you yet, old fellow. You wouldn't be wanting something plain, but the moment your master sits down to his dinner they'll give you the same as what he gets.

OSIP. What would you mean by something plain?

MISHKA. Cabbage soup, porridge, or meat pies.

OSIP. That'll do fine: cabbage soup, porridge and meat pies! I don't mind, I'll eat whatever there is. Come on, let's shift this thing. Is there another way out, over there?

MISHKA. There is, yes. [*They carry the trunk into a side room.*]

SCENE V

[CONSTABLES *open the double doors. Enter* KHLESTAKOV, *followed by the* MAYOR, *the* WARDEN OF CHARITIES, *the* INSPECTOR OF SCHOOLS, DOBCHINSKY *and* BOBCHINSKY *with a plaster on his nose. The* MAYOR *points out a scrap of paper on the floor to the* CONSTABLES: *they leap over and whip it up, colliding with one another in their haste.*]

KHLESTAKOV. Well, that's quite some hospital! I must say I'm impressed by the way you show your visitors round. In the other towns they never showed me a thing.

MAYOR. If I may dare to suggest an explanation, in other towns the officials are often more concerned with, so to speak, lining their pockets. Here, on the other hand, we think of little else but how to earn the approval of our superiors by our vigilance and good example.

KHLESTAKOV. Excellent lunch. Completely gorged myself. Do you lunch like that every day?

MAYOR. On the contrary, specially cooked for our charming guest.

KHLESTAKOV. I do love eating, I must say. But then what's life for, but to cull the blooms of pleasure. What was that delicious fish?

WARDEN OF CHARITIES [*scurrying up*]. Salt cod, Your Excellency— labberdaan.*

KHLESTAKOV. Really? Very tasty. Where was it we ate—in the hospital, right?

WARDEN OF CHARITIES. Quite right, sir, in the charitable institution.

KHLESTAKOV. Yes, I remember seeing some beds there. Didn't seem to be many patients though. Have they all recovered?

WARDEN OF CHARITIES. About a dozen left, the rest have recovered. It's the way the place is run. Since I took over the management—you may find this hard to believe, but all the patients have been recovering like flies. The moment they set foot in the hospital they feel fit as a fiddle. Not so much through medication as through honesty and good order.

MAYOR. But, if you don't mind my saying, all that's nothing compared to the duties of a mayor. So many things to deal with: cleaning the streets, repairs, renovations... problems enough to flummox the cleverest of men, but, thank the Lord, it's all in order here. I can think of mayors whose only concern would be that little bit on the side but no, as God's my judge, when I lie down to sleep, my prayer is 'Lord God, please let my superiors see my zeal and be pleased with me!' Whether they choose to reward me or not, that's up to them, of course, but at least I'll rest easy. When order reigns in the town, the streets are swept, the convicts well looked after, not too many drunkards about... What more could I want? It's not awards and decorations I'm after. They're attractive to some, I know, but for me, virtue is its own reward.

WARDEN OF CHARITIES [*aside*]. Just listen to that, the hypocrite! Talk about the gift of the gab!

KHLESTAKOV. Oh, very true! I must confess I dabble in philosophy a bit myself. An occasional bit of prose... the odd stanza or two, you know the sort of thing.

BOBCHINSKY [*to* DOBCHINSKY]. So perfectly true, Pyotr Ivanovich! The way he puts things is so... you can tell he's studied the sciences, can't you?

KHLESTAKOV. But tell me, don't you have any amusements in this town? Societies, you know, where you could get together for a game of cards?

MAYOR [*aside*]. Oho, my fine fellow, I can see what you're sniffing at! [*Aloud.*] Heaven forbid! I wouldn't stand for that sort of thing in our town! I've never picked up a card in my life, I don't even know how to play any of these card games. I can't bear to look at them calmly, and if I should be unlucky enough to see a king of diamonds or something like that I feel such revulsion I literally have to spit. I built a house of cards one day, to amuse the children, you know, and had nightmares about the damned things all night! Heaven help us! To think of all the valuable time people waste on them!

INSPECTOR OF SCHOOLS [*aside*]. He only took a hundred roubles off me last night, the lying toad.

MAYOR. My time is better spent in the service of the state.

KHLESTAKOV. Well, I don't think you're being entirely fair. It depends on the view you take of a thing. Of course, if you're the sort of chap who sticks just when you should treble your stake... No, no, there's a lot of fun can be gained from a hand of cards.

SCENE VI

[*The same, with* ANNA ANDREEVNA *and* MARIA ANTONOVNA.]

MAYOR. Your Excellency, allow me to introduce my wife, and my daughter.

KHLESTAKOV [*bowing*]. I am overjoyed, Madame, to enjoy... so to speak... the pleasure of your company.

ANNA ANDREEVNA. Our pleasure is the greater, to have such a distinguished guest.

KHLESTAKOV [*posturing*]. Permit me to insist, Madame, that the pleasure is entirely mine.

ANNA ANDREEVNA. Really sir, you're such a flatterer. Won't you please be seated?

KHLESTAKOV. Merely to stand beside you is already a delight, Madame, but if you absolutely insist, I shall sit. [*Sits.*] What contentment to be seated at your fair side.

ANNA ANDREEVNA. But no, no, you cannot really intend such words for my ears. For one used to life in St Petersburg, such peregrination must be most disagreeable.

KHLESTAKOV. Odious in the extreme, Madame. Accustomed to life as one is, *comprenez-vous*, in the *haut monde*, to suddenly find oneself *en route*: dirty inns, a cultural desert... I must admit, if it hadn't been for this happy occasion, which [*glancing at* ANNA ANDREEVNA *and posturing*]... makes it worthwhile...

ANNA ANDREEVNA. Indeed, it must be most disagreeable for you.

KHLESTAKOV. At this moment, madame, I find it the opposite of disagreeable.

ANNA ANDREEVNA. Oh sir! You flatter me, I'm sure.

KHLESTAKOV. And what more fitting object could one find for flattery?

ANNA ANDREEVNA. But I am a country person.

KHLESTAKOV. Ah! The country, to be sure, has its little... hills and
valleys. But it's true one can't compare it with St Petersburg! Ah,
St Petersburg! That's the life! You may think that I'm just a copy
clerk, but in fact the head of my department and I are as thick as
thieves. He'll clap me on the shoulder, just like that, and say:
'Come round to dinner, old sport!' I only poke my head into the
office for two minutes at a time to say: 'do this, do that!' and the
copy clerk, such a rat, scratches away, tr, tr... They even wanted
to make me a collegiate assessor,* but, I thought, 'what's the
use?'—and turned the promotion down. And the porter's forever
chasing after me with his brush: 'Allow me, sir, I'll just give your
boots a shine.' [*To the* MAYOR.] Why are you all standing, gentlemen? Do please sit!

[*Together*] {
MAYOR. We know our place. Your Excellency.
WARDEN OF CHARITIES. We'd rather stand.
INSPECTOR OF SCHOOLS. Please don't trouble yourself.
}

KHLESTAKOV. Oh for heaven's sake, sit down. [MAYOR *and others all
sit*.] I don't hold with standing on ceremony. On the contrary: I
always go out of my way to be inconspicuous. But it's impossible,
quite impossible! As soon as I turn the corner they all start
saying: 'Look: it's Ivan Alexandrovich!' Do you know, once they
took me for the Commander-in-Chief. The soldiers all came
rushing out of their guardroom and presented arms. And afterwards their officer—who's a close friend of mine—said to
me: 'You know, old chap, we were all quite sure you were the
C-in-C!'

ANNA ANDREEVNA. Good heavens, who would have thought it!

KHLESTAKOV. Oh yes, I'm known all round. I know all the pretty
actresses, of course. I write the odd little vaudeville for them, you
know. Yes, I know a lot of literary types too. Pushkin and I are
great chums. I bump into him every so often: 'How's it going,
Push, old boy?' I say. 'Middling, old chap,' he says, 'fair to
middling.' Old Pushkin's quite a wag, I can tell you.

ANNA ANDREEVNA. So you're a writer too? How wonderful to be so
talented! Do you write for the magazines?

KHLESTAKOV. Oh yes, I do a bit for the magazines. But then I've knocked off so many things: *The Marriage of Figaro*, *Robert le Diable*, *Norma*. I can't even remember what half of them are called. It happened quite by chance, actually. Those blasted theatre managers were always after me: 'Do please write us something, old fellow.' So I thought, 'What the hell: I'll give it a try.' Do you know, I sat down that very same evening and wrote the lot. Astounded them all. Yes, well, I've always had a great facility for thought. All that stuff by Baron Brambeus, *The Frigate of Hope*, *Moscow Telegraph*... They're all mine really.

ANNA ANDREEVNA. You don't mean to say that you're Baron Brambeus?

KHLESTAKOV. Yes, I correct all their bits and pieces at one time or another. Smirdin gives me forty thousand a year for it.

ANNA ANDREEVNA. Tell me, would *Yury Miloslavsky** be yours as well?

KHLESTAKOV. Oh yes, that's one of mine.

ANNA ANDREEVNA. There! I knew it must be.

MARIA ANTONOVNA. But, Mama, it says on the cover that it was written by Mr Zagoskin.

ANNA ANDREEVNA. You would have to make trouble, wouldn't you?

KHLESTAKOV. Yes, of course, it is by Zagoskin. But there's another *Yury Miloslavsky*, and that one's by me.

ANNA ANDREEVNA. Well I'm certain it was yours I read—it's so beautifully written!

KHLESTAKOV. I must admit, I just live for literature. I keep the best house in St Petersburg. Everybody knows it: 'That's Ivan Alexandrovich's house,' they say. [*Addressing all.*] Gentlemen, if you're ever in St Petersburg I beg you to do me the kindness of visiting me. I give balls too, you know.

ANNA ANDREEVNA. I can just imagine how grand and refined they must be!

KHLESTAKOV. They're really quite beyond description. On the table I'll have a watermelon, for example—one watermelon, costing seven hundred roubles! I have soup brought in the pot by steamer from Paris, and the aroma when you lift the lid—out of this world. I'm always at a ball somewhere or other. Or else we make up a four for whist: the Foreign Minister, the French Ambassador, the German Ambassador, and me. Sometimes we keep on playing until we're ready to drop. I just have enough strength to dash up the stairs to my rooms on the fourth floor and say to the cook: 'Here, Mavrushka, take my coat...' Good heavens, what am I saying—I mean the first floor of course. Why, the staircase alone is worth... And you should see the hall, in the morning, even before I wake up. Simply teeming and buzzing with counts and princes—bzz, bzz... just like a swarm of bees. Sometimes the Prime Minister himself looks in. [*The* MAYOR *and all the others rise to their feet, awestruck.*] I'm even addressed on my dispatches: 'Your Excellency'. I was in charge of a government department once for a while. Queer business it was, the director simply vanished into thin air, no one knew where. So, of course, there was the usual bickering about who should take over. All sorts of generals volunteered but as soon as they got a taste of it—no, it was too difficult. At first sight you'd think the job was easy—but take a closer look—the devil of a business. So in the end there was nothing for it: they had to send for me. They sent messengers and couriers all over the city—couriers, couriers, and more couriers—you've no idea. Thirty-five thousand couriers in all! 'Well, what's the problem,' I asked. 'Ivan Alexandrovich, come and take charge of the department!' I must admit, I was a bit taken aback. They caught me in my dressing-gown. I wanted to turn it down—then I realized it might get to the ears of His Majesty and I didn't want to blot my copybook... 'All right,' I said, 'I'll do it if you insist, but I'm warning you, none of your lip now! You have to be on your toes with me!... Or else...' And— let me tell you—the moment I walked into that department, you'd have thought an earthquake had struck: they were all trembling in their boots. Every one of them. [*The* MAYOR *and his crew shake with fear.* KHLESTAKOV *gets more worked up still.*] No, I'm not to be trifled with. I put the fear of God into them. Even the Cabinet's scared stiff of me. And I should think so too! I'm like that! I don't take no for an answer. That's what I tell them all. I know my own mind, I do. No doors are barred to me. I drop in at the Palace every day. Tomorrow they're promoting me to

FIELD-MARSH... [*Slips and almost sprawls on the floor, but the officials catch him and support him respectfully.*]

MAYOR [*stepping up, shaking from head to foot, can hardly speak*]. Woo... woo...

KHLESTAKOV [*quickly and abruptly.*] Well, what is it?

MAYOR. Woo... Woo... Wooya...

KHLESTAKOV [*in the same tone*]. I can't understand a word you're saying, it's all rubbish.

MAYOR. Wooya... Exency... Excellency like to rest? Room's ready and everything you need.

KHLESTAKOV. Nonsense! Don't need a rest... Well, all right. I suppose, if you like. ...A very good lunch, gentlemen. Very good. Well done. [*Declaims.*] Labberdaan! Labberdaan! [*Exit into side room followed by* MAYOR.]

SCENE VII

[*The same, without* KHLESTAKOV *and* MAYOR.]

BOBCHINSKY [*to* DOBCHINSKY]. Now there's a man for you, Pyotr Ivanovich! That's what it means to be a real man! I've never been in the presence of such an important personage before! I almost died of fright. What would you say his rank was?

BOBCHINSKY. Oh, I should think almost a general.

BOBCHINSKY. A general! A general couldn't even unloose his shoes. The generalissimo at least. Did you hear the way he put the wind up the Cabinet? Come on, let's run and tell Lyapkin-Tyapkin and Korobkin. Excuse us, Anna Andreevna.

DOBCHINSKY. Excuse us, ma'am! [*Exeunt* DOBCHINSKY *and* BOBCHINSKY.]

WARDEN OF CHARITIES [*to* INSPECTOR OF SCHOOLS]. I'm terrified, simply terrified—and I can't understand why. We're not even in our uniforms. What if he comes back to his senses and sends off a report to St Petersburg? [*Exit with* INSPECTOR OF SCHOOLS, *pensively.*] Excuse us, ma'am.

SCENE VIII

[ANNA ANDREEVNA *and* MARIA ANTONOVNA.]

ANNA ANDREEVNA. What a charming man!

MARIA ANTONOVNA. What a darling!

ANNA ANDREEVNA. But such refined manners! You can see he's a real person of culture. Such style and finesse! Oh it's superb! I simply adore young men like that! I'm quite overcome! And what's more, he was rather taken with me, I noticed he couldn't take his eyes off me!

MARIA ANTONOVNA. Oh, mama, it was me he was looking at!

ANNA ANDREEVNA. Now please, my dear, no more of your nonsense today. I haven't time for it.

MARIA ANTONOVNA. No, mama, really he was!

ANNA ANDREEVNA. Heavens above, girl, will you never stop picking quarrels! What would he be looking at you for? What earthly reason would he have for looking at you?

MARIA ANTONOVNA. I tell you he was looking at me, mama. When he started talking about literature he looked straight at me, and then when he told us how he played whist with the ambassadors he looked at me too.

ANNA ANDREEVNA. Well perhaps he threw the odd glance in your direction but it was only politeness: 'Ah yes,' he thought, 'it's about time I had a look at her...'

SCENE IX

[*The same, with* MAYOR.]

MAYOR [*enters on tiptoe*]. Shh! Shh!

ANNA ANDREEVNA. What is it?

MAYOR. I wish we hadn't given him so much to drink. Suppose even half of what he said is true? [*Thinks.*] And why shouldn't it be true? 'In vino veritas,' as they say: the truth always slips out when one's had a few. Of course he's embroidered it a bit, but then you never hear a speech these days without a few lies in it. Plays cards with ministers, calls at the Palace... In fact, the more you think about it... My God, it makes my head spin; I feel as if I'm perched on the top of a steeple, or standing with my head in a noose.

ANNA ANDREEVNA. Well I wasn't the least bit intimidated: I just saw in him a man of breeding and culture, and I don't care a straw about his rank.

MAYOR. Pshaw! Women! That's the long and the short of it. Fripperies and tripperies are all you can think of. There's no knowing what you'll blurt out next, and you'll get off with a thrashing, but I'll be for the chop! Carrying on with him like that! As if he were some common-or-garden Dobchinsky!

ANNA ANDREEVNA. I would advise you not to concern yourself on that account. We women know things that you don't. [*Looks at daughter.*]

MAYOR [*aside*]. Oh there's no use talking to those two! What a kettle of fish! I can hardly think straight for fear! [*Opens door and talks through it.*] Mishka, run and call those two constables here, Svistunov and Derzhimorda: they're somewhere out by the gate. [*After brief silence.*] It's a rum business all the same. He's not even anything to look at, so thin and scrawny—you'd never guess who he was! If he was a military man you'd spot him for what he is, but in a tailcoat he looks like a fly with its wings clipped. Though I must say he put on a grand performance at the inn this morning. All that posturing and la-de-dah—I'd never have seen through him. But he gave himself away in the end. These youngsters can never keep their mouths shut for long.

SCENE X

[*The same, with* OSIP. *They dash towards him, beckoning him.*]

ANNA ANDREEVNA. Ah do come here, my good man!

MAYOR. Hush, you! Well? Well? Is he asleep?

OSIP. Not quite, just having a bit of a yawn and a stretch.

ANNA ANDREEVNA. Tell me, what's your name?

OSIP. Osip, ma'am.

MAYOR [*to* WIFE and DAUGHTER]. Now that's quite enough from you! [*To* OSIP.] Tell me, my good man, did they feed you properly?

OSIP. Yes, thank you, Your Honour, they did. Very well, too.

ANNA ANDREEVNA. Now tell me this. At home, I imagine, there'd be quite a few counts and princes visiting your master?

OSIP [*aside*]. What should I say? Seeing as how they fed me so well, they might feed me even better. [*Aloud.*] Oh yes, ma'am, we get them all, counts too.

MARIA ANTONOVNA. He's very handsome, your master, Osip dear!

ANNA ANDREEVNA. Now tell me, Osip, is your master...

MAYOR. That's quite enough! You're just interfering with your idle chatter. Tell me, my man...

ANNA ANDREEVNA. What's your master's rank?

OSIP. Oh, the usual sort of rank.

MAYOR. For God's sake, you and your stupid questions! Can't you see that we have a serious matter to discuss? Now tell me, about your master, is he really strict? Does he give a lot of stick?

OSIP. Oh yes, he's very keen on order. He likes things just so.

MAYOR. I must say, I like your face. You look like a good chap to me. Well now...

ANNA ANDREEVNA. Tell me, Osip, does he go about in uniform at home, or...

MAYOR. Shut up, will you, you chatterboxes! There's a man's life at stake here... [*To* OSIP.] Listen, my friend, I've taken a real liking to you. Now an extra glass of tea is always welcome when one's travelling in this cold weather. Here's a couple of roubles for your trouble.

OSIP [*taking money*]. Thanking you kindly. May God reward you for helping a poor man.

MAYOR. Good, good, glad to be of service. Now what...

ANNA ANDREEVNA. What sort of eyes does your master like best, Osip?

MARIA ANTONOVNA. Osip darling, hasn't your master got the sweetest little nose!

MAYOR. Stop that, now! Let me speak. [*To* OSIP.] Now tell me, my friend, what sort of things does your master notice, you know, what does he like when he's travelling?

OSIP. Well, it's all according to how he looks at things. Most of all he likes to be well looked after, and well entertained.

MAYOR. Well looked after, eh?

OSIP. Yes, he likes that. Now take me, I'm only a serf, but he always sees to it that I'm well treated. Swear to God! Sometimes we'll just be leaving a place and he'll say to me: 'Well, Osip, did they look after you well?' 'Rotten, Your Honour,' I'll say. 'Indeed! So he's a bad host, Osip. Just remind me of his name when we get home.' But usually I think [*with a dismissive wave of his hand*]: 'What the hell.' I'm an easy-going sort of bloke, Your Honour.

MAYOR. You're a good man, Osip, and you talk good sense. I gave you something for a cup of tea, didn't I? Let me give you a bit more for a bun.

OSIP. You're too generous, Your Honour. [*Puts money away.*] I'll drink your health.

ANNA ANDREEVNA. Come to my room, Osip. I've got a little something for you too.

MARIA ANTONOVNA. Osip, dear Osip, kiss your master for me! [*Slight cough heard from* KHLESTAKOV *in other room.*]

MAYOR. Shh! [*Goes on tiptoe. Everyone talks in a whisper.*] For God's sake—we mustn't make a sound! Run along now, you two, we've had enough of you.

ANNA ANDREEVNA. Let's go, Masha! There's something I want to tell you that I noticed about our guest, but it'll have to wait till we're alone.

MAYOR. Those women would talk the hind leg off a donkey. [*Turning to* OSIP.] Now, my friend...

SCENE XI

[*The same, with* DERZHIMORDA *and* SVISTUNOV.]

MAYOR. You clumsy bears, clumping in here with your boots! Like someone unloading a cart! Where the devil have you been gallivanting?

DERZHIMORDA. Acting upon instructions received.

MAYOR. Shh! Quiet! [*Claps his hand over* DERZHIMORDA'S *mouth.*] Cawing like a crow! [*Imitates him.*] 'Acting upon instructions received'! Loud-mouthed oaf! [*To* OSIP.] Now, my friend, you run along and get things ready for your master. Ask for anything in the house you want. [*Exit* OSIP.] And as for you two—go and stand by the front door and don't budge. And don't let anyone in, especially not those damned shopkeepers! If you so much as let one of them in, I'll... The moment you see one of them come near with a petition, or even looking like the sort of person who might have a petition, grab him by the scruff of his neck and boot him out! Like this! [*Demonstrates with a kick.*] You hear? Now get on with it! Shh!... Shhh!... [*Exit on tiptoe after constables.*]

ACT IV

Same room in MAYOR's *house.*

SCENE I

[*Enter cautiously, almost on tiptoe: the* JUDGE, WARDEN OF
CHARITIES, POSTMASTER, INSPECTOR OF SCHOOLS,
DOBCHINSKY *and* BOBCHINSKY, *all in full dress uniform. En-
tire scene conducted in hushed voices.*]

JUDGE [*arranges them all in a semi-circle*]. Look, for heaven's sake,
gentlemen, hurry up and get into formation. And let's have a bit
more order! Don't forget this is a man who visits at the Palace,
God help us, and tears strips off the Cabinet. Get on a military
footing, now—You must be on a military footing! No, no, you
come to this end, Pyotr Ivanovich, and you, Pyotr Ivanovich, go
to that end. [*Both* PYOTR IVANOVICHES *scurry about on tiptoe.*]

WARDEN OF CHARITIES. It's up to you, but I think we should
arrange something.

JUDGE. Arrange what?

WARDEN OF CHARITIES. Well, you know what I mean.

JUDGE. Slip him a couple?

WARDEN OF CHARITIES. Well yes, even slip him a couple.

JUDGE. Too damned dangerous! He's a man of state, he might raise
the roof. Though we could disguise it a bit—we could say it was
a donation from the local gentry towards some public monument.

POSTMASTER. Or we could say: 'Look, this is some money that's
come through the post and we don't know who it belongs to.'

WARDEN OF CHARITIES. You watch he doesn't send you through
the post to a rather distant province! Those sort of things just
aren't done in a properly run community. Why are we all here in
a squadron? We ought to be paying our respects one at a time, so
we each get a sort of... er... tête-à-tête with him, and what the
ears don't hear and so on... That's how things are done in a

properly run society. And I think you should go first, Ammos Fyodorovich.

JUDGE. Me? No I think you should be first. After all it was in your hospital that our distinguished visitor broke bread.

WARDEN OF CHARITIES. Actually, Luka Lukich would be more appropriate, representing science and the enlightenment of youth.

INSPECTOR OF SCHOOLS. I couldn't, gentlemen. Really I couldn't. It's the way I was brought up, you see. As soon as someone one step higher in rank says anything to me my heart leaps into my mouth and I can't move my tongue. No, gentlemen, you'll have to excuse me, really I couldn't!

WARDEN OF CHARITIES. Well that leaves you, Ammos Fyodorovich. Master of the polished phrase. Cicero himself couldn't do better.

JUDGE. Whatever next? I ask you: Cicero! Just because I get a bit carried away sometimes about my hounds!

ALL [*urging him*]. No, not just about your dogs, you can go on about the Tower of Babel, about anything. Don't let us down, Ammos Fyodorovich, don't desert us, be our patron! Please, Ammos Fyodorovich!

JUDGE. Do please leave off, gentlemen! [*At this moment footsteps and coughs are heard from* KHLESTAKOV's *room. All scramble for the door, jostling one another in their anxiety to get out. Stifled yelps are heard:*]

BOBCHINSKY'S VOICE. Ouch! Pyotr Ivanovich! Watch where you're going—that's my foot!

WARDEN OF CHARITIES' VOICE. Let me through, gentlemen, take it easy now, you're crushing me.

[*More yelps of* 'Ow!' 'Ouch!'; *finally all squeeze out and the stage is empty.*]

SCENE II

[*Enter* KHLESTAKOV, *alone, with bleary eyes.*]

KHLESTAKOV. I must have slept like a top! Where do they get those feather-beds and eiderdowns, I wonder?—I'm dripping with sweat. My head's pounding like a gong—I reckon they must have slipped me something at lunch yesterday. It looks as if I could have quite a pleasant time here. There's nothing like hospitality, especially when it's provided out of the goodness of people's hearts and not with some ulterior motive. The Mayor's daughter's not a bad-looking crumpet, either, and even the old lady would do at a pinch... I don't know, one way and another I rather fancy this place.

SCENE III

[KHLESTAKOV and JUDGE.]

JUDGE [*stopping as he enters, to himself*]. Oh my God, please help me, my knees are giving way. [*Aloud, drawing himself up and putting his hand on his sword.*] May I have the honour of introducing myself: Collegiate Assessor and Justice of the district court Lyapkin-Tyapkin.

KHLESTAKOV. Please take a seat. So you're the local beak?

JUDGE. Appointed in 1816 for a three-year term by the will of the local gentry, and I have remained in office till this day.

KHLESTAKOV. And tell me, is it a profitable business, being a judge?

JUDGE. Awarded the order of St Vladimir, Fourth Class, after nine years of duty, with a commendation from the authorities. [*Aside.*] This money's burning a hole in my hand.

KHLESTAKOV. Yes, I like the Vladimir. Far more the thing than the St Anne,* don't you think?

JUDGE [*holding his clenched fist forward a little. Aside*]. Dear God in Heaven, I feel like I'm sitting on hot coals.

KHLESTAKOV. What's that you've got in your hand?

JUDGE [*starts and drops money on the floor*]. What? Er... nothing!

KHLESTAKOV. Nothing? But isn't that some money you've dropped?

JUDGE [*shaking all over*]. Oh no, sir! Not at all. [*Aside.*] Oh my God, now it's my turn to sit in the dock! I can hear the rattle of the gaol-cart!

KHLESTAKOV [*picking it up*]. It is money, you know.

JUDGE [*aside*]. It's all over. I'm done for now.

KHLESTAKOV. I tell you what, Judge—why don't you lend me this for a while?

JUDGE [*hastily*]. Why... why... of course! With pleasure! [*Aside.*] Holy Mother of God, get me through this!

KHLESTAKOV. I ran a bit short on the road, d'you see, what with one thing and another. But I'll send it to you as soon as I get to my estate.

JUDGE. Oh please, Your Excellency, don't give it another thought— it's a great honour for me in any case. I endeavour at all times... to serve the authorities... to the full extent of my abilities, weak though they may be... [*Rising from his chair, standing to attention.*] I shall not presume to trouble you further with my presence. Has Your Excellency any instructions for me?

KHLESTAKOV. Instructions?

JUDGE. I thought perhaps you might have some instructions for the district court?

KHLESTAKOV. Why no, I shan't be needing the district court now.

JUDGE [*exit bowing, aside*]. God be praised—I've saved the day!

KHLESTAKOV [*upon* JUDGE*'s exit*]. A nice fellow, that judge!

SCENE IV

[POSTMASTER *enters stiffly, in uniform, holding his sword.*]

POSTMASTER. May I have the honour to present myself: Postmaster and Aulic Councillor Shpyokin.

KHLESTAKOV. Pleased to meet you. Nothing I like better than good company. Do sit down. Lived here all your life, have you?

POSTMASTER. That is correct, sir.

KHLESTAKOV. I must say I'm very taken with your town. Of course it's no metropolis, but what the hell! It's not the capital, is it? I say, it's not the capital, is it?

POSTMASTER. No sir, quite right, sir.

KHLESTAKOV. Of course, it's only in the capital that you find the *bon ton*, and you get away from the provincial yokels. Isn't that so? What do you think?

POSTMASTER. Oh, quite correct, sir. [*Aside.*] He's not a bit high and mighty. Asks my opinion about everything.

KHLESTAKOV. But even so, one can be quite well off in a small town, wouldn't you say?

POSTMASTER. Oh yes, quite right, sir.

KHLESTAKOV. I mean it depends what you ask for. All you need is a bit of respect and the knowledge that people really like you— don't you think?

POSTMASTER. Exactly my own view, sir.

KHLESTAKOV. I must admit I'm glad you share my opinion. People often find me a bit odd, but it's just the way I am. [*Looking him in the eyes, to himself.*] Maybe this one's good for a touch, too. [*Aloud.*] You know, it's a most peculiar thing but I cleaned myself out on the way here. Haven't a bean left. Imagine! You couldn't perhaps lend me three hundred roubles, could you?

POSTMASTER. What? Why, with the greatest pleasure. There you are, sir. I am always glad to be of service.

KHLESTAKOV. Most grateful. I must admit, I hate having to deny myself things when I'm travelling. Why should I, anyway? Don't you agree?

POSTMASTER. Oh absolutely, sir. [*Stands, draws himself erect and puts his hand on his sword.*] I shall not presume to trouble you further with my presence. Perhaps Your Excellency has some observations pertaining to the postal administration?

KHLESTAKOV. No, no, none at all.

[POSTMASTER *bows himself out.*]

KHLESTAKOV [*Lighting a cigar*]. That postmaster's not a bad sort of chap either. Obliging, at any rate. That's the sort of fellow I like.

SCENE V

[KHLESTAKOV *and* INSPECTOR OF SCHOOLS, *who is virtually shoved into the room. A voice behind him says, in a stage whisper,* 'Get in, you coward!']

INSPECTOR OF SCHOOLS [*drawing himself up, trembling, and clutching his sword*]. Have the honour to present myself: Titular Councillor Khlopov, Inspector of Schools.

KHLESTAKOV. Delighted! Sit down, sit down. Have a cigar, won't you? [*Hands him a cigar.*]

INSPECTOR OF SCHOOLS [*to himself in indecision*]. Oh God! Never expected this! Do I take it or not?

KHLESTAKOV. Go on, take one, they're not bad little cigars. Not a patch on St Petersburg ones, of course. I pay twenty-five roubles a hundred for mine. When you've smoked one you just want to kiss your hands. Here, light up. [*Gives him a candle.*]

[INSPECTOR OF SCHOOLS *attempts to light it and starts shaking.*]

KHLESTAKOV. That's the wrong end!

INSPECTOR OF SCHOOLS [*drops cigar in fright, spits, and says to himself in despair*]. Oh heavens above, my cursed shyness again! Ruined everything.

KHLESTAKOV. I can see you're no connoisseur of cigars. I'm afraid they're one of my weaknesses. That and the fair sex of course. I can't resist a pretty woman. What about you? Which do you prefer: blondes or brunettes? [INSPECTOR OF SCHOOLS *is totally lost for a reply.*] I say, which do you prefer, blondes or brunettes?

INSPECTOR OF SCHOOLS. I wouldn't presume to know, sir.

KHLESTAKOV. No, no. Don't evade the issue! I'm anxious to know your preferences.

INSPECTOR OF SCHOOLS. Sir... Your Excellency... I beg to submit... [*Aside.*] God Almighty, what am I saying!

KHLESTAKOV. Ha! You won't let on. You've clearly had a tangle with some little brunette. That's right, isn't it? Admit it!

[INSPECTOR OF SCHOOLS *is speechless.*]

KHLESTAKOV. Aha! You're blushing! You see! You see! So why wouldn't you tell me?

INSPECTOR OF SCHOOLS. I was afraid, Your Hon... Your Ex... Your Highn... [*Aside.*] My confounded tongue's let me down again!

KHLESTAKOV. Afraid eh? Yes, there is something in my eyes that strikes fear into people's hearts. At least, I know for a fact that no woman alive is able to resist them, wouldn't you agree?

INSPECTOR OF SCHOOLS. Oh absolutely, sir.

KHLESTAKOV. Do you know, it's a most peculiar thing, I'm completely skint. Lost the lot on the road. You couldn't lend me three hundred roubles, could you?

INSPECTOR OF SCHOOLS [*delving into his pockets, to himself*]. Where is it? I've lost it, I've lost it! Oh, thank heavens, here it is. [*Takes out notes and hands them over, trembling.*]

KHLESTAKOV. Much obliged to you.

INSPECTOR OF SCHOOLS [*drawing himself up, hand on sword*]. I shall not presume to trouble you further with my presence.

KHLESTAKOV. Cheerio, then.

INSPECTOR OF SCHOOLS [*aside, hurrying out, almost at a run*]. Phew! Thank God for that! Now let's hope he won't look at the classrooms.

SCENE VI

[KHLESTAKOV *and* WARDEN OF CHARITIES, *standing stiffly, hand on sword.*]

WARDEN OF CHARITIES. May I have the honour of presenting myself, Excellency? Warden of Charities, Aulic Councillor Zemlyanika.

KHLESTAKOV. How d'you do. Sit down please.

WARDEN OF CHARITIES. I recently had the honour to receive you personally at the charitable institutions under my supervision.

KHLESTAKOV. So you did. I remember. Splendid lunch you gave us.

WARDEN OF CHARITIES. It is an honour to be able to exert oneself in the service of one's country.

KHLESTAKOV. I must admit, I have a great weakness for *haute cuisine*. Tell me, weren't you a little shorter yesterday?

WARDEN OF CHARITIES. Quite possibly. [*Brief silence.*] I never spare myself in the performance of my duty. [*Edges closer with his chair, and talks in hushed voice.*] Which is more than can be said for the postmaster here; he never lifts his finger. There are the most fearful delays in the postal service. You may feel it warrants an investigation. And the judge too, who was here just before me, he spends his whole time hunting hares, keeps dogs in the court-house, and his private life, if I dare mention such things in your presence—and indeed I must, for the sake of the nation, for all that he may be a friend and a relative—his private life is simply scandalous. There's one landowner here, Dobchinsky by name— Your Excellency has met him, I believe—well, the moment Dobchinsky leaves his house the judge pops in to see his wife— it's true, I swear... Try and have a look at the children; not one of them looks like Dobchinsky: they're all, even the girl, the spitting image of the judge.

KHLESTAKOV. You don't say! I'd never have thought it!

WARDEN OF CHARITIES. And as for our school inspector... I simply don't know how the authorities could have appointed him. He's worse than a Jacobin,* and he fills our children's heads with such subversive ideas that I couldn't even bring myself to tell you about them! Perhaps Your Excellency would prefer me to put this down in writing?

KHLESTAKOV. Yes, do that. That's an excellent idea. I like to have something amusing to read when I'm bored... What's your name again? My memory, you know...

WARDEN OF CHARITIES. Zemlyanika.

KHLESTAKOV. Ah yes! Zemlyanika. And tell me, do you have any children?

WARDEN OF CHARITIES. Er... yes, five, Your Excellency, two already grown up.

KHLESTAKOV. You don't say! And what are they... er?...

WARDEN OF CHARITIES. Is Your Excellency so gracious as to be asking their names?

KHLESTAKOV. Yes, what are they called?

WARDEN OF CHARITIES. Nikolai, Ivan, Yelizaveta, Maria, and Peripeteia.

KHLESTAKOV. Very nice too.

WARDEN OF CHARITIES. I shall not presume to trouble you further with my presence, and to take up your time, which is designated for sacred duties... [*Bowing his way out.*]

KHLESTAKOV [*accompanying him*]. No, no, not at all, what you said was most entertaining. Please come another time... I should be delighted... [*Turns back and opening door, calls after him.*] Hey you! What did you say your name was? I didn't catch your first names.

WARDEN OF CHARITIES. Artemy Filippovich.

KHLESTAKOV. Look here, Artemy Filippovich, you won't believe this but I'm cleaned out of ready cash. Haven't a copeck left on me. You couldn't lend me four hundred roubles?

WARDEN OF CHARITIES. Yes, of course.

KHLESTAKOV. Well now, isn't that a stroke of luck! I'm most obliged to you.

SCENE VII

[KHLESTAKOV, BOBCHINSKY, *and* DOBCHINSKY.]

BOBCHINSKY. May I have the honour to present myself: Pyotr Ivanovich Bobchinsky, member of the local citizenry.

DOBCHINSKY. Landowner Pyotr Ivanovich Dobchinsky.

KHLESTAKOV. Ah yes, I've seen you before. You're the one who had the fall, aren't you? How's the nose?

BOBCHINSKY. Oh please don't disturb yourself on my account, it's healed up now, thank God!

KHLESTAKOV. Healed up, has it? That's good. [*Abruptly.*] Got any money on you?

BOBCHINSKY. Money? What money?

KHLESTAKOV [*quickly and loudly*]. For a loan. A thousand roubles or so.

BOBCHINSKY. Honest to God, I haven't anything like that much. What about you, Pyotr Ivanovich?

DOBCHINSKY. I'm afraid not—not on me, because my money, if Your Excellency is so good as to be interested, has been lodged with the Board of Public Charities.

KHLESTAKOV. Well, if you haven't got a thousand, you can give me a hundred.

BOBCHINSKY [*rummaging in pockets*]. Have you got a hundred, Pyotr Ivanovich? All I've got is forty in notes.

DOBCHINSKY [*examining his wallet*]. Twenty-five roubles, that's the lot.

BOBCHINSKY. You'd better look more carefully, Pyotr Ivanovich! I know you've got a hole in your right pocket, and some may have slipped down into the lining.

DOBCHINSKY [*looking*]. No, really. There's nothing there, I'm afraid.

KHLESTAKOV. Well, never mind. I'll make do with what you've got. Give me the sixty-five roubles. It'll have to do. [*Takes the money.*]

DOBCHINSKY. If I might make so bold as to ask Your Excellency's assistance with regard to a rather delicate matter.

KHLESTAKOV. What is it?

DOBCHINSKY. It really is extremely delicate, Your Excellency: you see my eldest boy, if you'll pardon the phrase, was born out of wedlock.

KHLESTAKOV. Indeed?

DOBCHINSKY. Well, that is, in a manner of speaking, you see, because he was born to me just as if it were in wedlock, if you take my meaning, Your Excellency, and then of course, as was proper, I sealed the bonds of matrimony. And so now, if you will be so good as to see what I mean, I want him to be my son legally and to take my name, Dobchinsky.

KHLESTAKOV. Fine, let him take it! What's the problem?

DOBCHINSKY. I wouldn't have troubled you with it, but you know he's such a gifted boy, you feel sorry for him! Such a clever little chap: he should go far... He can recite poems already and if he ever gets hold of a penknife he can carve you a little horse and cart as quickly as any conjuror. Pyotr Ivanovich can bear me out.

BOBCHINSKY. Yes, he's a talented boy.

KHLESTAKOV. Good! Good! I'll do what I can, I'll talk to... I'll try... I'll fix something up, yes... [*Turns to* BOBCHINSKY.] And have you anything to tell me?

BOBCHINSKY. Well, actually I do have one request which I humbly ask of you.

KHLESTAKOV. What is it?

BOBCHINSKY. When you return to St Petersburg, I beg you just to say to all those high and mighty people, those senators and admirals, say to them: 'Your Highness,' or 'Your Excellency' or whatever... 'In such-and-such a town there lives a man called Pyotr Ivanovich Bobchinsky'. Just tell them that: 'There lives a man called Pyotr Ivanovich Bobchinsky.'

KHLESTAKOV. Very well.

BOBCHINSKY. And if you should come across His Majesty, if you could just mention to him, that... just say: 'Your Imperial Highness, in such-and-such a town there lives a man called Pyotr Ivanovich Bobchinsky.'

KHLESTAKOV. Very well.

DOBCHINSKY. Do forgive us for burdening you thus with our presence.

BOBCHINSKY. Do forgive us for burdening you thus with our presence.

KHLESTAKOV. Please don't mention it! It was a pleasure. [*Shows them out.*]

SCENE VIII

[KHLESTAKOV *alone.*]

There are a lot of officials here. They seem to have taken me for some government chappie. I suppose I did lead them on a bit yesterday. What a bunch of cabbageheads! I must write and tell Tryapichkin in St Petersburg all about it: he writes those articles, he can really go to town on this lot! Hey, Osip! Bring me some paper and ink. [OSIP *pops head round door saying:* 'Right away'.] Once old Tryapichkin gets his teeth into someone he really rips them to pieces. He wouldn't spare his own father for a good joke, and he likes the feel of money, too. These officials aren't a bad lot, really. Obliging with their loans, at any rate. Let's just see how much I've got: three hundred from the judge, three hundred from the postmaster, six hundred, seven, eight... ugh! what a filthy note! nine hundred.... Over a thousand! Just let me run into that double-dealing captain now. We'll see who gets the upper hand now!

SCENE IX

[KHLESTAKOV *and* OSIP, *with paper and ink.*]

KHLESTAKOV. Well, you oaf, you see what sort of a reception they're giving me? [*Begins writing.*]

OSIP. Yes, you can say that again! But there's just one thing, Ivan Alexandrovich.

KHLESTAKOV. What's that?

OSIP. Let's scarper. Honest to God, it's time we were off!

KHLESTAKOV. Nonsense! Why?

OSIP. I think we should, that's all. We've had a good splurge, the last two days; let's get out while the going's good. What's the point of knocking around with this lot, anyway? To hell with them! Our luck might turn and someone else could arrive at any minute... For God's sake, Ivan Alexandrovich! They've got some fine horses here—we could be off like greased lightning!

KHLESTAKOV [*writing*]. No: I want to stick around a bit. Tomorrow maybe.

OSIP. Tomorrow may be too late. For God's sake, let's be off now, Ivan Alexandrovich. They may be rolling out the red carpet for you now, but the sooner we do a bunk the better. It's only because they think you're somebody else... Your old man's going to blow his top if we don't get a move on. And with these horses they wouldn't see us for dust.

KHLESTAKOV [*writing*]. Oh all right. But take this letter along first, and you might as well order the horses at the same time. Make sure they give us good horses. Tell the coachmen I'll give them a rouble apiece if they drive like cavalry charges! And sing songs! [*Continues writing.*] Just wait till Tryapichkin reads this. He'll die laughing...

OSIP. I'll send one of the men here with it, sir, while I get on with the packing, so we don't waste any time.

KHLESTAKOV [*writing*]. Very well. Only get me a candle.

OSIP [*exit, off*]. Hey, listen, you! You're to take a letter down to the post office when it's ready and tell the postmaster he's to take it without money. And tell them to send round the best troika, the one the government messengers use—and my master won't pay for that either: tell them it's official. Now step on it, or His Lordship will be furious. Wait—the letter's not finished yet.

KHLESTAKOV [*still writing*]. I wonder where he's living now—Post Office Street or Gorokhovaya?* He also likes changing his address frequently—when the rent's overdue. I'll take a chance on Post Office Street. [*Folds and addresses it.*]

[OSIP *brings a candle.* KHLESTAKOV *seals the letter. Voice of* DERZHIMORDA *heard saying:* 'Where do you think you're going, fuzz-face? I've got orders not to admit anybody.']

KHLESTAKOV [*gives letter to* OSIP]. Here, take it.

SHOPKEEPERS [*off*]. You can't keep us out, we've come on business. It's urgent. Let us in, officer.

DERZHIMORDA [*off*]. Off with you! Go on, beat it! He won't receive you, he's asleep.

[*Noise increases.*]

KHLESTAKOV. What's that noise, Osip? See what it is, will you.

OSIP [*looking out of window*]. It's some tradesmen who want to come in, and the copper won't let them. They're waving bits of paper: seems they want to see you.

KHLESTAKOV [*going to window*]. Well, my friends, what can I do for you?

SHOPKEEPERS [*off*]. We appeal to you, Your Lordship. Allow us to present a petition.

KHLESTAKOV. Let them in, let them in! Osip, tell them they can come in. [*Exit* OSIP.]

KHLESTAKOV (*receives petitions through the window, opens one of them and reads*). 'To His Most Noble Eminence the Lord High Financier from the shopkeeper Abdulin...' What the devil is all this?— There's no such title.

SCENE X

[KHLESTAKOV *and* SHOPKEEPERS, *with basket of wine and sugar loaves.*]

KHLESTAKOV. What can I do for you, friends?

SHOPKEEPERS. We humbly beg your noble favour!

KHLESTAKOV. Well, what's the problem?

SHOPKEEPERS. Don't ruin us, sir! Deliver us from our yoke of unjust oppression.

KHLESTAKOV. Who's oppressing you?

ONE OF THE SHOPKEEPERS. It's all the Mayor's doing, sir. There never was a mayor like him, your lordship. The abuses he gets away with—you wouldn't believe it. He'll ruin us with all the soldiers he billets in our homes. The way he treats us! He pulls our beards and calls us Tartars. Honest to God! As if we didn't show him proper respect! But we always do our duty: a little bit of cloth to make a dress for his wife and his daughter—we've got no objection to that. But that's not enough for him, oh no: he comes into the shop and grabs whatever takes his fancy. He sees a length of cloth and says: 'Ah, my dear chap, that's a nice bit of cloth: send it round to me, will you?' So we send it, and there goes fifty yards of material.

KHLESTAKOV. You don't say! What a scoundrel!

SHOPKEEPERS. Scoundrel's the word! You have to hide everything away when he comes into the shop. He's not at all particular, either: he'll take any old rubbish! Prunes that have sat in the barrel for seven years, that even my assistant wouldn't touch, and he eats them by the handful. We give him all sorts of presents on his name-day, St Antony's, but he's not content with that and tells us he's having another name day, on St Onuphrius's. Which means more presents.

KHLESTAKOV. Why, the man's an out-and-out rogue!

SHOPKEEPERS. You can say that again! And if any man dares say a word against him he'll billet a whole regiment on him. Or he'll lock him up in his own house. 'I can't have you flogged,' he says, 'I can't have you tortured—that's against the law, but this way I can have you on bread and water!'

KHLESTAKOV. The man's a monster! He could go to Siberia for less than that!

SHOPKEEPERS. Siberia or further—anywhere you choose to send him, so long as it's far away from us. Now Your Honour, please accept this humble token of our hospitality, just a little sugar and wine.

KHLESTAKOV. Good heavens no! I wouldn't dream of it. I never accept bribes. But if you offered to lend me three hundred roubles, for instance, that would be quite a different matter. Loans I can accept.

SHOPKEEPERS. By all means, good father! [*They take out money.*] But why only three hundred? Better still, take five hundred, but do please help us.

KHLESTAKOV. Oh well, if you insist. It is only a loan, after all...

SHOPKEEPERS [*hand money to him on a silver tray*]. And won't you take the salver with it?

KHLESTAKOV. Well, I don't mind if I do.

SHOPKEEPERS [*bowing*]. And please take some sugar as well, sir.

KHLESTAKOV. No, no, I never take bribes...

OSIP. Oh go on, take it, Your Excellency. You never know when you might need a bit of sugar on the road. Here, I'll take it—the loaves and the package. Yes, give me the lot. What's that there? A piece of string? Give it here, a bit of string always comes in handy. If bits fall off the cart, you can lash them back on.

SHOPKEEPERS. Please look kindly on our plea, Your Grace. If you won't help us, we don't know what will happen! We might just as well stick our heads in the noose!

KHLESTAKOV. Rest assured, good people! I'll do everything I can.

[*Exeunt* SHOPKEEPERS. WOMAN*'s* VOICE *is heard:* 'Now don't you dare stop me! I'll lodge a complaint against you with His Excellency! Ouch! Stop shoving, that hurts!']

KHLESTAKOV. Who's that? [*Goes to window.*] What's the matter, woman?

VOICES OF TWO WOMEN. Have mercy, father, I beg you! Hear my plea, Your Lordship.

KHLESTAKOV [*speaking through window*]. Let her in.

SCENE XI

[KHLESTAKOV, LOCKSMITH'S WIFE *and* SERGEANT'S WIDOW.]

LOCKSMITH'S WIFE [*bowing deeply*]. Have mercy on us...

SERGEANT'S WIDOW. Have mercy on us...

KHLESTAKOV. Well, good women, who are you?

SERGEANT'S WIDOW. Ivanova, Your Worship, widow of Sergeant Ivanov.

LOCKSMITH'S WIFE. Fevronya Petrovna Poshlyopkina, Your Honour, wife of locksmith Poshlyopkin...

KHLESTAKOV. Wait, one at a time. What's the problem?

LOCKSMITH'S WIFE. Have mercy, father: I have a complaint against the Mayor! May God rot his soul! And may his children, and his own thieving self, and his uncles and aunts all rot in hell!

KHLESTAKOV. Goodness—what for?

LOCKSMITH'S WIFE. The swine!—he had my husband conscripted into the army even though his turn hadn't come up! And he can't be called up by law, anyway: he's married.

KHLESTAKOV. Well then, how could he do it?

LOCKSMITH'S WIFE. He can do it, the scoundrel, and he did it— may God damn him to eternal hell! May he, and his aunt, if he's got one, meet a sticky end, and if his father's still alive I hope he also kicks the bucket, the scoundrel, or chokes on his porridge! He was supposed to take the tailor's son, who's a drunkard anyway, but the boy's parents gave him an expensive present, so he went after the shopkeeper Panteleeva's son, and Panteleeva sent three bolts of cloth to his wife, so he moves on to me. 'What do you need your husband for?' he says, 'he's no use to you.' That's for me to say, whether he's any use or not, you scoundrel! 'He's a thief,' he says, 'he may not have stolen anything yet, but he will do sooner or later, and next year he'll be conscripted anyway.' The crook!—How am I supposed to manage without my husband? I'm weak, you rotten swine! I hope none of your family ever sees the light of day again! And if you've got a mother-in-law, I hope your mother-in-law...

KHLESTAKOV. Very well, very well. And what about you? [*Showing* LOCKSMITH'S WIFE *out.*]

LOCKSMITH'S WIFE [*making her exit*]. Please don't forget, good father! Be merciful!

SERGEANT'S WIDOW. It's about the Mayor, Your Honour...

KHLESTAKOV. Well, what is it? Keep it brief.

SERGEANT'S WIDOW. He had me flogged, as God's my witness, he did.

KHLESTAKOV. How come?

SERGEANT'S WIDOW. It was all a mistake, Your Worship. Some peasant women were quarrelling in the market, and the police didn't get there till it was all over and they had to arrest someone, so they just grabbed me. And they gave me such a thrashing, I couldn't sit down for two days.

KHLESTAKOV. Well, what do you want me to do about it?

SERGEANT'S WIDOW. Of course there's nothing can be done about it now. But you could make him pay damages. I could do with some good luck right now and spare cash is always welcome...

KHLESTAKOV. Very well, very well. I'll see to it, run along now. [*Hands clutching petitions are thrust through the window.*] Not more of them? [*Goes to window.*] No, go away! I don't want them! Take them away, for God's sake. [*Moves away.*] I'm sick to death of them! Don't let them in, Osip.

OSIP [*shouts through window*]. Go away! Scram! That's the lot for today! Come back tomorrow! [*Door opens to reveal a figure in a frieze coat, unshaven, with a swollen lip, and bandaged cheek. Behind him others are visible in the background.*] Where do you think you're going? Beat it! [*Thrusts back the first of them, pushing him by the stomach. Exit with them, slamming the door behind him.*]

SCENE XII

[KHLESTAKOV *and* MARIA ANTONOVNA.]

MARIA ANTONOVNA. Oh!

KHLESTAKOV. Did something give you a fright, mamselle?

MARIA ANTONOVNA. No, nothing.

KHLESTAKOV [*putting on airs*]. I am indeed flattered, mamselle, to think that you should have thought me the sort of man who... May I ask where you were going?

MARIA ANTONOVNA. I wasn't going anywhere, really.

KHLESTAKOV. And for what particular purpose were you not going anywhere?

MARIA ANTONOVNA. I was wondering if mama might be here.

KHLESTAKOV. No, but I'm curious to know why exactly you should be going nowhere?

MARIA ANTONOVNA. I'm being a nuisance, keeping you from your important affairs.

KHLESTAKOV [*posturing*]. But your eyes are more important than any affairs. How could you be a nuisance? No: you couldn't be a nuisance if you tried; on the contrary, you can bring me pleasure.

MARIA ANTONOVNA. That must be the way they speak in St Petersburg.

KHLESTAKOV. What other style would suit so exquisite a creature? May I give myself the happiness of offering you a chair? What am I saying? You deserve a throne.

MARIA ANTONOVNA. I don't know really. I ought to be going. [*Sits.*]

KHLESTAKOV. What a beautiful scarf you're wearing.

MARIA ANTONOVNA. Oh! You city people always make fun of us provincials.

KHLESTAKOV. Oh that I were that scarf, that I might thus embrace your lily-white neck.

MARIA ANTONOVNA. I just don't know what you're talking about. A scarf, did you say?... What extraordinary weather we're having today!

KHLESTAKOV. Your lips, mamselle, are much more extraordinary than any weather.

MARIA ANTONOVNA. Oh, you do say such things!... I want to ask you to write some verses in my album. I'm sure you know a lot of verses, don't you?

KHLESTAKOV. Your wish, signorina, is my command. What sort of verses would you like?

MARIA ANTONOVNA. Oh, any sort—just something good, and new.

KHLESTAKOV. Ah yes, verses! I know so many.

MARIA ANTONOVNA. Well, tell me which ones you'll write for me.

KHLESTAKOV. Why bother? I can remember them without reciting them.

MARIA ANTONOVNA. But I do so love poetry.

KHLESTAKOV. I know so many different kinds. Well, if you insist... how about this: 'Oh man, that thou shouldst thus vainly vent thy scorn upon the Gods...'* And there are others, too, only I can't quite call them to mind now. Anyway, to get to the point. Rather let me tell you about the love I feel when I gaze into your eyes. [*Moves his chair closer.*]

MARIA ANTONOVNA. Love! I don't understand what that is... I've never known what love means... [*Moves chair away.*]

KHLESTAKOV [*moves chair closer*]. Why do you move away? It's much more comfortable to sit close together.

MARIA ANTONOVNA [*moves away*]. Why sit close together, when it's the same further away.

KHLESTAKOV [*moving closer*]. But why be further apart, when it's the same to sit together.

MARIA ANTONOVNA [*moves away*]. But what's the purpose of all this?

KHLESTAKOV [*moving closer*]. It's all in the mind, you see. You only think we're close: just imagine that we're far apart instead. Oh what bliss, mamselle, if I could enfold you in my arms and press you to my heart.

MARIA ANTONOVNA [*looking out of window*]. What was that bird that just flew past? Was it a magpie?

KHLESTAKOV [*kisses her on the shoulder and looks out of the window*]. A magpie, yes.

MARIA ANTONOVNA [*jumps up in indignation*]. Now that's really too much!... What nerve!...

KHLESTAKOV [*restraining her*]. Forgive me, dear lady, it was love, the purest love that made me do it.

MARIA ANTONOVNA. You must take me for a real country maid... [*Attempts to leave.*]

KHLESTAKOV [*continues to restrain her*]. No, it was love, really, it was love. I only meant it in fun. Forgive me, Maria Antonovna, please forgive me! I'll even go down on my knees to seek your forgiveness. [*Falls to his knees.*] I beg you to forgive me. You see, I'm on my knees.

SCENE XIII

[*The same, with* ANNA ANDREEVNA.]

ANNA ANDREEVNA [*seeing Khlestakov on his knees*]. Heavens! Quel spectacle!

KHLESTAKOV [*rising*]. Damnation!

ANNA ANDREEVNA [*to her daughter*]. Well, young lady, what's the meaning of this? What kind of behaviour is this?

MARIA ANTONOVNA. Mama, I...

ANNA ANDREEVNA. Leave the room, do you hear! Go on, out! And don't dare show your face in here again.. [*Exit* MARIA ANTONOVNA *in tears.*] Forgive me, but I must say, I am surprised, Your Excellency.

KHLESTAKOV [*aside*]. She's quite a tasty morsel, herself... Hm... not at all bad. [*Throws himself on his knees.*] Madame, you must know that I'm consumed with love.

ANNA ANDREEVNA. What are you doing on your knees? Dear me, do please stand up—the floor's not at all clean!

KHLESTAKOV. No, on my knees, I must be on my knees. I have to know what is to be my fate—whether life or death.

ANNA ANDREEVNA. Forgive me, but I'm afraid I don't quite take your meaning. If I'm not mistaken, you're making some sort of declaration about my daughter?

KHLESTAKOV. No, no, it's you I'm in love with—you! My life hangs by a thread. If you don't requite my undying love I shall be unworthy of earthly existence. With my bosom aflame I ask for your hand.

ANNA ANDREEVNA. But I must point out, I am—to some extent, that is... a married woman.

KHLESTAKOV. Why, that doesn't matter! True love knows no barriers. The heart is a law unto itself, as Karamzin* says. Together we'll flee—to the shade of a distant brook... your hand, I beg you, your hand!

SCENE XIV

[*The same, with* MARIA ANTONOVNA, *who suddenly rushes in.*]

MARIA ANTONOVNA. Mama, papa says you're to... [*Seeing* KHLESTAKOV *on his knees, shrieks.*] Heavens! Quel spectacle!

ANNA ANDREEVNA. Why you... well... what do you think you're doing? Little flibberty-gibbet! Dashing in here like a scalded cat! And what are you so surprised about? I can't (imagine) what nonsense you've got in your head. Nobody would think you were 18 years old. You're just like a child of 3. When are you going to learn a bit of sense and start behaving like a properly brought-up young lady? When will you learn the rules of good conduct?

MARIA ANTONOVNA [*through her tears*]. Mama, really, I didn't know...

ANNA ANDREEVNA. You have nothing between your ears, that's why! You're no better than those Lyapkin-Tyapkin girls. Why you always have to copy them, I can't imagine. There must be better examples you can find. Take your mother, for instance.

KHLESTAKOV [*grasping the daughter's hand*]. Anna Andreevna, I beg you not to stand in the way of our happiness. Give your blessing to our constant love!

ANNA ANDREEVNA [*astonished*]. I don't... You mean she's the one?

KHLESTAKOV. Tell me at once. Is it life?... or death?

ANNA ANDREEVNA. Now look what you've done, you little fool. All because of you, you little wretch, our distinguished guest goes down on his knees in front of me and you come dashing in like a mad thing. By rights I should say no. I ought to refuse my consent: you're not worthy of such happiness.

MARIA ANTONOVNA. I won't do it again, Mama, really I won't.

SCENE XV

[*The same, with the* MAYOR, *who enters, breathless.*]

MAYOR. Mercy, Your Excellency! Spare me! Don't ruin me!

KHLESTAKOV. What's the matter?

MAYOR. The shopkeepers have been complaining to Your Excellency. Not half of what they say is true, I give you my word of honour, they're all liars and cheats. And the sergeant's widow who said I had her flogged, she's lying too, I swear to God: she flogged herself.

KHLESTAKOV. To hell with the sergeant's widow—I have other matters to deal with now.

MAYOR. Don't believe them, Your Excellency. They're all such liars... any child could see through them. The whole town knows that they're outright liars. And as for swindling, allow me to inform you: that lot are swindlers such as the world has never seen before.

ANNA ANDREEVNA. I don't think you're aware of the honour Ivan Alexandrovich is doing us. He's asking for our daughter's hand in marriage.

MAYOR, What?.... Have you lost your mind, woman? You don't know what you're saying. Please don't be angry, Your Excellency: she's a little touched. Just like her late mother.

KHLESTAKOV. But it's true: I am asking for her hand. I'm in love.

MAYOR. Your Excellency... I can't believe it.

ANNA ANDREEVNA. But he's telling you.

KHLESTAKOV. I'm quite serious... My love for her could drive me from my senses.

MAYOR. I daren't believe it, I'm unworthy of such an honour.

KHLESTAKOV. But if you do not give your consent I shall not be responsible for my actions.

MAYOR. I can't believe it: Your Excellency is having a little fun?

ANNA ANDREEVNA. Oh you nincompoop! Why don't you listen to what the gentleman's telling you?

MAYOR. I can't believe it.

KHLESTAKOV. Your consent, your consent! I'm a desperate man, I'll do anything: when I shoot myself you'll find yourself in court.

MAYOR. Oh, my God! No, please, I'm innocent, innocent in body and soul. Please don't be angry. I beg you to do as Your Excellency pleases. I can't think straight. My head's in a whirl... God only knows what's going on. I'm sure I'm making a complete ass of myself.

ANNA ANDREEVNA. Well, go on, give them your blessing.

[KHLESTAKOV *brings* MARIA ANTONOVNA *to the* MAYOR.]

MAYOR. May God bless you both, but I'm innocent, I swear.

[KHLESTAKOV *kisses* MARIA ANTONOVNA.]

MAYOR [*looking on*]. What the devil? Well, I never! [*Wipes his eyes.*] They're kissing each other! Dear God, they're kissing each other! It's true, they're engaged! [*Shrieking and jumping for joy.*] Whoopee, Anton! Whoopee, Anton! This is your lucky day!

SCENE XVI

[*The same, with* OSIP.]

OSIP. The horses are ready.

KHLESTAKOV. Er, right... I'll be there in a minute.

MAYOR. I say, is Your Excellency leaving?

KHLESTAKOV. Er, yes, I'm just off.

MAYOR. But, did you not... I mean... did Your Excellency not mention something about—er—a wedding?

KHLESTAKOV. Oh that, yes... I shan't be a minute... a day or two, to see my uncle, you know, a rich old boy... Be back tomorrow.

MAYOR. Of course. We would not presume to delay you and we look forward to your safe return.

KHLESTAKOV. Yes, of course. I'll be right back. Goodbye, my love... Oh... words fail me! Farewell, my darling! [*Kisses her hand.*]

MAYOR. Will you be needing anything for the road? Your Excellency was—er—a little short of money?

KHLESTAKOV. Oh no, why should I need any money?... [*Thinking a moment.*] Then again, perhaps I could do with a little.

MAYOR. How much would you be needing?

KHLESTAKOV. Well, let's see, you lent me two hundred—I mean four hundred—I don't want to take advantage of your mistake—so, shall we say the same again, to bring it up to a round eight hundred?

MAYOR. Certainly! [*Takes money out of wallet.*] What's more, all in nice, brand-new notes.

KHLESTAKOV. So they are. [*Examining money.*] How splendid. As they say, new notes bring new luck.

MAYOR. They do, indeed.

KHLESTAKOV. Well, cheerio, Anton Antonovich! Much obliged for all your hospitality. I must say, I've never had such a good reception anywhere else before. Farewell, Anna Andreevna! Farewell my darling, Maria Antonovna! [*Exeunt.*]

[*Voices heard off.*]

VOICE OF KHLESTAKOV. Farewell, my angel, Maria Antonovna!

VOICE OF MAYOR. What's all this? Surely you're not travelling in the post-chaise?

VOICE OF KHLESTAKOV. Oh yes, that's how I always travel. Springs give me a headache.

VOICE OF COACHMAN. Whoa!

VOICE OF MAYOR. Well, at least take something to spread on the seat. If you like I'll get you a rug?

VOICE OF KHLESTAKOV. No, what for? It doesn't matter. Though I suppose you could give me a rug.

VOICE OF MAYOR. Hey, Avdotya! Go to the store-room and get the best rug, the one with the blue ground, the Persian one. And run!

VOICE OF COACHMAN. Whoa!

VOICE OF MAYOR. When are we to expect Your Excellency?

VOICE OF KHLESTAKOV. Tomorrow or the day after.

VOICE OF OSIP. Ah, is that the rug? Good—now put it over here! And let's have a bit of hay on that side.

VOICE OF COACHMAN. Whoa!

VOICE OF OSIP. No, this side! Here, a bit more! Good! That'll be just fine! [*Pats rug.*] Now, will Your Honour be seated?

VOICE OF KHLESTAKOV. Cheerio, Anton Antonovich!

VOICE OF MAYOR. Goodbye, Your Excellency!

VOICES OF WOMEN. Goodbye, Ivan Alexandrovich!

VOICE OF KHLESTAKOV. Cheerio, mother!

VOICE OF COACHMAN. Giddyap, my beauties! [*Ringing of bells. Curtain comes down.*]

ACT V

Same room.

SCENE I

[MAYOR, ANNA ANDREEVNA *and* MARIA ANTONOVNA.]

MAYOR. Well, Anna Andreevna, how about that, eh? Never imagined anything like that, did you? A fine rich catch, dammit! You
have to admit: it's beyond your wildest dreams, isn't it? One
moment you're just any old mayor's wife, the next—damn it
all!—you're mother-in-law to a fine young devil like that...

ANNA ANDREEVNA. On the contrary; I knew right from the start. It
may seem incredible to you, because you're so uncouth. You've
never mixed with genteel people before.

MAYOR. I'm a genteel person myself, I'll have you know. No, but
just think, Anna Andreevna, we're birds of a quite a different
feather now, eh? Flying high we are now, damn it all! Oho, just
you wait, I'm going to make it sticky for those toads, those snakes
in the grass with their petitioning and informing. Hey, you out
there! [*Enter* CONSTABLE.] Ah, it's you—Ivan Karpovich! Listen:
get out there and fetch those shopkeepers, there's a good fellow.
I've got them now, the scum! How dare they complain about me!
I'll teach those two-faced Jews! You wait, my little doves, I'll give
you something to complain about. So far I've only had you by the
whiskers: wait till I get hold of your beards! I want the name of
every single person who came complaining about me, and every
one of those scribbling rats that wrote out their petitions. And
make sure the people of this town all know how God has chosen
to honour their mayor, that I'm giving my daughter in marriage
not to some common squirt, but to a man such as the world has
never seen before, a man who can do anything! Anything! Shout
it from the rooftops, ring the bells till they crack, this is your
mayor's great day! [*Exit* CONSTABLE.] So what about it, Anna
Andreevna? Where do you want to live then? Here or in St P?

ANNA ANDREEVNA. In St Petersburg, of course! You don't imagine one could stay on here!

MAYOR. If you say St P, St P it shall be. Mind you, it wouldn't be too bad here, either. Expect I'd have to chuck in being mayor, eh, Anna Andreevna?

ANNA ANDREEVNA. Naturellement! How could one be mayor now?

MAYOR. I say, Anna Andreevna, do you think I might land a plum job in St Petersburg? You never know, what with his being a crony of all those ministers, and calling at the palace, he could pull a few strings and in time I might end up a general. Eh, what about that, Anna Andreevna? Do you think I'll make it to general?

ANNA ANDREEVNA. I should certainly hope so!

MAYOR. It'd be capital to be a general, damn it! Complete with sash and all. What sash do you prefer, Anna Andreevna, the red or the blue?*

ANNA ANDREEVNA. The blue, of course.

MAYOR. Just listen to that! There's nothing wrong with the red, either. You know the great thing about being a general? Suppose you want to travel somewhere: couriers and adjutants gallop on ahead—'Horses! Horses for the General!' All those councillors, captains and mayors just sit and wait and wait for horses and you don't give a hoot. You're off to dine with the governor and the mayor can sit and stew—ha, ha, ha! [*Doubles up with laughter.*] That's the best thing about it, damn it!

ANNA ANDREEVNA. It's always the coarse things that appeal to you. You'll have to bear in mind that our life is going to be completely different now. No more riff-raff like this lot for your friends. No more dog-crazy judges for you to go hunting with, or Zemlyanikas. You're going to mix with counts and society people, the *crème de la crème*. And to tell you the truth, I'm not sure how you'll manage: sometimes you come out with the sort of words you'd never hear in the beau monde.

MAYOR. So what? Words can do no harm.

ANNA ANDREEVNA. That may be true for some common-or-garden mayor—but life there's completely different.

MAYOR. It certainly is! They have these two fish dishes there—a kind of eels and smelts—it makes your mouth water just to look at them!

ANNA ANDREEVNA. Huh! Fish—that's all he can think about! But I shall want to have the best house in the capital, and when you come into my room there'll be such an exquisite aroma you'll have to shut your eyes tight. [*Screws eyes shut and sniffs.*] Ah, that's wonderful!

SCENE II

[*The same, with* SHOPKEEPERS.]

MAYOR. Ah, there you are, my little lambs!

SHOPKEEPERS [*bowing*]. We wish you health and happiness, Your Honour.

MAYOR. Well, how are my little doves? How's business, eh? Well, teapot hawkers and cloth-peddlers, make complaints about me, would you? You arch diddlers, master fiddlers, prize-winning swindling rogues, decided to complain, did you? So where's it got you now? I know, you thought they'd put me in gaol!... The devil take your filthy rotten souls to hell...

ANNA ANDREEVNA. Anton! Really, what language!

MAYOR [*snaps at her*]. Never mind my language! Now, I've got news for you: that government inspector you ran whining to is going to marry my daughter. Well? What do you say now? Now I'll... wait till I get my hands on you! Cheating innocent people... You get government contracts so you can swindle the nation out of a hundred thousand: you supply rotten old cloth, and then you make a generous donation, you swine, of fifteen yards, and expect a decoration for it? If they ever found out, they'd give you what for... Fancy yourselves, don't you: 'I may be a shopkeeper,' you say, 'but I'm as good as any aristocrat.' Why, an aristocrat—you snoutfaces—an aristocrat studies the sciences; maybe they do whip him at school but at least he learns some manners. But you! You're born thieves and you get beaten by your masters because you can't cheat properly. You're giving short change before you can say the Lord's prayer; and as soon as your paunch fills out and your pockets begin to bulge you start giving yourself airs and graces! Ridiculous! Strutting about, just because you can swill down sixteen samovars of tea a day. Well, I spit on your heads and on your airs and graces!

SHOPKEEPERS [*bowing*]. We're very sorry, Anton Antonovich.

MAYOR. Complain about me, would you? And who let you charge twenty thousand for the timber used to build the bridge when the stuff wasn't even worth a hundred? It was me, goat-beard, me! Forgotten, have you? I only have to say the word, and it'll be off to Siberia for you. Hear that, eh?

ONE OF THE SHOPKEEPERS. Honest to God, we're sorry, Anton Antonovich. The devil led us astray, Your Honour. We swear we'll never complain again. Please don't be angry with us—we'll do anything you say.

MAYOR. 'Don't be angry,' you say? Yes, you can crawl and grovel now! Because I've landed on my feet. But if things had gone just a little more your way, you'd have trodden my face into the mud, you swine, and dumped logs on top of me for good measure.

SHOPKEEPERS [*bowing deeply*]. Don't ruin us, Anton Antonovich!

MAYOR. 'Don't ruin us!' Now it's 'don't ruin us', but what were you saying before? I'd like to take you all and... [*Waves his hand.*] Well, I hope God forgives you! That's all I can say! Count yourselves lucky I don't harbour grudges, but from now on you'd better watch your step! I'm not giving my daughter away to any old nobleman, so make sure you come up with some decent wedding presents, d'you hear? And none of your old pickled herrings and loaves of sugar, this time, do you hear? Now beat it. [*Exeunt* SHOPKEEPERS.]

SCENE III

[*The same, with* JUDGE, WARDEN OF CHARITIES, *and, later,* RASTAKOVSKY.]

JUDGE [*still in doorway*]. Are we to believe the rumours, Anton Antonovich? That an extraordinary piece of good fortune has come your way?

WARDEN OF CHARITIES. Allow me to congratulate you on your extraordinary good fortune. I was genuinely overjoyed when I heard the news. [*Goes up to kiss* ANNA ANDREEVNA*'s hand.*] Anna Andreevna! [*Kissing* MARIA ANTONOVNA*'s hand.*] Maria Antonovna!

RASTAKOVSKY [*enters*]. Congratulations, Anton Antonovich! May God grant you and the happy couple a long life and may He multiply your posterity with grandchildren and great-grandchildren! Anna Andreevna! [*Kissing* ANNA ANDREEVNA*'s hand.*] Maria Antonovna! [*Kissing* MARIA ANTONOVNA*'s hand.*]

SCENE IV

[*The same, with* KOROBKIN, *his* WIFE, *and* LYULYUKOV.]

KOROBKIN. Sincerest congratulations, indeed, Anton Antonovich! Anna Andreevna! [*Kissing* ANNA ANDREEVNA*'s hand.*] Maria Antonovna! [*Kissing* MARIA ANTONOVNA*'s hand.*]

KOROBKIN'S WIFE. My sincerest congratulations, Anna Andreevna, on your new happiness.

LYULYUKOV. Allow me to congratulate you, Anna Andreevna! [*Kisses* ANNA ANDREEVNA*'s hand and then, turning to the audiences, tuts and waggishly shakes his head.*] Maria Antonovna! My congratulations! [*Kisses her hand and casts spectators same waggish look.*]

SCENE V

[*Enter large number of* GUESTS *in tails and frock-coats who first kiss* ANNA ANDREEVNA*'s hand, saying* 'Anna Andreevna', *then* MARIA ANTONOVNA*'s saying* 'Maria Antonovna'. *Enter* BOBCHINSKY *and* DOBCHINSKY, *colliding in doorway.*]

BOBCHINSKY. Allow me to offer you my sincerest congratulations!

DOBCHINSKY. Anton Antonovich, allow me to offer you my sincerest congratulations!

BOBCHINSKY. On your extreme good fortune!

DOBCHINSKY. Anna Andreevna!

BOBCHINSKY. Anna Andreevna! [*They bend over* ANNA ANDREEVNA's *hand at the same time and bump their foreheads.*]

DOBCHINSKY. Maria Antonovna! [*Kisses her hand.*] Allow me to offer you my sincerest congratulations. You will experience happiness beyond description and float about in gold dresses and drink exquisite soup and spend your time most agreeably.

BOBCHINSKY [*interrupting*]. Allow me to congratulate you, Maria Antonovna. I wish you riches beyond measure and masses and masses of roubles and a teeny-tiny baby boy just like this [*demonstrating*]—so he can sit in the palm of your hand! And he'll sit there and yell—Wah! Wah! Wah!

SCENE VI

[*Enter several more* GUESTS, *who kiss the ladies' hands,* INSPECTOR OF SCHOOLS *and* WIFE.]

INSPECTOR OF SCHOOLS. Allow me to offer you...

HIS WIFE [*rushing up*]. My congratulations, Anna Andreevna! [*They kiss.*] I was simply overjoyed, let me tell you. 'Anna Andreevna's daughter is betrothed' they said. 'Goodness me!' I thought, and I was so thrilled I said to my husband, 'Listen, Lukanchik,' I said, 'you'll never guess what a wonderful thing's happened to Anna Andreevna!' 'Goodness,' I thought, 'thank heavens!' And I said to him: 'I'm so excited I simply can't wait to see Anna Andreevna...' 'Goodness me', I thought, 'Anna Andreevna's been hoping to find her daughter a good match, and this is exactly what she wanted.' And my dear, I was so overjoyed that I couldn't speak. I was crying, tears just streaming down my face. And Luka Lukich says: 'But why on earth are you bawling, Nastenka?' 'Lukanchik,' I said, 'I really don't know', and the tears were just coming down in torrents.

MAYOR. Please, ladies and gentlemen, do be seated. Hey, Mishka! Bring some more chairs. [*The guests sit.*]

SCENE VII

[*The same, with* CHIEF OF POLICE *and* CONSTABLES.]

CHIEF OF POLICE. Allow me to congratulate you, Your Excellency, and wish you many long years of prosperity!

MAYOR. Thank you, thank you! Please be seated, gentlemen. [*They sit.*]

JUDGE. Well, aren't you going to tell us how it happened, Anton Antonovich? Describe the course of events, eh?

MAYOR. It was an extraordinary course of events: His Excellency saw fit to make the proposal himself.

ANNA ANDREEVNA. What's more, in the most respectful and delicate way. I just wish you could have heard the way he said it. 'Anna Andreevna,' he said, 'it's out of a deep respect I have for your virtues.' Such an outstanding, well-bred gentleman, with the noblest principles! 'I assure you, Anna Andreevna, my life is not worth a copeck, I'm doing this only through esteem for your rare qualities.'

MARIA ANTONOVNA. Oh Mama, you know he said that to me.

ANNA ANDREEVNA. Silence, girl, mind your own business! 'Anna Andreevna', he said, 'I am struck with wonder...' Oh, he showered me with such compliments and when I was about to say, 'But we cannot presume to hope for such an honour', he suddenly fell on his knees in front of me and said in the most noble way, 'Anna Andreevna, tell me you reciprocate my feelings or I shall have to put an end to my life.'

MARIA ANTONOVNA. Really, Mama, he was saying that about me.

ANNA ANDREEVNA. Well, maybe it was about you as well, I never said it wasn't.

MAYOR. He had us really alarmed, you know. Said he was going to shoot himself. 'I'll shoot myself, I'll shoot myself,' he said.

MANY OF THE GUESTS. You don't say!

JUDGE. Well I never!

INSPECTOR OF SCHOOLS. It's the proper course of destiny!

WARDEN OF CHARITIES. Destiny, my elbow! It's the just deserts of true service. [*Aside.*] It's always the biggest pig who's first to the trough!

JUDGE. I think I'd be prepared to sell you that puppy, Anton Antonovich, the one you were enquiring about before.

MAYOR. I've no need for puppies now.

JUDGE. Well if not that one perhaps we could agree on another one.

KOROBKIN'S WIFE. My dear Anna Andreevna, I'm so happy for you, you simply can't imagine!

KOROBKIN. But where, if I might ask, is our distinguished guest at the moment? Did I hear that he's left town?

MAYOR. Yes, he's just gone off for a day on some extremely important business.

ANNA ANDREEVNA. To his uncle, to seek his blessing.

MAYOR. Yes, to seek his blessing; but tomorrow he'll be... [*Sneezes. Loud clamour of:* 'Bless you!'] Thank you! But he'll be back to... [*Sneezes. Clamour. Various voices can be heard above the general din.*]

CHIEF OF POLICE. Very good health to Your Honour!

BOBCHINSKY. A hundred years and a sack of gold coins!

DOBCHINSKY. May God prolong your years to forty times forty!

WARDEN OF CHARITIES. I hope it chokes you!

KOROBKIN'S WIFE. Go and rot in hell!

MAYOR. Thank you, thank you. And the same to you, all of you.

ANNA ANDREEVNA. Of course we shall be moving to St Petersburg now. Here, you know, the air's so... I have to say it... so provincial. It really is most disagreeable. And as for my husband... they'll make him a general, of course.

MAYOR. Yes, gentlemen, I must confess I rather fancy being a general, dammit!

WARDEN OF CHARITIES. Please God they make you one.

RASTAKOVSKY. To God all things are possible.

JUDGE. Big ships need deep waters.

WARDEN OF CHARITIES. And honour is paid to true service.

JUDGE [*aside*]. That'll be the day when they make him a general! Making him a general is like putting a saddle on a cow! No, my brother, you've got a long way to go yet. There are plenty ahead of you still, with far cleaner copy-books.

WARDEN OF CHARITIES [*aside*]. Look at that—promoting himself general already! You never know, he may just get there. He's pompous enough, that's for sure. [*Turns to* MAYOR.] You won't forget us then, will you, Anton Antonovich?

JUDGE. If there was any sort of trouble around here, you'd stick up for us, wouldn't you?

KOROBKIN. I'll be taking my boy to St Petersburg next year to enter him into government service. Can I count on your giving him a helping hand and acting as father to the poor little orphan, for my sake?

MAYOR. I shall do all that lies within my powers.

ANNA ANDREEVNA. You're always much too ready to make promises. Anton. First of all, you'll have no time for that sort of thing. And besides, why should you burden yourself with such promises?

MAYOR. Well, why not, my sweet, I might occasionally have time.

ANNA ANDREEVNA. Even if you did, you can't go around offering a helping hand to every man and his dog.

KOROBKIN'S WIFE. Do you hear how she runs us down?

LADY GUEST. What of it?—She's always been like that. Set a pig at table and it'll put its trotters in the plate...

SCENE VIII

[*The same, with* POSTMASTER *breathless, clutching a letter with its seal broken.*]

POSTMASTER. I say, everyone—a most extraordinary thing! The man we thought was a government inspector was no such thing.

ALL. What do you mean, no such thing?

POSTMASTER. He's not a government inspector at all, it's all revealed in this letter.

MAYOR. What? What d'you mean? What letter?

POSTMASTER. This letter. He wrote it himself. It was like this: they brought a letter down to the post office. I looked at the address and it says 'Post Office Street'.* I was petrified. 'That's it,' I thought, 'he's found something wrong with our postal department and he's sent in a report.' So I took it and opened it.

MAYOR. How could you do such a thing?

POSTMASTER. Honestly, I really don't know. I was impelled by some supernatural force. I was on the point of calling the courier to send it off by special express delivery, but I was overcome with a curiosity such as I've never felt before. Just couldn't hold myself back. Couldn't stop myself. In one ear I could hear a voice telling me: 'Don't open it—it's more than your life's worth!' and in the other some devil kept on whispering: 'Go on, open it up!' The sealing wax was burning a hole in my hand—but when I opened it I felt myself freeze, honest to God. My hands trembled and my head started to swim.

MAYOR. But how dare you open the mail of such a powerful, important personage?

POSTMASTER. But that's the whole point! He's not at all powerful, or important. He's not even a personage!

MAYOR. Well, what is he then, according to you?

POSTMASTER. He's a nobody... a little squirt, that's all.

MAYOR [*angrily*]. How dare you call him a nobody, a little squirt, how dare you? I'll have you arrested.

POSTMASTER. Who, you?

MAYOR. Yes, me.

POSTMASTER. You haven't got the authority.

MAYOR. You are clearly not aware that he is to marry my daughter, whereupon I shall be a dignitary myself and I shall pack you off to Siberia!

POSTMASTER. I'd forget about Siberia if I were you, Anton Antonovich. Siberia's a long way from here! I think I'd better read you the letter. Shall I read the letter, ladies and gentlemen?

ALL. Yes, yes, read it!

POSTMASTER [*reads*]. 'My dear Tryapichkin, I must write and tell you the incredible things that have been happening to me. On my way out here I was completely fleeced by an infantry captain, so I was stranded, and on the point of being chucked in gaol by the innkeeper, when suddenly, on account of my Petersburg clothes and looks, the whole town took me for some Governor-General. So here I am at the Mayor's, living off the fat of the land, chasing after his wife and daughter—the only trouble is, I can't decide who to go for first... maybe I should begin with the mother, because she looks the accommodating type...

'Remember that time when we were both down on our luck, scrounging and sponging, and that pastry cook threw me out of his shop because I charged my pies to the king of England? It's a different tune here, I can tell you! They all lend me as much money as I want. You'd die laughing—they're such buffoons. You write those literary titbits, you should stick this lot in a story. Take the mayor for instance, stupid as a cart horse...'

MAYOR. Rubbish, you're making it up.

POSTMASTER [*showing letter*]. Read it yourself then.

MAYOR [*reads*]. '... stupid as a cart horse.' It's impossible! You wrote it yourself!

POSTMASTER. Come on, how could I have written it?

WARDEN OF CHARITIES. Read on!

INSPECTOR OF SCHOOLS. Yes, go on, read it.

POSTMASTER [*continues*]. 'The mayor, for instance, stupid as a cart horse...'

MAYOR. You don't have to repeat it, damn you. It was quite bad enough the first time.

POSTMASTER [*continues*].... Hm... mm... mm 'a cart horse. The postmaster's quite a character, too...' [*Stops reading.*] He says something rather rude about me, too.

MAYOR. Go on, read it!

POSTMASTER. Why should I?

MAYOR. Because it was your confounded idea to read it in the first place, that's why! Read it all!

WARDEN OF CHARITIES. Give it here, I'll read it. [*Puts on spectacles and reads.*] 'The postmaster's the spitting image of old Mikheev, our night-watchman, and I should imagine he drinks like a fish, too, the scoundrel.'

POSTMASTER [*to audience*]. Young whippersnapper! He should be flogged.

WARDEN OF CHARITIES [*continues reading*]. 'As for the so-called superintendent of charitable insti... insti...' [*Stammers.*]

KOROBKIN. Why have you stopped?

WARDEN OF CHARITIES. The... er... handwriting's hard to read... Anyway it's clear that he's a thorough rogue.

KOROBKIN. I'll read it, my eyes are better than yours. [*Grabs letter.*]

WARDEN OF CHARITIES [*holding on to letter*]. No, we can skip this bit, it gets legible again lower down.

KOROBKIN. Here, I'll read it.

WARDEN OF CHARITIES. No, I will; it's quite legible further on.

POSTMASTER. Oh no, you don't. You read the whole thing, we've been reading it all.

ALL. Give it to him, Artemy Filippovich, give him the letter. [*To Korobkin.*] You read it, Ivan Kuzmich.

WARDEN OF CHARITIES. All right, all right. [*Hands over letter.*] We've got to here... [*Covers part of letter with thumb.*] Read from here. [*All crowd round.*]

POSTMASTER. Read it, read it! No nonsense now, read the lot.

KOROBKIN [*reads*]. 'Superintendent of charitable institutions, one Zemlyanika, looks like a pig in a skull-cap.'

WARDEN OF CHARITIES. It's not even witty! A pig in a skull-cap, I ask you; who ever heard of a pig in a skull-cap!

KOROBKIN [*continues*]. 'The inspector of schools reeks from head to foot of onions.'

INSPECTOR OF SCHOOLS [*to audience.*] What nonsense! I've never eaten an onion in my life!

JUDGE [*aside*]. Well thank God he's said nothing about me, at any rate.

KOROBKIN [*reads*]. 'And the judge...'

JUDGE. Damnation! [*Aloud.*] Honestly, gentlemen, this letter's far too long. It's damned tedious listening to all this rubbish.

INSPECTOR OF SCHOOLS. Oh no it's not!

POSTMASTER. Oh no! Read on.

WARDEN OF CHARITIES. Oh no! Just keep on reading.

KOROBKIN [*continues*]. 'And the judge, Lyapkin-Tyapkin, is most decidedly... movay... tone...' (*Stops.*) Must be a French word.

JUDGE. And the devil only knows what it means! Bad enough to be called a crook, but that may mean something worse!

KOROBKIN [*carries on reading*]. 'But on the whole they're not a bad lot, hospitable too. Cheerio for now, Tryapichkin, old sport, I've decided to follow your example and take up literature. It's a bore living like this, there's no getting away from it, one must have food for the soul. One simply has to concern oneself with higher things. Write to me in Saratov, Podkatilovka village.' [*Folds letter and reads address.*] 'To the Honourable Ivan Vasilievich Tryapichkin Esq., St Petersburg, Post Office Street, No. 97, third floor, first on the right.'

ONE OF THE LADIES. What a dreadful indignity!

MAYOR. Now I'm done for, good and proper. It's all up with me, now! I can't see a thing... all I can see is a mass of pigs' snouts, instead of faces, just pigs' snouts... Bring him back! Bring him back! [*Waves arms about.*]

POSTMASTER. No chance! To add insult to injury, I told the stationmaster to give him the fastest horses we've got and as if that wasn't enough I went and gave him a priority warrant!

KOROBKIN'S WIFE. What a mess! What a frightful fiasco!

JUDGE. And the devil of it is, gentlemen, that I lent him three hundred roubles.

WARDEN OF CHARITIES. So did I.

POSTMASTER [*sighs*]. So did I.

BOBCHINSKY. And Pyotr Ivanovich and I lent him sixty-five in notes, so we did.

JUDGE [*spreading his hands in consternation*]. But how did it happen, gentlemen? That's what I want to know. How did we make such asses of ourselves?

MAYOR [*striking his forehead*]. How could I be such an idiot? I'm starting to dote, like an old mule! Thirty years I've been in the service and there's never been a shopkeeper or contractor could get the better of me; I've outsmarted the sharpest crooks, I've cheated sharks and foxes wily enough to rook the entire human race. I've hoodwinked three governors! Governors! [*In disgust.*] And that's not the half of it...

ANNA ANDREEVNA. But this is impossible, Anton, he's betrothed to our Masha.

MAYOR [*enraged*]. 'Betrothed'! A fig for your betrothal! Don't give me that betrothal nonsense now! [*In desperation.*] All right. Look at me. Look, just look, all of you—the whole world, all Christendom—look up and see the Mayor, see what a fool he's made of himself! Fool! Halfwit! Imbecile! [*Shakes fist at himself.*] Blockhead! Taking that pup, that little squirt for a brass hat. Think of him now, trumpeting it all down the highway! He'll spread the story to the four corners of the earth! I shall be the laughing stock of the country. And as if that weren't sufficient, some hack, some penny-a-liner will come along and stick us all in a comedy. That's the worst of it! They'll spare nothing! They'll take no notice of rank, or reputation; anything to raise a few cheap laughs and to make the rabble clap. What are you laughing at? You're laughing at yourselves, that's what!... You, eugh! [*Stamps with rage.*] I'd like to get my hands on those scribblers! Penpushers! Dirty liberals! Devil's spawn! I'd trample the lot of you, grind you to powder and scatter you to the four winds! [*Swiping his fist and pounding the floor with his heel. After a brief silence.*] I still can't think straight. When God punishes someone it seems he takes away his reason first. Was there anything about that guttersnipe that remotely resembled a government inspector? Nothing! Not even one little finger! And suddenly it's all 'the government inspector', 'the government inspector'! So who first got it into his head that he was a government inspector? Tell me that!

WARDEN OF CHARITIES [*spreading his arms*]. For the life of me I couldn't say how it happened. Some fog must have got into our minds.

JUDGE. I'll tell you who started it! They started it, those two smart alecks! [*Pointing at* DOBCHINSKY *and* BOBCHINSKY.]

BOBCHINSKY. No, it wasn't me. I never dreamt of it.

DOBCHINSKY. I never said a thing!

WARDEN OF CHARITIES. It was them! Of course it was them.

INSPECTOR OF SCHOOLS. So it was. They dashed in here from the inn like a pair of lunatics, shouting: 'He's here, he's here, and he's not spending any money!' A prize rabbit you caught!

MAYOR. It had to be you, didn't it? The town gossips and scandalmongers!

WARDEN OF CHARITIES. Damn you both to hell! And your inspector with you!

MAYOR. You do nothing but run around spreading panic, you blathering magpies!

JUDGE. Gibbering monkeys!

INSPECTOR OF SCHOOLS. Fatheads!

WARDEN OF CHARITIES. Potbellied toadstools! [*All crowd round.*]

BOBCHINSKY. As God's my witness it wasn't me, it was Pyotr Ivanovich.

DOBCHINSKY. Oh no, Pyotr Ivanovich, it was you who started it...

BOBCHINSKY. Oh no, it wasn't, it was you, you said it first...

FINAL SCENE

[*The same, with* GENDARME.]

GENDARME. A government inspector has arrived by decree of the tsar from St Petersburg. He demands that you attend him immediately at the inn.

[*Everyone is thunderstruck by these words. An exclamation of astonishment is uttered simultaneously by the ladies; the entire company suddenly shifts position and is turned to stone.*]

DUMB SCENE

The MAYOR *stands like a pillar in the middle, his arms outstretched, his head thrust back. To the right are his wife and daughter, arrested in motion towards him; next in line is the* POSTMASTER, *contorted into a question mark, facing the audience; next comes the* INSPEC- TOR OF SCHOOLS, *with a look of naïve bewilderment; next to him, at the very edge of the stage, stand three ladies, leaning against one another with the most satirical expression on their faces, clearly directed at the* MAYOR's *family. To the left of the* MAYOR *are: the* WARDEN OF CHARITIES, *his head cocked to one side, as if listening for some- thing; next to him the* JUDGE, *arms outstretched, squatting almost on the floor, his lips pursed as if to whistle, or to say 'Well, this is a pretty kettle of fish!' Next to him stands* KOROBKIN, *facing the audience, his eyes screwed up and a look of contempt on his face directed at the* MAYOR; *next to him, at the edge of the stage, stand* BOBCHINSKY *and* DOBCHINSKY, *their arms stretched out towards each other, their mouths wide open, their eyes popping. The other guests are merely turned into pillars. The petrified company retains this disposition for almost a minute and a half. The curtain comes down.*

EXPLANATORY NOTES

PETERSBURG TALES

The stories gathered in this volume, together with the two cycles *Village Evenings Near Dikanka* and *Mirgorod*, make up the full complement of Gogol's completed stories. In addition, there are a number of unfinished pieces, the most substantial of which is the heavily didactic story 'Rome', and a large opus of writing on art, history, religion, and other subjects.

Five of these stories—'Nevsky Prospect', 'The Nose', 'The Portrait', 'The Overcoat', and 'Diary of a Madman'—have as their setting St Petersburg and have come to be known as Gogol's Petersburg Tales, although the author himself never grouped the stories together with that title. The title has stuck, however, and the grouping is irresistible, so it has been retained here, but with the addition of 'The Carriage'. Although 'The Carriage' has a provincial setting and, strictly speaking, is not a Petersburg story, the stylistic affinities it has with the other stories, its portrayal of crassness (*poshlost'*, a theme so beloved of Gogol), the obsession with rank, and a host of other characteristically Gogolian features, would seem to justify its inclusion. Gogol himself included 'The Carriage' in one volume with these stories (and in the order used here) in the third volume of his collected works of 1842.

Gogol's shift in these stories to themes of the city and the civil service reflects developments in his own biography: in 1829 he joined the civil service, to earn the 'cursed, vile money' he needed to live, serving first in the Department of Administration and Public Buildings, then in the Department of Crown Property, but he resigned in March 1831. In 1830 he took lodgings in a district of St Petersburg, near Gorokhovaya Street, where members of the petty bourgeoisie (*meshchanstvo*) and civil servant classes lived and which is described in 'Diary of a Madman'. Here too lives the barber Ivan Yakovlevich of 'The Nose'—not far from his noseless client, Major Kovalyov—and Poprishchin, hero of 'Diary of a Madman', wanders about this same district, stopping in wonder before the very building in which Gogol lived, the Zverkov house, on the corner of Stolyarny Lane and the Yekaterininsky Canal.

Although Gogol's sojourn among the officials of St Petersburg was relatively brief, the impression made on him was to be unforgettable and it informs all his subsequent work. The influential nineteenth-century critic Belinsky wrote that, in the mores of the middle estate of St Petersburg, Gogol discovered 'a deep and mighty poetry'; less contentiously, the writer and historian Alexander Herzen noted that Gogol documents the pathological anatomy of the Russian functionary, the *chinovnik*, representative of the social class which Lenin described as an army of spiders, spinning the webs in which the common folk of Imperial Russia were trapped and struggled like flies.

Nevsky Prospect

This story, like 'The Portrait' and 'Diary of a Madman', first appeared in the collection *Arabesques*, published in 1835, which also contained a number of essays on art and other subjects. In the version used here, passages which were struck out or changed at the censors' insistence have been restored, notably the scene of Pirogov's thrashing. Pushkin protested against the excision of that scene, which he believed essential to the effect of the 'evening Mazurka' scene in the story.

The story was composed over the years 1831–4, and underwent a number of changes that resulted in the toning down of its Gothic qualities, strongly apparent in an earlier, unfinished version entitled 'The Dread Hand', and the strengthening of its realism. It stands as an overture to the other Petersburg Tales, introducing themes which will occur again and again: the tragic collapse of idealism, the triumph of everything crass, the conflict between the artist and society, and of course the treacherous, but fascinating, life of the city. The great Russian poet Alexander Pushkin, who did much to promote Gogol in the literary establishment, hailed it as the 'fullest' story of the cycle.

3 *Nevsky Prospect*: as is soon apparent to the reader, Nevsky Prospect is St Petersburg's main thoroughfare and—to a perhaps greater extent than equivalent streets in other European capitals—the nerve centre of the city. The street is also a masterpiece of urban architecture and planning. Unlike so many other major streets in Russian cities, its name was never changed in the Soviet era; perhaps this story had some part in staying the commissars' hands.

4 *department*: in pre-revolutionary Russia, a department of the complex government service created by Peter the Great in 1711.

peaked cap instead of a hat: the common folk wore peaked caps; hats were the headgear of gentlemen.

5 *Foreign Collegium*: service which in the tsarist government performed the functions of a modern ministry of foreign affairs. In creating a new administration for Russia, Peter the Great instituted a system of twelve 'Colleges', which functioned as the departments of government (see the College of Inspectors in 'The Nose'). The buildings occupied by

these colleges were subsequently taken over by the new University of St Petersburg and the road on which they stand renamed University Embankment.

6 *Admiralty Spire*: copper-clad spire which crowns the Admiralty building, on the right bank of the Neva and centred on Nevsky Prospect, so that it can be seen from any point along that avenue.

7 *Titular, aulic, and other councillors*: different ranks on the table instituted in 1722 by Peter the Great for the Russian civil service and modelled on the German system. The full Table of Ranks is reproduced on p. xli.

frieze-cloth greatcoat: uniform greatcoats—*shineli*—were worn by all those in service, military or civilian, including, in tsarist Russia, functionaries, seminarists, and even domestic servants. The quality of the cloth would depend on the status of the wearer; thus, frieze coats would have been the garb of the lower orders.

8 *Politseisky Bridge*: literally 'Police Bridge', and originally known as the 'Green Bridge', it was renamed because of its proximity to the house of Chicherin, then chief of police. After the Revolution it was renamed Narodny ('People's') Bridge. See the map on p. xl.

Perugino's Bianca: Perugino was the byname of Pietro Vannucci (1446–1523), painter of the Umbrian school, whose figures are notable for their sweetness and serenity and who, at one time, was Raphael's teacher; while Perugino has no work entitled Bianca, this probably refers to the Madonna in the fresco of the Adoration of the Magi in the chapel of Santa Maria dei Bianchi in Città della Pieve, near Chiusi.

17 *Kammerjunkers*: rank of courtier, introduced by Tsar Paul I in 1797; the Oberkammerherr, or Senior Chamberlain, had authority over twelve Kammerherrs, or Chamberlains, twelve Kammerjunkers, or Gentlemen of the Bedchamber, and forty-eight pages.

Kammerherr: see previous note.

24 *Okhta cemetery*: Okhta is an area of St Petersburg on the right bank of the Neva, i.e. across the river from Nevsky Prospect, and so named after the Lesser and Greater Okhta rivers, tributaries of the Neva.

Capuchin monk: Roman Catholic order of friars, which broke away from the Dominicans in the early sixteenth century and became very active in foreign missions; so named from the Italian *cappuccino* for 'little hood'.

26 *Bulgarin . . . A. A. Orlov*: Faddei Venediktovich Bulgarin (1789–1859), member of the conservative literary establishment and publisher of such reactionary journals as *Severnaya pchela* (*Northern Bee*) and *Syn*

otechestva (Son of the Fatherland), in which he attacked progressive writers, including Pushkin, Belinsky, and Gogol; Nikolai Ivanovich Grech (1787–1867), grammarian and associate of Bulgarin; Alexander Anifimovich Orlov, poet and author of didactic pamphlets. Gogol reveals the philistinism of the members of this class of officers by having them yoke Pushkin, whom he idolized, together with the odious Bulgarin and Grech.

26 *Filatka vaudeville*: reference to the frivolous dramatic entertainment, *Filatka and Miroshka—the Rivals, or Four Bridegrooms and One Bride*, by the actor and playwright Grigoriev the Younger, which was first staged in 1831 and delighted audiences with its comic portrayal of the life of the common man.

Dmitry Donskoy and Woe from Wit: *Dmitry Donskoy* is a historical tragedy in the classical style about the Grand Duke of Moscow and Vladimir, Dmitry Donskoy, by the playwright Vladislav Aleksandrovich Ozerov (1769–1816), the author of a number of dramatic works in the classical and sentimental idiom which enjoyed great, but short-lived, popularity; *Woe from Wit* is an outstanding comedy by the Russian playwright and diplomat Alexander Griboedov (1795–1829); see also note to p. 58.

a cannon and a unicorn: the difference between these two objects may in fact be less than the reader—and Pirogov's audience—expect: a 'unicorn' was a piece of Russian ordnance, a type of howitzer, first cast in 1577, for the firing of balls and explosive missiles up to a range of four kilometres and so named because of the unicorn motif cast in its barrel.

28 *rapé*: or 'rappee', a coarse variety of snuff obtained by rasping a piece of tobacco.

30 *'Gensie zum kitchen!'*: Schiller's German is similarly ungrammatical and macaronic in the Russian original.

34 *General Staff . . . State Council*: supreme Russian military and legislative authorities, respectively, before the 1917 Revolution.

Northern Bee: *Severnaya pchela*, a St Petersburg newspaper founded and published from 1825 to 1865 by Bulgarin (see note to p. 26, above). In 1831 it became a daily, with Grech as co-editor; because of its founder's unwavering support for the status quo, the *Northern Bee* was the only private newspaper allowed to print political news and the only paper read at court.

College of Inspectors: in the first half of the nineteenth century, the State body in charge of accounting and statistics; see note to p. 5.

35 *Lafayette*: Marie Joseph Paul Yves Roch Gilbert du Motier, Marquis de Lafayette (1757–1834), French general and political leader, who fought beside Washington in the American Civil War and was appointed commander of the National Guard after the storming of the Bastille; among other achievements, Lafayette is credited with the design of the modern French flag.

The Nose

The composition of this remarkable and disturbing story dates back to late 1832, but it was not completed until 1836. It was published later that year in Pushkin's new journal *Sovremennik* (*Contemporary*), after it had been rejected by the journal *Moskovsky nablyudatel'* (*Moscow Observer*) as too vulgar and sordid (*gryaznoy*). This story brought Gogol into his first open conflict with the censors: see, in particular, the note below on the Kazan Cathedral episode.

Pushkin records that Gogol was loath to publish it but finally let himself be persuaded by the poet, who was delighted by the story's originality. An early version of the story has Kovalyov awakening at the end from a dream, but Gogol later rejected this conventional denouement, replacing it with a truly Gogolian ending, with a baffled author and the usual surprising twists and *non sequitur*s.

Influences behind the creation of this story include the writers Sterne, Tieck, Veltmann, Zschokke, Hoffmann, and, in particular, Chamisso with his *Peter Schlemiel*. In addition, the story was prompted by a vogue current at that time in *belles-lettres* and the press for stories—real and fanciful—about noses, and is foreshadowed by the cobbler Hoffmann's narrowly averted rhinotomy in 'Nevsky Prospect'. One of the stories given currency in the press of Gogol's day featured a man persecuted by his colleagues because of the size of his nose. Indeed, the vogue is a perennial one, for, even at the time this edition was being prepared—in 1994—newspapers carried a report of a man in Denver whose nose was bitten off in a bar-room brawl and swiftly reattached by a doctor, who warned, however, that sometimes reattached noses 'don't take'. Gogol's story stands both as a commentary to and parody on such accounts of severed and vanishing noses: it is the *ne plus ultra* of all nose stories.

37 *Voznesensky Avenue*: renamed Mayorov Avenue in 1923; the original name was restored in 1991. For this and other place-names, see the map on p. xl.

38 *Collegiate Assessor*: rank in the Petrine civil service, equivalent to the military rank of major. The complete Table of Ranks is reproduced on p. xli.

39 *Isakievsky Bridge*: an early floating bridge across the Neva, also known as Nevsky Bridge, built in 1727 and destroyed by fire in 1916.

40 *acquire their position in the Caucasus*: the acquisition of such ranks was facilitated in the Caucasus by the anarchy and corruption rife among the local authorities in that distant outpost of the empire. This was one of several deprecatory observations found unacceptable by the censors and excised from tsarist editions.

42 *Kazan Cathedral*: cruciform cathedral in the Classical style, built by the architect Voronikhin in the manner of St Peter's in Rome and completed in 1811. The cathedral has two sweeping colonnades and faces on to Nevsky Prospect. It was named 'Kazan' in honour of its holiest property, the miraculous icon of the Kazan Mother of God. During the Soviet era the authorities converted the cathedral into a museum of atheism (or 'Museum of the History of Atheism and Religion', as it was officially named). It was restored to the Russian Orthodox Church during Mr Gorbachev's presidency. This episode too was considered offensive by the censors; anticipating their response, Gogol wrote to a friend: 'If the stupid censors object to the "nose" visiting the Kazan Cathedral, I could take him to a Catholic church. But I can't believe they could be that witless.' They were: they even insisted that it take place not in a church at all, but in a shopping arcade, the Gostiny Dvor.

43 *Voskresensky Bridge*: a floating bridge across the Neva, in existence from 1786 to 1879.

45 *Politseisky Bridge*: see note to p. 8; *Anichkov Bridge*: fine extant bridge on Nevsky, across the Fontanka. The original stone bridge, completed in 1715, was embellished in 1841 with four equestrian statues, depicting rearing horses restrained by athletes, designed by Baron Klodt von Jurgensburg.

Board of Public Order: institution in tsarist Russia responsible for the administration of the municipal police service and headed by the mayor. The Boards, which were founded in 1782, monitored compliance with the law and also exercised some judicial functions. The last such Board, in St Petersburg, was abolished in 1877.

49 *Northern Bee*: Gogol takes the opportunity to denigrate a journal which had conducted a campaign against him and other prominent writers; see note to p. 34.

50 *Berezinsky shag*: make of cheap tobacco, presumably named after the Berezina, a river which flows into the Dnieper.

57 *Junker's emporium*: fashionable store in St Petersburg; there were several prominent families in St Petersburg at that time with the name Junker.

58 *Khozrev–Mirza*: Persian prince who led an embassy to St Petersburg following the murder of the Russian ambassador to Teheran, the play-wright Alexander Griboedov (see note to p. 26). During his visit to the Russian capital, Khozrev-Mirza stayed in the Tavrichesky Palace, originally built for Prince Potyomkin, who was given the title Prince of Tauria ('Tavrichesky') for having annexed the Crimea (historically known as Tauria) to the Russian empire. The park in which the Palace is situated is known as the Tavrichesky Gardens.

60 *Gostiny Dvor*: a shopping arcade on Nevsky Prospect, built by the architects Rastrelli and Valin-Delamot between 1761 and 1785. It retained its name throughout the Soviet era and is a major centre of commercial activity even today.

The Portrait

The most didactic and artistically the least satisfying story of this group, 'The Portrait' was written between 1834 and 1842 and first published in the collection *Arabesques* in 1835. That version was substantially changed and expanded and the new version published in the journal *Sovremennik* (*Contemporary*) in 1842. In this story, Gogol attempts a high seriousness with not entirely happy consequences. The influences on the story are many: notably the German Romantics, Wackenroder (particularly his fragmentary writings on art) and Hoffmann, as well as Maturin and Balzac. Gogol takes the conventional parable of the artist who sacrifices the pursuit of truth and beauty on the altar of Mammon, and ends with a message about the redemptive power of art. While the story's long, homiletic passages and high moral tone may seem to detract from its interest, they do at least demonstrate the author's passionate views about art and the role of the artist, and the story's *longueurs* are, in any event, considerably redeemed by its incidental description of the milieu inhabited by the artist-hero and his manservant.

The story reveals Gogol's keen interest in fine art, and his knowledge of—in particular—Italian painters as well as the whole subject of the purpose of art and the perils of the slavish reproduction of reality. During his long sojourns in Italy, Gogol largely spent his time in the company of Russian painters, and developed a particularly high regard for the model, as he saw it, set by the painter Aleksandr Andreevich Ivanov (1806–58), who lived for twenty-eight years in Rome, twenty of which he spent in the completion of a single canvas, the monumental *Appearance of Christ to the People*.

62 *Shchukin Dvor*: lit. 'Pike's Yard'; second largest market in St Petersburg at that time, situated between Chernyshev Lane and Sadovaya Street.

62 *Khozrev-Mirza*: see note to p. 58.

Tsarevna Miliktrisa Kirbityevna: a figure from Russian folklore, widely featured in the popular *lubok* broadsheets, the crudely printed chap-books referred to here. Miliktrisa was the beautiful but treacherous mother of the virtuous knight Bova Korolevich.

Okhta: see note to p. 24.

63 *Yeruslan Lazarevich . . . Foma and Yeryoma*: Yeruslan Lazarevich is a character from Russian folklore; Foma and Yeryoma were good-for-nothing, clumsy brothers, who also featured extensively in *lubok* stories. The phrase 'Foma and Yeryoma' is used as a catch-all expression, comparable to the English 'Tom, Dick and Harry'.

65 *Fifteenth Line on Vasilyevsky Island*: the streets on Vasilyevsky Island, a district of St Petersburg (see map on p. xxxviii), are referred to as 'lines'.

69 *Vasari*: Giorgio Vasari (1511–74), Italian architect, writer, and painter in the Mannerist style, best known for his entertaining *Lives of the Artists*, the work referred to here.

74 *Kolomna*: district of St Petersburg on the right bank of the Fontanka and at its confluence with the Yekaterininsky Canal (see map on p. xl). In Gogol's day Kolomna was on the outskirts of the city.

75 *Prince Kutuzov*: general who commanded the Russian forces in the Russo-Turkish war of 1811 and the Patriotic War of 1812–13 against Napoleon; enjoyed great popularity among the people but was dis-trusted by Alexander I.

78 *golden-eye drake*: I take the liberty of 'resurrecting' a dead Russian metaphor for pomposity and swagger, as the bird in question is the author's namesake, the 'gogol' (*Bucephala clangula*), which makes an earlier appearance at the end of Gogol's Cossack tale, 'Taras Bulba'.

80 *by his forename and patronymic*: perhaps surprisingly, it is a mark of respect for Russians to be referred to, or addressed, by their forename and patronymic, rather than by their surname; the use of honorific titles, such as 'Mr', has never caught on in Russia—even the strenu-ously promoted *tovarishch* ('comrade') never really entered common parlance. Characteristically, in Gogol's inverted world, the honour is also conferred on an animal (Agrafena Ivanovna, in 'The Carriage').

87 *Corinna, Undine, or Aspasia*: Corinna is the heroine of Mme de Staël's *Corinne ou l'Italie*; Undine of the eponymous *Novelle* by the German Romantic La Motte Fouqué; and Aspasia the mistress of the Greek statesman Pericles, renowned for her intelligence, erudition, and beauty.

94 *demon which Pushkin portrays in his verse*: reference to Pushkin's poem 'Demon', which begins: 'In those days when all life's impressions were new to me . . .'.

96 *Gostiny Dvor arcade*: see note to p. 60.

98 *Senate*: set up by Peter the Great in 1711 as the supreme administrative, legislative, and judicial organ of Imperial Russia, subordinated directly and exclusively to the tsar; by Gogol's time its powers had been considerably eroded and were largely confined to the judicial area; following the great reforms of 1864 its functions were reduced to those of a Supreme Court; the Senate building forms one half of a grand edifice on Senate Square, joined by an arch to the Holy Synod.

Meshchanskaya Street: literally 'Petty Bourgeois Street', renamed Citizens' Street and Plekhanov Street in the Soviet era; it was in this district that many members of the minor official class of St Petersburg made their homes and here too that Gogol himself lived during his brief career in the civil service; see map on p. xl.

99 *Kalinkin Bridge*: more correctly known as the Staro-Kalinkin Bridge, the last bridge across the Fontanka before it falls into the Neva.

102 *Grandison*: embodiment of virtue and nobility, the benevolent hero of Samuel Richardson's novel *The History of Sir Charles Grandison*, which, together with Richardson's other novels, enjoyed great popularity in Russia.

The Overcoat

Widely considered to be Gogol's greatest short story, 'The Overcoat' is also his last and a belated addition to the cycle of Petersburg Tales. The author worked on the story intermittently over the years 1839–1841, and it was first published in the third volume of his collected works in 1842. The garment in question—a *shinel*—is really a greatcoat, the uniform garb of all those in service (see note to p. 7), but the story has become familiar in English as Gogol's 'Overcoat', so I have kept that form here.

'The Overcoat' is thought to have been inspired by an anecdote—related in Gogol's presence—about a clerk with a passion for hunting, who underwent severe privations to save up for a gun, only to lose this cherished new acquisition on his very first hunting expedition. In a state of shock and deep depression the unfortunate clerk takes to his bed and goes into a rapid decline. He is rescued from this only by the efforts of friends, who club together to buy him a new gun. According to the testimony of witnesses, the story made a deep impression on Gogol.

In addition, we know from the author's own letters that he had first-hand experience of the hardship and discomfort endured by his hero, during his own years in government service in St Petersburg. This experience furnished the material for the descriptions of this milieu throughout these stories.

The unmistakable social message of 'The Overcoat' was felt keenly by his contemporaries: thus, in his autobiography, *My Past and Thoughts*, Alexander

Herzen records a friend's reaction to the story: 'That ghost on the bridge pulls the coat off the back of each and every one of us.' The well-known observation. 'We all came from under Gogol's "Overcoat"', ascribed variously to Dostoevsky and Turgenev, conveys the debt owed by Russian literature to this story.

115 *department*: see note to p. 4.

rank . . . Titular Councillor: reference to the complex system of ranks and privileges devised by Peter the Great for the new government service; the full Table of Ranks is reproduced on p. xli.

116 *Belobryushkova*: an improbable-sounding surname, derived from the Russian for 'white-bellied', yet one which, in Gogol's fantastic world, seems somehow quite plausible (cf. the name 'Bashmachkin', mentioned earlier in the story, to which the author provides his own gloss). Similar examples of motivated names abound in his works.

Akaky Akakievich: from the Greek *akakos*, 'innocuous'—a prophetically appropriate name for its bearer; its Western equivalent would be Acacius. The custom of naming children from names of saints in the calendar is strongly adhered to in the Russian Orthodox Church, whose calendar offers a very great number of saints (there are no less than nine Akakys, for instance); hence the custom of observing 'name-days'—celebrating the feast-day of the saint after whom a person is named, which, if the correct naming procedure is followed at birth, will in any case be the same day as that person's birthday.

120 *Falconet*: Étienne Maurice Falconet, French sculptor who created the famous equestrian monument to Peter the Great in Senate Square, St Petersburg, completed in 1782 and immortalized in Pushkin's poem 'The Bronze Horseman'. In this beautiful statue, which depicts a rearing mounted horse, the sculptor has solved the mechanical problem posed by the need to support the massive weight of a bronze horse and rider on its relatively flimsy base by resting the horse's tail on a rock and incorporating a serpent, sculpted by F. G. Gordeev, into the base of the monument—so that the sculpture is supported by three points. One of these, the tail, is much more substantial than the horse's slender hind legs; hence the joke to which the author refers.

121 *he started going by the name Petrovich after he had been granted his release*: serfs customarily used only their given names; only after gaining his freedom could a serf use a family name, such as the patronymic form here.

lace cap rather than a headscarf: the lace cap, *chepchik*, was the headgear of ladies of a certain standing, while peasant women would have worn headscarves.

141 *Kalinkin Bridge*: see note to p. 99.

145 *Kolomna district*: see note to p. 74.

Obukhov Bridge: stone drawbridge over the Fontanka, no longer in existence.

The Carriage

Written in 1835 and sent to Pushkin for inclusion in a planned almanac which never materialized, 'The Carriage' is Gogol's shortest story and often overlooked in collections of his work because it has no obvious connection with any of the cycles. Although it is not set in St Petersburg, it is—as I explain above—included with the other stories for the close thematic and stylistic kinship it has with them and in accordance with the author's own precedent.

The Carriage was highly praised by Tolstoy, who said he was 'tempted to call it Gogol's best work', and by Chekhov, who said the story was worth 200,000 roubles, and—for all it slightness—it shows Gogol at his best. Like other compositions by Gogol, the germ of the story is provided by an anecdote, in this case about a loud-mouthed and absent-minded landowner. The hero bears similarities to both the fawning Chichikov and the braggart Nozdryov of *Dead Souls*, on which Gogol had already started working at this time. The dreary provincial setting and the inanity (*pustota*, as Gogol terms it) of its characters similarly foreshadow the worlds of *Dead Souls* and *The Government Inspector*. With its unremarkable subject and slender plot line, the story would seem to offer little scope to the author's talents, yet, as Gogol himself remarks, 'the greater a poet one must be to draw from a thing that which is extraordinary'.

While the story pleased both Pushkin and Belinsky, contemporary critics passed over its publication in almost complete silence, so preoccupied were they with *The Government Inspector*, which had its first performance in early 1836.

147 *pood*: pre-revolutionary unit of measure; equivalent to 36 lb. avoirdupois.

148 *faro*: or *faraon*, a card game in which stakes are placed on every one of the fifty-two cards.

calashes: in view of the importance of carriages as part of the paraphernalia of Gogol's world, along with items of clothing, culinary dishes, dogs, and other domestic animals, some explanation of the terms used in these translations would perhaps be of assistance to the modern reader. The Russian word they usually translate is given in brackets.

britschka (brichka): a small, open carriage with a calash top and a space for reclining.

bon-voyage (bonvoyazh): a four-wheeled touring-car, similar to a phaeton, suitable for longer journeys; the name is presumably derived from a manufacturer's name.

cabriolet (kolyasochka): a light, two-wheeled carriage, drawn by a single horse and furnished with a leather hood and apron.

calash (kolyaska): the vehicle featured in the title of this story; however, as the story has become known under the more anodyne title 'The Carriage', I have retained that form here. The calash was first developed in Eastern Europe and known by many names in English—*galeche, gallesh, calesh* etc., derived from a Slavonic word, possibly Czech, cognate with the Russian *kolyaska*—and a variety of the calash, holding one passenger only, became popular in Quebec under the name *calèche*. The calash was a light carriage with a removable, folding hood; sometimes the word 'calash' is used for such a hood.

chaise (kolyaska, kolyasochka): a more general term, which applies to an open carriage, sometimes with two and sometimes with four wheels, also known, respectively, as a phaeton and a curricle.

droshky (drozhki): a Russian-made, low four-wheeled carriage, without a top, and equipped with a narrow bench for a seat on which passengers sat astride or sideways; the droshky was commonly used for hire.

gig (tarataika): a small sprung carriage, usually two-wheeled, also known as a trap or spring-cart.

tarantass (tarantass): a four-wheeled Russian carriage without springs on a long flexible wooden chassis, described by an early traveller to Siberia as a 'roofless, seatless, springless tumbril mounted on poles which connect two wooden axle-trees' (H. Landell, *Through Siberia*, 1882).

troika (troika): a Russian vehicle drawn by three horses abreast and capable of great speed. The troika features in a celebrated epic simile in Gogol's *Dead Souls*, in which Russia is seen as a troika careering madly, dangerously down the road of history.

148 *Tambov and Simbirsk*: large provincial towns of the Russian empire, south-east and east, respectively, of Moscow; Simbirsk was the birthplace of Goncharov, author of the novel *Oblomov*, and, some sixty years later, of Vladimir Lenin (whose real name was Ulyanov) and was renamed Ulyanovsk in the latter's honour during the Soviet era.

149 *Château Lafite*: one of the great wines of France. A bottle of 1806 Château Lafite was sold in Chicago in 1980 for $31,000.

153 *1812 campaign*: reference to the invasion of Russia by Napoleon with his *grande armée*, which took place some twenty-three years before the writing of this story.

Diary of a Madman

This story was written in 1833–4 and first published in the collection *Arabesques* in 1835. It occasioned serious clashes with the censors, which were only resolved by Gogol's agreeing—in his own words—'to discard the best passages'. 'Best' or not, the passages are many and substantial, and include: the dog Madgie's disquisition about medals and orders and her comparison between the Kammerjunker and Trésor, the remark that only noblemen know how to write and any mention of the Emperor or—rather more puzzling—Dominicans and Capuchins. (At the censors' insistence, the Capuchins became shaven-headed grandees, and the king of France, with a wart under his nose, the Dey of Algiers.) All these passages have been restored in this translation, which follows the text of the Academy edition.

The story was clearly prompted by a growing general interest at that time in the social problem of insanity, fed by a surfeit of newspaper stories about lunatic asylums and their inmates; literary precedents include Odoevsky's cycle *The Madhouse*. In addition, stories about Spain and the disturbances in that country following the death of Ferdinand VII were common in the Russian press in the 1830s.

As always, Gogol goes beyond the conventional limits of his subject-matter, and—largely thanks to his graphic use here of the *skaz* technique, with a single, exteriorized narrator—creates a story whose combination of the grotesque and the compassionate cannot fail to disturb the reader. The story was well received by the critics, especially Belinsky, who found it—with its marriage of grotesque mockery and poetic profundity, of caricature and philosophy—'worthy of the brush [*sic*] of Shakespeare'. The reader's laughter, he wrote, is 'laughter at a madman whose rantings at once provoke our ridicule and rouse our compassion'.

158 *department*: see note to p. 4.

   gubernia administration . . . civil and treasury chambers: the *gubernia* was an administrative division, introduced by Peter I in 1708; initially there were eight such *gubernias* in the country, each headed by a governor, and by Gogol's day the number had risen to over fifty; the civil and treasury chambers were organs of central government and the treasury chamber, which came under the Ministry of Finance, was responsible for the administration of Crown property and construction work.

160 *Polkan*: while 'Polkan' is a standard canine name in Russian, comparable to the English Fido or Rover, it was then—and still is—fashionable in Russia to give dogs foreign names; these names, especially the French ones, suggest that we are dealing here with a better class of dog

   Gorokhovaya Street . . . Meshchanskaya . . . Stolyarnaya . . . Kokushkin Bridge: it was in this neighbourhood that Gogol had his second apartment in St Petersburg, near the Kokushkin Bridge; the neighbourhood was largely inhabited by members of the civil servant class and the petty bourgeoisie.

160 *Zverkov house*: this was the building in which Gogol had his own lodgings in 1830, situated on Stolyarny Lane near the Kokushkin bridge over the Yekaterininsky (now Griboedov) Canal; it was a well-known building at that time, as one of the few five-storey houses in the town, but it no longer stands.

161 *the Bee*: see note to p. 34.

162 *'My sweetheart . . . I did sigh'*: lines from a lyric popular at the end of the eighteenth century by the poet and playwright Nikolai Petrovich Nikolev (1758–1815).

   aulic councillor: see the Table of Ranks on p. xli.

163 *Rutsch*: fashionable St Petersburg tailor of the time.

   Filatka: heroine of the Russian vaudeville *Filatka and Miroshka—the Rivals, or Four Bridegrooms and One Bride*, see note to p. 26.

168 *Kammerjunker*: see note to p. 17.

170 *definitely a Mason*: the Masonic movement gained considerable ground in Russia in the eighteenth century but, like any independent movement, was viewed by the authorities with great hostility and was outlawed in 1792; the prohibition was lifted by Tsar Paul I but reimposed in 1822. Masons were accused of complicity in the Decembrist uprising of 1825. There are extensive passages in Tolstoy's *War and Peace* describing his hero Pierre Bezukhov's flirtation with Masonism.

171 *doña*: the young lady in question is Ferdinand VII's under-age daughter Isabella, who was raised to the throne in 1833; her succession was contested by her uncle Don Carlos, who also pretended to the throne: critics have observed that Poprishchin may be conflating the Don Carlos of 1833 with the sixteenth-century Don Carlos, who in Schiller's play—well known in Russia—is handed over to the Inquisition, like Poprishchin himself (or at least so he imagines).

172 *Philip II*: (1527–98), king of Spain, who reigned from 1556 to 1598 and was notorious for his alleged cruelty, but was considered by modern historians not to have been the bloodthirsty tyrant portrayed by his enemies and later writers.

   Capuchin monk: see note to p. 24.

177 *that scoundrel Polignac*: reference to Jules Armand, prince de Polignac (1780–1847), French politician whose actions as prime minister helped precipitate the July Revolution of 1830.

PLAYS

From an early age, Gogol demonstrated a keen interest in the theatre; his father was an amateur playwright and even at school Gogol directed and acted in a number of plays. His first foray into drama was a comedy, *The Order of St Vladimir, Class III*, which he began in 1832 and then abandoned. The three surviving scenes were subsequently published as three separate one-acters: *Morning of a Busy Man*, *The Lawsuit*, and *The Servants' Quarters*. As well as the two completed plays included in this volume, *Marriage* and *The Government Inspector*, Gogol also wrote a short play *Gamblers*, which—while complete in form—remained unfinished as a literary work and was described by Gogol as a 'comic scene'. In addition, he started a historical drama on Alfred the Great, which remained fragmentary, and another on a Cossack theme, which he burnt before it was far advanced.

Besides works for performance, Gogol also wrote extensively on the theatre, including two pieces which relate to his own stage compositions: 'Leaving the Theatre after the Performance of a New Play' and 'The Denouement of the Government Inspector'. The first of these is constructed in dramatic form, as a dialogue between various characters, including the 'Author', but it is meant to be read and pondered, rather than staged. 'Leaving the Theatre' can be seen as a catalogue of responses to Gogol's work; it contains some significant observations, including the expression of regret by the Author that no one has noticed the single positive character in his work: laughter.

The flowering of literature, including drama, came relatively late to Russia, and while there was a considerable repertoire of plays in existence at the time Gogol turned his own creative attention to the stage, most of these— although they enjoyed great popularity at the time—were highly derivative and generally mediocre works and have long since been forgotten. Exceptions are Fonvizin's plays *The Minor* and *The Brigadier*, Griboedov's *Woe from Wit*, and Pushkin's *Little Tragedies* and *Boris Godunov* (although the last mentioned are rarely performed as plays: the *Little Tragedies* are generally thought not to have been written for the stage, while *Boris Godunov* is best known as an opera, in Mussorgsky's version).

Marriage

Gogol started work on this play in 1833, and a first version, entitled *The Bridegrooms*, was completed in 1834. The conception of this first draft was fundamentally changed and the play extensively rewritten for the version that has come down to us as *Marriage*. The author was initially reluctant to commit it to the stage, and he took the text abroad with him on his travels, even appearing loath to discuss it with his friends and fellow writers. On his return to Russia in 1840 he brought a more or less finished version, to which he made a few further corrections. In addition, a few passages fell victim to the censors' scissors (including the reference to someone living with the Chief Secretary of the Senate and the adjective *sodomny*—'sodomitic', but rendered here as 'b—— awful', used by Fyokla, the matchmaker).

The play was first staged at the Aleksandrovsky Theatre in St Petersburg on 9 December 1842, as part of a three-play benefit performance. For the most part the actors—used to playing vaudeville—performed extremely badly. The audience also found it difficult to accept the relative plotlessness of the play, the lack of dramatic movement and denouement. A slight hissing greeted the final curtain. Belinsky attended the first performance and ruefully declared it a victory for Gogol's detractors. Subsequent performances in 1842–3 were increasingly successful and the play soon established itself in the repertoire of Russian theatre. In many respects it foreshadows the work of Ostrovsky, with his comedy of mores, and breaks new ground in its use of—and departure from—conventions of drama. At the same time, Gogol still draws on theatrical tradition, adapting the vaudeville themes of the unsuccessful matchmaker and the indecisive suitor, and echoing material from the now forgotten comedy *The Ditherer*, by Khmelnitsky. The play is more episodic than *The Government Inspector*; here the importance of character outweighs that of intrigue, while in *The Government Inspector* the two are more evenly balanced. The critic Bulgarin (see note to p. 26, above), aptly described it as 'scènes à tiroirs'.

The merchant milieu and the exploration of such social themes as the uneasy relationship between the nobility and the merchant class are encountered elsewhere in Gogol's work, notably in 'Nevsky Prospect' and 'The Portrait'. In general, the merchants fare better than the artistocracy—though only just—and it is interesting that as Gogol worked on the play he softened the satire of the merchantry. Other echoes may be detected here too, such as the diffidence of Ivan Shponka, from the *Dikanka* stories, particularly in the conversation between the suitor and the bride in both works.

The play has become widely known in English under the title *Marriage*, but the word 'marriage' is slightly misleading here as a rendering of the Russian *zhenit'ba*. What is meant is not marriage, *zhenit'*, but the process of *getting* married, the *business* of marriage—the *-ba* of *zhenit'ba*. In his monograph on Gogol, Nabokov renders this title as *Getting Married*; were it not for the established usage, I would have preferred the translation *Marriage Business*.

181 *written in 1833*: this is Gogol's own annotation, so retained here, although the play was only begun in 1833, and not completed until some ten years later.

182 *court councillor*: seventh in order in the Petrine Table of Ranks, equivalent to the military rank of colonel. For the full Table, see p. xli.

Pancake: in Russian *Yaichnitsa*, literally an egg dish, consisting of one or more eggs fried in a skillet and not turned. This is another example of the extraordinary, yet somehow plausible, names Gogol gives his characters; examples abound in *The Government Inspector*. As a rule, I have preferred not to translate proper names, even when 'motivated', as here, but an elaborate pun on the name Yaichnitsa in Act I, scene xvi, forces the translator's hand and accounts for the translation 'Pancake', rather than the perhaps more accurate 'Fried Egg', or even 'Omelette'. Many of the names in this play carry some sort of connotation; often the intention is only to ridicule the bearer with his ridiculous handle, but there are some instances where the name might appear motivated by a corresponding character trait: for example, Podkolyosin suggests *pod koleso*, 'under the wheel'; Brandakhlystova—*brandakhlyst*, a loafer; Kuperdyagina—*skuperdyaga*, a skinflint; Zhevakin—*zhevat'*, to chew or, figuratively, to ramble on about something; some require no gloss, however, as they are as preposterous in English as they are in Russian (Baltazar Baltazarovich).

187 *Moscow quarter . . . Vyborg Side*: districts of St Petersburg; see map on p. xxxviii.

191 *Shestilavochnaya . . . Peski . . . Mylny Lane*: Shestilavochnaya—lit. Street of Six Shops—renamed Mayakovsky Street in the Soviet era; Peski—lit. Sands—a district of St Petersburg; Mylny Lany—lit. Soap Lane.

199 *. . . that you want to spit*: the custom of spitting has more extensive social connotations, at least than in the English cultural context; Russians spit not merely as a sign of disgust, but also, for example, to avert evil or bad luck—where we touch wood, the Russian spits three times.

201 *governor . . . senator*: a governor was an appointed official, who administered the provinces of the empire; senators were members of the Senate (see note to p. 96), who gained their seats through a complex process of indirect and successive elections.

204 *Pavel Petrovich was tsar*: Tsar Paul I succeeded his mother, Catherine II, to the Russian throne for a brief reign (1796–1801), conspicuous for the vagaries of his foreign policy and the tyranny which he exercised over his subjects at home. He was deposed by a coup conducted with the approval of his son and heir Alexander; during the coup he was strangled.

206 *Dustbin, Sloshkin . . . Rottenov . . . Hole*: as with 'Pancake', I have been compelled by the text to depart from usual practice, and to attempt English renderings of these strange and typically Gogolian names:

Pomoikin—from *pomoika*, 'rubbish-dump'; Yaryzhkin—from *yaryga*, 'constable', or, in dialect, 'drunkard'; Perepreev—from *perepret'*, 'to rot'; Dyrka—from *dyra*, 'hole'.

210 *Gostiny Dvor*: see note to p. 60.

213 *Petrov Street... the Eighteenth Line*: Petrov Street was renamed Dubrovskaya Street in the Soviet era; the Eighteenth Line is a street on Vasilievsky Island; see note to p. 65.

222 *Senate*: see note to p. 96.

227 *service record*: all government employees, including members of the armed forces, kept such records, which gave details of their place and length of service, performance, etc., and had to be presented to a new supervisor when changing workplace.

232 *Kazan Cathedral*: neo-classical cathedral on Nevsky, the venue for Major Kovalyov's ill-fated reunion with his errant nose, in 'The Nose' (see note to p. 42).

Yekaterinhof: the Yekaterinhof Palace outside St Petersburg, built by Peter the Great in 1711 as a gift for his wife, the Empress Catherine. Every year festivities were held here on 1 May and on Trinity Sunday.

241 *Kanavka... Semyonov Bridge*: Kanavka is from the Russian *kanava*, a ditch or canal; the Semyonov Bridge is probably the Simeonovsky Bridge, renamed Belinsky Bridge in 1923.

The Government Inspector

In contrast to *Marriage*, on which Gogol worked intermittently for some nine years, *The Government Inspector* was conceived, written, and finished in a remarkable seven weeks of creative activity in 1834. On 7 October Gogol wrote to Pushkin with the following request: 'Do me a favour—give me a plot, anything funny or not funny, but a real Russian story. Right now I'm itching to write a comedy... and I swear, it'll be as funny as hell!' Pushkin obliged with various anecdotes about mistaken identity, including an experience of his own, in which he was taken for a government official. There are grounds to believe that, had he not ceded the plot to Gogol, Pushkin might have used the material for a work of his own. Be that as it may, the poet—who was later to contribute the idea behind *Dead Souls*—played a crucial role in the creation of what is undoubtedly Russia's greatest comedy.

The play was first performed on 19 April 1836 and while the pantomime-like interpretation appalled the author, the performance was attended by the tsar, who enjoyed it immensely, despite—or because of—the misinterpretation, sent his family to see it at its third performance, and enjoined his ministers to see it too, thus ensuring the play's official acceptance. Gogol further refined the text for publication and a final version—used for this translation—was published in his collected works of 1842. The play's un-flattering portrayal of provincial life and official corruption, which led to its being described by Alexander Herzen as a 'terrible indictment of contem-porary Russia, comparable to the exposure of seventeenth-century Russia by Kotoshikhin', meant that *The Government Inspector* was vigorously pro-moted in Soviet literary dogma as a work of critical realism and a biting satire on tsarist corruption; it can be argued equally plausibly, however, that the play is devoid of any moral message as there is no retribution enacted on stage, all the characters are equally contemptible and venal, and there is a general absence of didacticism.

The universal appeal of *The Government Inspector* is attested to by the ease with which it can be made to fit different contexts; there have been successful adaptations for the African stage and the Italian cinema, there has even been a Hollywood musical, starring Danny Kaye as Khlestakov. A memorable British performance was staged by Peter Hall with the Royal Shakespeare Company in 1966, with Paul Scofield in the role of Khlestakov. The play has bequeathed to the Russian culture and language a number of archetypes; thus the names Khlestakov, Derzhimorda, Bobchinsky and Dobchinsky, Lyapkin-Tyapkin, and others were adopted as derogatory epithets for certain types of class enemy and used by Lenin and Stalin in their polemics. Finally, while it is not set in St Petersburg, the idea of St Petersburg, the enigmatic, animistic city explored in the Tales, the distant, glittering capital from which government inspectors travel forth to root out corruption in the provinces, to which the Mayor and his family will move to join other genteel souls—this idea pervades, informs, and dominates the play.

246 *Characters*: the names of the characters in *The Government Inspector* are, almost without exception, motivated to some degree or other. In accordance with the practice followed throughout these translations, I have merely transliterated them, with the inevitable loss of some comic effect. In a stage production, it might be more acceptable to translate the names, but for this printed version the reader is asked, yet again, to refer to the endnotes. As noted above (see note to p. 116), the de-notation of the characters' names is not always significant: the inten-tion may merely be to ridicule a pompous character by giving him a preposterous handle, and we should not attach too much importance to the exact 'meaning' of the name. Sometimes the name sounds as ab-surd in English as in Russian; that, alas, is the happy exception. Some names suggest a specific character trait, and here we are forced to resort to endnotes. This is true of most of the motivated names in this play. To illustrate, I give an indication of the meaning of these names

and for some, the translation used in a production at the Oxford Playhouse in 1975. The production was directed by Gordon MacDougall, and based on an earlier and adapted version of this translation.

Skvoznik-Dmukhanovsky (Mayor): *skvoznik*—a draught, or, figuratively, a sly customer, and *dmukhati* (Ukrainian)—to blow or to whack. The suggestion is one of a devious and voluble man, who is also a windbag, fond of blowing his own trumpet

Khlopov (Inspector of Schools): *kholop*—a serf and *khlopat'*—to smack or make a loud bang or empty noise: Flogov

Lyapkin-Tyapkin (Judge): *tyap-lyap*—any-old-how: Slapkin-Dashkin

Zemlyanika (Warden of Charities): wild strawberry: Strawberry

Shpyokin (Postmaster): *shpion*—spy, *shpik*—secret agent: Snoopin

Khlestakov: *khlestat'*—to lash

Huebner (Physician—in Russian this name is transliterated as *Gibner*): *gibnut'*—to perish

Lyulyukov (retired official): *lyulyukat'*—to lull to sleep

Svistunov (Constable): *svistnut'*—to whistle, also to clout: Fistikov

Derzhimorda (Constable): *derzhat' mordu*—to shut one's trap

Pugovitsyn (Constable): *pugovitsa*—button, also *pugat'*—to scare

Ukhovyortov (Constable): *ukho*—ear, *vertet'*—to twist

Poshlyopkina (Locksmith's wife): *poshlyopat'*—to slap: Slapcheekina

Tryapichkin (Khlestakov's writer friend): *tryapki*—rags: Trashkin

Rastakovsky (retired official): *rastochitel'*—usurer

Korobkin (retired official): *korobka*—box

Perhaps the last word on this topic should go to Nabokov, who says that Khlestakov's name 'conveys to the Russian reader an effect of lightness and rashness, a prattling tongue, the swish of a slim walking cane, the slapping sound of playing cards, the braggadocio of a nincompoop and the dashing ways of a ladykiller (minus the capacity for completing this or any other action).' A daunting task for a translator to try and emulate!

252 *what the Voltaireans say*: the followers of the French writer and philosopher Voltaire (1694–1778) were characterized by their sceptical views on social and religious matters; as here, the term was widely used in Russia to denote any subversive elements in society.

253 *Marshal*: the marshal was a local official, elected to represent the local nobility before the tsar.

255 *Moscow Gazette*: an official newspaper, founded in 1756.

257 *Saratov province*: administrative region to the south-east and some one thousand versts distant from Moscow; the provincial town, Saratov, is on the Volga.

258 *St Basil the Egyptian*: the prevailing view is that this is St Basil the Great, whose feast-day is celebrated in the Russian Orthodox Church on 1 January; this indicates, however, that the play is set in deep winter, which seems improbable in view of the use of carriages, droshkies, and postchaises and the absence of any sleighs.

Acts of John the Mason: considered by Russian editors of Gogol to be a reference to an English Masonic text translated into Russian in the eighteenth century; could also refer to *Self-Knowledge*, by John Mason (published 1745), widely known in Russia.

264 *on the stove*: traditionally, Russian houses were heated by wood-burning stoves built into large brick structures in the centre of the room, often tiled, and fitted with benches and recesses on which people could sit and even lie and sleep.

Shchukin market: see note to Shchukin Dvor on p. 62, above.

267 *Penza . . . faro*: Penza—a large provincial town, some one hundred versts to the north of Saratov (see note to p. 257, above); faro—a card game (see note to p. 148, above).

Robert le Diable: lavish and exotic work by the operatic composer Giacomo Meyerbeer (1791–1864), written in 1831—his first French opera and immensely popular in its day.

268 *Jochim*: fashionable carriage-dealer in St Petersburg at that time.

271 *Kholmogory*: town near Archangel in the far north of Russia which was an important trading centre from the fifteenth century; its dealers were famed for the quality of their beef.

274 *St Vladimir*: the Order of St Vladimir, prince and equal of the Apostles, was a decoration of the 4th class, instituted in 1782 and awarded for state service; it took the form of a ribbon.

283 *labberdaan*: the Dutch name for a type of dried, salt cod, similar to bacalao; the word is as unfamiliar to the Russian ear as to the English.

286 *collegiate assessor*: rank in the civil service equivalent to the military rank of Major; see the complete Table of Ranks on p. xli.

287 *Robert le Diable . . . Yury Miloslavsky*: Robert le Diable—see note above, to p. 267; *Frigate Hope* was a story by the fashionable Romantic poet Alexander Bestuzhev-Marlinsky (1797–1837), and not Baron Brambeus, *nom de plume* of Osip Senkovsky (1800–58), a hack journalist and critic despised by Gogol, editor of the journal *Library for Reading*; A. F. Smirdin (1795–1857) respected St Petersburg bookseller and publisher of the *Library for Reading*; *Yury Miloslavsky*—a historical novel, à la Walter Scott, by Mikhail Zagoskin.

297 *Vladimir . . . St Anne*: Order of St Vladimir—see note, above, to p. 274; Order of St Anne, instituted in 1797, originally an order of Schleswig-Holstein; the award was given to military officers for bravery and took the form of a cross worn on the hilt of the sword.

302 *Jacobin*: adherent of a radical French political organization.

307 *Post Office Street or Gorokhovaya*: streets in the district of St Petersburg where members of the functionary classes (including Gogol himself, in 1830) tended to live; see note to p. 160 and map on p. xl.

313 *Oh man . . . Gods*: Khlestakov is quoting from an ode by the great eighteenth-century scientist and poet, Lomonosov—presumably a poem learnt at school and the only verse he can now recall. In production a different approach might be used; thus, in the Oxford Playhouse version, Khlestakov declaimed—inaccurately and somewhat anachronistically— 'Say not, the struggle naught availeth', misremembering lines by Arthur Hugh Clough.

315 *Karamzin*: Nikolai Karamzin (1766–1826), noted historian and man of letters, leader of the Russian Sentimentalist school; the reference here is to his work *Bornholm Island*.

322 *the red or the blue*: the red sash was awarded with the order of St Alexander Nevsky and the blue with the order of St Andrew the Apostle, which was higher.

330 *Post Office Street*: this street is so-named because the postal headquarters stand on it; hence the Postmaster's alarm on seeing the address; Gogol enjoys a private joke, by giving Tryapichkin's house the same number as his own, 97.